Praise for *The Return of Black Douglas*

"Intriguing... Bestseller Coffman spins a rewarding love story between her two intelligent, stubborn protagonists, keeping their relationship fresh and their conflicts credible... a satisfying time-travel romance."

—*Publishers Weekly*

"Coffman's exciting tale is full of action, danger, passion, and drama... A must-read for medieval and time-travel fans alike."

—*RT Book Reviews*, 4 stars

"Coffman's delightful time-travel romance will leave readers wanting more."

—*Booklist*

"Irresistible... Time travel, hunky men, educated women, a good old-fashioned war of wills... all these things put together make for one heck of a good book!"

—*Romance Reader at Heart*

"Coffman does a remarkable job of painting the background of the Scottish Highlands. The dialogue is superb."

—*Minding Spot*

"Delightfully infused with suspense, humor, heartache, an entertaining plot, well-drawn characters, and a wily ghost, this story is a keeper."

—*Romance Junkies*

"The plot was extraordinary. Elaine Coffman brought sixteenth-century Scotland to life with amazing detail... Each page held something wonderful."

—*The Royal Reviews*

"A wonderful journey to the Scotland of the past with a hero to die for and a heroine who matches him—*The Return of Black Douglas* has it all."

—*Linda Banche, Romance Author*

"A delightful fantasy. Romantic, titillating, and exciting."

—*Beyond Her Book*

"Great time-travel romance... filled with handsome Highlanders and strong, intelligent women who love them... Coffman's ability to recreate the time period, customs, and culture sets this novel apart."

—*Debbie's Book Bag*

"Intensely thought provoking... the sort of book readers can become emotionally invested in."

—*Romance Fiction on Suite101.com*

"Imagine being thrown into the sixteenth century, into a warrior's arms—scary but hot. A great little love story with a twist."

—*Bookloons*

"Full of handsome Highlanders... a pure escapist story."

—*Celtic Lady's Ramblings*

Lord
OF THE
BLACK ISLE

ELAINE COFFMAN

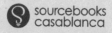

sourcebooks
casablanca

Published by Sourcebooks Casablanca, an imprint of Sourcebooks, Inc.
P.O. Box 4410, Naperville, Illinois 60567-4410
(630) 961-3900
FAX: (630) 961-2168
www.sourcebooks.com

Printed and bound in Canada
WC 10 9 8 7 6 5 4 3 2

I have found power in the mysteries of thought,
exaltation in the changing of the Muses;
I have been versed in the reasonings of men;
but Fate is stronger than anything I have known.

—*Alcestis* (438 BC)
   Euripides (484 BC–406 BC)
   Greek tragic dramatist

Prologue

Love will find a way
through paths where wolves fear to prey.

—"The Giaour" (1813)
  Lord Byron (1788–1824)
  English poet

Màrrach Castle
Isle of Mull
Scotland, 1516

A BLOODRED MOON HUNG AS IF SUSPENDED OVER A velvety black sky. From the swells of the Atlantic below, a blue mist rose, spangled and spiraled. It curled like a cat's tail around dark castle turrets. It drifted lower, to creep silently over roof tiles to an open window casement and slide quietly into the bedchamber below. As hushed as a vapor, it floated toward the bed where she slept, passing like a cold chill over her still form, as softly as the caressing hand of a lover seeking warmth.

Inside that bedchamber, Elisabeth Douglas slept fitfully, plagued by a dream. Out of the shadows, a blackbird came, sharp claws extended, searching for someone to love and possess. Terrified of its stark blackness,

she lay tangled in pale, gauzy bedding, a prisoner of
the night. She closed her eyes against the frightening
sight and listened to the dreadful flap of wings, coming
closer and closer. Caressed by the sweep of sleek black
featherings that touched her, she could only watch with
speechless dread as the night turned black as pitch and
the stars went into hiding.

She yearned for the pure light of morning to cleanse
the effects of this blight that covered her like a curse.
She wanted to open the window and see sunlight spangled upon the sea, and to listen to the song of birds on
the chimney singing to the sky, yet all she heard was the
pounding in her heart, a throbbing beat in her head, and
the sound of sand bleeding through the wall and onto the
floor, the passing crystals of time running out.

Slowly, ever slowly, the bloodred moon began to
sink beneath the horizon to ride upon a wine-dark sea,
until the earth was cast slowly into inky oblivion...

And into her world rode the black knight upon a
demon black horse.

Chapter 1

Had we never lov'd sae kindly,
Had we never lov'd sae blindly,
Never met—or never parted—
We had ne'er been broken-hearted.

—"Ae Fond Kiss" (1791)
  Robert Burns (1759–1796)
  Scottish poet

ISOBELLA MACKINNON HAD NEVER SEEN HER SISTER,
Elisabeth Douglas, look more beautiful than she did at
this moment. "You look as graceful as a plumy egret,"
she said. "If only you could see yourself. Oh, how I wish
we had a full-length mirror."

"I don't need a mirror, Izzy. I can see myself in your
eyes." Elisabeth looked down at the dress and declared,
"It looks as fragile as fairy wings."

Isobella nodded. "Just think, if you married in our
time, you would be in a boring white gown and about to
marry some dude from the twenty-first century."

Elisabeth laughed. "Oh spare me, for that reminds
me of how much I wanted to throttle you the day we
came back in time and found ourselves in a glen full
of warring knights. Remember how the Black Douglas
stood there, looking positively bewildered when he saw

I had accompanied you? I'm still ashamed of the fit I threw when I found out he couldn't send me back. And I was so angry at you, too. Do you remember how I said I would love to punch you, flat out?"

Izzy laughed and said, "Yes, and I was afraid you were mad enough to do it!"

"I know it's a little late, but I feel I should apologize for being so hard on you, Izzy. How would I dream that jumping back six centuries in time would change my life for the best? Please don't feel like I gave anything up, because I didn't. I'm still a doctor, and I am needed here so much more than I could ever be in our time."

"I know, but I wish it could have happened a year later, after you finished your last year at Johns Hopkins. I know it was hard to give up your position as chief resident."

Elisabeth hugged her and said, "Yes, but look what I got in return."

Isobella's eyes sparkled as she said, "I'd better get going so I can get dressed before I start crying from happiness and get tears all over my new dress." She started toward the door, then stopped and turned. "You aren't sorry about the way things worked out... I mean, if you had it to do over again, only this time if you had a choice, would you choose to come back?"

Elisabeth's smile was brilliant. "Without hesitation," she said, and watched Isobella slip through the door, looking happier than a smiley face.

After Izzy was gone, Elisabeth dressed quickly, glanced at her wedding dress again, and sat down on the bed, her heart bursting with happiness as she fell back, thinking about her future. An hour later, she was still lying on the bed, enraptured in her thoughts about her life at Màrrach Castle, which included the marriage of Izzy to Alysandir, Chief of Clan Mackinnon. And now here she was, a year and a half later, about to marry his brother Ronan.

I don't deserve to be so happy. No one does…

Poor Elisabeth. She needn't have worried about being so happy, for personal turmoil was about to come her way. When it came to the future of Elisabeth Rhiannon Douglas, Fate had other plans…

———

Later that evening, Elisabeth sat on her bed, too exhausted to cry any more. Suddenly, the door opened and Isobella rushed into the room, threw her arms around Elisabeth, and said, "Oh my God, Elisabeth! I'm so sorry. I don't know what to think, because I know nothing can ease the pain you are feeling. Oh, what can I say? What can I do? What can any of us do?"

With a stone face and a broken heart, Elisabeth lifted eyes that were void of life, as she replied, "Nothing. There is absolutely nothing you or anyone can do." She sighed. "Oh, Izzy, they lie when they say love conquers all. I loved and he loved, but that was not enough. My love for him was like quicksilver slipping through my hands, and there was nothing I could do to stop it."

Elisabeth stood and walked to the window. "Why couldn't I marry the man I loved as you did? Oh, I don't know why I ask you that when the Black Douglas is the only one who can answer it, and he is making his ghostly presence very scarce around here. Not that I blame him.

He knows I wouldn't be very nice to him. You haven't seen him, have you?"

Isobella shook her head. "Not so much as a ruffled leaf or a draft blowing down the chimney."

Elisabeth nodded and crossed her arms in front of herself as she began pacing back and forth.

Isobella watched her... back and forth... back and forth... and wondered how she, or anyone, could explain why, on the eve of his wedding, Ronan was ordered to marry the daughter of the Earl of Bosworth. Isobella had never felt so inadequate, and it pained her to see the way Elisabeth pressed her fists against the knots in her stomach, just before she spoke.

"I wish to God he had thrown me aside for another or lost his feeling for me. That I could have suffered and gotten over," Elisabeth said. "But this? How does one get over knowing we were separated by an edict from the King's regent?"

Isobella walked to the window and stood beside her sister, still at a loss for words.

"Oh, Izzy, how can I face tomorrow and all the to-morrows that follow? My life is over."

Isobella gave her a shake. "No, it isn't! You mustn't say that because it isn't true. You have been wounded deeply, but you will heal in time. And while you wait for the healing to come, you must stay busy. Yes, you love him, but he was not your first love."

Elisabeth jerked back as if she had been slapped. "*Not* my first love?" she said. "Izzy, how can you say that?"

"I can because it's true. Medicine was your first love. Focus on that, and you will find your healing."

Elisabeth sighed, lost in her thoughts, and then, after

a few minutes, she realized Izzy was right. She was in danger of allowing her grief to take over. *Elisabeth, you have more self-discipline than that, and you cannot allow your pain to ruin your life. What would you tell a heartbroken patient?* She knew the answer to that, just as she knew the answer to what would save her.

She turned to Izzy and said, "You're right. If anything can save me from ongoing despair, it's medicine."

"I'm so glad to hear you say that," Izzy said. "You are a doctor, a healer, and a damn good one, or you wouldn't have been appointed chief resident. It's like you told me once—find your bearings and you will regain your life."

Elisabeth smiled sadly, remembering when she said that, never knowing she would one day heed her own advice. She was a healer, and although she had suffered a terrible loss, she could spare others the painful heartbreak of losing a loved one by devoting herself to her calling. She would lose herself in caring for others. She would return to her first love, medicine. And there she would find solace, if not happiness; peace, in lieu of love. "I think I became so enamored with being in love that I quite forgot about medicine. Remember that quote Dad had framed over his desk?"

Isobella nodded. "It had something to do with timing, I think."

"Yes, that's the one," Elisabeth said. *"Timing... and picking up the pieces when all is said and done—or something to that effect."* She sighed and looked off. "You know, that's very similar to what Ronan once told me."

Isobella waited a moment, then asked, "And what was that?"

"Things do come at their appointed time through all the changing seasons of life."

Chapter 2

Mr. Turnbull had predicted evil consequences...
and was now doing the best in his power to bring
about the verification of his own prophecies.

—Phineas Finn (1867)
  Anthony Trollope (1815–1882)
  British novelist

Aisling Castle
The Black Isle, Scotland

THE BLACK ISLE, OR *AN T-EILEAN DUBH*, AS IT IS CALLED
in Gaelic, is a study in contradictions. It is not truly an
island, but a peninsula surrounded on three sides by
three firths—Cromarty Firth to the north, Beauly Firth
to the south, and Moray Firth to the east. And it is not
really black, although some believe it obtained its name
because snow does not lie in the winter, so the point of
the promontory looks black against the snow gleaming
on the higher ridges.

Steeped in history, Aisling Castle sits inland, nestled
on a rocky outcrop of cliffs and woodlands, with a
view of Moray Firth. The castle is decorously skirted
by majestic conifers and girdled with steep, jutting
boulders. A hidden glen not far away sends a torrent

of white-foaming water falling over lime-rich rocks of rapids and under a fallen rowan tree before peacefully flowing into the dark silence of a deep pool.

One can hear the falls at Fairy Glen before they can be seen, or hear the cry of a golden eagle as it flies over broad-leaved woodlands set in the steep-sided valley. It is where the gentle greens of moss-colored glens give way to sea fjords and deep, blue lochs where the Picts once hunted lynx and bear. In ancient times, this land was called Pittanochtie, a Pictish name for which the translation has been long lost, for the Pictish language has been extinct for hundreds of years.

It is an enchanted place, beautiful, mysterious, and rich in history, where soldiers stand guard over grand castles, unaware that most of them will one day lie in ruins. In the winter, the land lies silent and cold beneath snow or the frozen dew of hoarfrost. In the summer, the fields are fertile and green, some covered in fields of broom and whin, others lined with thick forests, covered with oak, hazel, and pine; a place where deer and wild pigs roam, carefully trying to avoid the prowl of a hungry wolf. Here, eagles are plentiful, as are ptarmigan and raven, which fly far above herds of red deer, or an occasional wildcat, haughty, aristocratic, and reclusive.

On this particular day, David Murray was returning from a successful hunt, as he rode through a thickly wooded valley. Before long, the sun would slip behind the black fringe of trees and darkened fields as the golden orb dropped from sight. But at this moment, the entrance to Aisling Castle was still sun-warmed from the west, defended by a barbican and high curtain walls, topped with corner turrets that took advantage of all that lay below.

There was something romantic about this time of day, when night creatures would soon begin to stir in the huddle of hills, as if competing with the roar of a nearby burn, teeming with trout. David was not thinking about burns or castles this day as he rode toward Aisling, for his mind was on his tyrannical father and the pressure David was under for his "stubborn refusal to wed and produce an heir," as his father called it.

It had only been a fortnight when the Duke of Ballinbreich had proposed, for a second time, a wedding between David and his daughter, Fenella Gordon. Although David liked her as a family friend, he announced his dislike of taking Fenella to wife in the same breath that he informed his father that he would not wed her if the king himself ordered it, simply because he did not love her.

David had left Aisling Castle early the next morning, before his father arose and sent for him for another brow-beating session. Now he was returning home, and he knew his father would be waiting for him. It was the normal way of things between the two of them: David displeasing his father in everything he did until David would ride away, only to face his father lashing out with accusations when he returned.

Behind him, David's cousins were leading pack horses with three fine stags slung over their backs, along with four fat capercaillies. These were the same cousins his father referred to as his irresponsible kinsmen. Unlike David, his cousins ignored the harsh words of the earl, for they were accustomed to hearing that the earl was greatly disappointed and coldly censorious of his only surviving son and heir.

In spite of his difficult father, David was anxious to be home after the weeklong hunt. They had ridden through miry bogs and muddy tracks for some time now, and had fought a skirmish with the McNabbs, which had placed David in the position of having to kill two of their number. He and his cousins were close to home now, for they soon splashed across Markie Burn and followed the narrow track past the old church and graveyard. A short time later, they rode through the open gate of Aisling Castle.

Overhead, birds shrieked, and he watched the lazy circling of sparrow hawks and doubted even his father would be pressed to find something to criticize about such a boon as three stags and six capercaillies. In the distance, the muted cry of fulmars and jackdaws broke the silence as David dismounted and smiled at his sister, Ailis, who hurried out to greet him as she always did, pausing just long enough to see the spoils of their hunt and then hurrying to greet her brother.

"Och, David! 'Tis a fine trio o' red deer ye have brought us. All and sundry will be looking forward to having something besides fish for our next meal. Father will be pleased to hear ye had such good fortune."

Turning his head with a skeptical sneer, David replied, "The Earl of Kinloss... pleased with something I did? 'Tis surely a jest, sister."

Ailis rose on her toes to give him a kiss on the cheek. "When have I ever been known to jest?" She laughed gaily—a bit too gaily for David, who knew she was trying to lighten the moment. "Aye, jest I did, but I didna say he would be pleased wi' *ye*, but with the knowledge that he wouldna have to eat fish for a while."

David started to turn toward the hall, but Ailis placed a hand upon his sleeve. "Dinna go into the hall just now, David. Wait a while and give him time to let the flames burn down. He is still verra upset wi' ye."

"'Tis nothing new ye speak of, Ailis. The mere sound o' my name distresses him."

"'Tis better that he speaks o' it, David. Ye ken the distress that doesna show on the face lies in the heart. Ye anger him because ye refuse to bend and become what he wants. Faith! Sometimes I wonder if ye dinna do it a purpose."

David smiled while his eyes searched hers. "Mayhap I do gouge the old toad now and then. 'Tis difficult to always be on the receiving end of his harshness, criticism, and disapproval, and yet remain mute."

"Just try, David. Please?"

Ailis started to say something else, but David kissed her on the forehead. "When could I ever refuse ye anything, Ailis?"

Ailis stared at her younger brother, the fifth born of nine children, and wondered if there was something cursed about being the fifth, for it did seem her brother was born at the wrong time, to the wrong family, under the wrong circumstances. How else could she explain her father's cruelty? True, he grieved over the deaths of their three brothers, but why would he punish his only remaining son by withholding anything resembling fatherly love, guidance, pride, understanding, or encouragement?

She often thought that had it not been for the love of

his mother and, after her death, the love of his sisters, David would have had less regard for his life than the little he now possessed, for he was deliberately defiant with his life, he was fearlessly brave, and his caring for others before himself made him a dangerous man, a valiant knight, a good leader, and a wonderful brother.

Ailis grieved for David, because she knew he was a man in pain. She could not help but respect the way David handled himself with their father, for when it got to be more than he could take, instead of having words with the earl, David and his cousins would go hunting.

There were times in the past that she was certain the castle would explode from all the game being processed. But the clan members were thankful and held David in high regard, for the Murrays were known for their benevolence toward all their clansmen, and none ever went hungry. The earl's son had on many occasions ridden among the common folk with his cousins and pack animals loaded with game, which they handed out themselves.

Ailis remembered David's younger years, before one could see the indifferent gaze in his eyes and the scornful countenance, for it had been a time when he was quick to excite laughter in others with a wry face or to break out with the delightful sound of his own wonderful laugh or to take up the pipes and play a jig. And his beautiful, smoldering voice could soothe a snarling wolf.

She worried, too, that David would never marry, for he rejected every opportunity and ignored his father's efforts to unite him with daughters of powerful Scots, which was a shame in a way, for women adored him, with his black hair and smoldering eyes, the tall frame with the deerhound sleekness, his handsome visage, and the broodingly rebellious hero they saw who aroused their desire to a fever pitch. There was nary a knight in the Highlands who could best him when it came to skill with a sword.

David had known many women, but he'd never met one he couldn't walk away from. He knew the glowing coals of desire, the yearning pull of lust, and the fiercely hot flames of making love, which ended as quickly as they came. He never got close to women, other than those in his family. He'd simply learned to keep part of himself separate when it came to them. And even then, when women heard of his proficiency in lovemaking, his devotion to bringing them pleasure, and the detachment that came later, they still thought they could be the one to win his undying love and devotion. Faith! Ailis was beginning to wonder if any woman could.

"Where is he? By God, I will have a word with him! Send him to see me the moment he arrives!"

At the sound of his father's booming voice, David paused ever so briefly and then continued up the stairs, obviously mindful of the ominous staccato of an angry tread approaching from below. "There ye are, slinking into the castle. Did ye come in the back way?"

David continued up the stairs, having chosen not to respond.

"David, I will have a word wi' ye! Now!"

David paused, then turned and descended a few stairs and stopped. He looked down upon the earl and, by doing so, had the vantage point—something he knew would not escape his father's critical eye.

The earl waited with his customary stern demeanor, tightly drawn lips, and icy blue eyes. "Have ye naught to say?"

"Nae, Father. I dinna ha' any ammunition to give ye today so that ye may fire it back at me. 'Twould be of no use anyway, fer ye have yer opinion of me and naught I can say or do would change it."

"And ye can live with that? Knowing ye are a worthless son and an insult to the Murray name?"

"I *have* lived with it since I was a boy. I am what ye made me to be, a man like ye... cold, uncaring, and arrogant." His beautiful, fathomless eyes conveyed everything he felt, everything he could not say.

"If only it had been ye that died instead of yer brothers."

David nodded. "For once we have found something upon which we can agree."

"For the love of God! I canna understand why ye are so difficult... why ye must butt heads wi' me at every turn!"

David turned and continued up the stairs, but the earl was not finished with him. "Ye willna turn away until I give ye leave. I am not finished wi' ye!"

As was his usual way of dealing with the earl, David did not respond and continued on his way. A moment later, he heard the angry tread of his father's footsteps upon the stairs and the too-familiar sound of his harshly spoken words.

"By the hand o' God, I canna disown ye and prevent ye from becoming the Earl of Kinloss, but I can see that ye rot in a dungeon! I willna rest until I find a way to make ye pay for yer insolence. Mark my words well, for ye will rue this day!"

"I canna regret it any more than I already do," David replied. Suddenly, someone screamed, and he turned in time to see his father fighting for balance just before he tumbled backwards and fell down the stairs.

By the time David reached his father's side, a pool of blood was widening beneath the earl's head, and David knew his father had at last found a way to make him pay, just as he had said.

In the ensuing days, David felt tremendous guilt as the castle bustled with the preparations for the funeral of the Earl of Kinloss, and if he could have grieved at all, it would not have been for the loss of a father, but the loss of the kind of father he might have been.

In the end, he felt some satisfaction in knowing his father got exactly what he wanted, for David did rue this day.

Chapter 3

Sometimes being a friend means mastering the art of timing.
There is a time for silence.
A time to let go and allow people
to hurl themselves into their own destiny.
And a time to prepare to pick up the pieces when it's all over.

—*The Women of Brewster Place* (1982)
   Gloria Naylor (1950–)
   U.S. novelist, producer, and playwright

Isle of Mull, Scotland
A few months later

GROWING UP, ELISABETH HAD ALWAYS HEARD THAT the history of Scotland was complex. She'd never dreamed that by going back six hundred years, she would discover for herself just how complex it was... forbiddingly so.

Scotland was a puzzle of ten thousand pieces in which one tried to painstakingly find some semblance of order, shape, and color to be able to put it all together, forming a country, for according to her archaeologist sister, Isobella, Scotland had been known by many names: Albion, Alba, Alban, Pretanikai Nesoi, Cruithintuait, Pictland, Caledonia, 'O chrich Chat co Foirciu, and Scotland.

It possessed a history that was powerful, sad, strong, persuasive, potently addictive, melancholic, and not easy to see clearly or understand without the skill of discernment. For how can you make a whole out of so many sad fragments? How can one assemble the bits and pieces of tradition, sprinkled with falsehoods, peppered with truths and scratches of Pictish symbols that no one has been able to translate, or the fragments of long-forgotten facts, faded memories, superstitions, myths, Druidic beliefs, Catholic documents, Roman writings, Viking legends—and then heap it all together and call it Scotland?

Scotland, Elisabeth decided, was still complex, for its people were as muddled as its past, with Picts, Celts, Norse, Danes, and Angles all coming together in a mix of language, history, and culture, rolled up with a mountainous landscape that rose out of the North Sea like a clenched fist.

No wonder she was confused. Making a decision wasn't as easy as it sounded, for after Ronan was torn from her future and her life, how slowly the days passed and bled into weeks, and the weeks became months, and the months became blurry until Elisabeth realized she had lost track of time.

Lethargy gripped her and passed through her like the fingers of thieves, stealing her spirit and stripping away her very soul. Life had no purpose. Inwardly, she was washed out and empty. The world was callous and cruel, and it left her indifferent. If only she could care... for something. And for a while she stayed busy, but now there were no ailments within the castle. Not even the animals suffered from any malady. And the sympathy others expressed and the sorrow she saw in their eyes whenever she passed were a constant reminder.

And pity was definitely not what she needed.

It was as if God had been busy and lost track of her—and the Black Douglas, too. She tried taking walks along the beach beneath Màrrach Castle, but the weather was turning cooler and the sky overcast, and she found herself more melancholy upon her return than she was before she left. She accompanied Isobella down to the caves where she was excavating, but that only reminded her of Ronan and memories of them helping Isobella and then picnicking on the beach afterward, and lying on the damp sand and feeling the luxurious weight of Ronan lying over her.

It is time fer ye to go... The words floated across Elisabeth's mind, but she pushed them away for she knew where they came from and she wasn't in the mood to talk to the Black Douglas right now. She was very angry with him, and if he would show himself in human form, rather than as a meddlesome vapor, she would love to punch him flat out! However, she knew in her heart it was time for her to leave Màrrach and to find her own way in the world waiting out there.

But now the question was, where would she go? She knew no one, save the MacLeans, who had captured her in the past and held her prisoner, and the Mackinnons, who had rescued her and welcomed her as part of their family.

Day by day, she felt the urge to leave, for remaining here was not in the best interests of either her or Isobella. Although she was finally past the pain of losing Ronan, there were still so many reminders of him everywhere. She needed a fresh start, a change, an opportunity to present itself. *You are a physician.* But there was always the possibility that leaving would be the worst thing that she could do. *What if I end up in a worse situation than I am now?* Then she wondered just how much worse things could be. She was slowly dying inside. She needed a new life. She needed to practice medicine, and if medicine would not come to her, she would go to medicine.

She rubbed her temples, wondering how she would ever solve this dilemma. Finally she thought: Go… leave… you know it will be best for Isobella and for you, and only time will tell if you made the right decision. Time is, after all, a great healer. And, if you fail, you can always return to Màrrach. She decided she would sleep on it, and if she still felt the same in the morning, she would leave as soon as possible.

She did sleep on it, and when she awoke, she had breakfast in her room, then dressed and went in search of Isobella, who would be sewing or knitting baby clothes in the solar this time of the morning.

On her way there, she passed the nurse carrying Isobella's baby boy, and she stopped a moment to croon over the beautiful, sleeping child, before she continued on her way. She had not gone far when she met Alysandir's brother Drust coming down the stairs. He inquired how she was doing, and they paused a moment to talk. She wanted to know what he thought, so she told him of her decision and why she felt leaving was best. "Do you think I am wrong to do so?"

"Nay, I dinna. I ken ye know yersel' better than anyone," Drust said. "I dinna see there is much aboot

Màrrach to help get yer mind off of my brother and on to making a new life fer yersel'. 'Tis no' an easy time ye will have o' it, no matter where ye go, but I think leaving here will give ye time to start yer life over, and that is the best choice available to ye right now. Have ye any plans as to what ye will do or where ye will go?"

"No, I only know I want to use my medical training. So it makes sense to go wherever I feel I would be needed. I have even thought about opening a hospital somewhere."

"Och! If it is a hospital ye be wanting, ye should go to Soutra Aisle. It is part o' the House of the Holy Trinity, which includes a monastery of friars."

Her heart began to pound with excitement at the mention of a hospital, for she had no idea there were hospitals in Scotland. "Soutra Aisle? Tell me more, please, for it may be exactly what I need."

"'Tis a church of the Augustinian Order, and they have the largest hospital in Scotland. 'Tis on a well-traveled road between the border and Edinburgh."

Filled with an adrenaline rush, she grabbed him with a big hug. "Drust, you are an angel. That is exactly what I needed to hear. I know I can be of help to them."

"Weel, it isna a place for women, ye see, fer there are no nuns there, but dinna be forgetting that our uncle, Lachlan Mackinnon, is the abbot at Iona. I ken he would write ye a letter to persuade the friars there to take ye in for a short while so ye could learn from them, and then ye could be on yer way to finding yer own place."

"Oh, Drust, that is an excellent idea! Would you see if you could get such a letter from your uncle? I would love it if the monks helped me familiarize myself with the medicines and procedures they use."

"They are na monks, though. They are friars."

Not being Catholic, she did not know the difference, so she asked.

"Both monks and friars give up all personal property and take vows of poverty, but monks live cloistered in monasteries, away from normal life. Friars live among the people, and they belong to an order rather than a certain monastery."

"Oh, I had no idea there was a distinct difference. I will pray the friars will lean favorably toward me."

"I will pray for that also," Drust said. "And I will ask Alysandir to write to our uncle, and then Colin and I will take the letter to Iona."

She gave him a bigger hug this time. "How can I thank you, Drust?"

"I canna let ye thank me without giving ye a warning. Ye should be careful how ye go aboot it, fer there could be those that would see yer knowledge as coming from the deil and that would get ye in a heap o' trouble. Mayhap it would be best to pay a call upon the parish priest, or even better, I shall accompany ye to Soutra Aisle with a few men. We will have to wait until we receive the letter from Lachlan, but in the meantime, ye can prepare yer things fer travel—but dinna take all o' yer things, or ye would surely fill Soutra Aisle until there was no room fer the patients."

She laughed, endeared by his humor, his way of raising her spirits. "I will miss you, Drust."

"Aye, and I will miss ye as well, but 'tis not going to be the last we see o' each other, ye ken."

She smiled, feeling more optimistic than she had since the dreaded news about Ronan's marriage had arrived. "You have set my heart at ease, for I was worried about how I would find the right place to go and how I would get there. But please don't say anything yet to your sisters. I want to break the news first to Isobella."

"Leave everything to me. I will speak with Alysandir as soon as he returns."

She bid him good-bye and continued on her way to the solar, where she found her sister alone.

Isobella glanced up when Elisabeth walked in. "Good morning!" She looked more closely at her sister's face. "Getting up your nerve to try knitting, or is something else on your mind?"

"I have decided to leave Màrrach," Elisabeth said, her eyes meeting Isobella's.

Isobella looked startled and then said, "Oh, Elisabeth! I shall miss you terribly, you know, but it's probably the best thing for you. I'm glad, really I am. Have you decided where to go?"

Elisabeth laughed at the excitement in Izzy's voice and told her about Soutra Aisle, setting her mind at ease.

Isobella was beaming. "Elisabeth, that is simply wonderful, and with an introduction from Lachlan, you will be accepted readily. But I will only let you go if you promise to stay in touch."

———

Elisabeth spent the rest of the morning in the solar, stitching tiny, white linen gowns. Ronan flashed through her mind a time or two, and she wondered how he fared, and how things were between him and his bride. Only now, when she thought about such, she no longer felt the burn of the tears that spilled down her cheeks or the wrenching pain in her heart. Time had begun to work its magic, and she changed the direction of her thoughts from Ronan to herself.

That night, she thought about the things she should take with her to Soutra Aisle, which had to be few, considering she only had a saddle pouch to carry them. Remembering Drust's admonishment about taking too much, she smiled. She thought about the letter she would have from Lachlan Mackinnon, and it hit her that she was going out on her own among total strangers. She recalled her thwarted hopes and unfulfilled desires, and realized her future was not her own.

I will be satisfied with my new life, but never again will I be truly happy. She caught herself and decided this was the last time she would give credence to such thoughts. From here on out, she would be positive, and that meant being more careful to rein herself in before she sunk into melancholia, even if it was the fate of some people to be ill-destined. It was also time to say a final good-bye to Ronan, for his name had become a repetitious litany that had lingered in the back of her mind long enough. She had made great strides to rid herself of the grief and memories that had been her constant companions.

Looking back, she still found it hard to believe that loving and grieving could hurt so much. It had been like a wound that bled constantly, and during those darkest days, she wondered if there would ever come a time when she could sit down beside it and embrace her loss as one would a long-lost friend. Grieving for him had made Ronan seem much larger and more perfect in her mind than he had been when they were together.

In suffering, she had managed to forget even his little faults, the imperfections, the flaws she saw in him, until he was idealized like a statue in marble in a shadowed niche in her mind.

Of course, there were times when she still missed him or the sound of his laughter; the way his eyes smoldered when he took her in his arms; the feel of his hand upon her skin; the delicious weight of him when he came to her; the smoothness of his skin, the manly fragrance belonging only to him. Only now, she did not cry in order to cleanse the pain that held her in its grip.

She arose from the bed, lit a candle, and poured herself a goblet of something she thought of as an uneducated ancestor of wine, then dragged a blanket to the fire and wrapped herself in it. She saw this as an official separation ritual and the toasting of a new birth. She sipped the wine and stared at the low-burning flames until they were naught more than glowing embers. She sighed deeply, told herself for the umpteenth time she had made the right decision to leave and to focus on her future, and was soon fast asleep in the chair.

Early the next morning, she took a long walk down the beach. When she grew weary; she sat down on a rocky ledge and stared at the mesmerizing movement of the ocean.

"He who busies himsel' with two things drowns."

She sucked in enough air to fill a balloon and turned around so quickly that she got a small crick in her neck, for she knew exactly who that voice belonged to. Massaging the crick, she looked around but did not see any sign of the Black Douglas, but she did see a mounted rider coming toward her, and as it drew closer she began to frown suspiciously.

Through the fog of a cool summer morning and the gauzy haze of history, he rode closer, the Black Douglas, in full armor and riding a black horse. He was obviously dressed for battle, which struck her as curious.

Dressed in full knight's regalia, he was truly a splendidly magnificent man: handsome and not tall by twenty-first-century standards, but tall for the sixteenth-century male, muscular, yet slender, with dark blue eyes and hair of the blackest black. But the more she stared, the more she realized that something wasn't right. She continued to study him, trying to decide what was different, and then she realized his tunic was black, not blue, and also missing were the three white stars. In fact, *everything was black*... his chausses, his over-the-knee boots, his surcoat, and even his chain mail hauberk was black, as was his helmet.

When he drew rein near her, she asked, "What happened to your blue tunic with the three white stars? Why are you in full armor when there is no sign of a battle anywhere around here?"

"Weel, I had a notion ye wouldna be too happy to see me, and ye would be ready to confront me in a battle over recent occurrences in yer life. Am I wrong?"

She laughed outright. Then gaining control, she said, "No, you are not wrong, and I would love to do more than confront you. I truly think I could take your sword and run you through."

"Aye, and there ye have it."

"There I have what?"

"Ye have the reason why I ha' come in full armor.

I came prepared to meet ye on the battlefield. 'Twas fitting that I should come dressed in black, I think, to go wi' my black heart."

Elisabeth remembered a ranting she hurled at him and his meddlesome ways when she was feeling as low as a receding tide and had accused him of having the blackest heart in the history of mankind. Suddenly, she burst out laughing. She couldn't help herself. Sometimes he was so mortal, contemporary, and downright hilarious that she could not stay angry at him. And today, especially, he was such a jovial soul, in spite of his black attire. His attempt at humor went a long way to soften her anger at him, although it did nothing to ease her trepidation.

Here he was, if not in the flesh, close to it and looking quite magnificent, she thought, but of course, she wouldn't tell him, the reprobate whom she had not seen since he paid her a visit the night Alysandir was wounded, rescuing her from the MacLeans at Duart Castle. "I don't suppose I need to ask if you know about what happened with Ronan," she said.

"Aye, and I ken ye shed many a tear and grieved greatly, fer we could hear you a couple of centuries back. Naught could be that bad."

"That is easy for you to say. Your heart wasn't broken."

"Ahhh, the 'precious porcelain of human clay.'"

She frowned suspiciously. "Do you know Lord Byron?"

Up went his brows with surprise, which was followed by a rumbling laugh that seemed to have begun low, perhaps in his feet, and grew louder as it rose to the top, gathering speed as it went, rather like champagne ready to blow its cork. "Nay, lass, I know him not, but I did read *Don Juan*."

"*Humph!*" she said. Then as an afterthought, she added, "*Don Juan*... It figures, for I have heard about you and your unrestrained life."

"Mayhap—'tis no secret that I wasna celibate all my life."

That got her attention. "Are you going to tell me about the Countess of Sussex? Is this true confessions time?"

"Mayhap it is; mayhap 'tis not. But I might be convinced to join ye on that rocky ledge and confess along wi' ye. Do ye wish to partake?"

She stared at her feet. "I don't think there is anything in it for me. Besides, I don't kiss and tell."

"If it eases yer mind, Ronan Mackinnon suffers the same as ye."

Her head jerked up. "You have spoken to him?"

His blue eyes were alight with humor, as he said, "Nay lass, I dinna spend my time floating aboot and visiting wi' all and sundry."

"No, you just go around pestering helpless and defenseless women."

"Do I now? Ha' ye seen any of those helpless, defenseless women aboot?" He looked around, as if searching. "I should like to see what one looks like."

He was venturing off into a direction where she did not want to go, so she changed the subject. "Then how do you know he suffers as well?"

"'Twas merely an observation I made. I can observe without making my presence known."

"Apparently," she said, quite huffily.

"'Heav'n has no Rage like Love to Hatred turn'd, Nor Hell a Fury, like a Woman scorn'd.'"

"Obviously quoted by a female friend of yours," she

said, fighting the urge to smile. He laughed and she refused to think about just how wonderful his deeply baritone laugh was, and then she wondered if he could read her mind and decided not to go there.

"Ye are still miffed that I didna pay ye the same number o' visits as I did Isobella?"

"You can barely call a couple of short twirls through my life a visit. And you did show a *strong* preference for visiting my twin."

"That wouldna be yer eyes of green talking now, would it?"

"Well, the two of you were rather chummy, while I was left with the MacLeans for ages without a clue as to what was going on…"

"'Twas not yer time for me to involve myself wi' ye."

"Oh, now I get it. One must suffer horribly before you pay them a call."

"Nay, I didna visit ye much because it wasna yer time, and I dinna recall yer horrible bouts o' suffering."

"I may not have suffered, per se, but *I'm* the one who got all the grief, while Izzy was living a relatively relaxed life. If you remember, I spent most of my time in the clutches of Angus MacLean, as his captive. There was even an opportunity for Izzy to follow her archaeological calling, while I was never afforded anything equal, and before you say that the treating of Alysandir and Braden were opportunities for me to practice medicine, they definitely were merely isolated events."

"And I seem to recollect the MacLean having ye doon to the great hall to sup wi' him on many an occasion. And ye had yer freedom to go about Duart Castle at will, did ye not?"

She purposefully ignored that last question. "I'm not going to put a dog in that fight," she said, "but I will say that I think you owe me."

He gave her that look, which she was becoming accustomed to, when he raised his brows and his face bore an expression that lay somewhere between amusement and being amazed at her gall. "And what would it take to soothe yer ruffled feathers and cause ye to purr like a kitten?"

She gazed off for a moment and lifted her eyes skyward, as if seeking some sort of divine suggestion, then she said, "I was thinking that something given in recompense for my having the short end of the straw—and before you disagree with that, let me remind you that not only was I held prisoner while Izzy was free as a breeze, but she also married the man of her dreams, while I had mine cruelly yanked out of my life before we could wed."

"Mayhap ye are taking the cart afore the horse, fer yer fate is not always in my hands, and the time for a turning point in yer life may lie in yer future, not in the events of the past. Mayhap ye should consider that instead of allowing things to happen, ye might endeavor to influence yer future by making wise choices."

She felt like she had been hit in the face with a pie. She was speechless. "I get the feeling you are referring to my staying at Màrrach and letting things happen, rather than leaving here and making a new life for myself."

"I believe yer contemporary way of putting it would be, if what ye are doing isna working, why do ye keep doing it? Why not try something new? Ye have trod upon the soil of Mull long enough. Follow yer heart. Seek yer passion, and there ye will find yer future."

"So, this is my big moment? My time to 'strut and fret my hour upon the stage and then be heard no more,' as Shakespeare said?"

"Eiridh ton air uisge balbh."

"You *know* I don't speak Gaelic. A translation is needed."

"A wave will rise on quiet water."

"Since you are being frank, I feel I have to be honest. I never expected you to show yourself around me after I left Màrrach. You were always Isobella's sidekick, not mine, and to be frank, you were never very nice to me."

"Ahhh, the scornful words of the sour grape variety."

"Of late, all my grapes seem to be sour," she said, sounding pathetically woeful even to her ears.

"Everything at its appointed time, lass," he said, and then he laughed and said again, "Everything at its appointed time. Dinna be so eager to get the bit between yer teeth. 'Twas Isobella's moment in the sun and shadows, not yours."

She clapped her hands on her hips and narrowed her eyes suspiciously before she said, "For having been born in the thirteenth century, you have an amazing vocabulary."

"I dinna spend all my time moldering."

Her brows went up. "Oh? Do you sit in on college courses?"

"Aye, I have from time to time. And I have been known to visit libraries, but I dinna check oot books."

She laughed heartily and thought it had been a while since she had done so. How she wished the laughter in her heart would last, but no one was that fortunate.

"Faith! 'Tis a relief, lass, to hear yer laughter. I was

beginning to think I would have to camp oot her for a few days to accomplish that. Ye are no' as quick to bring to humor as yer sister."

"Isobella is the muse of laughter in our family."

"'Twould not hurt ye to pick up a bit o' it."

Her glum spirits were returning, and with a certain curiosity. "I hope Ronan does not suffer still."

"Like ye, he has accepted his fate, and he understands that ye are both innocent in this matter."

Her head jerked around and she eyed him suspiciously. "Did you cause this to happen?"

"Nae, I didna."

"Did you know it would happen?"

"Aye."

"I don't suppose it was something you could change."

"Nay, lass. Would that I could, but I canna change yer destiny."

She frowned and asked, "Well, can't you ease the pain of it a wee bit?"

"I have been trying to do so for the past half hour."

She laughed. "Apparently, it's working."

"Weel, working wi' ye is more like the tide—it comes in and it goes oot. And so ye are off for Soutra Aisle. 'Tis a good choice ye ha' made, for yer medical skills are sorely needed. Many a babe in the Highlands is afflicted with the coughing sickness ye call whooping cough."

"Believe me... I will be more than glad to return to medicine."

"Ye may not feel that way fer long."

"If you mean I will be busy, that's wonderful! I'm glad to know I'm headed in the right direction."

"And now that ye realize that yer world isna going to end in the near future, I will bid ye adieu."

"Will you visit me at Soutra Aisle?"

"Mayhap, I will…"

"But what if…"

Before she could finish her sentence, he mounted his great black charger and turned away, just as his image began to shimmer and grow dim. A moment later, she saw the outline of a knight on a great black horse riding down the beach until it was absorbed into the sunlight.

The only reminder that he had been here at all was a lovely fragrance that seemed to accompany her as she turned and made her way back to the castle.

Later that evening, after supper was over, she lay in her bed, gazing through the open window, and watched the moon slip slowly into place beneath a scattering of stars as it settled over Màrrach Castle. Silent, round, and brilliant, its light was a shimmering moonbeam that slipped as softly as a babe's breath into her room, and Elisabeth slept a charmed sleep, deep in the land of shadows.

―――∿――――

The next morning, she awoke from that bower of peace called slumber and remembered that as a child she called it the land of Nod for their mother told her children that it was a magical place where children went to sleep. She stretched, feeling at peace with the world and, more importantly, with herself.

Full of a mixture of excitement and energy, she dressed, ate breakfast, and arrived in the solar before the others. Once everyone had gathered, Elisabeth put down her mending, which she had been given, because her other talents were found to be so lacking that she was appointed chief mender. Some might consider that humiliating, but Elisabeth saw it as a blessing, for she could practice her surgery stitches, although wishing as she did that she had a nice bowl of oranges to practice on.

She waited until after the chatter died down, before she glanced at Isobella, looking lovely in a dress of a deep golden color, with the sun shining down upon her head like a radiant halo, which made her look like an angel. Motherhood became her, and if possible, she was even more beautiful than before.

Next, she glanced at the expectant but puzzled faces of each of the sisters of Alysandir: Marion, Sybilla, Barbara, and the youngest, flame-haired Margaret. "I know all of you suspect something is going on here, and it is. I have decided the best thing for me is to leave Màrrach.

"I don't think I need to explain the reasons why, just as I know I don't have to tell you that I will miss each of you in a thousand different ways. I do not see this as a separation, for a part of each of you will go with me, and I promise I shall come back to visit and hope you will do likewise once I am settled."

She then answered a barrage of questions from the Mackinnon sisters. "Where are you going?" Marion asked.

Elisabeth replied, "To Soutra Aisle and the hospital there."

Barbara raised her brows. "Soutra Aisle? But that is a friary... but ye must have been told that already, so that makes me think ye ha' the help of our uncle Lachlan."

Elisabeth laughed. "I had hoped that, at least once

before I left, I could pull the wool over your eyes. I see that is not the case. And, yes, your uncle has given me a letter of introduction."

Barbara nodded. "I shan't ask why ye have chosen this path, fer I would have done the same thing. I ken it is safe to say for all of us gathered here that we shall miss ye as much as a sister, and we send ye with our prayers fer much happiness to be waiting fer ye at the end o' yer journey."

Elisabeth, who rarely cried, felt her eyes fill to the brim as she stood and hugged each one of them.

Chapter 4

The best laid schemes o' Mice an' Men
go oft astray.

—"To a Mouse" (1785)
  Robert Burns (1759–1796)
  Scottish poet and songwriter

SHE SHOULD HAVE KNOWN WHEN THE TRIP TO SOUTRA
Aisle started off exactly as planned that something was
bound to go wrong, for didn't bad things come in twos?
Or was it threes?

Elisabeth, accompanied by four of Alysandir
Mackinnon's brothers—Drust, Colin, Gavin, and
Grim—had been riding in a misting rain that seemed
never ending, when as quickly as it came, it was over.
Warmed now by the sun and the nice feel of her clothes
drying, she settled into pleasant conversation with the
Mackinnons, forgetting that history often repeats itself.

Suddenly, a cry rang out and what seemed to be an
entire brigade of men rode out of the cover of trees.
When she saw the black hair of the one in the lead,
Elisabeth's heart plummeted. Not Angus MacLean, her
heart cried. She thought she was done, once and for all,
with the MacLeans capturing her and holding her prisoner. Faith! It happened so often that it was becoming

quite ordinary, a daily chore like brushing your teeth.
But instead of brushing your teeth, you mount a horse
and shortly thereafter you are captured by the MacLeans
and taken to Duart Castle and held prisoner. However,
she had to admit that her accommodations were always
first-class there and Angus did, quite frequently, invite
her to join him for supper.

But how in God's name, she wondered, did Angus
MacLean find her? She had a quick memory of the day
the Black Douglas had brought her and Isobella back in
time and how he had abandoned them in a glen without
so much as a featherweight of advice. The MacLeans
captured Elisabeth and took her to Duart Castle, while
Alysandir Mackinnon rescued Isobella after she had
taken a tumble off the side of a crag. The MacLeans
treated Elisabeth well, but Angus refused to allow her
to be with her sister, which kept them apart for months
at a time. When old Angus MacLean wasn't using her
as a pawn, she served as a prod to gouge Alysandir
Mackinnon, for Angus knew Isobella would be begging him to reunite her with her sister, and knowing
Angus, he probably received great satisfaction from
that bit of knowledge.

And now, after all this time, it would seem history
was going to repeat itself and she would find herself
right back in the hands of Angus MacLean. Elisabeth
had no time for further thought, for she heard the *whoosh*
of MacLean blades being drawn all around them. She
spurred her horse and cut in front of the Mackinnons,
saying, "I'll not have an ounce of your blood spilled
over this. You know that I have spent more than enough
time as the MacLean's captive, and we both know he

will not do me harm. I am only a way for him to poke and prod Alysandir."

Angus MacLean's black hair and beard seemed to ride ahead of him, and behind Angus were ten or so of his men, who rode forward and drew rein beside him. Angus smiled and leaned forward, crossing his arms over the pommel of the saddle, the reins dangling loosely in his hand. He looked her over, then exclaimed, "Well... well... well... what ha' we here? 'Twould seem we ha' been blessed wi' a bit o' guid fortune, for we ha' found our wee, lost lassie, and she is looking no worse for the wear."

Angus sat back and dipped his head toward her and then cast a glance in the direction of the Mackinnons, waiting in readiness as he took his time letting his gaze move slowly over each of them, and then he said, "I had no' expected to come upon such fair game, and I regret to inform ye that I will take my lass back now."

He smiled and looked around the clearing, inhaling the rain-freshened air. "'Tis a fine, fine morning to be oot and aboot, and I find I rather like having such a lovely surprise gifted upon me. I am most grateful for finding my stray lassie when I least expected it, and I thank ye kindly for taking such guid care o' her, as I can see she is in the bloom o' health. And a welcome sight for these old sore eyes to see, she is." He paused for a moment and then made a big to-do about scratching his head, as if puzzled about something. Then he said, "I ha' been given the opportunity to capitalize on my adversary's blunder, for what was the Mackinnon thinking when he let ye leave Màrrach with such a small escort?"

Elisabeth spoke quickly, not wanting the Mackinnons

to become embroiled in this affair. "He probably wasn't thinking you would still be spying on me after my having been back at Màrrach so long, but the truth is, I did not want a large escort, and I begged him to keep our group small."

Angus scratched his chin and leaned forward once again. "'Twas no' spying that brought us here, lass, for we are returning from lending our swords to show support for Alasdair Craig, the Duke of Galloway. There's trouble a-brewing at Ardnamurchan again, for the McDonalds and the McLains are once again rattling their claymores and butting heads like a couple o' hard-headed rams."

He glanced around to his men and asked, "Indeed, is it no' our guid fortune to have happened upon Elisabeth Douglas quite by chance, and not because of any plans we made to do so?"

Naturally, his men nodded eagerly, and Elisabeth knew they would have given the same eager nod of agreement if MacLean had asked them if mud tasted good.

MacLean continued, saying, "However, no one can say I'm a man who doesna take advantage of a gift when it presents itself. 'Twould be foolish indeed, to do so. 'Twas a fortunate set o' circumstances to be sure, for we can take ye without wasting a dram o' yer bluid or ours." He looked toward the Mackinnons, who still had not sheathed their swords. "Put yer swords away, laddies. The Mackinnon wouldna have his brothers make such a foolish stand when they are so greatly outnumbered. We will take the lass, and ye can hie yourselves back to Màrrach and tell Alysandir Mackinnon that Angus MacLean took his lass back to Duart Castle."

Elisabeth felt as if the warm spring air had turned suddenly frigid and her blood ran cold. This couldn't be happening to her. Not now. She wanted to do something with her life other than waste it as a prisoner of the MacLeans. She blinked to hold back tears, angry at herself for showing such cowardice. She glanced toward her friends and said, "Please, do as he says. I will not have your blood on my hands. Return to Màrrach and let Alysandir decide how he wants to handle things."

Drust started to speak, but Elisabeth shook her head and said, "Go... all of you. Go now and don't come back. Naturally, I am not the least bit happy to have this unwelcome and unexpected change in my plans, but I know the odds are not in our favor and that I will not be harmed. Please go. I beg you!"

She watched as they sheathed their swords and rode away, the sun glinting off their mail like a farewell salute. And then they were gone, swallowed by the dense beech trees and leaving nothing behind, save the wrenching heaviness that settled over her.

Why, she wondered. *Why is there always an obstruction to my making any progress with my life? What purpose can be served by keeping me a prisoner? And why couldn't you, Sir James, have done something to prevent it? And don't give me all that malarkey about it being my fate. I'm sick and tired of that phrase!*

There wasn't so much as a leaf that fluttered or a breeze that stirred, and she knew she had been completely abandoned to her fate.

"Come, lass. We've not so far to go afore we stop to rest the horses," the MacLean said.

She turned her horse and fell in with them, while

mentally trying to soften the edge of her disappointment over her plans having gone so awry. *Dear God, I don't know why this is happening to me again, or what, if anything beneficial can come of it. There is so much good I could do if I could go to Soutra, if I were given the chance to practice medicine. I could save lives, instead of wasting my life in captivity, and all because of an old man's grudge. Please, send me a miracle and put a speedy end to the circumstances I find myself in.*

And then she wondered if her vacuous vapor of a ghost was hanging around as an invisible observer, but no matter what she thought or how much she pleaded, he kept his distance, without so much as a rumble of thunder in the distance. *Fine, go ahead and wait. Then you can come out after the battle is over and shoot the wounded.*

They rode on and she finally ran out of things to mentally vent about, and about that time, they came to a fairly wide burn that flowed into a narrow, heather-splashed clearing that opened in the thickness of trees and bracken. In the distance she could hear a tumbling waterfall. She looked around the glen and then at the men around her, dressed in the garb of knighthood, their swords polished and gleaming, their eyes keen and ears alert, and she wondered if there was an idyllic place in all of Scotland that had not been tempered by conflict.

Life here was hard, for Scotland was a place swept by rain and strong winds, dotted with solitary lakes and magnificent waterfalls, and surrounded by a coastline battered on three sides by an unforgiving sea. The weather was unbelievably unpredictable and, more often than not, rainy or cold, or both.

She was wondering if they were truly stopping here

when at last the MacLean dismounted, and while his men tended to their horses, Angus came toward her. "Ye may dismount now, lass, and stretch yer weary legs a wee bit afore we take to the saddle again. We will rest the horses fer a time and have a bit o' nourishment fer ourselves."

She wanted to vent her anger, but she knew it would do no good. Whatever they had planned, it would not be changed by anything she said, so she held her tongue and dismounted. She removed her saddle pouch, not trusting her letter to Lachlan Mackinnon to fate, which heretofore had not been very kind to her. She handed the reins to one of the men, who led her horse away.

Without a word or looking at the MacLean, Elisabeth turned away and walked toward the trees and sat on a chair-sized rock in the shade, mindful that she could get skin cancer in the sixteenth century as easily as in the twenty-first. She realized, too, that the Mackinnons had ridden away with some of her belongings in the pouches behind their saddles, so the only possessions she had now were behind her saddle, which was precious little. Well, it served the old codger right, and it pleased her beyond measure to think Angus would have to provide her with a new wardrobe. She had already decided she was going to be very, very picky.

She sighed and glanced around the glen, wondering how she always seemed to stay in the frying pan, only this time she had jumped smack into the fire. Out of one mess and into another... her life seemed to be a long stretch of hopscotching all over the place and making very little progress doing it. She decided to stretch her legs and maybe just keep on stretching them until she found an avenue of escape. It was worth a try, so she casually glanced toward Angus MacLean and found him talking to one of his men.

"I need a moment of privacy, if you don't mind," she said, approaching him.

Without speaking to her, he nodded and turned back to his clansman, so she made her way toward the burn and followed it for a while before she turned into the trees that lined it. She had not ventured far when she jerked to a standstill, for she saw a man on the other side of the burn.

Judging by what she could see of him, he seemed to be as naked as the day he was born, but as her luck would have it, the interesting part of him was hidden behind a tumble of boulders. She walked on a bit further before she paused to remove her shoes and placed them beside the saddle pouch. She waded into the shockingly cold water, just far enough to wet her feet. She splashed a little water on her face and glanced around her before she scooped a couple of handfuls to drink.

Once she waded back and put on her boots, she glanced around and checked the sun to get her bearings. Looking down the shadowy bank of the burn, she decided to head that way, hoping the MacLeans wouldn't come looking for her anytime soon. She prayed the burn widened enough that she could even try floating down it, which would be faster than climbing through all the undergrowth that lined it.

Utter silence surrounded her as she picked up her pouch and moved deeper into the trees, keeping an eye on the naked man as she drew even with him and she saw... plenty, and it all appeared to be in magnificent working order, for he was just about the most splendid example of manhood as she had ever seen—and she was, after all, a doctor and had seen a great deal of the male anatomy. In fact, the rest of him looked good enough to bump old David off his pedestal in the Piazza della Signoria and take his place.

She paused to partake of life's offering and felt not one iota of embarrassment as she stared stupidly, with her mouth gaping like a backwoodsman on his first visit to town, but she would have to say in her defense that she was polite enough to chastise herself from time to time for gawking. And then she reminded herself that she shouldn't waste her precious time to pause and gawk, for the MacLeans could be searching for her at this very moment. But what woman in her right mind wouldn't look when afforded such an opportunity?

She was thinking that he was a prime candidate to help her get her mind off Ronan and being left at the altar, so to speak. Yes, if this black-haired Scot, proud as Lucifer before the fall and naked as a needle in broad daylight, couldn't get her mind off her recent predicament with the MacLeans, there had to be something wrong with her.

Of course, she was just talking big, for she wasn't on the verge of going over to his side of the burn and striking up a conversation, for that could be a good way to end up with her head on a pike. Still, she had to hand it to him, for he was one fine specimen of a young, healthy male in any century. It was a good omen, for she knew her feelings, when it came to men, weren't as dead as she thought.

All and all, Scotland was looking better and better all the time, for who wouldn't enjoy the site of a gloriously naked man without a smidgen of modesty? Of course, he was unaware that she was watching him with heart-thumping relish and drooling from the other side of the burn, while at the same time feeling Shakespeare was right on target when he wrote "Can one desire too much of a good thing?" Apparently not, for there he was, luring her like the scent of something sweet and forbidden, and desire rose within her like a burning flame begging to be fed.

She studied the beautiful musculature of his chest, the ripple of muscle when he moved, and then the rather melancholy face and long, dark, damp hair while she was, thinking... Something about him seemed familiar... for surely he had stepped right out of a dream. He was wearing only chausses—his bearing haughty and proud. She closed her eyes for a moment to clear the mental image of him from her mind, for she was certain he was a figment of her imagination, but when she opened her eyes, he was still there. No vision, but a mortal who stepped out of a dream right into reality.

For a brief moment, they were like Adam and Eve alone in the Garden of Eden, but then she came to her senses and realized that they might be alone now, but the MacLeans were sure to be looking for her and more than likely hot on her trail, so it was time to move on and leave this enchanted spot. With a sigh of disappointment, she regretted she had to turn away. She truly wished she could enjoy the scenery longer, but she had to put some distance between herself and the MacLeans if she ever hoped to escape.

She turned away and continued to follow the winding burn, careful to stay near the water's edge and on the rocks that lined it so she left no footprints. As she walked, she kept thinking about long, dark hair and well-honed muscles, and promptly fell over a log.

At that exact moment, she heard a rustling in the bracken and knew the MacLeans had caught up with her. She pounded the ground out of frustration and was starting to get up when she felt a hand clamp around her wrist and she was hauled ignominiously to her feet. She searched her mind for an excuse, knowing full well that Angus MacLean was going to be furious with her, and she was now wishing she had not tarried to look at the stranger.

"What do ye think ye are doing oot here? Are ye daft, woman?"

It wasn't the voice of MacLean but of one of his soldiers. She glared at the hand gripping her wrist, and then, without looking at him, she said, "I must be. I'm talking to you, aren't I?"

"Ye would do well to mind yer tongue. What are ye doing roaming aboot here alone and afoot? Ha' ye no sense?"

None of MacLean's men would ask her such a question, so Elisabeth turned her head and stared into the handsome, chiseled face of a man with the darkest blue eyes she'd ever seen, so dark, they were almost purple. But her wrist was starting to feel the loss of circulation.

"*Ouch!* You're cracking my wrist, you ogre," she said angrily, and saw he looked irritated enough to really and truly put her head on a pike. And suddenly, she saw the way he was looking at her and she knew he was thinking about her having seen him sans clothing. *Well, if he thinks I'm going to mention it, he has a long wait.*

However, she would have to admit that she was truly embarrassed to know he had seen her, and she could not help the rosy stain of mortification she felt spreading over her cheeks.

He removed his hand, ignoring the way she rubbed her wrist. "Who are ye, and what are ye doing out here alone?"

She waved her hands, hoping to quiet him, as she glanced back the way she had come, praying she had not been followed. "Shhh... they will hear you."

He looked like he wasn't buying whatever she was selling, so she tried again. "Please, I was captured by the MacLeans of Mull. I managed to escape, but they are not far behind me. Please, let me go before they come looking for me, for they will most assuredly haul me back to Duart Castle and hold me indefinitely as their prisoner. Believe me, they have taken me captive before, more than once. I can tell you now that it wasn't a lot of fun, so I was hoping to be spared the indignity of it again."

He stared at her as though he was talking to someone from Mars, so she tried smiling at him.

The hardness of his gaze softened somewhat as he asked, "What is this word 'fun'?"

Good Lord, she thought. *I'm about to be captured and he wants to play vocabulary?* She decided the best thing to do was to give him a quick synonym...

Entertaining... "Fun means the same thing as entertaining," she said, quickly glancing behind her.

"Then why didna ye say entertaining if it means the same? Why have two wirds with the same meaning?"

She was ready to throw her arms up in the air from exasperation. All she knew was that she had to end this running dialogue or they would be here all day, and time was something she did not have. "Look, I will explain that to you later," she said, "but right now, I have to get away from here... and fast!" She turned to leave, but he caught her by the arm, more firmly this time.

"Listen! I am sure you mean well, but if you don't want to fight a dozen MacLeans, you should really let me go. Please! I don't want to be their prisoner again!"

"Where is yer home, lass?"

"The Isle of Mull, but I'm on my way to Soutra Aisle to study medicine there."

He jerked her arm, which pulled her against him, and she stared into his angry face just as he said, "Ye lie! Soutra Aisle is a friary and they allow no women there."

"They will allow me, for I have a letter from Lachlan Mackinnon, the abbot at Iona. I am going to Soutra to familiarize myself with the herbs and medicines the friars use and to learn their methods of treating the sick and infirm. And you really are cracking my wrist."

Without saying a word, he hauled her against him and slung her over his shoulder like she was spoils taken in a raid. He carried her to the burn and waded across with the warmth of his hand spread across her posterior, and none too gently, mind you. However, she remained silent about the impropriety of that indignation, for she knew it would do no good to complain about it. Besides, he might just dump her in the burn and ride off without her, and she desperately needed his help, for anything seemed far better than being back in the clutches of Angus MacLean.

He did not put her down until he reached his horse, which was, appropriately, a black beast, just like its owner, and like his horse, the owner was, she would have to admit, a prime specimen. She drank in the sight of him as he saddled his horse, mesmerized by the play of muscles working in harmony to perform such a task and satisfied that he could not see her enjoying every moment of every little movement he made. She sighed, for it was like something from a movie. Here he was, a man to teach Hollywood's favorite idol a thing or two about playing the role of the hero. And why not, for this was no role-playing pseudo hero. This knight was the genuine article, the kind of man all modern heroes would try to emulate and never in a million years come close to.

Like the Mackinnons, he wore the regalia of a knight, for he was dressed in chausses, a hauberk, and over that, a tunic, which would set any woman's heart aflutter— and those long leather boots that came over the knee... Well, they seemed to put him right smack at the top of the desirability list, as far as she was concerned. She saw plenty of such boots at Màrrach, of course, but she had never seen them on him, and he did wear a knight's garb the way it was meant to be worn. Women in the twenty-first century did not know what they were missing. Sexy... sexy... sexy...

He was very good-looking, which would be enough to get him noticed. But he also had that certain something that made him stand apart from all others. It was something remarkable that made a woman notice a man the minute he entered the room, something that drew her to him and made her feel like she was melting inside. He was masculine and confident, and possessed a manner that said he was sure of himself and comfortable with himself and his place in the world around him. He had already proved he wasn't afraid to step forward and make decisions, even on the spur of the moment. And if there was anything she needed, it was a man capable of doing just that.

Her gaze went back to the coat of arms on his tunic, for there was something about the shield with the blue background and the three white stars... she frowned, recalling that the shield of the Black Douglas had a blue bar at the top with three white stars across it. Two and two were starting to make four, because strange things had been happening and they were beginning to bear the marks of the meddling of that vacuous vapor who seemed to take an inordinate amount of pleasure in poking his nose in the lives of others.

"Are you a Douglas?"

He seemed surprised by that question. "Nae, I am of Clan Murray. What reason would ye ha' to think my name was Douglas?"

She had already committed herself, so she might as well finish it. "It's the blue bar with three white stars on your tunic. The arms of the Black Douglas are on a blue background with three stars."

"Aye, 'tis said we both have Flemish ancestors."

His ancestors could have been cannibals for all she cared, for he was simply a delight to look at, and she would have to say that his hawkish nose and the sensual fullness of the mouth below were quite distracting. The best part was that she was attracted to him, and that made her feel human again after suffering over her loss of Ronan, for she realized she had suffered his loss for some time. Apparently, she was truly over the worst of it now, for she was fascinated by the way her knight simply oozed masculinity.

He mounted his horse, and she was flooded with disappointment, for she knew he was going to ride off, taking his honor and his good looks with him, and leave her here to fend for herself. She was on the road to feeling sorry for herself, but before she could ask if he intended to ride off and leave her, he leaned forward, clasped her about the waist and hauled her up into his lap, and said, "Ye will ha' to put yer leg over to ride astride."

She was already doing that when he spoke, and she replied, "I know how to ride. I learned when I was four years old."

She could have sworn she felt his body shake a bit, which, to her, indicated a chuckle, but since she had no way of knowing, she decided to call it a chuckle, which made her feel more relaxed with him. She exhaled a long sigh and took back every dark thought, each critical word she had said about Sir James Douglas, for rescued by this dark knight was far superior to being in the clutches of the MacLeans, in spite of her being ninety-nine percent certain that running into the MacLeans was not happenstance.

She frowned at that thought, for she was trying to decide what Sir James hoped to gain by causing the MacLeans to ride into her life again, just as they had the day she and Isobella first set foot on the Isle of Mull. Was it his intent for the MacLeans to capture her so this knight of Clan Murray could rescue her? But try as she might, she could see no purpose in it, for this knight certainly had nothing to do with medicine. She decided to give up trying to read the mind of a ghost, for everything he did sounded a bit far-fetched, but then, "far-fetched" was familiar ground for Sir James, and he could navigate it blindfolded—if he was in human form, of course.

Either way, things were definitely looking better. But they should be thinking about putting some distance between them and the MacLeans, for no matter how good a warrior he was, the two of them would be quite outnumbered.

"I forgot to mention that the MacLeans are large in number."

"'Tis naught to worry aboot, lass, for we shall be well away from here afore they arrive, and if we should encounter them, Angus MacLean is no threat to me."

"Maybe not to you, but he is a *big* threat to me," she said, "and he will fight you or anyone else to get me in his clutches again."

"Nae, he willna, fer his sister is married to my uncle, and he will no' harm ye while ye are under my protection."

She couldn't have been more relieved if a helicopter landed in front of them and offered them a ride, with a free lunch and a movie. She sighed with relief but then realized he was not saying he would keep her with him, even if the MacLean wanted her back. "You aren't going to hand me over to them, are you?"

"Nae, I dinna plan on it," he said. "Is there some reason why I should? Or mayhap there is a particular reason why ye want to stay wi' me."

She refused to tackle that one truthfully, on the grounds that it most certainly would incriminate her, so she simply said, "You are the lesser of two evils."

He actually laughed, and it was a beautiful, rich sound that ended too soon.

She waited for a moment or two, but when he said nothing more, she had to ask, "Just what do you plan on doing with me?"

"Ye said ye were on yer way to Soutra Aisle, did ye not? So that is where I will take ye."

She sighed happily and settled back against him. She closed her eyes, thinking about all that had happened to her of late. Life had certainly been one big adventure after another since she arrived. She found herself thinking that if she was sent back to her time, there were so many things about living here amongst these Scots that she would truly miss and being hauled around with her back resting on a hunk of a Scottish warrior from the past was definitely at the top of the list.

"Ye have an odd manner o' speech. Where did ye learn it?"

"From my father… he traveled a great deal and lost much of his accent when his became mingled with many other tongues." *Please don't ask me anything more…*

"And yer name?"

"Elisabeth Rhiannon Douglas." She was prepared for a comeback, but he remained mute. She wondered what he was thinking, but she wasn't about to ask. However, she did hope the Murrays didn't have some centuries-old feud going against the Douglases.

They rode for what seemed to her a long time, and perhaps it was, for the brilliant orange orb of sun was dropping lower and turning the sky a rusty red. Then, as if growing heavier, it began sinking into the treetops. Something about it reminded her of the crimson-colored flesh of a blood orange, which made her realize she was starving. She hadn't eaten since a very early breakfast, and she hoped he didn't hear her stomach growling or her ribs clanking together.

When the early evening began to settle around them, she broke the silence. "I hate to sound unappreciative for your kindness in rescuing me, but I am hungry... or to be more accurate, I am starving and my stomach thinks my throat has been cut."

He didn't say anything, and she would have to say she was disappointed that he kept on riding. After a while, she began to feel a bit sleepy, so she closed her eyes, vaguely aware that her head flopped backwards. Her only thought was that he could shove it away if he liked... and that was her last thought as she drifted off to sleep.

She had no way of knowing how long she dozed, for when she opened her eyes, they were no longer moving, and it was not yet completely dark. She was staring up at a handsome face, uncomfortably close due to his having shifted her so she was nestled in the crook of his arm. She wondered just how long he had been sitting there on his horse and staring down at her face.

For a moment, she was completely incapacitated by the intimacy of being held in his arms like this with her face just inches from his. The way he never took his gaze from her face made her feel spellbound, and it left her hopelessly adrift in the fathomless blue-violet sea of his eyes. She felt powerless and unable to move or turn her head, and she wondered if he was a cohort of the Black Douglas and she was under a spell, for everything about him was mesmerizing.

She wanted to ask him to help her down, but if she had learned anything in the time she had been here, it was that a woman was more effective when it came to men if she employed diplomacy, and if one tossed in a dash of helplessness, even better. However, helplessness was not in her vocabulary, and looking at him, she didn't think diplomacy would serve her any better than trying to wrestle herself out of his grip. In the end, she tried the practical approach.

"My backbone will be permanently fused to this saddle if you don't release me and put me down."

"What is this word 'fused'?"

"It means to bring two things together so they are physically united." As soon as the words left her mouth, she wanted to grab them back, but she would have settled for him to simply have missed the obvious innuendo, or at least be gentleman enough to ignore it.

One look at him with the raised brows and the laughter dancing in his eyes told her she struck out on both. She wished she could simply stick her head in the sand. *Elisabeth, you are an idiot, pure and simple, and no one would ever accuse you of engaging your brain before your mouth.*

Thankfully, he did not add a verbal jab to the visual one he had already given her. Instead, he said, "Mayhap I will take that under serious consideration, once I have answered a question that has been plaguing me since I saw ye spying on me in the river."

She gasped, ready to declare her innocence about spying, but decided instead to swallow the words that crowded at the back of her throat, for she needed to be careful about how she handled things with him, and that included how much information she provided him. For a moment she couldn't decide which of those she was going to respond to: the accusation that she was spying, or what it was that had been plaguing him. She opted for the latter, not grasping the fact that she had compromised herself, when she asked, "And what question would that be?"

The words no more than left her mouth when she noticed the way he was looking at her, and she stood there like a charmed snake while he lowered his head and when she gazed into his eyes she understood her mistake, for she was unable to look away.

Her heart began to pound. She could have shoved him away. She should have turned her head. She could have said she didn't kiss on the first date. She could have said or done any of a dozen things, but she simply stared like a trapped rabbit, mesmerized as she gazed into his eyes. She humiliated herself further when she allowed a faint little groan to escape, just as his head lowered and his mouth took hers, and truthfully, she was not sure if the groan was born of desire or of feeling like an ensnared varmint about to be skinned. Not that it mattered, for her eyes drifted closed of their own accord. He kissed her lightly, then he pulled back.

It did not occur to her until later that he had kissed her lightly as an inquiry that she could reject by turning her head away or accept by doing exactly as she did, and this time, when he lowered his head, he kissed her in the fullest sense of the word. She remembered a fleeting thought that there were kisses and there were kisses and this was definitely a kiss... one that sent her world wobbling off kilter, so unexpected it was. And yet, it wasn't so different from kisses she had experienced before, which had to mean it was the kisser and not the kiss, per se, that she found exciting. And even more unexpected and surprising was how very much she enjoyed it, for her body was responding big time.

The kiss was slow, lingering, and thorough... very thorough, to be exact. He traced her lips and drew her lower lip into his mouth, and the sensuality of it made her dig her hands into his tunic to keep her balance in a world that had suddenly gone off track. It must have struck him as humorous, for he pulled back just enough to brush his lips across hers lightly, and as he did, she sighed, thinking she was so very happy to find she enjoyed kissing him as much as she did.

But, she had to admit, that wasn't your average kiss, and he definitely wasn't just your run-of-the-mill Highlander. He was obviously an educated man of good breeding who had all the trappings of a bona fide catch, so she couldn't fault him one iota. And the thought of their parting ways was not a pleasant thought, for there was some really powerful chemistry going on here.

She wasn't a child, and not one to mourn over someone for the rest of her life. She had loved Ronan, but he was wed to another now, and she knew he would have fulfilled his obligations as a husband, whether he wanted to or not. There would always be a place in her heart for him, but now there was room enough for another, and this knight seemed to fill the bill.

She knew the best way for her to pick up the pieces and start anew was to go on with her life, and if that meant kissing this stranger, then so be it. She knew that as a knight, he followed a code of honor and that meant she would not be harmed, nor would he force himself upon her. So, what was wrong with a little harmless kissing, especially when it was for such a good cause... well, she needed to see if she had really dealt with losing Ronan and moved on, didn't she?

Elisabeth, just who do you think you are fooling?

She had never been the shy type, but she seemed to have all the characteristics of it now, for she felt... well, *tremulous*. Yes, definitely the symptoms were there, for she was a trembling, quivering, dry-mouthed lump of timid reserve that made her feel completely witless. While she sat there, looking up at him like she was searching for her brain, he lifted his hand to her cheek and gently stroked it with the back of his fingers, and that opened Pandora's box, while a flurry of butterflies seemed to be loose in her stomach.

She stopped breathing when his hand skimmed lightly over the skin of her throat. Her eyes fluttered and then closed when his index finger came out to follow the curve of her bodice, lightly skimming over the swell of her breasts. And it stopped there long enough for his mouth to capture hers, while his hand cupped her breast, finding and caressing the point that sent waves of sensation coursing through her. The sensation was so powerful she groaned, for her body seemed to be flooded with liquid warmth.

Just when the kiss seemed to go on forever, it ended and reality began to settle around her. Embarrassed now, her eyes flew open and she saw him watching her, knowing he had touched her in a throat-catching way that made her natural instincts take over. She was breathing heavily. Her throat was dry. There wasn't an intelligent thought in her brain... well, other than the thought that she wanted him to kiss her again.

He must have been thinking along those same lines, for he was having feelings he thought long dormant, while a gentle wave of emotion filled his battle-hardened body and seemed to glow like a hot coal inside him. He was acutely aware of everything around him, for the sun seemed brighter, the air fresher, the birds noisier, the trees fuller leafed and a darker shade of green, and the heat of desire within him greater and more powerful than he had, heretofore, experienced.

It was as if every part of his body had joined forces in order to make him more acutely aware of her—the feel of her skin, the scent of her hair, the softness of her breast, the slender curves of her body, the ripple of ribs. His mind jerked back to awareness when she grabbed his hand and said, "That will do, Lancelot."

He dismounted and hauled her out of the saddle. She made the mistake of looking up at him and saw he was studying her face intently, looking for clues... of what? The last vestiges of her aching desire for him? And he must have seen how she was not yet recovered from the intimacy they shared. Did he know how difficult it was for her to end it, or how intensely she wanted to make love to him? Was he aware of his hand that was mere inches away from having the proof of her desire when she stopped him?

Or, were his thoughts returning to normal and his sharp eyes searching hers for a hint of her truthfulness? Her deceit? Her moral values?

She, meanwhile, was still stuck on how she reacted to him, how she melted when he touched her, and how a little part of her wished he would simply ride off into the sunset and take her with him.

Still holding her in his arms, he looked down at her and asked, "What are ye hiding? And dinna think aboot lying. I will have the truth."

Back to that, are we? Just when I thought both of us were happily diverted. "I hide nothing. I have answered your questions honestly." *Well, maybe not the one about my accent.*

There was something in his gaze that was overpowering and, because of that, a little frightening. She realized their little interlude of passion had not only cooled, but the lava was now rock hard. With a sigh, she realized she was not Alice, and this was not Wonderland. Nothing like a swift kick of reality to one's backside to change the slant of things. "You can put me down now."

He made a grunting noise and lowered her to her feet, and she started to turn away and yelped, "*Owwwww*." Her hand went immediately to her head, and she discovered her hair had caught in a link of his mail shirt. She yanked it loose, almost scalping herself in the process, for the mail was as rough as a Brillo pad. She wondered how it felt on bare skin, but then she remembered the thick, linen shirt knights always wore beneath the hauberk.

Rubbing her head, she looked around the clearing and heard the bubble of a burn nearby. She stretched, trying to get her mind off what had passed between them and wishing for more. Chastising herself, she decided she needed a diversion—like getting the kinks out of her mind and body. She wished she had a pair of shorts and tennis shoes so she could jog along behind him and his horse for a few miles. She wondered if she would ever be able to run again, for the terrain here was rough and the shoes quite the most cumbersome clodhoppers imaginable. She almost smiled when she thought about what he would do if she started doing a few exercises. He would probably think she was having some kind of seizure, especially in the garb of the long dress she wore, or perhaps he would think she was conjuring up some kind of charm or spell.

He stood a foot or so away, content to remain stoically silent and observant, as if he was intentionally trying to make her uncomfortable. If he was, it was working. She looked around. The sun had disappeared, and the evening was beginning to settle in, accompanied by the sounds of night creatures buzzing about. It was a dose of reality, and the howl of a wolf in the distance filled her with loneliness. She knew that would not do, so she asked, "Do you know how far it is to Soutra Aisle from here?"

His head tilted to one side and his brows went up, but he did not answer straightaway. She was about to ask the question again, when he said, "I will have ye there on the morrow."

He said nothing more, and a lull stretched between them like an empty hammock, so she made another attempt at conversation. "Thank you for helping me. I hope I haven't put you to a great deal of trouble or taken you too far out of your way. Where were you going?"

"Does it matter to ye?"

"No, of course not. Why would I care where you go? I was only making conversation and I realize the effort was wasted, so forget what I said and I will keep my big, fat mouth shut."

"I am on my way to Elcho Priory," he said, his voice flat and toneless.

She laughed and saw the way his face hardened just before he asked, "Ye find something humorous aboot a priory?"

"No, of course not! I'm sorry. I wasn't laughing at you, but at our situation. I am going to Soutra Aisle, where there are only friars. You are going to Elcho Priory, which is a priory of nuns. It seems it should be the other way around. I have told you why I am going to Soutra Aisle. Can you tell me why you are going to the priory?"

That guarded mask of secrecy slipped back into place, and he asked, "Is my business there important to ye?"

"Oh, for Pete's sake!" She threw up her hands. "Never mind! I don't want to know, and if you try to tell me, I swear I will stuff my fingers in my ears. I'm too tired to try and humor an ogre. I wasn't trying to pry into your personal affairs. I was trying to be polite and engage you in a civilized conversation between two educated human beings, but I can tell by your ignorance of it that civilized conversation is something that has not yet reached the part of the world you live in. So, I'm going to go wash some of the dirt from my face and hands, with hopes that you enjoy your time free of me."

By the time she returned, he had his horse unsaddled and kindling gathered for a fire. He handed her two oatcakes and a strip of what she hopefully assumed was dried beef, for she could use a bit of protein about now. She almost smiled, imagining what he would do if she started telling him about the benefits of eating protein and how it would be good for him, in that it was a building block of bones, muscles, cartilage, skin, and blood, not to mention repairing tissues, or that it was a macronutrient, which meant the body needed large amounts of it. Her mind wandered off on another tangent, occupying her while she waited for him to start something that resembled a conversation. Finally, when none was forthcoming, she said, "I'm curious as to why you were bathing in the burn earlier today, instead of waiting to do it now."

"'Twas warmer then than now."

Well, there was certainly nothing like hitting one in the solar plexus with an obvious answer. She clenched her jaw against a cleverly delivered retort and diverted her thoughts to the topic of the solar plexus, that large network of sympathetic nerves and ganglia located in the peritoneal cavity behind the stomach and having branching tracts that supply nerves to the abdominal viscera. And with a hint of feeling a supreme moment, she added a definition for him… *the pit of the stomach*.

It was effective, but not so effective that she stopped wishing there was a hole somewhere that she could crawl into and pull the dirt over her head. She was through trying to engage in anything that resembled conversation with him. She would not utter a peep, unless she had a question, which was not bloody likely. So, she looked around as she munched on an oatcake that had as much flavor as a boiled sock. It amazed her that something that was almost pure oatmeal and probably recently made could taste like something her sister Isobella would have unearthed while digging in an ancient Celtic mound.

Forgetting her vow of silence, she asked, "Is there

anything to drink, or do I grab a little ice floating down the burn and eat it?"

He seemed amused, which was about as sensual as any woman could handle without letting her mind wander off into imaginings of what it would be like to make love with him, which, to be honest, she had already considered. But instead of giving him a clever reply, he beat her to the punch by saying, "'Tis a pity for sure that there isna any ice in the burn, for I would enjoy watching ye eat it."

She clasped her hands together and placed them between her knees as she looked around the glen. Her mind was exhausted and devoid of any clever thoughts or interesting topics for conversation, and not feeling particularly sleepy, she guessed looking around was about her only option. She noticed his saddle and plaid near what appeared to be a shallow cave. Nearby was an old wattle-and-daub hut with a partially collapsed roof of dingy thatch, which was exactly the kind of thing Isobella would have done cartwheels to inspect. It occurred to Elisabeth just how much she had learned about archaeology through her sister since coming to Scotland, for there was a time when she would have guessed wattle was a stepped-on duck.

She had to turn sideways a bit to see, off to one side, where the cold waters of the boulder-strewn burn flowed, and she was reminded of the icy effect of washing her hands and being harshly reminded of his wisdom in bathing beneath the warming rays of sunlight earlier in the day.

After he turned down her offer to help him build a fire, she entered the cave and found it to be larger than she expected. She could see the remains of older fires and some markings on the cave walls, but she had learned enough from helping Isobella in the caves she excavated on the Isle of Mull to know that these markings were not those of the ancient Celts or Picts. They were done much later. Farther over were some scattered bones, including a few at the back of the cave that she identified as human—two of which belonged to an infant. She wondered at the cause of death.

She heard a sound and turned to see him spreading his plaid just inside the cave, not far from the fire. She guessed she was going to sleep beside him, as Isobella said she had when Alysandir rescued her.

"Ye will have to share my plaid."

Oh, gee, what a bummer…my having to share a plaid with a totally delectable man who could generate sexual tension picking his teeth. She gave the plaid a resigned look and sighed woefully. "Well, I suppose it beats sleeping on a pile of dirty leaves."

Standing at the mouth of the cave, highlighted by firelight, he seemed larger, darker, and fiercer than in daylight, to the point that she could almost believe he had morphed into some immortal being, an ancient Celt perhaps, angry at her intrusion to this place, or dressed in his knights regalia as he was, he could have been Thor, the god of thunder. Perhaps she should have accepted the ancient Celtic necklace that Alysandir Mackinnon had offered her, telling her how such a necklace was thought to ward off evil.

"You have yet to tell me who you are," she said, her gaze on the plaid.

"Why do ye want to know?"

"I don't. I've changed my mind. Keep your identity to yourself."

"Then why did ye ask?"

She was truly sorry that she had brought it up. But she was committed now so she replied, "It seemed proper to at least know the name of a man I would be sleeping beside, but I realize how foolish that is, since it is quite commonplace to sleep with no-name strangers. Faith! I do it all the time."

He said nothing but continued to look at her, neither smiling nor saying anything. There was, however, the barest hint of amusement in his eyes. But his face was still stony and his features dramatized by the firelight. His eyes looked as black as pitch, and the dark blue surcoat he wore gave him a netherworld appearance that made her think she wouldn't have been surprised if he sprouted giant wings and flew right over her head. Then she wondered if this place was haunted, for it was certainly getting to her in a weird sort of way. She felt she was an outsider here, that somehow she was upsetting the balance of things ancient and probably causing a few rocks to hurl down the side of a crag somewhere nearby.

"David Murray, at yer service, mistress," he said, then added, "Come, hie yersel' over here and sit doon while I retrieve something from my pouch."

She watched David Murray At Yer Service as he walked toward his saddle. His horse was neither tied nor tethered, as was the way of many Highlanders, whose horses, miraculous as it seemed, would not stray. Perhaps Highlanders had the same effect upon women, for she was thinking along those same lines. She forced further thoughts away from him. Being quite knowledgeable about horses herself, she thought the Scots' hobblers were unbelievable horses, for they were small, active, and able to travel great distances over the most difficult and boggy countryside. What her father wouldn't give for a couple of hobbler studs to breed with mares on their ranch.

She suddenly felt a stab of loneliness for the world she had left behind… six hundred years into the future, but it wasn't the same kind of loneliness she felt when she was first yanked back in time. This had become her world now, and these Scots were her people, and she knew her skills as a physician were needed beyond anything she would have found in the twenty-first century. Only he did not seem the least interested in being one of her people. Still, it was the nature of humans to think upon their slippers when their feet began to hurt.

To get her mind back on the current century, she studied the way he walked, with a certain fluid ease and long stride. She liked the long-shanked, muscled leanness of him, for he was well put together, tall and slender with just the right amount of strength in the legs and arms where it was needed. His walk was about as close to a cowboy swagger as one could get in Early Renaissance Scotland. She realized she truly liked his build, for it seemed much more masculine to her than that of the twenty-first-century males who hung out at the gym building body mass that they would never use.

She glanced at his sword, trying to remember what Isobella told her about the swords of this time period, but all she recalled was it was long, double handled, and very well kept, for it fairly gleamed. Because of the size and double handle, she thought a fair guess would be that it was a claymore, but she had been wrong before. She turned her attention back to David, thinking that she knew he was a man of honor, self-discipline, bravery, and strong mental bearing, for she had witnessed his calm demeanor, and knowing that he was a knight, she knew he would embody these traits. Simply said, he had that superior kind of manner that one would envy, and in many ways he reminded her of Alysandir, for they were both Highlanders of Celtic, or in David's case, Celtic-Flemish stock, and they both lived by the same code, that of a knight.

Her study was cut short when he returned with a small pouch and a silver cup, and she watched as he poured what she thought was probably mead or *uisge beatha*, the ancestor of the Scots whisky of the twenty-first century.

He offered the cup to her. When she hesitated, he said, "Drink it doon, mistress. 'Twill ease the effects of travel and grant ye a peaceful sleep."

She tilted her head to one side and gave him a serious stare, as if trying to see the inner workings of his mind. "I'm afraid I would have to have several of these in order to have a peaceful sleep with a total stranger."

His comeback was quick, sharp, and to the point. "Then mayhap I shouldna remain a stranger."

She gulped and almost choked, but recovered quickly enough that she hoped he did not see it. "Don't get your hopes up," she said as she took the cup from him. She could tell by the fumes that it was whisky, and she felt the burn in her nose when she sipped it. She smiled, thinking back to another time, far, far away.

"What pleasures ye?"

"Nothing… it was just a memory."

"Ye would prefer not to tell me of this memory?"

She took another sip. "I was remembering a time when my sister and I were much younger, and we drank some of our father's whisky… actually, a *lot* of our father's whisky, and we couldn't seem to stop talking and singing, and everything made us laugh… until the next day, when we thought we were dying."

He almost smiled; in fact there was a hint of amusement in his eyes. "Aye, it robs the mind of wit."

She finished the whisky and handed him the cup. "Your turn," she said, and watched him fill the cup and take a few sips. Before he could say anything, she rose to her feet. "I think the whisky is having the desired effect, and I would like to lie down before I fall down, so if you would be so kind as to tell me if I am permitted to go to sleep now."

"Aye," he said in his usual reticent manner, and nodded toward his plaid.

"Thank you," she said, and toddled off, feeling quite mellow, warm, and quite sleepy.

She had a vague memory of having lain down before she fell asleep. She wasn't certain how long she slept before she became vaguely aware of him lying down beside her, closer to the cave opening, which meant he would greet any wolves that stopped by for a visit. That bit of information warmed her to the core and with a sigh, and she smiled and felt her muscles relax.

As for him, David spent a great part of his time studying Elisabeth as a spectator would, for he quietly and carefully noted her behavior—quiet and careful observation being a valuable source of information. She was beautiful, but what intrigued him more was that there was something different, yet incomparably extraordinary about her. David was not the kind of man who was given to hasty assumptions about a woman who caught his eye or happened to stand out when compared to others. Yet this one was a strange sort, different from the multitudes, which made her quite unlike any woman he had met, and that went beyond the fact of her strange speech. He decided he would find out more about her before making his final decision on whether to believe or trust her.

He was also a man with a man's urgings and needs. He did have a good eye for beauty, and she definitely was a beauty who instantly caught his attention and held it. As he observed her, he found himself wondering if she was real or whether he was conjuring up a fantasy, for there was an almost ethereal quality about her that made him want to know more about her: who she was, and where she came from. And because he desired her, part of him wondered if she was truly a mortal or simply one who called home any place where the celestial spheres gathered. He found all of this a bit vexing because he could not find a place in his mind where she seemed to fit into his world.

There was much to like about the lass. He was captivated by her hands. They were graceful, pale, and slim, but they moved with such seemingly effortless beauty and charm of movement that he felt spellbound simply watching her perform simple tasks... the brushing away of an errant wisp of hair, the way she held the reins in her hand, the way her hands encircled the cup when she drank. They were not the hands of an ordinary woman, even one of great breeding, for he sensed they held a magical quality.

Her motions were deft and fluid, purposeful and yet full of grace. When she moved, he was reminded of the reeds at the loch, and the way they bent and danced at the water's edge. She was unusual and that captivated him; mysteriously elusive and that made him wary and cautious. He felt himself drawn to her, not only by his masculine attraction to her, but by some unknown, stronger force. All he had to do was to close his eyes and he could see her as she had looked when he caught his first glimpse of her with her face bathed in sunlight. She had exquisite skin, the color and texture of cream that rises to the top of milk.

Watching her when she was asleep was like studying a painting of the Madonna, for light played upon her heart-shaped face and lent a shimmering quality to the porcelainlike texture of her skin. All that was missing was a bowl of fruit on a table beside her. But the rest of her... his body stirred. She should be lying upon a tapestry heavily embroidered with red and gold thread. But it was the resplendent glow of her face that convinced him that something wholesome, pure, and giving dwelled within the heart and soul of her.

Was she simply a beautiful mortal that he happened upon, or was she an enchantress who bewitched him with a spell that rendered him unable to resist? When he first saw her, he was struck with the urge to capture her and toss her over his saddle and ride away with her, to find a place where he could place her that she would be his and his alone to enjoy. Even now, watching her sleep, he had visions of what she would look like lying there completely bare, and the thought of it stirred him.

He might have gone on thinking along these lines, had she not stirred and turned in her sleep, her skirt catching beneath her and exposing a long length of leg. He groaned and closed his eyes; then after a few minutes he stood and removed his hauberk, mail shirt, and belt. Then he dropped down beside her and lay there in the sheer agony of inextinguishable desire long after he drew his plaid over them.

At some point during the night, she felt cold and she tried to pull her skirts down to better cover her cold feet, which did nothing to warm the chill of the rest of her. She had a vague thought that she should scoot a little closer to him, when he suddenly turned over and pulled her against him. She put her head on his arm and snuggled close to him, wondering how he managed to be so warm while she was frozen to the core. She was almost asleep when she felt the press of his kiss against her hair, and that one innocent, chaste act endeared him to the core of her and told her what kind of man he was. She knew he desired her to the point he was in torment, for she had seen it in his eyes. He could have easily taken whatever he wanted from her.

But he did not...

That was her last thought until the early dawn, when he prodded her with his boot and she opened her eyes to the glow of a fire reflecting off the cave walls.

"'Tis time to go, Mistress Douglas, or we willna reach Soutra Aisle afore sundown."

Chapter 5

Life is mostly froth and bubble;
Two things stand like stone,
Kindness in another's trouble,
Courage in your own.

—"Ye Weary Wayfarer" (1866)
   Adam Lindsay Gordon (1833–1870)
   Australian poet

DERE STREET WAS THE MEDIEVAL NAME FOR THE ancient Roman road Via Regia, which was for centuries the main route from York, England, to the Firth of Forth, near Edinburgh. Close to this main route was one of the biggest and most famous hospitals in Europe, known as the House of the Holy Trinity.

The House of the Holy Trinity, founded in 1160, was a complex of hospital and monastic buildings with a friary run by Augustinian friars. Also known as the Hospice of Soutra, or Soutra Aisle, it was well endowed, powerful, and a refuge for travelers, pilgrims, fugitives, the needy and the sick, with estates that covered twenty square miles.

After another day of travel, Elisabeth got her first glimpse of this famous medieval hospital, and her first impression was how very different it looked from the lone surviving building and scattered rubble that were all that existed of it when she and Isobella visited it in the twenty-first century. But she couldn't very well tell David Murray that. And speaking of David Murray, he didn't exactly drop her, point to where Soutra Aisle was, and ride off, but he came close to it. Although he did deliver her to the hospital, he immediately said, with a brief apology, that he wanted to reach Elcho Priory before nightfall. And then he made ready for his immediate departure.

She did not want him to leave, and she did manage to detain him a moment longer by offering her thanks and appreciation for his chivalrous behavior. "I owe you a debt of gratitude," she said, "and I truly hope I shall one day have the opportunity to repay you. I shudder to think where I would be now, had you not befriended me. I shall never forget your kindness in coming to my aid."

"'Twas naught more that any honorable man would do," he said. "'Tis my hope that all will go well wi' ye during yer time at Soutra Aisle, Mistress Douglas."

She started to step back to tell him good-bye, but she was almost rendered speechless, for his cool, unassuming words did not, by any means, match the burning coals of desire she saw in his eyes. For a moment she remained in place, her hand on his boot as he looked down at her, for she was trapped in a moment of pure animal magnetism that passed like an electrical current between them. It paralyzed her to know he could mesmerize her by the sheer force of his larger-than-life presence, his desire for her, and the powerful force of knighthood that surrounded him like a mantle. It was as if she were snared in a bubble of time, held by a spider's thread spun in a golden field of stubble.

The purpled dye of his eyes was so hypnotic that she lingered in a neutral state of mental bondage, unable to break the charm of enchanted fascination she was under. She felt helplessly exposed by the liquid heat that seemed to melt away the fragments of her clothing until she was completely nude, standing beside him.

She was not immune to it, for she was suffused with warmth and a desire so powerful that she wanted to ask him to take her with him. *Ask him… go on. Ask him…* a voice in her head cried out. She moistened her lips, indecision eating away at her.

A cloud gathered overhead and thunder rumbled. The scent of rain hung heavily in the air, and if Sir James had been there, she would have told him to go chase a runaway star and mind his own business.

Maybe he was doing just that…

The thought was sobering. "God go with you," she said, and stepped back. She looked up at him with a smile that was genuinely warm. She was answered with a molten heat of desire that fairly glowed in the depth of his eyes, and for a moment she thought he was going to yank her into the saddle with him and ride away.

Her desire for him matched his and they both knew it, but in the end, honor and duty won out.

Her knees almost buckled when reality set in, and a moment later, he gave her a nod and spurred his horse into a full gallop. She knew that the last she would ever see of David Murray At Your Service was his dark blue cape billowing around him like the flapping wings of some giant, mythical bird, and she watched it until it faded from sight. She found it odd, but she felt a sense of loss, knowing he had come into her life for a brief period and then, just as quickly, passed out of it. Things like that happened all the time in one's life, yet this one left her with a particularly empty feeling, as if she missed him, which seemed absurdly impossible since she never truly knew him.

For some time she stood there, unable to move, for never had she met a man who charmed and captivated her attention as he had. She would always call him dear for filling her with such desire that she knew she had moved beyond the sadness of the past, and she would always think of this moment at Soutra Aisle as very special. For it had healed her broken spirit and rekindled her deep desire to heal. She would never forget him, and then she smiled, recalling genetics and the phenomenon of imprinting, when ducklings and chicks, upon hatching, would follow and become attached to the first moving object they encountered.

Only, in her case, she most assuredly socially bonded with David Murray, and then she watched him ride away, leaving her in a strange place among strange people, and she knew this was home, at least for a while.

With a sigh, she turned back to the friar who came outside to greet her, and she followed him inside. She withdrew the letter of introduction from Alysandir Mackinnon's uncle, Lachlan Mackinnon, and gave it to the Abbot. After learning she was related to the Mackinnons and reading the letter from their uncle, Elisabeth was well received and warmly welcomed by the friars. The Master of the Hospital seemed especially honored to have the opportunity to teach her what they knew, and he began to tell her how much they needed women to help with the smaller hospitals at nunneries, these hospitals being more like the clinics of her time.

This was where her new life began, and she promised herself she would learn as much as she could from the friars regarding methods, medicines, disinfectants, and the general medical and surgical knowledge that was available in this time period. However, she would have to admit that she did feel a sense of continued emptiness over her knight in shining armor and the memory of him riding over the rim of a hill to be absorbed into the bright orb of a setting sun resting there. If she was going to be kidnapped, why it couldn't have been by someone like David Murray?

And speaking of kidnappings, it did seem that since she arrived in Scotland, her life had dealt mostly with kidnappings, disappointments, and losses. She sniffed, having used up her allotted time to feel sorry for herself, and nodded her thanks at Father Andrew Galbraith, who handed her a kerchief. "In case you ha' a need fer it," he said.

"Thank you. I suppose I am not as good at hiding my emotions as I thought," she said, smiling up at him.

"Leaving is never easy, lass, because we always leave a part of ourselves behind. But soon we learn to part with the things we can part with and bring with us the things we hold too dear. Sometimes it helps to look forward and not behind, for there is always in front of us something new to be experienced. After all, that is why ye left, is it not... to learn something new?"

How could she not smile at the optimism in his voice and the cheerful manner in which he spoke? "You shall be my new best friend," she said quite seriously, and Father Andrew laughed.

"I can think of nothing that would pleasure me more, but remember that Job endured everything until his friends offered him comfort."

She gave him a curious stare, and when he said nothing, she asked, "So, tell me. What happened to him?"

"He grew impatient."

Oh, if you only know just how impatient I am to see again the knight who just rode away. She laughed. "You remind me of my father, who always tempered my impatience by telling me 'Nature, time, and patience are the three great physicians.'"

Father Andrew smiled and said, "A wise man, he."

She took a deep breath and looked around. The worst was over. She had said her good-byes to Ronan, her sister, all the Mackinnons, and the prince of princes who had rescued her from the clutches of the MacLeans, and now she was at Soutra Aisle, about to begin a brand-new adventure in her life. She had no idea just where it would take her or how it would all play out in the end, but for now, she was elated that it was a brand-new beginning, where she could put the pain and lack of purpose she experienced in the past behind her. She looked up at Father Andrew's round, beaming face and smiled. She considered it a welcoming gift, for she knew she would find in him a boon companion.

She had read much regarding the history of medicine, especially medieval medicine, in college and medical school. After her arrival in Scotland, she learned from Isobella that, because of the advancement of science and technology, archaeological excavations were proving that medieval healers in Scotland were not only aware of but also used much, much more than a few remedial herbs, as previously thought.

In Father Andrew, she had a constant companion who took an inordinate amount of pleasure in helping her, and what he didn't know he was most eager to find out. He was also eager to learn more about her medical abilities and information, but she was careful not to reveal too much, which would make him curious as to how she came to have such advanced knowledge. This was, after all, a religious hospital, and this was the age of suspicion when heretics were burned for nothing more than having beliefs that contradicted the established religious teachings.

Fortunately for her, she was the novice here, and Father Andrew, with his warm brown eyes and funny stories about his childhood, and gentle, blue-eyed Father Geoffrey, who had studied medicine in Italy, did most of her instruction. It was a time of learning for her in just about the most inhospitable place one could conjure up, for the squalls from the sea rolled in without warning and with great frequency. But she was so busy that she did not have much time to dwell on the lonely setting or the inclement weather, for the hospital was on the old Roman Road known as Dere Street, which ran from England to Edinburgh and the friars at Soutra Aisle gave succor to many a traveler.

Father Geoffrey enlightened her: "The Augustinian Order is highly respected for its hospitals." That went along with Isobella's comment that "they were the greatest practitioners of herbal medicine, and they ran more hospitals in the Middle Ages than any other order."

Once she rolled up her sleeves and set to work, Elisabeth was truly awed to discover there were so many medicines available. To date, she had identified some 230 plant species with medicinal applications, which Father Geoffrey carefully wrote down for her, complete with a precise and complete recipe for mixing each of them.

"If ye want to ease pain, mix opium with animal grease and rub it on the skin," Father Geoffrey said, "and when measuring, ye should recite the Ave Maria," which she decided amounted to about fifteen seconds.

"Next, I will teach ye to mix opium with wine for amputations," Father Andrew said.

The most astonishing thing was, according to her own conclusions, that the friars might have had more to do with female patients than originally thought, for in their supplies, there was a container of the deadly ergot fungus and berries of the juniper bush. She knew that black ergots were found only in the resting stage of a parasitic fungus that attacked cereal crops. But ergot also contains alkaloids, like ergometrine, which can cause catastrophic uterine contractions.

When she walked in the garden one afternoon with Father Geoffrey, she recognized something she knew. "Juniper bushes!" she said, remembering some that grew on their ranch in Texas.

"Aye, they represent the Tree of Life," he said.

She nodded and said nothing, but she knew that juniper was also a uterine stimulant and had been mentioned in conjunction with abortions as far back as Dioscorides in first-century Greece, for he wrote that a drug made from the root "is applied as a pessary with honey to draw down the embryo."

Father Geoffrey did not say such procedures were done at Soutra Aisle, but he did tell her that ergot and juniper were thought to help with childbirth or to end it. She knew this was dangerous territory for him, because Augustinian friars were strictly forbidden to practice midwifery. She did recall also that Isobella once told her that often such things were found during archaeological digs at medieval hospitals, where they unearthed fragments of bones from fetuses, which would suggest it was probably done in some places. Elisabeth pretended not to make the connection, however.

One herb that was very helpful was tormentil, which was used for parasitic worms, and it contained tannin, chinovic acid, and glycosides that could alleviate diarrhea and internal bleeding. Recalling the size of the swords the knights used and the wounds she had seen at Màrrach, she knew anything to help internal bleeding would be a godsend.

One afternoon, while in the apothecary, she did discover some pages that read as if they might have been copied from some ancient book of medicine, so she inquired about it to Father Symon. He was more of a bookworm than the others, and she could tell her curiosity pleased him immensely.

"Aye, 'tis from *De Materia Medica*," he said, "Dioscorides's five encyclopedias on herbal medicine and pharmacopeia. We use many of the herbs he referenced, and we shall teach ye the use of all of them if ye are here long enough."

And teach them they did, for she learned rhubarb was not only a laxative, as used in modern times, but also was used in this time period for digestive, kidney, bladder, spleen, and liver problems. Skullcap was used as a headache remedy, lungwort for tuberculosis. Wild carrot was good for coughs and convulsions; the teasel root possessed cleansing properties, and by boiling the herb's roots in wine, it was an effective treatment of fistulas as well as warts. The fruit of a yellow-barked shrub was of great value to treat "yellow diseases," which meant jaundice.

Father Geoffrey took her with him into the hospital one afternoon, where a patient had a bleeding gash on his thigh. He showed her how to heat oil, water, or metal and then touch it to the wound to seal off the blood vessels.

Later she told him, "With all the fighting and clan battles that occur, I am interested in treatment for wounds, especially when the wounds begin to fester."

"Ahhh," Father Geoffrey said. "Ye must become friends with *Erythraea centaurium*, good for wounds, lung disorders, and blood spitting. And there are honey, garlic, and vinegar for those that fester."

Soutra Aisle was never meant to be a permanent place for her, but only a stop to educate her, for being a woman she could not stay there for long. When the time came for her to take her leave, they gifted her with more recipes and notes for mixing other medicines they used, as well as seeds to start her hospital garden, including seeds for the poisonous herbs black henbane, opium poppy, and hemlock, and a box to keep them under lock and key.

In all, she spent three months at Soutra, and from what she learned, she realized that this period in time had been grossly misjudged, for their medical knowledge reached far beyond what modern medicine thought, but the opposite was also true, for when it came to sanitation and disease control, they were basically still very medieval.

Throughout her time at Soutra, there always lingered in her mind the knowledge that her allotted time would come to an end, since there was no nunnery here. And when it was time for her to go, it seemed far too soon and caught her completely off guard. The sad occasion was made sadder still when the friars gave a dinner for her and, as a parting gift, authorized six of the friars to escort her to St. Leonard's Augustinian Nunnery in Perth.

With her letter of introduction from Lachlan Mackinnon and another from the Master of the Hospital at Soutra, they made the journey north, learning on the way of an outbreak at St. Leonard's.

"'Tis kinkhoast," Father Symon said.

"'Tis a dreaded cough," Father Thomas added.

Pertussis... but he wouldn't know that term. "Ah... whooping cough," Elisabeth said, then realized he wouldn't know that term either.

"Mayhap that is another name fer it," Father Thomas said. "I have heard it is called chin-cough in England."

At last they arrived in Perth and made their way to the nunnery, where they were genuinely welcomed and seen as a gift from God. Because of the outbreak of kinkhoast, Elisabeth went to work immediately, thinking her friends would be there to help for a while. But, as Father Geoffrey said, "Our staying would only prolong yer becoming acquainted with yer new home," he said, then seeming a bit embarrassed, he reached into his cloak and withdrew a small leather pouch. When she opened it, she was stunned to see a golden cross studded with tiny diamonds on a gold chain, which he said the Master of the Hospital at Soutra had blessed.

"Oh, this is beautiful, but I could not accept something like this from you. It is priceless," she said, truly overwhelmed.

"It belonged to my sister. I have kept it since her death, for she wanted me to give it one day 'to a woman who is beautiful within and without.'"

Of course, she started to cry when Father Geoffrey placed it around her neck. Then Father William, Father Symon, and Father Thomas gathered around her and gifted her with a book of herbs, a pair of medical scissors, and vials and bottles of medicines, one of which she could use straightaway to treat the large number of children stricken with whooping cough.

One of the biggest boons from her time at Soutra was learning that the plant squill was used to treat whooping cough, and fortunately it was in one of her bottles. She knew from medical school that it was still in use in modern times as standardized sea onion powder for many other ailments—asthma, digestive problems, rheumatism, skin conditions, menstrual ailments, heart problems, back pain, hemorrhoids, and wounds. A typical dose was 0.1 to 0.5 grams, and one had to administer it carefully, for there could be side effects.

They took a short tour to the parts where the friars were allowed to go, and she learned the hospital at St. Leonard's was much smaller than Soutra Aisle, and the nuns were not as advanced in their medical knowledge. Comparing the two was like comparing a small clinic to a hospital in the twenty-first century.

All too soon, it was time for the friars to leave, and for some time after her friends had all departed, she found herself staring at the place where she had seen them last, her hand squeezing the cross at her throat, and swallowing to ease the knot there, as she considered herself the luckiest person in the world.

She turned and started to go to the abbey to pray, but as she looked around, she realized there was no better abbey than the beautiful bower where she stood. She dropped down on her knees, still clutching her cross, and thanked God for sending her here, for she knew in her heart it was not a mistake. This is not the path she would have chosen, for being away from Màrrach and her sister was difficult, but she knew she now stood upon firm ground.

She could see her way clearly now, for she knew there was a peaceful and perfect rightness to it, as if she had followed her yellow brick road. That did not mean she had no apprehensions or that she was unafraid. Nor did it mean this would be her home forever, unless she chose to take the vow of a nun. But for now, she would help those in need, practice this new kind of medicine, and pray for a time in her life when something would be permanent. *In the meantime*, she thought, *this is where I am needed*, and she felt an overpowering rightness to her circumstances.

Perhaps things were working out as they were meant to be. She was a doctor and she was needed, and there was little opportunity to practice on the Isle of Mull for it was sparsely populated and Màrrach was isolated. She knew now that leaving there was her opportunity to find a part of Scotland that provided her an opportunity to do what she had trained for. "This is where I was meant to be. This is where I belong, at least for the time being."

Apparently, she was wrong about that last statement, for her future lay elsewhere, and as a storm strikes without warning, she would be caught by surprise.

Chapter 6

I have found power in the mysteries of thought,
exaltation in the changing of the Muses;
I have been versed in the reasonings of men;
but Fate is stronger than anything I have known.

—*Alcestis* (438 BC)
    Euripides (484 BC–406 BC)
    Greek tragic dramatist

IT WAS OVER A MONTH LATER, ON A DARK, MOONLESS
night, when Elisabeth entered the storage room. She put
her candle down as she searched for her basket of herbs.
Finding it, she slipped her arm through it and was about
to pick up the candle when two knights burst into the
room and, asking her forgiveness, pulled her from the
room and into the torch-lit outer enclosure.

There, in the priory yard, she saw six mounted knights
and two saddled horses. She swallowed hard, fighting
the sense of panic rising in her throat. Of all the places
she thought she would be safe, it was in a nunnery. Who
were they and were they taking her? Had MacLean
found where she was and sent his knights? Had someone
accused her of sorcery? She was frightened, but before
she could ask who they were and where she was being
taken, she suddenly found herself thrust into one of the

saddles. She was starting to cry out when she noticed the prioress was hurrying toward her, but not in an alarmed manner. Did the prioress know these knights?

She put her hand on Elisabeth's knee and patted it. "Dinna fret, Elisabeth. These men are knights in the service of the Earl of Kinloss. His sister is the prioress at Elcho Priory. She was taken to her home on the Black Isle several days ago. It is feared she is dying of a fever. The earl has sent his men here to escort ye to Aisling Castle to care for the prioress."

"But why me, when they are much closer to the priory at Beauly?"

"The earl has heard there was healer who has performed miracles with the sick at Elcho Priory."

"But Elcho is here in Perth, not so terribly far from St. Leonard's. Why didn't they bring her here instead of taking her all the way to the Black Isle?"

"They didna know aboot ye at the time, and the prioress had asked to be taken back home to Aisling Castle so she could die there."

"If the fever is advanced, there is nothing I can do. She may be dead before I arrive. I am needed here, where my presence will make a difference to those not so gravely ill."

"'Tis naught I can do," the prioress said. "The knights have their orders and they are signed by the abbot of Fearn Abbey."

One of the knights rode up beside her and stopped. "Come mistress. We must be on our way."

She nodded at the prioress. The metal bit clanked as she turned the horse and rode alongside the knight riding next to her. Did he have orders to keep pace beside her? Surely they did not think she would ride off in the dark alone. She rubbed the back of her neck. She was already tired from a long day. She did not relish an even longer moonlight ride followed by however many days it would take to reach the Black Isle, especially riding with a hardened group of knights with frozen expressions of dark pride upon their faces. They looked as if they would rather be anywhere else but here.

Well, at least we have something in common...

All in all, it took almost three days of hard riding to reach the place near Inverness where they would cross the firth to the Black Isle, and another half day to reach their destination. Elisabeth was exhausted by the time they arrived at Aisling Castle. Weary to the bone, she had lost all track of time, for they traveled straight through, only stopping long enough to feed and rest the horses and eat, with very few stops to take anything that even remotely resembled a nap. It was late in the afternoon when she was pulled from the saddle, and when she was grabbed under the arms from behind, her knees gave way.

"Yer a hardy lass, I will grant ye that," said the knight who caught her, and she recognized by his voice that he was the stern-faced one who had ridden beside her.

She was starting to respond when her head began to buzz and she dropped to the ground.

Lord David Murray, the Earl of Kinloss, was staring morosely into the fire when he received word that the healer from Elcho Priory had arrived. He did not expect to see her being carried into the hall like a sack of oats tossed over a shoulder. "Has she caught the fever?" he asked.

"Nae, in truth we didna give the lass time to rest or provide her with naught to eat but a few oatcakes. I ken the fast pace o' the journey withoot sleep was too much for her."

Lord Kinloss walked closer and stared at the dirty bit of humanity in the arms of his closest friend and cousin, Duncan Murray, and he was shocked to see the face of the woman he rescued and took to Soutra Aisle a few months ago.

"Is she asleep or did ye have to cuff her to bend her to yer will?"

Duncan chuckled. "Nae, she is no' a defiant lass, but that may not be true when she awakes, for she has had a time o' it and she wasna too happy to come here." Duncan paused and looked from the girl to his cousin. "Have ye met the lass before?"

David was hardly listening to Duncan, for he could not believe this was the same woman he had been unable to forget, and now she was here under his care. He was curious as to how she had made such a reputation for herself in such a short time. But Duncan was looking at him strangely, so he nodded and said, "Aye, I ha' met the lass. 'Tis a long story," he said, distracted by the long length of trim legs dangling beneath the blue garment she wore. He recalled how many nights he had lain awake with the memory of her uncovered leg during the night they spent in the cave and what agony it had been to lie beside her and have her not.

Duncan laughed. "Weel, I ha' plenty o' time to hear yer tale aboot the lass. Mayhap ye can tell me later."

David continued to stare at her, recalling the achingly familiar face, for even when it was dirty, she was still a beauty. He longed to touch her auburn hair, rich as golden sable. He said nothing, but he did wonder what she would do when she realized he was the one who had her brought to Aisling Castle.

"'Twas not a happy lass we had, ye ken, fer she wasna pleased aboot being hauled here like so much baggage, withoot a bath or a change o' clothes, and at such a fast pace. Faith! I am in awe that the lass made it as far as Aisling afore she dropped like a stone from lack o' sleep."

Duncan glanced toward the stairs. "Shall I carry her above stairs and let her sleep a while?"

"Nae, yer tired after such a trip yersel'. Go get some rest. Let me have the lass, and I will take her up to the room that has been readied for her."

Duncan wasn't so tired that he couldn't grin widely at the words his cousin uttered, so he raised his brows in a questioning manner and then laughed when his cousin paid him no mind.

Ignoring Duncan, Lord Kinloss gathered Elisabeth into his arms and carried her up the stairs and down the long hallway, then paused long enough to nudge open the door to the room, which was next door to the room of his youngest sister, Ailis.

The draperies were open and the afternoon sunlight was dropping below the windowsill. As he started across the room to place her upon the bed, she stirred and opened her eyes and said, calmly as ye please, "What are you doing here?"

"I was aboot to ask ye the same question," he replied. "Ye didna tell me ye were a healer."

He saw the dazed look of confusion upon her face as she looked around, as if she was trying to decide just where *here* was. Then her eyes narrowed and she asked, "Do you live here?"

"Aye, 'tis my home and I welcome ye to it."

She looked around with a suspicious frown. "Just who are you?"

"David Murray, the 3rd Earl of Kinloss," he replied as he leisurely absorbed the perfect beauty of her dirty face. He had regretted not taking more time to deliver her to Soutra Aisle, and after he left her, he had the devil's own time getting her off his mind. And now, like a gift from the gods, she was in his arms, and he could not think of a better place for her to be.

"The Earl of Kinloss? You are an earl?"

"Aye, since the death of my father, the 2nd Earl of Kinloss."

She yawned and he could see she was trying to stay awake. "Why didn't you tell me?"

"I did not think it important at the time, just as ye did not think it important to tell me of yer past."

"So, what am I supposed to call you?" she asked. "Your Majesty?"

He detected no contempt or scorn in her tone, so he supposed she truly did not know. He smiled. "Nay, I am no that high on the peerage charts. An earl is addressed as a lord, or in my case, Lord Kinloss, or Lord David Murray, Earl of Kinloss, or the Earl of Kinloss, or simply Kinloss."

"I will never get that straight," she said, thinking she would refer to him as "your brother" or "your cousin" or "the earl." Then she let that ride to get on to more important things. "Are you the one who ordered those knights to haul me away from the hospital?"

"Aye, although I understand yer discomfort, my sister is gravely ill. My cousins did deliver a letter signed by the abbot of Fearn Abbey, asking fer ye to be released unto my care," he said. "I had hoped that would allay any fears ye had."

"I was still taken against my will, and I was *not* informed of the letter before they burst into the room and hauled me out to the courtyard and plopped me on a horse, scaring me to death." She frowned and he remembered her eyes were as green as bracken and still as beautiful as his memory of them.

"Weel, I apologize for the rudeness o' my cousins and I will address it with them."

"Well, if your sister is as ill as you say, we are wasting precious time. I am filthy with the grime of travel. I will need a bath before I can see to her. Can you arrange it?"

"Aye, I will see to it," he said, as he lowered her to her feet, then turned and left the room. He closed the door and started down the hallway as a slow smile settled momentarily upon his lips, then vanished, for Lord David Murray, Earl of Kinloss, was said to never smile.

He went downstairs and spoke to the steward regarding a bath for her and also fresh clothing, since she did not have time to pack anything. Then he went to the room of his sister, Caitrina, or Mother Dominique, as the nuns called her once she became prioress. He paused beside her still form. Although she was a small-boned woman, she looked terribly small and frail, for she had lost much weight. He looked down upon her, lying so still, and wondered if she was even breathing. He remembered the pillow fights they had in this very room,

so many years ago when they were naught more than
saplings and his three brothers were still alive. And now,
she was fighting for her life, but he would not let her die.
He brought the green-eyed lass to rid her of this illness
so she would not be another sibling that he had to lay in
the ground.

He did not know if she could hear him, but he said,
"I have brought the healer from St. Leonard's, and she
will examine ye on the morrow. Ye will be better soon,
Caitrina. You will see."

He kissed her pale hand, which was quite warm, and
paused. Her fever was higher and her breathing more
labored. He decided to bring the healer to her tonight,
but when he knocked on the door to Elisabeth's room,
she did not answer. He knocked again, then opened the
door and stepped into the room. He saw the tub of used
water and her asleep upon the top of the bed, wearing
the dress Ailis had given him. A nightgown was folded
at the end of the bed.

He remembered the coarseness of the garment she
had worn, which was quite similar to what the nuns
wore; only hers was of a pale blue color. He tried to
imagine what she would look like in a gown like the
women wore at court, with the low décolletage, for she
was blessed with enough to grace such a gown.

He hated to wake her, but Caitrina needed seeing
to. He was about to put a hand on her shoulder when
she opened her eyes. She rolled to her side and sat up,
then looked around the room and down at the dress she
wore, as if she was trying to get everything straight in
her mind.

"Thank you for the bath and the clothes. I could not

examine any sick person when I was not clean. The sick... they are more susceptible to illness than those who are healthy. If I touched your sister as I was, without bathing, I could give her the germs of another illness."

He stared blankly at her, wondering what gibberish she was speaking. What was this "susceptible" and "germ" she spoke of?

She realized he probably did not understand what she was saying, for she had encountered this problem before, while a prisoner of the MacLeans on the Isle of Mull and again at Soutra and St. Leonard's. She released a long breath, and although he had opened his mouth to respond, he closed it when she spoke. "'Susceptible' means, in the way I was speaking, that someone might be affected by something or capable of having something on or in their body that is harmful to others. A germ is something one cannot see, for it is smaller than a grain of sand, but it is there and it can cause disease."

He was staring at her blankly. She paused. "Do you speak French?"

"Aye."

She took a deep breath. "A germ is like an invisible seed. In fact the word comes from the French word *germe*, which, as you know, means seed or sprout, which is from the word..."

"*Gignere*, 'to beget,'" he said. "Ye washed away these invisible seeds when ye bathed?"

Elisabeth nodded. "Yes, cleanliness is a very important part of maintaining good health."

"Ye have a strange way o' talking, mistress, and yer accent is strange. And fer a doctor, ye have unheard-of ideas and words aboot yer medicine. Where do ye come from, or are ye like yer invisible seed and ye sprout where ere ye please?"

She smiled and said, "I suppose it does sound as though I do. Now, why don't you take me to see your sister? Her name is Caitrina, I believe."

"Aye, although she is known as Sister Dominique by the nuns."

She stood and said, "Lead the way, Lord Kinloss," and he was struck again by how beautiful she was, with the curly hair and a face that could easily grace a fine Italian painting. But after noticing what nice things she did to the dress she was wearing, he decided she would do even better as a nude statue born of pale marble at the hands of Michelangelo.

When they walked into Caitrina's room, Elisabeth knew immediately that things did not look good, for she could hear the shallow, rapid breathing and the rattling coughing spasms. She hurried to Caitrina's bedside and made the usual observations, hampered greatly by having no up-to-date medical supplies. Even without a thermometer, the burning heat of Caitrina's skin told Elisabeth the fever was quite high, and she observed that Caitrina was also having chills. And then she noticed that her lips and nail beds were blue, which was a sign of a lack of oxygen.

This is not looking good… not at all, she thought…

She put her fingers on Caitrina's pulse. The pulse rate was high: one hundred beats a minute. "How long has she been ill?"

"She has been here aboot a week," David said.

"And before that? When she was at the priory, how long had she been ill?"

"'Twas said she had been ill for aboot a week, with fever and shivering and a pain in her back."

"Was she coughing when she arrived?"

"Aye, but 'twas no' as bad as it is now."

Elisabeth was thinking that the symptoms of bacterial pneumonia usually begin quite suddenly, often after a milder infection like influenza or a cold. Besides Caitrina's sweating, there was the shortness of breath, the nasal flaring and wheezing, and the cyanosis of her lips and nail beds.

Elisabeth couldn't be certain without the proof found with lab results, but the symptoms all pointed toward streptococcus pneumonia. That, coupled with the high rate of Caitrina's breathing, meant things looked bad for both of them; for she knew if she did not save the earl's sister, her own life could be in danger as well.

Pushing such thoughts away, Elisabeth took a respiratory count and found the rate to be twenty-two beats a minute, again in line with streptococcus pneumonia. She sighed regretfully, for Caitrina's white blood cell count would have been especially helpful, and so would the ten or so other tests normally run to evaluate such an illness. The worst part of it was that even if she had the tools to give a positive diagnosis, she had no antibiotics, and her collection of herbs and primitive drugs were not sufficient to deal with an illness of the magnitude of streptococcus pneumonia, especially in its advanced stages, if that was for certain what Caitrina had.

What Elisabeth did know was that the prioress was

dying, and she did what she could to ease Caitrina's suffering, in spite of the agony of knowing that an anti-biotic like erythromycin or amoxicillin, if given in time, would have saved her.

Later, when Lord Kinloss came by, she stepped into the hallway to speak to him, explaining her suspicions that it was a grave illness and that there was no medicine available to cure it. "I am so sorry to say this, but there is nothing I can do to save her. I can only give her some-thing to ease her pain and help her rest."

He looked as if he had been struck a fatal blow, and she had never experienced anything that she hated more than being the bearer of the news that brought him more grief. She wondered what he was thinking when he turned away quickly and strode down the hall and down the stairs.

Elisabeth stayed by Caitrina's bed for the next two days, taking her meals in the room and sleeping in the chair by her bed each night, leaving only long enough to bathe and change clothes before returning. She had been using cannabis hemp that was grown in the garden at Soutra around the clock as a painkiller, and while Caitrina slept, Elisabeth would catch an occasional nap in the bedside chair.

On the second day, Elisabeth could hear the change in Caitrina's breathing. She took her pale hand and held it in hers, as she leaned forward and said, "I don't know if you can hear me, but I want you to know there was so little I could do by the time I arrived. If only I had seen you when you first became ill, things might have been different. My heart is heavy and I grieve for my inability to do more, and I am so sorry for the grief my failure will cause your family.

"I have the knowledge to save you, but I have not the advancement of science and the tools available in my time to work with. And, I don't know why I am saying all of this to you, for I know it makes no sense. I am sorry, so sorry that I failed you. Please forgive me. I just want you to know that it is all in God's hands now, and I know that with your faith, that is a blessed place for you to be."

To Elisabeth's astonishment, there was the slightest movement of Caitrina's hand and a featherlight squeeze. Elisabeth stood and held the hand of the prioress to her heart and kissed her forehead. "Go with God," Elisabeth whispered, and lay the hand of the prioress upon her chest.

She heard a noise, and looked toward the door and saw the Earl of Kinloss standing there. Had he heard what she said? Had he seen his sister squeeze her hand? When he turned abruptly away, without so much as a nod in her direction, she decided he had not.

Things were eerily quiet that night, but by the first rays of early morning, she knew by the rattle in her breathing that Caitrina was nearing death and she sent for her brother and family members.

Elisabeth was standing beside Caitrina, pressing a moist cloth to her parched lips, when the family members began to gather. No one spoke as they settled into place in a semicircle around the bed. Elisabeth laid her cloth down and was making a move to leave the room when Lord Kinloss put his hand upon her shoulder, preventing it, as he said, "There is no reason fer ye to leave now."

Elisabeth nodded and took a step back, then lowered her head, her focus upon the last minutes of the life of

the prioress of Elcho Priory. And as death reached out
and touched Caitrina's heart, and they heard the low
death rattle of her last breath, Elisabeth knew her sight-
less eyes were now dazzled by the brightness of light
and the mighty ways of God.

Chapter 7

O! what a deal of scorn looks beautiful.
In the contempt and anger of his lip.

—*Twelfth Night*, Act III, Scene 1 (1602)
  William Shakespeare (1564–1616)
  English poet and playwright

SLEEP, THE TWIN OF DEATH, EVADED HER.

It was the first time Elisabeth had a sleepless night since the days after Ronan was cruelly ripped from her life, and in spite of being exhausted still, she was glad to see the first tender fingers of morning creep between the gaps in the drapery, heralding a brand-new day.

She sat up in bed, elbows resting on her knees, and thought about all that had happened to her of late, and how she had been hopscotching around Scotland. Although a fun, sightseeing tour it was not.

So many emotions swirled around in her head. Regret, of course, was at the forefront of her mind: regret that there were such poor medical advancements in this time period, regret that she was not brought here sooner, regret that she was not able to see Caitrina before she was brought back home to Aisling Castle, regret that she did not have more time so she had a fighting chance to formulate some sort of antibiotic when it might have made a difference, regret that Caitrina was already knocking at death's door by the time she arrived; and a deep, despairing sorrow that such a beautiful, dedicated young woman had to meet such a tragic end.

And she also wondered what the Earl of Kinloss would do to her, now that Caitrina had died.

On the morning of her third day at Aisling Castle, she was awakened by one of the maids who brought her a black dress and told her the earl said she was to put it on. "Ye are to come below stairs once ye are dressed. Will ye be wanting any help wi' yer hair, mistress?"

Elisabeth eyed the extremely plain dress and knew it would look severe, somber, and very black upon her, but what did it matter? She preferred not to stand out. "No, I can manage, thank you."

She put the dress on and worried about how it fit, but there was no full-length mirror, so she would never know if it hung on her like socks on a rooster, as her grandmother used to say. That left her feeling as lost as a blind person in a dark room as far as her appearance went. What she could tell was that the dress was way too short, for she could see her shoes sticking out like the ruby slippers on the Wicked Witch of the West after the house fell on her.

She eyed the French hood and wished she had a way to put her hair up. She would give anything for a rubber band or even a few hairpins, and even a sliver of a mirror would have been nice. Since she had none of these things, she ran her fingers through her hair as best she could, put the hood on and hoped she placed it right, and hoped that it would suffice.

With a sigh, she went downstairs and found a

large number of people gathered in the great hall,
with Caitlin's coffin to one side of the great fireplace.
A priest stood beside the coffin, and nearby she saw
Lord Kinloss's sister, Ailis, standing next to him, then
Duncan and the four other knights who had accompa-
nied her from St. Leonard's.

Without realizing she was doing so, she stared at
Lord Kinloss, who looked quite splendid in trim black
breeches, tall boots, and a black velvet doublet. He
was tall and would be as deliciously handsome as she
thought he was when he rescued her if he wasn't consumed by grief.

She decided the title of Earl of Kinloss did suit him, for
he had a bearing that was both noble and commanding,
and he stood apart from everyone else in the room. Had
she not met him before, she would have thought him a
man with a haughty attitude, as if he considered himself
to be better than all the others gathered there, but she remembered the man who rescued her and was glad she had
met him then, for she understood that he could be kind
and caring. With a quick, indrawn breath, she realized
she had been staring at him, and when their gazes met,
he returned her stare with one that was impassively cold.

If it had been another person or another time, anger
might have surged through her blood, heating it to the
boiling point over his arrogant disregard of the fact that
she had done all she could. But grief dealt harshly with
those who lost a loved one. She caught a glimpse of
herself in a small mirror and realized how ill-fitting the
black gown was and how nothing about it suited her.
Thankfully, she could not see how dreadfully short it
was on her, and God only knew how horrid her hair

must look. She didn't need self-criticism, so she quickly looked down at the floor and kept her gaze there during the long mass.

When it was finally over, she turned away, more than ready to return to her room, and almost bumped into someone. When she lifted her head, she was shocked to see Lord Kinloss standing before her. She turned, intending to bypass him and continue on her way upstairs, but his hand lashed out and caught her by the arm. "Ye will accompany us to see Caitrina laid to rest. I would have ye see what yer failure to cure her has wrought."

Elisabeth gasped as his words cut into the quick of her. "It would seem your anger toward me would only be appeased if I joined her in death, and even then, I'm not sure you would be satisfied. I see no purpose to my going to her burial. It should be a private time for you and your family. I will only be a distraction. And no matter what you think, I am not as callous as you think, nor is my heart made of stone. I have my own sorrow over her death, and it pains me greatly to lose someone I had under my care. But I am only human and I cannot perform miracles, and I can assure you that only a miracle would have saved Caitrina. Now, if you will excuse me, I will return to my room and retire early so that I might leave this inhospitable place and be out of your hair at daybreak."

"Ye will accompany us to the cemetery, and as for leaving on the morrow, ye may put that thought out of yer mind completely. So, ready yersel', mistress, for the trek."

"You cannot force me to go."

His face hardened. "Aye, mistress, that I can, and I

will do so if needs be," he said, his voice low and threatening. "Ye *will* join us, for ye will regret it if ye dinna."

Elisabeth wondered what happened to the gentle knight who rescued her, but she knew the pain of losing a loved one did affect people in different ways. Perhaps, for some reason he blamed himself and was taking it out on her. Before she had another thought, he turned away and she fell in at the back of the group departing the castle and followed them to the cemetery.

The funeral was a terribly sad one for her, and she could not help the tears that rolled down her face. They were not tears of guilt but rather sadness for one so lovely and so young, and for the brother and sister who had seen to the burial of both their parents and so many of their siblings, for Elisabeth was appalled to see the names of so many of them in the cemetery. All were siblings of Ailis and Lord Kinloss, and as she read the names, William, Hugh, Janet, Archibald, Mara, and Grainne, her heart went out to the two of them for the suffering and loss they had endured, and she was shamed to have been so curt and angry at him. She reminded herself that grief was understood only by those who suffered.

She had no idea and no imagining of how one could deal with such loss. Of nine siblings, only two remained. With a sigh, she lifted her head and stared upward into the leafy bower of a large tree a few feet away, with hopes that it would serve to take her mind off the sadness that engulfed this place of mourning.

But that did not help, so she stood there with her head downcast and took a deep breath as she wiped the path of tears from her face. Later, when the tears subsided, she lifted her head and found David still staring at her with a cold look of disdain. He looked as tall and dark as the outline of the stone-hewn castle behind him, and just as enduring and cold.

Bah! What did she care what he looked like? He was nothing to her except a pain in the posterior. She quickly turned her head and thought of her own family, centuries away, who were as dead to her as his were to him. The reminder that she would never see them again sent a sharp pain to her heart. All she had was her sister, Isobella, and her heart seemed to thud painfully slowly as she felt her twin's absence acutely.

When the priest began to speak, she tried to follow the words, but her mind kept drifting off. It was only when she heard the softly muted murmur of talking that she realized the service was over. Stone faced, and unnaturally pale, she watched each of the family members toss a handful of dirt upon the wooden coffin as they turned away to begin the journey back to Aisling Castle. She waited a moment before she adjusted the black headdress and veil, and when the last family member walked through the cemetery gate, she gathered up her skirt to tread as heavily upon the muddy sod as she did on her feelings.

They were almost to the castle when she felt someone take her arm, and she turned quickly, expecting to see Lord Kinloss ready to haul her off to the dungeon. Instead, she saw the pale face of Ailis, who managed a wan smile to go with the soft look in her lovely blue eyes.

"I ken my brother's wirds are harsh and fall unkindly upon ye, but dinna judge him too harshly. We have suffered so many losses that grief and funerals have become

a way of life for us. Caitrina's death was especially difficult for him because they were twins."

Elisabeth was shocked to hear about them being
twins and wondered why he did not mention it. "I'm
sorry you have suffered so much. I cannot imagine such
a loss," she said, feeling a deep sorrow that any family
should suffer so.

Elisabeth caught sight of David ahead of them, walking with Duncan and four other men about the same age.
Even his walk was authoritative. "It seems your brother
has found a group of friends his age to give him some
feeling of brotherhood."

"Nae, not friends," Ailis said. "'Tis family, for they
are our cousins, Duncan, Branan, Cailean, Taran, and
Aleyn. Our fathers were brothers. They havena any family save us."

"And you are the only girl." Elisabeth wanted to kick
herself because she was ashamed she reminded Ailis
that she was, now that Caitrina was gone, the only girl.

Ailis did not smile, but her eyes did shine with a
gleam of humor. "Aye, 'tis me against the six o' them,
so it will be nice to have ye here, just to help balance
things oot a wee bit."

"Ahhh, a buffer," Elisabeth said, thinking a sense of
humor was always nice to serve as a cushion against the
shock of reality.

"Do ye have brothers?" Ailis asked.

Elisabeth nodded. "Yes, I have two younger brothers." She decided not to tell her their names were John
and James, or that she had a younger sister, Anna, and
they all lived six centuries in the future, or that her twin
was married to the Chief of Clan Mackinnon. As her

father always said, "Never expose your cards before you have to."

Ailis lifted the skirts of her gown to step over a puddle. Elisabeth, in her too-short gown, did not have to and Ailis must have taken note, for she said, "I shall see to having some new clothing made fer ye that is better suited to yer height. The gown ye wear… it belonged to Caitrina afore she became a nun. She was no' so tall as ye."

They walked on for some time, lost in conversation, until Elisabeth realized they had drawn quite close to Lord Kinloss and his cousins. The two of them slowed their pace, but not before they heard Duncan say, "So, tell me, why didn't ye send the lass back, instead of making her attend the funeral?"

"Duncan, are ye daft?" one of them said. "Ye ha' only to take one glance at her to see she is more than just a comely lass. She looks like she stepped from a painting. Ye could look far and wide and no' find a more beautiful woman."

"Beauty is no' a reason to be elevated or worshipped," David said, "and I find her quite plain." But his cousins glanced at each other, as if doubting his words, just before he added, "Beauty comes from within, and she is too bold, too opinionated, and too outspoken."

"Ye better not let her hear ye say that, or ye might end up the proud owner of a black eye!" Duncan said.

David was quick to reply: "And ye might have one yersel' if ye care to mention that again."

Elisabeth and Ailis fell back even further, and they were the last to arrive back at Aisling Castle. She breathed a sigh of relief, knowing she could slip away

and seek the comfort of her room, for she was still unbelievably tired from the trip and the time she had spent
in the room with Caitrina.

It wasn't until she was inside the castle keep that she
realized she had muddy shoes and dirty stockings, and
she could feel the heat of embarrassment upon her face.
She hoped to slip quietly inside and disappear into her
room, but the men were all gathered around the entry to
the great hall when Ailis and Elisabeth entered.

Ailis stopped and said, "Elisabeth, I want you to meet
my cousins. Duncan Murray you have met. Standing
next to him are Aleyn, Taran, Branan, and Cailean."

Elisabeth greeted them with a remark that they were
a fine-looking lot and that they were all from the well-
favored side of the family, and felt she at least got in a
bit of a gouge for the remark of Lord Kinloss about her
being quite plain.

The five cousins glanced at David, who stood slightly
behind her but far enough away that she could not see
his face. The cousins beamed with delight, for it was
obvious they wanted to laugh but not so soon after the
burial of their cousin.

Elisabeth would have given anything to see David's
face, but she did not want to give him the satisfaction of
thinking that she even cared. She decided it was time to
retire and said, "If you will excuse me, I think I shall—"

David cut her off. "If ye harbor any thoughts aboot
retiring early, mistress, I would not advise it." He turned
and motioned to his cousins to follow, and she was relieved to see them go.

"Is he always like this?" Elisabeth asked.

Ailis watched her brother leave before she said,

"Although it pains me to say so, he can be, but that isn't the real David. He has not had an easy time of it and never really wanted to inherit the title. Our father was horribly harsh and critical of him, and in spite of that, David never raised his voice to him. I thank God every night that our cousins are here, for I dinna ken how he would be able to live here with just the two of us. It would be unbearably sad. Our cousins are quite jolly most of the time and always teasing and laughing. It is good for David to have his spirits lightened. I know ye wouldna believe it, but he was once as happy and teasing as they."

Elisabeth could not help wondering what he had been like back then, but she pushed such thoughts aside and went with Ailis to sit at the end of a long table, thankfully at the opposite end from where David sat. That did not, however, prevent him from holding Elisabeth in his gaze almost the entire time they were there. So she focused her attention on just about anything she could to get her mind off him, for if she were honest with herself, she was still terribly attracted to him, just as much as that day she first saw him. And since coming here, she thought quite often just how wonderful it would be to kiss him again. But she glanced at his stone-hardened face and thought, *Not bloody likely!* She gave herself a mental slap for such thoughts, for they did nothing to ease her situation. Fortunately, Ailis was rather talkative, which was a blessing, for Elisabeth only had to add an occasional comment or nod now and then in agreement.

Once the meal was over, the talking began to die down, and Elisabeth desperately hoped it would soon be time to retire. She was unusually tired and knew

the stress of today's activities had taken their toll. At
that particular moment, everyone began to stand, and
not wanting to stand out, Elisabeth rose to her feet and
glanced at Ailis for some indication as to what would
happen next.

"Come, and I will walk upstairs with ye," Ailis said.
"I have no' the strength to remain down here any longer,
and I ken ye are tired as well. Most of those who remain
will be here for some time, and if they have whisky, they
will stay even longer."

As they walked, Elisabeth yearned to inquire about
Lord Kinloss but did not wish it to come across as pry-
ing, nor would she want to give even the remotest hint
that she was interested in him as a man. It was best
if he thought he did not interest her in the least, for it
would only make things more difficult. Yet, even as she
thought it, she could not seem to shake the memory of
when he kissed her, and she had most certainly kissed
him back.

"What about your mother? Was he close to her?"

Ailis's expression said she was surprised by the
question, and Elisabeth put her hand on Ailis's arm and
said, "Please forgive me. I did not mean to inquire about
things that are none of my affair."

Ailis smiled softly and replied, "David seemed to
regret it wasn't him that died, instead of his older brothers. I truly dinna ken how he dealt with our father's
criticism and managed to be respectful to a man who did
not deserve it. Nothing David did seemed to be enough
to please him. David is a remarkable warrior knight
and has fought bravely many times and suffered great
wounds, and there are none finer. He has all the qualities

of a good leader, and our clansmen love him for his fair and honest ways."

"I had no idea he was the youngest son. He seems older, but I can see how the things you have told me would make him appear that way."

"He can be difficult at times, but he is a fair and generous leader of Clan Murray and the people respect him. Ye willna find anyone with more dignity or a man more honorable. But, he is accustomed to being obeyed and never having his word questioned. When he gives an order, he expects it to be complied with. I ken that when he is quiet and sullen, he is at war with himself. Part of him feels he must be that way; part of him yearns to be warm and loving. It saddens me that he did not have anyone to show him more love and affection when he was younger. Our mother was always in poor health, and although she loved him dearly, she was abed a great deal of the time."

Elisabeth was shocked, to say the least, and quite at a loss for words. Ailis had said much for her to think about, and it did shed a great deal of light upon the character of Kinloss. Once they reached the door to her room, Elisabeth turned and took the hand of Ailis and said, "I thank you for sharing your thoughts on your brother. It makes him easier to understand. We are all, in some way, the victims of our past, and we are self-taught in the ways we develop to deal with it. I will see him in a different light, and I will now bid you a good night."

"Good night, Elisabeth. I am so verra glad ye are here. Please consider me your friend." She rose on her tiptoes and gave Elisabeth a kiss upon the cheek, then disappeared down the darkened hallway.

In her room, Elisabeth undressed quickly, pulled on a gown and washed her face, and never thought a bed could feel so good. She was emotionally drained, but sleep did not come to her right away, for thoughts of Lord Kinloss lingered in the back of her mind, and she could not help feeling pity for him. His was not an easy road to walk down, and she knew now that was why he was so hard on himself and everyone around him. He carried a great burden, and now he had lost his twin sister, which left him one remaining sibling. That would make anyone bitter. She realized she had seen him at his worst, for it was a terrible point in his life. That left her feeling small and petty for being so critical. She vowed to do her best to be more ladylike in the future.

She closed her eyes and was serenaded by the memory of a full, deep, sonorous voice that spoke Scots so deliciously that it seemed to fill every inch of a room, as would smoke from a clogged chimney. She thought of the way he looked today, with his melancholy face, the dark blue of his sad eyes, and the dark hair, all neatly wrapped up with his black cloak swirling about him.

What was it that made her feel both angry and sad whenever she thought of him? He seemed to be surrounded by an eternal fog of gloom, with his face set with an obstinate scowl as if he were determined not to accept any opinions other than his own or agree even a little with the wishes of others. Why did he stubbornly adhere to an opinion or course of action without allowing room for debate? And where on earth did he get his tight-lipped obstinacy? Couldn't he hear? Could he not see? And why was he so gentle and understanding when he rescued her? She couldn't help wondering which was the real Lord Kinloss, or would she, in time, discover one or two more?

And yet he was just about as sexy and compelling a man as she could recall meeting. Perhaps it was because he was such a strong and powerful figure. She sighed, closed her eyes, and said a prayer for the heartbroken earl and his family.

———

That would be the same heartbroken earl who decided the next day that she could not leave Aisling Castle.

"*What?*"

Elisabeth was certain she did not hear correctly. "Are you saying that you are holding me here because I did not save your sister? That is grossly and totally unfair! And mean! And it comes *after* I explained that it was impossible for *anyone* to save her at that point. Her illness had advanced beyond the point of no return. No one, short of God himself, could have saved her life. So, tell me, why am I being punished when I was taken against my will and brought here at breakneck speed, and I explained to you after I examined her that there was nothing humanly possible that could be done. It was too late before I arrived."

"That is not why I am keeping ye here."

"Then tell me, what reason could you have for keeping me here?"

"I find that it is guid to ha' a healer here, for we ha' no doctor nearby."

"You cannot force me to stay here and be your doctor."

"It is nothing that must be decided now. I ken yer

presence is good for Ailis, and she is verra fond o' ye.
I can see a change in her since ye arrived. And I ken ye
would be nearing the end of yer time at St. Leonard's
before too long and that ye would have to find a suitable
place to devote yersel' to healing."

"So, what happens next? Am I to whittle away my
time here until an opportunity to practice medicine appears?" She did not know why she was attacking him
on this, for she would never forget the intimacy that had
passed between them and how often she thought of him
after he left Soutra.

How could he tell her the truth? How could he make
her understand how the memory of her had tormented
him since he left her at Soutra Aisle? How could he make
her understand how he had relived the few moments he
had with her, or how the memory of having her lie beside
him on their journey was something he thought of over
and again. He wanted to lie with her even now, so shortly
after the death of his sister, but he wanted her to want it
as well, and he hoped that if he kept her here, she might
just come to care for him. He did not want to let her go,
and yet he could not give her a good reason for keeping
her here. In the end, he simply said, "Ye will remain here
until I decide what to do wi' ye."

"This makes no sense. If you would only be reason-
able, I am sure we…"

He brought his hand down and slammed it upon the
table. "Enough! My sister is barely in the ground. I dinna
want, nor do I have the time, to have this conversation
wi' ye at the this moment," he said, immediately realizing how hard he was being.

She crossed her arms over her middle. "You

certainly had enough time to give orders to hold me as your prisoner."

"Ye will remain here, mistress, and ye are no' being held as a prisoner. Ye are here until I give it some thought and broach the subject wi' ye, as I said."

She started to say something curt, but the tenderness she felt for him begged her to back off, to cut him some slack. Besides, you know you want to be with him, and it is okay to have your pride, but don't overdo it, she thought. After all, there might be sick people here needing her help, but there were also sick people who needed her back at St. Leonard's. And such a situation made her think too much about how she missed Isobella, but she had already decided to withhold that bit of information from him, for the last thing she wanted was to cause problems for Alysandir Mackinnon, who had always been so very kind to her.

In the end, Elisabeth decided to stay out of the earl's way, but by the time she reached her room, her feelings toward him softened, for she did care for him and she was attracted to him, and what difference did it make if she stayed here for a while longer?

Chapter 8

Jupiter, not wanting man's life to be wholly gloomy and grim,
has bestowed far more passion than reason—
you could reckon the ration as twenty-four to one.
Moreover, he confined reason to a cramped corner
of the head and left all the rest of the body to the passions.

—*Praise of Folly* (1509)
   Desiderius Erasmus (c. 1466–1536)
   Dutch humanist

WITH SUN-KISSED FLAMES OF AUBURN HAIR OF THE deepest hue, she was easy to spot, even when partially hidden behind the screen of trees running parallel to the garden wall. David stood at the window and watched her. She intrigued him, this strange-talking woman with the flashing green eyes and coppery hair. Who was this Elisabeth Douglas captured by the MacLeans—a lass who was a doctor at the Priory of St. Leonard's, by way of Soutra Aisle, who was a sister-in-law to Alysandir Mackinnon?

All in all, he knew precious little about her. It was said that a woman of auburn hair was of a gentle nature, and thus far she seemed to be so, but only time would confirm that. He had to admit he was doubtful, for he felt she would prove herself to be as difficult to deal with as a slaty ridge stubborned with iron. Aye, he knew precious little about her, but he would before he returned her to the priory.

Regarding her, he had a lot of questions and too few answers. Was she an angel in the guise of a doctor? Had she truly come to help, or was her reason of a darker nature? Aye, he needed answers, and before he let her go, he would have them.

Lastly, he thought about another, more important reason he kept her here, one born of the lustful thoughts he had for her, for he could not deny that he had thought of little else since first seeing her. His thoughts were too often filled with imaginings about what it would be like to make love to her until she cried out with pleasure. And something inside him told him she would be a woman who participated and was not shy to show her emotions. Simply put, he wanted her, and he wondered if he would be satisfied for long with merely making love to her. He could not deny the strong attraction he felt or the strange power she had over him—a power that made him want to keep her with him and wanted her to want it as much as he did.

She turned and looked toward the window where he stood, and he took a step back, lest she see him. He watched her walk through the garden gate and he turned away, for something about her reached out to him and drew him to her, so much that he went below stairs and out into the courtyard, where he turned toward the garden. He heard her laugh and it sent ripples of pleasure washing over him, drawing him deeper into the spell she cast about him like a gossamer net.

He stepped on a twig and heard her gasp as she turned

around. When she saw him, she released a pent-up breath, her hand going to press against her breast. He envied that hand…

"You scared me," she said, the fear not yet completely gone from her lovely eyes.

"I didna mean to frighten ye," he replied, feeling suddenly inadequate and speechless around her. "There is naught fer ye to fear within the castle walls. We are well protected, and the Black Isle is not plagued with as many warring clans as other parts o' the Highlands. And we ha' no MacLeans here."

She smiled at that and he felt awkward as a schoolboy. He looked around as a diversion, while he searched his mind for something to say. "Do ye like the garden?" he asked with a brooding shadow of inarticulateness, as his mind groped for words that would express all that he was feeling inside. Why was he quiet as a nun stumbling around in the dark with her when it came to expressing his personal feelings, yet with other subjects or expressing his displeasure toward her, he felt no limitations?

She laughed and repeated his question. "Do I like the garden? How could I not? I find it as glorious as a sunset, as calming as a visit with old friends."

He felt the pull of her again, surrounding him this time like the silken thread of a spider reaching out to wrap itself around him, drawing him closer to spin him in a cocoon. Once there, he would never escape, and that made him consider if he would ever want to. And then he wondered, why her? Why this puzzling woman he barely knew?

As if sensing his discomfort, she pulled a glossy leaf

from a tree and twirled it between her fingers. "I truly love your garden, for it is remindful of our garden at home, only ours was much larger, but then, the weather there is milder than it is here, so our growing season was also longer." Her eyes widened suddenly and she said, "I should return now."

She started around him, but he caught her by the arm. "There is no reason fer ye to leave simply because I am here or for ye to fear me. In spite o' what ye think, ye are safe wi' me." He wanted to smile, for the expression on her face said she did not feel the least bit safe with him at all. Was that because she feared what he would do or what she might be persuaded to do? "Tell me of your garden at home."

She seemed to relax a bit, and he was pleased to know his words had eased her discomfort.

"It is a lovely place, not far from the river. The swings my sister and I used as children are still there, or at least they were before we came here."

Many of her words were foreign to him and spoken too rapidly. "What is this swing ye speak of?" He noticed how her lovely eyes seem to grow brighter, as if warmed by his interest.

"Oh... well, you tie two lengths of rope on a sturdy branch of a tree, about this far apart," she said, showing him. "And you take a smooth plank of wood and put two holes in it on each end, like this, and run the rope through it and knot it on the bottom. Then you can sit in it and push yourself back with your feet. Then when you lift your feet, the rope will swing you forward, letting you move through the air quickly, then bring you back. It's something children love."

"And ye love it as well?"

She smiled. "Oh, I do love it! I've been known to swing quite a few times, even as an adult. Perhaps that is because we are reluctant sometimes to let go of the things we remember as having brought us pleasure."

"Where learned ye this?"

She looked uncomfortable and glanced quickly toward the castle, and he said, "Ye canna return until I give ye leave. Answer my question."

"I learned it from my father."

"Who is yer father?"

She said nothing.

"I will ask ye once more. Who is yer father?"

"Robert James Douglas."

"A Lowlander…" He said the word as if it was something he wanted to spit from his mouth. "Where does yer family reside?"

"I would rather tell you later, Lord Kinloss."

The title sounded terribly strange coming from her, and he knew it was not something that came naturally to her. "Ye may call me David, if it suits ye. I am no' so formal wi' my family and this is my home and not the English court, where ye must bow or curtsy to those of higher rank."

She was about to remind him that she was neither family, nor a permanent resident in his home, but calling him David was much easier and more to her liking than Lord Kinloss, which sounded like a pedigreed Afghan hound at a dog show.

"Why should I wait when I want yer answers now?" he asked.

"Because you won't believe me when I tell you, and

I'd rather go to bed tonight not worrying about when you are going to lop off my head."

He tried, unsuccessfully, to hold back the smile that captured his mouth. His hand came out, and he cupped her chin and tilted her head upward so she looked directly at him. He searched her eyes and studied her face momentarily, then replied, "'Twould be an unforgivable sin to separate the face of Helen of Troy from the body of Venus. Now, tell me aboot yer strange speech, for 'tis no' Gaelic or English, so how come ye by it?"

She broke eye contact with him and looked down as she said, "It is the way they speak where I come from."

"And where is this place ye speak of?"

He observed signs of her discomfort when she glanced around, as if she was seeking a place of solace or a foxhole to run into. "If I promise to tell you everything soon, will that suffice?"

"Nae, lass. I want yer answer now."

She pulled a leaf from a tree and twirled it in her hands, gazing off for a moment. He knew she was trying to mentally separate herself from a difficult situation, but he felt no sympathy and would grant her no pardon. He watched her walk to a low-hanging bough and sit upon it. Her eyes grew wide when it creaked, but she did not make a move to get up. She carefully avoided making eye contact with him by looking around the garden and then released a long sigh.

"My reluctance is not because I don't want to tell you, but because when I do, you won't believe me, and then you will have all sorts of erroneous suspicions about me. For that reason, I truly would rather return to

St. Leonard's and avoid such turmoil. You have no valid reason to keep me here."

"Rank doth have its privileges… I need no *valid* reason to keep ye here, mistress." He wondered why she was being so evasive. Was she afraid to tell him where she came from? He could not understand the way she seemed to fear him or, more so, fear what he might do if she told him the truth. How could asking her about her strange speech and where she was from cause so much distress? What was she hiding? "Why say ye that I willna believe ye? I am a learned man with much understanding."

She shook her head. "Believe me, what I could tell you would be far, far beyond your understanding or the understanding of any man in Scotland or the rest of the world, for that matter."

She spoke words that had no meaning to him as if they formed some sort of riddle he was to solve. "I am no ogre that ye must fear me. And ye willna leave here until ye tell me the way o' it, so why not tell me now?"

"It's a very long story."

"I have time for a verra long story."

She released a long sigh and gazed off. He could almost feel the sense of dread building up within her, and it puzzled him. He saw the way she clasped her hands in her lap, as if she truly feared what might happen to her if she was truthful and told him what he wanted to know. "Are ye a spy?"

He saw the instant look of surprise and shock upon her face… and it came too quickly to be anything other than an honest reaction, so he doubted her reason for withholding information was due to political artifice or evasion, but more to fear, which puzzled him. Had he been overly harsh with her? "Ye fear me, no?"

That only seemed to cause her more distress, for he did not miss the way she was wringing her hands. "I'm not afraid of you, per se, but of what you might do because I can promise you that you will not believe me. I am certain of it."

He did not understand her reluctance. She seemed in such distress that he wanted to take her in his arms and tell her she had naught to fear from him, that he could and would protect her, but he did not. Rather, he said, "I will promise to do my best to believe ye, and if ye tell me that ye were spawned by the deil himsel', I will do ye no harm. Ye have my word."

He saw the look of relief and resignation on her face, and he knew she was close to relenting, which meant she would give him the answer he sought. A sad longing embraced her and she turned her head to gaze toward the castle. "I am not from this world."

She said the words so quickly that it gave him pause. Then the words penetrated his consciousness and he was puzzled by what she meant. "What mean ye, that ye are na from this world?"

"I come from another place in another time… a time in the future."

His heart stilled. What she said was blasphemous and he told her so. "How managed ye to get by saying such at St. Leonard's?"

"I did not tell them because they never asked."

"Tell me of this world where it is that ye live. Does it have a name?"

"America."

That gave him a start, for he had knowledge of this America, but it had been discovered only twenty-three years or so ago. "I have heard of this place ye speak of, but ye canna be from there."

"Yes, I can, and I am, but my time is in the future… a long way in the future."

He did not know why he asked, "How far into the future?" He knew she was deceiving him with her lies, in spite of all her hand-wringing.

"Six hundred years."

"Ye lie! 'Tis blasphemy! Do ye take me for a dunce, thinking I would believe such a foolish story?"

"No. I *knew* you wouldn't believe it and I wouldn't believe it either, if it had not happened to me. I understand your doubt, but what reason would I have to lie about this? How else can you explain my strange way of speaking English or the medical knowledge I have? You will have to go on what I have done at St. Leonard's, but it can be verified. And there is this," she said, and pulled a ribbon that was tied around her neck, with a hole in a silver coin that dangled from it. She removed the ribbon and handed it to him.

"What is this coin ye give me?"

"It is an American silver dollar. On the front you can see the face of a woman with the word 'Liberty' written above her head and by her neck the words 'In God We Trust,' and below that is the date 1934. Now, if you turn it over…" and she did. "This is the American eagle, and here it says 'One Dollar,' and above the eagle's head it says 'United States of America' and below that, 'E Pluribus Unum,' which means—"

"Oot of many, one."

"Yes, 'out of many, one' refers to the fact that out of many individual states, one country was formed."

"Ye are from America in 1934."

"No, not 1934. That is the date the coin was made."

He handed the coin back to her, wanting to believe her, yet searching for another reason why she might have such a coin. "If ye came back in time, how did ye make it happen?"

"It wasn't something I chose, but rather something that happened to me and my sister." She went on to explain how she and Isobella traveled to Scotland because they wanted to visit places where their Scots ancestors lived. "We went to St. Bride's Kirk in Lanarkshire to see the tomb of Sir James, the Black Douglas. My sister was so moved by the sad story of how he was killed fighting the Moors near Theba, Spain, that she started to cry. She put her hand on his effigy, where his heart would have been, and said she was so sorry. Immediately, she jerked her hand back because the place she touched was warm.

"The next day, we visited Beloyn Castle to see the portrait of the Black Douglas that hung there. Isobella, feeling quite emotional again, put out her hand and touched the painting, where the cape curled around his boot, and she said, 'It's really you, isn't it?' She no more than said the words when everything went black."

Elisabeth paused and looked at him, as if trying to see how he was taking all she had said, but he kept his expression passive and said nothing, other than to tell her, "Go on with yer outrageous story."

"There isn't much more to it. When the darkness cleared, we found ourselves standing in the middle of nowhere familiar, and then I noticed a vaporous glowing light of a greenish color that began to take shape, until we could tell that it was the Black Douglas in his ghostly form."

"'Tis impossible! There are no ghosts!"

A look of utter and complete defeat settled upon her face. Eyes downcast, hands clasped tightly in her lap, she shrugged and looked away. He was touched by the sadness, laced with uncertainty and possibly fear, that he saw in her eyes when she looked back at him to say, "I said you wouldn't believe me. Now you understand why I was hesitant to tell you. Call it what you will, but it is the truth. There most certainly is at least one ghost that exists, and I have seen him here at Aisling."

He saw the moment she seemed to lose all hope, for he saw defeat in the way her shoulders slumped and her eyes were downcast, as if she was resigning herself to her fate. Did she truly believe he would harm her? He realized he was at a crossroads and he was undecided as to how to deal with this.

If he was firm and threw her words back in her face, if he pushed her and refused to believe her, she would withdraw and speak of it no more. He searched for a reason to believe her and decided that her story was so preposterous that there was no reason for her to make up such an outlandish story, for she knew full well he or any man would not believe her, just as she said.

"I did not ask to be brought here," she said, "and although I have come to love it here in Scotland, and I feel I have so much knowledge to share and use, I do not know if it is possible that I might suddenly find myself back home, or if I will spend the rest of my life here."

His tone softened. "Ye think it is possible that ye might return?"

"No, not really... I don't know, for Black Douglas is always evasive. Sometimes I wonder if he even knows how we came back to this time period, but I think it highly possible that he leads us down that path because he does not want to tell us everything and that is an easy way out. But I also know it happened, so I don't see why it could not happen again, and he has made comments about ghosting having its limits and boundaries as to what he can and cannot do. It is all a gray area, neither black nor white, but he is so charming and so likeable, rather like an indulgent grandfather, that one cannot help but love him."

She glanced at him to see if he would say anything, but he decided to let her talk as long as she wished without interruption.

"I suppose you could say I am telling the truth because I know my life is at stake if I tell you a lie, for you would find the truth eventually and that could be fatal for me. I don't want to die, believe me. There is too much good I can do here if I have the chance."

There was something sincere about the way she spoke, and there was also the look of honesty he saw in her eyes that made him want to believe her. And, she was right. To be caught lying could be a fatal choice. He would hear her out. "Pray continue wi' yer story."

"That's about it. We asked the Black Douglas where we were, and he said the Isle of Mull. When Isobella asked if he brought us here for a reason, and he nodded and said, 'As bidden.'"

"But ye didna say that ye bid him to bring ye here."

"That is because we didn't ask him to send us any-where, but then Isobella said, 'You mean you brought us here because I cried back at St. Bride's when we visited your crypt?' And he said 'Aye, yer tears reached out across the centuries to summon me. I might have been a mighty knight in the service of my king, but a woman's tears were ere my undoing.'"

He almost smiled at that. "Ye ha' a remarkable mem-ory when it suits ye."

"Believe me, I will never forget those words as long as I live."

"Finish yer story."

"We started talking about how we would get back to Edinburgh, and he said there were none of the means of transportation we had in our time and told us we were in Scotland in the year 1515. When we asked when we could go back, he said, 'Who knows? Mayhap never. Mayhap when the spirit moves me.' Naturally that made us angry, and I pointed out that I did not cry at his crypt and demanded to know why he brought me along. He replied it was because I was sticking to my sister like a leech.

"We didn't have time to ask anything else because we heard shouts and the clanging of swords and saw two opposing groups of knights fighting each other nearby. Worried, we asked if he was going to take us back to our time, or was he simply going to hand us over to the warring men. We couldn't believe it, but he simply smiled and his image began to grow dim and then it faded completely away."

"And that is the last ye saw of him?"

"Yes, he abandoned us in the glen. I did not see

him for quite some time, but he appeared to Isobella quite frequently and they became very close. He really is a most likeable man... er, ghost." She paused long enough to glance at him. "The men fighting in the glen turned out to be the MacLeans who were fighting the Mackinnons. I was captured by the MacLeans and taken to Duart Castle. Isobella was rescued by Alysandir Mackinnon and taken to Caisteal Màrrach."

"Where is yer sister now?"

She sighed heavily, as if she knew this moment was coming, yet hoped it would not. He waited.

"My sister is still at Màrrach. She is married to Alysandir Mackinnon."

That startled him. "The Mackinnon has heard yer story?"

"Yes, my sister told him, and like you, he did not believe her at first." She waited and when he said nothing more, she said, "I hope my telling you will cause you to let me return to St. Leonard's."

"Naught has changed in that regard," he said.

Her face wore a sad expression, and he admired her ability to bear her burden without angry words or tears, in spite of her disappointment. She was a strong lass and unlikely to be gentled as easily as a deerhound.

"Do you believe any part of what I have told you?"

He could hear the pleading tone of her voice and he was surprised by her words, and the hopeless look upon her face reached far into the innermost workings of his heart. Pity was not something he normally felt, nor did he allow it to move him, yet, he could not help feeling a gentle compassion and a tender sort of caring for her. The story of her sister being married to Alysandir

Mackinnon would be easy to verify, which, if true, would name her honest.

He decided he would withhold judgment until he had proof. "As ye said, yer story is too outrageous not to believe, for how could one make up such a story? And there is yer coin and yer knowledge and yer strange way o' speaking English. Therefore, I accept yer story as the truth until I can send word to the Mackinnon and receive a reply from him."

He could hear her breath of relief and saw the way the color seemed to come out of hiding to settle upon her fair face. Lord Kinloss stood and said, "Come, I will walk back wi' ye and we will speak no more if it now."

—~~~—

Elisabeth returned to the garden the next day, and to her surprise, she found a swing there. She looked around but saw no trace of Kinloss or anyone else, so she would wait to thank him later. She understood the swing was more than just a swing. It was his way of putting her at ease, of telling her she had nothing to fear from him, and it spoke volumes about the kind of man he was. He was educated, powerful, brave, devoted to his family, loved by his clansmen, and gentle. And that last trait touched her in a profound way.

With a smile, she went to the swing and seated herself, then realized it was more difficult to swing with a wad of petticoat and skirt tangled about her, but she finally managed to tame her skirts and try out the swing.

Hidden from sight, Kinloss stood behind the cover of a trailing vine drooping from the branches of a tree, not far away. He watched her swing and saw her fly out of the swing and fall. He dashed toward her and heard her laughing.

"Ye are no hurt from yer fall?"

Still laughing and quite breathless, she looked up through the leafy bower overhead, not bothering to get up and not bothered that he stood nearby watching her. She ignored that, for she was not ready to let him into her world, and truthfully, she did not know if she ever would be. And then she realized that perhaps that was because she had no world, for she was a woman with one foot in the present and one in the future, and she feared she might never be able to call either of them home.

So many memories, she thought. Memories of my childhood, my family, the Blanco River, my first horse, first car, first kiss, first love in high school, and how much she grieved over his being killed in Afghanistan two years after graduating from West Point... It all seemed so far away now and she felt the bite of a bittersweet longing for her past. That surprised her, for she thought herself resigned to the fact that she would never be going back.

She wouldn't go so far as to say she was sad. Melancholy would be a better word, for she was surrounded by a pensive and gentle sadness. She sighed deeply and closed her eyes, fighting for composure and telling herself that not even one miniscule tear better gather there.

He approached noiselessly and dropped down on one knee. "Ye are sad fer yer family."

She nodded. She did not want to discuss her family or her feelings, and she wondered where her usual boldness had bolted to and why it remained in hiding. She only knew she did not want to look at him, for she feared he would see more in her eyes than she was prepared to show him.

She looked away and did not respond, nor did she move. While she was mentally planning the best way to extricate herself from this uncomfortable situation, he leaned forward and kissed her so swiftly that she was caught completely off guard. Before she could draw a surprised breath, he drew her into his arms.

Her eyes flew open, just before his mouth captured hers a second time with surprising tenderness, moving slowly, exploring, and filling her with a sort of lethargy that kept her from pulling back or pushing him away. She enjoyed kissing him as much as she had when he rescued her from Angus MacLean, and it did not sit well with her to know she was this vulnerable... she, who was never, ever vulnerable because she was always and foremost in charge. How had he managed to gain the upper hand so swiftly and without words?

When the kiss ended, she rolled to her side and came to her feet about the same time he did.

"I did not come here to seduce ye, nor did I plan for that to happen," he said.

"Yes, well, sometimes the devil appears as a man of peace." She turned away and walked back to the swing, taking one of the ropes in her hand. She did not know why she had said that, and it bothered her to see her harsh words find a tender place to prick. She always had the habit of engaging her mouth before her brain.

It occurred to her that a man's world can be, at times, a rather bleak one, filled with doubt and confusion, where they must prove themselves to be what they are not and, at the same time, be talented at hiding their vulnerability, so as not to risk sharing it and, by doing so, finding themselves humiliated.

Like her, he was dealing with the loss of a loved one, and that alone makes one terribly vulnerable. She thought of his eyes, those remarkable eyes of dark violet blue, which played a sort of trickery when she looked into them, for there was a look of expectation, as if he knew things about her that she, herself, did not know.

She sighed. She had not handled things well. She did not want to make an enemy of him, for it would be far better for both of them if they could become amicable and live in harmony until such time as he stopped grieving, learned she was trustworthy, and decided to let her return to the priory.

The flip side of this was that she didn't have red hair for nothing, and she found the idea of waiting upon him disconcerting.

"David…" She turned to say as much to him and found she was standing in the garden alone.

After leaving her, David needed time to sort things out in his mind, for he did not want to act rashly. Not with her. So he chose not to return to the castle or to take a swim in the burn. Instead, he rode all the way down to Moray Firth. There, he found the water calming as he sat upon a large rock at the base of the hill and watched the play of dolphins frolicking without a care. He wondered what it would be like to be as carefree as they.

His gaze then settled upon a pod of seals, lazily basking in the afternoon sun, and he closed his eyes, absorbing the warmth and feeling the calming solace of it, while he directed his thoughts toward deciding what to do about the puzzlement of a woman called Elisabeth Douglas and her incredible story. He did not know why, but he found himself believing her. But then, she had not given him any cause *not* to believe her. And then he recalled one of the few words of wisdom his father had passed on to him:

"Remember, 'tis wise to exercise caution in all matters, and better to have a thousand enemies outside the castle than one enemy within."

He was reminded that one could never be too careful; therefore, on the morrow he would send one or two of his cousins to the Isle of Mull to hear the Mackinnon's story. He would wait to make his decision regarding Elisabeth Douglas until after they returned.

He frowned suddenly as he realized he would have to resort to duplicity, for he did not want the Mackinnon to think he was holding his sister-in-law captive. The thought did rankle, for he was a man mentally faithful to himself; a man who adhered firmly and devotedly to his beliefs, and honesty in all things was one of them. But, there were times when necessity overruled honesty, and only time would prove if he had been wise to do so.

In the meantime, he would give Elisabeth time to prove herself, and he hoped she would be both trustworthy and truthful.

Chapter 9

She shrank from words, thinking of the scars they leave,
which she would be left to tend when he had gone.
If he spoke the truth, she could not bear it;
if he tried to muffle it with tenderness,
she would look upon it as pity.

— "The Blush" (1958)
   Elizabeth Taylor (1912–1975)
   British novelist and short-story writer

AFTER BEING AROUND THE MACKINNONS WITH THEIR
large family of seven brothers and four sisters, it was
both unexpected and extraordinary to find herself thrust
into an almost all-male household, with only Ailis to
offer her companionship, along with five male cousins.
There was something not right about it, for it seemed ill
fitting, like a hastily sewn garment.

She mentioned such to Ailis, as she took Elisabeth on
a tour of Aisling Castle.

"I hope you are comfortable here, for I find your
companionship a blessing. Ye canna know how happy
I am to have ye here, for I have missed having another
woman that is part of the family. Caitrina was the first to
leave when she decided to serve the church, and then my
sister Janet died. After that, it seemed the dying would

never stop and when Mara died, I knew I would be next, but it turned out to be Caitrina."

Elisabeth replied, "Your family has endured so much. When I saw all of the graves that day at the cemetery… How can I explain it other than to say I cannot imagine losing so many members of your family? I kept asking myself how it was possible that you would lose four sisters. How did that happen? Was there a natural disaster? Was there a plague, a sickness that went through the family?"

Ailis shook her head. "It was many things. We lost Grainne and Mara to a fever. Grainne was the baby of the family. She was only nine when she died. Mara was thirteen. She died a week after Grainne left us. 'Twas fitting in a way, for the two o' them were verra close."

Elisabeth searched for consoling words, but words escaped her. Before she could think of something to say, Ailis led her to a room very much like a sitting room, and there she saw sewing baskets and needlepoint stretched upon frames, a cross-stitch of what looked like Aisling Castle, and farther over, a partially knit garment. She realized that these things were left by the dead sisters, and a wrenching sadness consumed her. It was unbelievable, but these things must have been sitting here just as their owners left them the last time they walked from this room, smiling and laughing, never dreaming they would not live long enough to finish them. "These belonged to your sisters?"

"Aye, everything is just as they left it," she replied, with a gaze around the room, and Elisabeth could almost feel the sadness of evoked memories reaching out to curl its arms around her.

Ailis took a deep breath. "This is where we all gathered, for each of us loved our time together away from the goings-on in the rest of the castle. I suppose I should put it all away, fer 'tis always a sadness that greets me whenever I come here."

"I will help you pack them away," Elisabeth said, for she could well understand the lure of this lovely, peaceful room, for it was smaller and more intimate than the solar, because it was not expected to accommodate so many people.

They returned to the solar, which was a room of comfort and status with a large fireplace, decorative woodwork, beautifully worked tapestries and wall hangings, and a Celtic prayer carefully cross-stitched by young hands.

Ailis drew back a bulky drape, and behind it was a painting of a large and happy family. Elisabeth's gaze rested upon the majestic image of Aisling Castle in the background. She counted a mother, father, and nine children. "This was your family portrait?"

"Aye, 'twas the last time we were all gathered like this, for Grainne died a few months after it was painted, and then, one by one, they all began to disappear."

Elisabeth, her heart pierced with the sadness of such overwhelming loss, asked, "What of your brothers?"

"Our brother William was killed in battle against Clan Ross. Archibald was badly wounded in the same battle and died a few weeks later. Three years later, Hugh was attacked by a dog while hunting and died of *canis furibundus*. 'Twas said the dog was cursed, for it went mad after it had eaten the sacrament."

Canis furibundus... Elisabeth stared at a delicately

wrought ebony screen, as she thought back to her years of taking Latin. *Canis furibundus*, mad dog, was nothing more than what the Romans magniloquently called, in layman's terms, rabies.

"And so, out of many children, only two," Ailis said. "I pray every night that naught will happen to David."

Elisabeth could understand the feeling of complete and utter loss that Ailis felt, for it was similar to the wrenching sense of loss she and her sister Isobella experienced over the loss of their family who would not even be born for several hundred years. She put her arms around Ailis and patted the braided coils of her silken strawberry-blonde hair. "I am sorry you know so much about suffering."

Ailis smiled wanly, looked away as if giving herself a mental shake, then said with a burst of newfound energy, "I almost forgot to tell ye that the semestair from Avoch, employed to make us dresses, gowns, and linen fer our beds, will be coming on the morrow."

Semestair? Elisabeth thought about that word a moment before she decided it had to be the word for *seamstress*. "That is very kind of you, but I won't be staying much longer so I don't really need new clothes, for I wear a habit at Elcho Priory," she said.

"Aye, ye do need to see the semestair," said Ailis, "fer David said ye wouldna be leaving Aisling anytime soon."

Elisabeth tried to hide her ruffled feelings, for she did not wish to drag sweet Ailis into an issue she had with her brother. But Elisabeth was angry about being kept here when it served no purpose. She was an educated woman. She had much to offer in the way of healing. She could save lives and change the way medicine was practiced if she wasn't held back by the likes of David Murray, the Earl of Kinloss. She wanted to learn and practice medicine, and she was very excited about the things she learned at Soutra Aisle. She had only begun to use them at Elcho Priory, and now that had all changed and she did not understand why. Why was she being denied the opportunity?

Suddenly, she had a very strong suspicion just who it was that might have caused all of it, for where was Black Douglas, and why did he allow all of this to happen?

After all, *she* had been kidnapped by the MacLeans and had her wedding canceled by the King's regent. Her fiancé was forced to marry the Earl of Bosworth's daughter, then she was almost kidnapped again by the MacLeans and now was basically kidnapped by the Earl of Kinloss. Just what did she need to do to get a little sympathy from Black Douglas… start moaning over the fact that she couldn't find *her* own Mr. Darcy, as Izzy did? "Fair is foul and foul is fair," to quote Shakespeare, for she thought of Douglas as their guardian and noble protector, but in her case, he was looking more and more like a devious plotter and anything but a champion for her cause.

Elisabeth realized suddenly that her thoughts had wandered off and Ailis was patiently waiting for them to wander back in her direction. "I'm sorry, Ailis, I fear I let my red hair get the best of me. Since it seems I will be staying at Aisling longer than I anticipated, you are right about my needing additional clothing. A visit from the semestair will be most welcome."

"I am going to the mews to exercise my hawk. Will ye accompany me?"

"Oh my, I know nothing about hawking," Elisabeth said.

"I can teach you," Ailis said. "In fact I would like very much to do that. It would be like having one of my sisters back."

"That was a lovely thing to say, Ailis."

When Ailis did not respond, Elisabeth knew she was waiting for her to finish, but Elisabeth did not plan on doing so until she saw the hopeful expression and knew she would be the worst sort of wretch if she cruelly said no. Idiot that she was, she blurted out a cheerful, "And of course I will go with you."

As they walked down to the mews, Ailis explained that the term "mews," in falconer's language, meant a place where hawks were put at the molting season, and where they cast their feathers. She also explained that hawks were in much demand; a good cast of hawks brought high prices and it was also expensive to keep them. "We dinna have as many as most, and I have heard that King Henry has partridges, pheasants, and herons, and will throw anyone who kills one into prison."

Elisabeth nodded, for that sounded like something old Henry VIII would do. He was so busy casting people into prison and lopping off heads that she was surprised to hear he had time for falcons.

"Perhaps another day we shall go out when they work the dogs," Ailis said, "for it is wonderful when a burn is frequented by game and the dogs flush out ducks or other small waterfowl and the handlers remove the hoods and cast off their hawks."

"I suppose one must be very practiced at this sort of thing to be good at it," Elisabeth said, searching for something to say and thinking she must concentrate on keeping abreast of things for the general diffusion of useful knowledge.

"Yes, there are those who canna tell a hawk from a hernshaw."

Well, that certainly hit home! "I'm afraid I'm one of them," Elisabeth replied. "What is a hernshaw?"

"'Tis a bird. It is known as a heron in England."

And so passed the afternoon, with Elisabeth advancing her intellectual capacity to encompass things she never dreamed she would remotely consider and finding it enjoyable because of the pleasure it brought to Ailis.

Later that evening when she was settled in her room, she thought about David and wondered how it was possible to feel both a strong attraction and a great deal of annoyance toward the same person. Perhaps it was nothing more than a sexual attraction that would die its own natural death over time. Or, what if it was an attraction she wanted to feel again and to go so far as to have a man in her life again?

She was at a loss as to how to explain her feelings for him even to herself. He was a man she barely knew, yet they had kissed quite thoroughly and very shortly after she met him. She was reminded that she hadn't participated in that kind of thrill kissing for many a year. She reminded herself, as well, that none of this really mattered, for whatever attraction *he* felt had evaporated when she could not perform a miracle and save Caitrina. And yet, he had kissed her by the swing...

Elisabeth was sympathetic concerning David, for he had suffered an inordinate amount of loss with the deaths of so many family members. Naturally he had wanted desperately to keep the two sisters who remained alive, but he ventured off course when he allowed his desperation to override his logic in forgetting that a doctor is a healer, not a performer of miracles.

And then he took it a step further, for now he not only blamed her but added to that punishment in the form of disallowing her to return to Elcho Priory. Such behavior confused her, for one moment he was holding her a virtual prisoner and the next he was kissing her, or to put it more plainly, one minute he acted like he was attracted to her and the next he completely ignored her. She was starting to feel like a yo-yo. It was strange how much one could learn about a person if they reflected on their observations while alone when all of the emotions were removed.

And what good did all of this reflection do? Nothing more than that she was beginning to fill out the blank page titled "Lord David Murray, 3rd Earl of Kinloss," which should at some point lead to understanding the complicated man he was. He was a proud man, and sometimes that pride could make him seem harsh, cold, and unfeeling. He had seen many of the family and friends he loved disappear out of his life long before they should have. But what saddened her the most was that he blamed himself for not only his father's death, but the deaths of his sisters as well.

He had assumed the title of earl upon his father's death, neither happy nor sad about being the only remaining son and therefore assuming the title. He simply accepted it because it was his duty to do so, and now that he had it, he would perform the role to the best of his ability. He had never been in love, so he had no baggage in that department. And the thing that twisted her heart the most was that his father had never gotten over the fact that of all his sons, David would be the one to stay alive and follow him as the Earl of Kinloss.

Thump… thump… thump…

Was that a sign of some sort from Sir James, she wondered. She paused, listening, but the sound did not come again, and her thoughts returned to Lord Kinloss once more.

She had a feeling he was not the kind of man to fall in love overnight. He was slow to trust, and probably even slower to open his heart and show a woman what lay secreted inside it. And she had no earthly idea why she was allotting so much time to this, for she was not going to be a permanent fixture around Aisling Castle. Her future lay elsewhere, and she intended to look for it.

That night, she lay awake for what seemed an eternity, looking at a full moon sliding through the window and casting a mellow, golden light over the entire room, which made it easy to lie awake thinking. Had she been wrong about her future? Was ministering to the sick something that would not be possible for her? And if it was, why were there so many things happening to prevent her from fulfilling her destiny to be a doctor? Was her life indeed hers, her life to live and make her own decisions and follow the leadings of her heart? Or was she nothing more than a puppet on a string, and the strings were being pulled by someone else?

She sat up and dangled her legs over the side of the bed, debating whether she should try once more to sleep or give up with the idea altogether. Then she stood and began to pace the room to see if that made her tired enough to sleep.

Over and over the words played in her head like a litany, until she wondered if she was becoming deranged, or was she hopelessly confused. How had she gone from being intelligent, self-possessed, pleasant, and resolute to stupid, confused, insecure, and indecisive in such a short time? *My life is running off in a direction I don't want to go, and I don't know how to turn it around. Am I not the master of my own ship, the heroine in my own play?*

"*What's done cannot be undone. To bed… to bed… to bed…*"

She turned around and brought her hand up to her chest as if that could still the frantic beating of her heart. "You took your sweet time showing yourself. I was beginning to think there was some truth to that story of you and the Countess of Sussex. Were you off gallivanting with her?"

Sir James crossed his arms and looked down at her with a grandfatherly expression. "Ye are upset."

She clapped her hands on her hips. "Gee whiz, how could that be true? Especially when things have been going so very, very well and you have been a peach to visit me frequently, just to see how I am faring?"

"Ye may not be upset, but ye are angry."

"I *know* I'm angry and I am also upset, so don't tell me you popped in here to tell me something I already know. You haven't exactly been involved in your own mischief, and I am not the kind to be enamored with being bounced around like a puppet on a string. I like order in my life. I like to make plans and execute them. I want to feel I have some control over my own destiny. I want to know what is going on here and how you intend to take care of the situation I find myself in. And lastly, just where in the devil have you been? I have needed help and guidance, and you have ignored me."

"I havena come to yer assistance because ye didna need assistance."

"I need assistance right now."

"Nae, lass, ye dinna need that. Ye are no' a lass who likes to be led along and told what to do. So, I ha' given ye the opportunity to make yer own way."

"Make my own way... hogwash! If I leapt off a bridge, thinking I could fly, would you sit back and let me break my fool neck?"

"There are some things I can do and some things I canna. If ye are determined to jump, I canna intervene."

"And yet you call my being held prisoner here an opportunity?" She was thinking she could die in this place and Isobella would never know.

He laughed, "Nae, lass, I would tell her."

"Are my thoughts public property?"

"Some o' them are."

She was wondering if a ghost could become senile—after all, he was certainly old enough.

"Nae, senility belongs to the living."

"Why don't I just sit down and think about what I want to say in our conversation, and you can do all the talking? Why are you here? Why did everything work out so well for Isobella, while I'm having nothing but obstacles in my path? She married the man she loved."

"As will ye."

Her eyes popped open. Well, that was more like it.

But then, he was probably just telling her that to humor her. And if there was anything Elisabeth hated with a capital *H*, it was being humored. "And to whom will I be married? And when?" she asked, not really believing him, so she wanted proof.

"When the time is ripe."

"Get a new pet reply. I'm tired of that one. Why are you being so hard on me?"

"He who will not be ruled by the rudder must be ruled by the rock. Ye are blaming me for your own wrong-headed decisions, when it isna my fault ye are doing too much thinking and not enough action."

"So in response to all my shortcomings, you come in here quoting Lady Macbeth? Am I supposed to go out and gather eyes of newt and toes of frogs?"

"Nae... unless it pleases ye to do so."

"Then you tell me, what does my current situation have to do with Lady Macbeth or Shakespeare? *Macbeth* is tragedy."

His brows raised, and a smile lifted the corners of his mouth, then, with a twinkle in his eye, he said, "Aye, 'tis true it is a tragedy. Which is naught more than a serious play with a tragic theme involving a heroic struggle and the downfall of the main character. Does that sound familiar?"

She gasped. "Downfall! Are you predicting my demise?"

"Nae, but one can be brought to ruin or to sorrow as a consequence of their actions, whether it be a tragic flaw, a moral weakness, or simply because they canna cope with unfavorable circumstances."

He was diving pretty deep with his rhetoric now, and she wasn't in the mood, so she changed the subject when she asked, "So, are you going to get me out of this mess or not?"

His eyes were bright as sapphires and there was laughter in them, which she chose to ignore, her plight being, in her mind, nothing to laugh about. He could not humor her with bright, shining, beautiful blue eyes—or they could turn red and flaming, but neither one would work. She wasn't being bought off so cheaply. She was getting smarter now. She wanted answers. And she was going to get them. "So, are you going to intervene?"

"Nae, I canna live yer life for ye, but I can give ye a poke and a prod now and then."

"I feel over-poked and prodded already. Have you not been watching? I've been bounced all over the place, kidnapped more than I want to remember by the MacLeans, and then hauled here at a miserable pace. So, what am I supposed to do?"

"Ye could stop feeling sorry for yersel'. Ye always had the ability to control yer destiny, but ye choose not to make changes but wait for change to happen."

"If you think I can simply fly out the window and walk away from here and not be hauled back…"

"Ye dinna listen, lass. 'Tis sometimes a problem fer ye, for yer mind races ahead o' my wirds."

Well, that sure slammed a damper on things. "Okay, I can take constructive criticism, so where am I off on all of this?"

"Destiny will happen. Ye either strive to find it, or ye sit back and wait fer it to find ye."

All the wind seemed to go out of her sails with a giant *whoosh!* For how could she fight what was foreordained? "Destiny packs quite a wallop, and I'm beginning to hate that word. It is an inexorable ruler and not fair in the least, for determination and physical ability have no authority over it. I do all the work and feel all the pain, and destiny gets the credit. It seems destiny is something gained through immense suffering. And I hate that!" And she stamped her foot for emphasis. "It makes me feel like a puppet. Destiny is an excuse for everything, even crime." She gave him a direct look. "It is all rather hopeless, isn't it?"

"Nae, lass, ye have no reason to be so doon aboot it. There is always room for optimism, ye ken. 'Tis no' so difficult when ye ken the formula."

That got her attention. "Formula? What formula is that?"

"Change what ye can change, and find a purpose in that which ye canna change."

"Find a purpose? Are you saying I am not going to leave here, so I have to dig in and make the most of it?"

"Ye are a creature born to make yer own choices, and I canna tell ye what yer future holds, but I can help ye to find it."

She thought of the words of Dryden: "'For present joys are more to flesh and blood than a dull prospect of a distant good.'"

The sparkle of his eyes lit up the room. "Aye, lass, now ye ha' discovered the way o' it. For a while there, I thought a Heilan' coo could sooner be broke to ride than fer ye to get the understanding o' it."

She smiled and said, "Well, that was a first... I've never, ever been compared to a Highland cow before." She was about to say more, but he smiled brilliantly, and his image began to sparkle like a million lighted pinpricks before it began to grow lighter and lighter until nothing remained, save the memory that he had been here.

She fell into bed, rolled over, punched the pillow into some sort of shape for her to sleep upon, and placing her head there, she closed her eyes, the words of the Black Douglas floating in and out of her consciousness. She yawned and fell into a deep sleep, unaware that it was due to a sweet breath of air that floated into the room and left her feeling strangely calm and comforted.

—⁓—

She awoke the next morning and decided that she could either spend the day feeling sorry for herself as she had been doing of late, or she could stiffen her spine and find something to do—beside waiting on Lord Difficult to see what his mercurial mood suggested. So, she dressed and went down to find something she could wrap in a kerchief and take with her, for she needed exercise and needed to be out of doors.

She put on a dark blue dress and discovered it was cut lower than the others she had worn, but it was simple, with a full skirt that would give her room to walk and climb, if need be, and she liked the color blue.

A short time later, she walked into the bustling kitchen. The castle cook, Mrs. Duffy, was a pleasant sort, with a round face and a cheery greeting: "Good morning to ye, Mistress Douglas. May I be offering ye a bit o' breakfast this fine mornin'? Would ye be likin' a nice, hot bowl o' porridge?"

Elisabeth pulled the kerchief out of her pocket and

offered it to Mrs. Duffy. "I would like something I can take outside with me, Mrs. Duffy, so porridge won't do."

"Ahhh, 'tis a blessed mornin' to be oot an' aboot now, that is for certain, for the sun is shining and there is nary a cloud in sight. I can wrap ye up a nice currant scone, wi' a spot o' butter, but let me get ye a cup o' tea to warm ye while ye wait."

"That would be lovely, thank you."

Elisabeth sat at the table in the kitchen and sipped her tea, finishing it about the time Mrs. Duffy brought her the kerchief.

"I put two scones there fer ye, in case ye wander aboot a wee bit longer than ye planned. 'Tis such a lovely day fer it."

"Thank you again, Mrs. Duffy. I will be on my way."

It was the first time Elisabeth had ventured out beyond the castle walls to familiarize herself with this part of the Black Isle, for it was quite different from the gray fortress that was Màrrach Castle, which seemed to rise out of the Atlantic with all the fury of a volcano, surrounded by a savage sea.

Compared to Màrrach, Aisling Castle was a study in stately tranquility. Built in the thirteenth century, it was a large fortified enclosure, known as a quadrilateral, with thick curtain walls twenty feet high, six square towers with parapets with embrasures for defense, and rampart walks that ran the length of the curtain walls. Entry was through a portcullis, and in the square towers there were pointed arch windows facing the courtyard. The inner bailey was quite large and there was room for a nice garden, but today she walked beneath the portcullis and out of the castle.

She had not walked too far when she saw a fairly large building through the trees, and her curiosity, getting the better of her, caused her to veer off the narrow trail and do a little investigating, it did seem strange that another building would be so close, yet outside the wall of the outer bailey.

At that moment, she realized it was an old, abandoned abbey of a decent size, with two smaller outbuildings and a burial ground adjacent to one side. Although it was not common knowledge, Isobella said abbeys usually had a burial crypt that was in the central court of the castle, with an opening and steps leading down to a hidden tunnel that ran to another crypt in the abbey. Suddenly, she remembered that when she first arrived, Ailis had told her there was a hidden tunnel, laughing as she told how she and her brothers and sisters would play in it when they were children.

Elisabeth paused to take in her surroundings, for the peaceful tranquility called out to her. The setting around Aisling Castle was as magnificent as it was idyllic and pastoral, with cattle and sheep grazing in pastures that had been cleared from a thick stand of trees on the southern slope, while the wooded glens were home to deer and wild boar, and not far away there were wildly tumbling falls that gave way to the placid meanderings of Markie Burn.

At that particular moment, David happened to be in his study, where he was staring out the window, deep in thought about Elisabeth and what to do with her. He wanted to keep her here but had no valid reason for doing so, and as a peer of the realm, he should allow her to go.

With a sigh, he was about to turn away when he caught sight of Elisabeth and watched her enter the old abbey. Suddenly, his brain felt as if it was struck by lightning, for he knew the perfect way to keep her here. She wanted to work in a hospital, so why not give her a hospital here at Aisling Castle? The old abbey would be a perfect place where she could design her hospital and conduct her work away from the castle. And a hospital here would provide a great service, for there was not another place to receive medical treatment nearby.

He turned away, thinking about what would be the best time and place to mention it to her, for he did not want to wait overly long.

Still intrigued by the abandoned abbey, Elisabeth found the door unlocked and pushed it open, shuddering when it scraped against the stone floor, the sound of it sending chills down her spine. Her first thought was that it would make a great haunted house.

Sunlight filtered through the windows to provide enough light for her to satisfy her curiosity, and she went first to inspect a raised dais at one end beneath an arched glass window that was, remarkably, still intact. The crypt was at the opposite end, which was probably where the tunnel from the castle ended. She stood there for a moment looking at the crypt and thinking she could hear, beneath the cold slab, the soft, sad music of the humanity that resided there, and she wondered about the nameless acts of kindness, the unremembered deeds, the moments of joy and kindness, and the depth of love they once knew. She wondered, too, what ailments they had died of, and then her heart began to pound and she had difficulty breathing, but she was not afraid, for she knew it wasn't the crypt or the tunnel that caused her mind to race.

But what did cause it was the sudden realization that this abbey would be the perfect place to set up a hospital. And that gave birth to an idea. If she couldn't go back to Elcho Priory to practice medicine, she could set up her own hospital here in this abbey, which was obviously not being used for anything. Her mind was racing now, and she was trying to think of the supplies she had brought with her. She still had her medicines the friars gave her, but she needed more to treat the larger number of people that this abbey could provide room for.

The only snag in the entire idea was convincing Lord Kinloss to let her put his abbey to good use, and a hospital meant there would be people coming and going, which was sure to not sit well with him. But when had she ever let something like that deter her, once she made up her mind?

She left the abbey and walked down a narrow pathway, and finding a tranquil spot, she sat upon a tumbledown rock wall and pondered how she could find sources for all the things she would need. The hospital at Soutra grew many of its own plants, so she could do the same, but for things like opium, she would have to rely upon ships that would bring such supplies into Edinburgh. She decided to see if Ailis could obtain pen and paper for her to list her supplies, and perhaps David would allow some of his men to make the trip back to Soutra to obtain seeds and such that she could use here until they could raise their own. They could also provide her with the best way to establish connections with the traders who brought things like opium and other ingredients that they could not grow or buy in Scotland. Lastly, she would need all of her supplies and belongings from Elcho Priory moved to Aisling Castle. But first she needed to speak to Lord Kinloss.

And speaking of Lord Kinloss, David was in his study pondering the best time and place to approach her with his idea, and decided there was no time like the present. He left the castle and was on his way to the abbey when he saw her walking toward him.

Elisabeth had just rounded a corner by a magnificent stand of pines surrounded by dense shrubs, so she did not see David until she almost bumped into him and lost her balance trying to avoid it. He reacted quickly and grabbed her before she took a tumble. Stunned, she took a deep breath and said breathlessly, "Thank you. I'm so glad you happened along."

"I was looking for ye but did not expect to find ye so quickly. Had I known it would end wi' ye in my arms, I would ha' come sooner."

She realized he was still holding her by both arms, with her clasped closely against him. She decided to change the subject and asked, "Why were you looking for me?"

"I have a proposition for ye."

Shocked, she took a step back, for she had an idea just what kind of proposition he had in mind. "And what might that be, Lord Kinloss?"

"I have come to offer ye the use of the abbey for a hospital. With a few changes, I think it could be made into a fine hospital, and there is great need for one in this part o' the Black Isle."

She was momentarily too stunned to speak, so she

simply stood there like a carved statue while her brain tried computing what this could mean. "And what would you want in return?"

His lips twitched, but he was all seriousness when he said, "Medical treatment for those who live near enough to travel here. What other reason would I have?" He paused a moment, and when she couldn't seem to put two words together, he said, "I thought you wanted to practice medicine. Do you find having your own hospital offensive? Have I insulted ye?"

His voice was both deep and rich, and she was reminded of the first time she heard him speak and how she thought she could sit for hours just listening to him read anything. She studied his slightly melancholy face, the deep violet-blue eyes, the almost unassuming appearance—as though he were lost in a swirling gloom of Highland fog. He seemed totally unaware of his animal magnetism, or his traditional, manly qualities that marked him as an excellent specimen of manhood. And that made him absolutely, positively adorable.

She wondered if he ever smiled since assuming the role of earl. She realized how much she missed the knight she had come to know after he rescued her from the MacLeans and took her on that short journey to Soutra Aisle. She tried to remember if she had heard him laugh even then, for try as she might, she could not conjure up a memory of what his laughter sounded like.

He was truly a study in understatement and could write the book on habitually uncommunicative speech and manner. He was simply so broodingly intense that his almost starchy reticence made him tremendously sympathetic. Yes, he was haughty and proud, but he carried a burden of tormenting grief that would have made Atlas buckle beneath the weight of it.

Elisabeth, if you so much as look like you are going to cry, you are a bigger idiot than I thought...

She realized at that moment that he was waiting for her to answer him. "Yes, it would make a perfect hospital, and it isn't being used for anything now. There is always a need for treating the illnesses of the infirm, and if there isn't a hospital close to here, then it would serve this area well. I have no womanly skills for needlework, I cannot sing, and I am not a student of the arts. But I am a very good doctor, and a place away from the normal routine of castle life would be a perfect place for me to work."

"And yer supplies? Where will those come from?"

"There is nothing around the abbey save the cemetery, which leaves plenty of room for a garden where we could grow some of the plants necessary for making medicines right here, much in the same manner as the friars did at Soutra Aisle, and the things we cannot grow we can obtain, as they did, from foreign traders coming into port at Edinburgh. I have the knowledge to compound the medicines and the education and training to administer them to treat various illnesses."

She almost mentioned how lives could be saved, but she caught herself in the nick of time, for that would serve as a reminder of his sister, and she did not want to go down that path. She realized she had been babbling away, and when she looked up to see how he was taking all of this, she was beyond shocked to see the barest ghost of a smile and an amused twinkling in his eyes.

But he did not say anything, and after a few minutes

of him simply staring at her, she was becoming a bit on edge. She decided she had waited enough and that it was time to cut to the chase, so she stood on tiptoe and gave him a totally spontaneous hug… a *big*, wrap-your-arms-around-his-middle hug, which went off okay until she made the mistake of looking up at him.

She took a step back and was trying to think of something to say to save herself, but whatever words were lingering in her mind disappeared faster than the morning mist in brilliant sunshine, and she was left with a dazed sort of confusion. She could not remember ever having a man look at her with a gaze that was both gentle and highly erotic, rather like a warm hand gently gliding over one's naked skin. His caressing eyes held hers, never blinking or looking away, but looking at her in a smoldering way that made her insides feel like they were melting. She was awfully glad she was sitting down. She could feel her heart hammering in her throat, but still his gaze held hers. The moment stretched between them, and the rest of the world seemed so very far away.

"Come here."

Come here… The words went over her like a warm palm, touching her as gently as a caress, as comfortable as a loving hug. Her mind was running away with imaginings. Her mouth was dry, her hands perspiring, and her breathing grew more rapid. Forgotten was the reason she came here to see him. Forgotten was her resentment over his keeping her here. Forgotten was her bitterness that came from the blame he wrongly placed upon her for the death of his sister.

She could feel the steady hammering of her pulse in her throat. Her mind went blank, for all rational thought was replaced by her contemplation of his vitality, his forcefulness, and the masculinity that seemed to radiate outward from him, surrounding her with thoughts she would rather not have at this particular moment when she was trying to appear levelheaded and businesslike. In truth, she was wishing he would take her in his arms and kiss her senseless, then strip both of them down to bare flesh and then replace the black and white images of what their lovemaking would be like with vivid color. And she would be forever haunted by the smoldering look in his eyes.

"Excuse me?"

"Come here."

Her mind grew foggy and her eyesight seemed to blur a bit, and she saw Mr. Darcy walk out of a small lake, wearing his soaked clothes, his hair wet, and looking totally precious walking toward her with a smoldering look. She blinked and Colin Firth disappeared, and David was sitting there looking as good as two holidays come together.

With a wobbly voice she asked, "Why?"

He smiled and she melted like a pat of butter in a hot skillet. "Come here and I will show ye."

She wanted to. Oh boy, did she ever, but she was hesitant, which surprised her.

"Do I disturb ye?"

Oh, you have no idea just how true that is... "Yes, you do."

"I wonder," he said softly, "why that is."

She shrugged. "If I knew, I wouldn't tell you."

He didn't smile, but his eyes did. "And why is that?"

"I don't think it wise to give advantage to the enemy."

That seemed to surprise him. "And I am your enemy?"

"I do not know you well enough to know for certain."

"Now, that is something that can be easily changed."

It was such a strange thing to see herself in a situation that she had no control over… she, Elisabeth Rhiannon Douglas, who was the queen of coolness in high school, the devil's own temptress in college, and a strong, independent, self-confident, and self-willed woman who thought nothing of challenging a man or a professor when speaking her mind in medical school. Only now, in the presence of this Scottish knight, she was out of sync with herself, for she was none of these things, and she realized what made him different and why he was so appealing to her. He was not one man, but many, for he challenged her and stood up to her, and no matter how tired he was or how much he suffered or what ordeals he faced or how many responsibilities clung to him like weights, he understood her and knew how to gentle her without breaking her spirit. He did not feel threatened by her, nor did he feel superior, and she was completely captivated by the knightly manliness of him and the knowledge that he would protect her if it meant losing his life to do so.

She frowned, deep in thought, for that skillet with the pat of butter was getting awfully hot and she was kidding herself if she said she was not attracted to him. Ergo, it did seem ridiculous for her to sit here like the Rock of Gibraltar when he wanted her over there where he was, and she thought that would be a dandy place to be for one who was terribly in need of a little consoling about now. However…

She never got beyond "however," however… for

suddenly, she felt his hand take hers, when she had not been aware that he had come to his feet or walked around the desk, and now he was taking the decision away from her by taking her hand in his and pulling her to her feet. It was such a simple, effortless thing to do, but it completely overwhelmed her. She could have handled his gentleness or taking her in his arms with a passionate embrace, but this, by virtue of its understatement, left her breathless, uncertain, and anticipating… what?

"Are ye afraid o' me?"

"No, of course not!" She closed her eyes, mentally browbeating herself for a reply that was too quick, too forceful, and spoken too loud. She could never remember being out of control around a man, but she was out of her comfort zone, over her head, and sinking faster than the *Titanic*.

He lifted her hand and brought it to his lips, then kissed each of her fingers, one by one, before she felt him trace her lips with his finger, then he trailed it lightly over her skin to the highly sensitive area of her neck just below her ear. Her breath caught, her eyes closed, and she swayed on her feet, only to be caught in his embrace as his mouth captured hers in a kiss that made her knees buckle.

He slipped an arm around her and pulled her closer, then turned her with her back to the bookcase. And just when she opened her mouth to say something ridiculous like *Let me go*, his body was pressed against hers and he kissed her deeply, his hands coming up to caress each side of her face, his fingers stroking her neck, and she whimpered just as her arms went around him.

He caught her leg and lifted it, and it curled around

the back of his leg like it had a mind of its own. She could feel the hardness of him pressing against her in just the right place that made her breathing erratic, and she had a vision them lying in bed with his thick dark hair rumpled from sleep, his voice low and throbbing with desire, his hands doing wonderful things to her body that made her scream from the pure pleasure of it, and yet he coaxed even more from her, far more even than she was willing to give.

And that unnerved her. Really unnerved her... for it was empowering and she did not want to give him that edge. Shaken now, down to her core, she knew she had to get out of here and away from him, or she would end up making love with him on the floor. But, his hand was touching her and he groaned at her readiness.

"Let me make love to ye."

She had to bite her tongue to keep from saying yes and sinking to the floor. True, she wanted him to the point of desperation, but not here and not like this. She knew there was something different about him that made her different when she was with him, and she wanted more than groping against the wall and sex on the floor.

She pushed him away. "I can't," she said, and turning, she almost ran to the door, and her hand was barely on the handle when she jerked the door open. Just as she started through it, he spoke.

"Aye, lass, ye canna... but ye will..."

Chapter 10

I would that you were all to me,
You that are just so much, no more.

—"Two in the Campagna" (1855)
  Robert Browning (1812–1889)
  British poet

AILIS POKED HER HEAD THROUGH THE DOOR, SMILED AT her brother, and said, "Elisabeth and I are back from the hospital, and we are aboot to take a turn around the grounds afore the sun goes doon. Would ye be wanting to join us?"

He looked up and watched her enter the room and smiled at the eager look on her face, like a child being promised a sweet. "I will receive more benefit from knowing ye are happy to have a female friend aboot, for it has been too long since ye have enjoyed the close companionship of another woman. Just promise me ye will laugh."

"Oh, I shall laugh. And then I will laugh, and laugh some more," she said, her words full of lightheartedness and merriment. She kissed him on the cheek, and with a swish of her skirt, she disappeared through the doorway.

He leaned back in the chair, feeling something he had not felt for many a year: complete peace, born of the feeling of pleasure that comes when a long-felt desire has been fulfilled. He would forever hold Elisabeth in high regard, for she had given him something he never thought to have, and that was his happy, smiling sister back.

He leaned back and propped his boots upon the desk, his hands folded behind his head, recalling the memory of Elisabeth standing by the door and how difficult it had been not to take her when he knew he could have. But she would have never forgiven him for manipulating her like that, and it pleased him to know that he won a victory by losing the battle.

It had been a long day, but then, it was always a long day when he had record keeping to be done, and meetings with the clansmen who ran the various day-to-day tasks that had to be performed in order to keep things running smoothly around the castle and with the Murray clansmen.

He never enjoyed the record keeping that went with the title of Earl of Kinloss. He much preferred the day-to-day running of castle interests and mingling with clansmen. He closed the large leather-bound ledger, glad to have today's postings finished. He stood and moved to a small table by a large, wooden chair and poured himself a wee dram o' Scots *uisge beatha*, that fiery nectar that the ancient Celts produced with great zeal and consumed enthusiastically. He took a swallow and savored the amber liquid, warm and mellow.

He couldn't understand why it took James IV until 1495 to issue the following decree in the Exchequer Rolls of 1494: "To Friar John Cor, by order of the King, to make aqua vitae VIII bolls of malt." He smiled, remembering when he explained this to Elisabeth and she wondered how much whisky could be made from eight bowls of malt, and he had to explain that a boll was a measurement of six imperial bushels. Whatever the meaning of the word, it was one of the many remarkable things this good king did for Scotland and Scots alike. The worst was getting himself killed at the Battle of Flodden Field three years ago.

David leaned back and put his feet on what he still thought of as his father's desk. He stared at the gray stone floor and remembered playing there as a child, back when his father was young and happy. He wasn't sure when his father began to change, or why. Perhaps it was a gradual thing that worsened with each child he buried. He took another sip and leaned his head back to stare at the vaulted ceiling and then at the sun shining through the mullioned window and casting illusory images on the stones. He closed his eyes and could almost feel the warmth seeping into his bones from the shimmering patterns the sun left there.

He had always liked this room, with its fireplace, fine furnishings, and beloved books, for Aisling boasted one of the largest libraries in the Highlands, and some of the scrolls of parchment and leather-bound books dated back to ancient times. He was surrounded by things he loved: yellowing paper, crackling parchment, a number of leather-bound reference tomes, the smell of ink and steaming tea, the scent of polish, and the perfume of a bouquet of flowers gathered by Ailis; the lingering dew of an early morning rain, the crumbs of an apple scone still sitting on his desk, and the scent of ancient oaken casks in the amber liquid he warmed in his hand.

His thoughts were interrupted by the sound of a

woman's laugh. Although it had been a long time since
he heard such, he recognized it right away as Ailis's, but
it was beyond him what she had to laugh about. He tried
to recall the last time he heard the sound of her joyful
laugh and decided it had to have been at least two years
ago. He stood and walked to the window and saw her
walking arm in arm with Elisabeth, their heads together
as they talked and laughed. It was a good sound, and one
Aisling Castle had done without for too long.

There was power in laughter, he decided, for he could
feel the effect of it faster than the whisky that warmed
him. He recalled how his father thought of laughter as
being connected to irreverence and lack of self-control,
and a woman's laughter... well, he thought it naught
but sheer folly and quite indelicate for a lady to partake
of. But now, listening to the sound of it, which had been
missing in his life for so long, he decided laughter was
medicine for the soul.

He was glad Elisabeth was here for many, many reasons and pleased that she and Ailis had become close,
but his attention wasn't really on his sister, but upon
Elisabeth, for they had stopped not far from his window
and they seemed to be looking at something on another
floor of the castle, or perhaps the roof. That gave him an
unobstructed view of her face from not very far away.
He was struck by her beautifully expressive green eyes,
the dark burgundy hues of her auburn hair, and somehow even the curl fit her, for like her, it had a strong
will of its own, was pleasing to look upon, and made
him want to wind his hands in it and pull her lovely face
close enough for a kiss.

The kiss would have to wait, he knew, for he hadn't

handled things with her too well, save his suggestion to use the abbey for a hospital. She was a very well-educated woman from another time where women were equally educated, and he had to admit her sharp mind, her intelligence, and her quick wit were what he most admired about her. He doubted he would ever grow tired of her or become bored in her company. This pleased him… at least for now. However, there was caution riding gently in the back of his mind, for he knew that she was also a formidable foe and a woman to be reckoned with, and any man who tried to bring her into his fold would not find the task easy.

He pushed such thoughts away and watched the two of them when they paused for a moment, and then Ailis hugged Elisabeth and departed. Elisabeth remained there for a moment, as if trying to decide if she wanted to go inside or somewhere else. Then she turned away and walked in the direction of the kennel and mew. He decided to follow her, thinking perhaps she heard that the bitch had whelped pups the night before.

He found her in one of the stalls where she had lowered herself, with her skirts billowed out around her, as she examined the tiny deerhound in her hand, then she put it down. She stroked the mother's head and said softly, "It's a fine litter of pups you have, and all six of them look fit and healthy."

He took a step closer, and when the hay rustled, she quickly turned her head. "Oh! You startled me."

"It was not intentional. I see ye have found the new litter of pups."

"Yes, I have always had a fondness for any kind of babies, be it human or animal."

"'Tis her third litter," he said. "She whelps guid pups."

Elisabeth stood and looked around as if she was searching for an escape route, and it pained him to think he had made her feel this way. He wanted her trust, not her fear or uneasiness around him... he simply wanted her. "I am sure ye must find Scotland rough and uncivilized."

"Yes, just like some of the people," she said, keeping her green eyes upon him and leaving little doubt as to who she was referring to.

He realized then that he had two choices. He could be angry, or he could see it as an example of her keen wit and sharp mind. He decided to lean toward the latter. He actually liked her outspoken ways, for he would never have to wonder where he stood with her. "Your sister... does she have this habit of speaking what she thinks?"

"To some degree, but she softens the bite of her words. It has always been a Douglas habit to be outspoken."

"Aye, I know aboot Douglas opinions."

She smiled. "I am speaking of the Douglases of the future."

"'Twould seem they havena changed all that much in six hundred years," he said.

Her brows went up. "So you do believe me about coming back in time?"

"Aye, for the time being, or until ye prove me wrong."

"You have sent your cousins to Màrrach to get the Mackinnon's word that what I say is true?"

"Aye, Duncan and Branan are on their way to Mull as we speak."

"Good."

"Hmmm," he said, thinking. "That is all ye have to say on the matter?"

"Yes, why?"

"I dinna remember ever hearing ye stop with only one word."

She opened her mouth and then shut it.

"Surely ye are not left with naught to say? Ye canna possibly have no opinion."

"I have an opinion, but I restrained myself."

"Why?"

"Because I saw there was no purpose to be served by my cutting you down to size."

Were all women where she came from this way? He was wondering how a man in her time ever managed to get through to a woman, how they progressed from fencing with words to communicating about matters of love and lovemaking. Her eyes were lovely, alive, and flashing with intelligence. She was both beautiful and desirable. And there was absolutely nothing demure or soft-spoken about her. She would challenge a man at every crossroad, and she was as stubborn as the most stoic Scot and much too strong. She was also too wise, too understanding, and too willful, too educated, and certainly too determined to have her own way. There was no way the two of them would ever get along, and yet, getting along with her was precisely what he wanted.

He was about to turn away, but her eyes stopped him. Those green eyes… there was something alluring about them that pulled a man in and devoured him. He could read so much about her in her eyes, for they were like a mirror to the inner workings of her being, a passageway to her heart and mind, that allowed him to see all the things she would rather he not see… her determination, the goodness of her soul, the fire of her spirit, the strength to grab onto something or someone and not let go, her joy of life, and something deeper that she kept hidden, something that caused her grief and deep sorrow, something that pained her still. But, the thing he wanted to see the most was not there, and that was what she truly thought of him. After all, he was holding her here at Aisling against her will.

He started to say something, but instead, his arms went around her and he covered her mouth with a kiss.

For a moment she responded, and then she broke the kiss and pushed him away. "I cannot be what you want me to be."

"And how would ye know what I want?"

She looked away, as if by doing so she could come to grips with the confusion she felt. She cared for him, but she wanted more out of life than to be seduced by every nobleman she encountered. His intentions could be honorable, or she could simply be someone he kept around for his pleasure. But the biggest fear she had was if they became lovers it would sabotage her work on the hospital, and that was something she wanted to do above all things. She put her hand to her head, where confusion reigned. She did not know what she wanted. The hospital, yes, but what about David? She could not answer that question. She would simply have to wait and see where things went from here.

The thought no more than entered her mind when things really went off in a different direction.

"Is there someone else?" he asked.

She was shocked at his question and it caught her off guard. She stared off into space for a moment, and then she said, "There was someone, yes."

"Someone from back in yer time, someone ye loved?
Is that why ye are sad? Ye have left your sweetheart
centuries in the future? 'Tis naught ye can do aboot that,
lass. Ye said yersel' that ye canna go back."

"He was not from my time. He is… was at Màrrach
Castle… and before you ask, his name is Ronan
Mackinnon… Alysandir Mackinnon's brother."

His face darkened and she saw the muscles clench
in his jaw. "I ken who Ronan Mackinnon is. 'Twas yer
marriage that the King's regent stopped when he ordered
Ronan to marry Bosworth's daughter, wasn't it?"

"Yes, shortly before the wedding."

"And that is why ye left and ye went to Soutra Aisle."

"Yes."

He was quiet, pensive for a moment, for he did feel
compassion for her, and he knew how that must have
pained her. "And ye were robbed of yer wedding night
and the man ye loved."

"Yes, without an opportunity to do more than to
say good-bye."

Her words were like salt to a wound, for he had imagined this beautiful, spirited woman would be his and
only his, and the thought that she had loved someone,
known someone before him cut to the heart of him. He
saw the way she was looking at him, waiting to see what
he would say. He could not speak of it in anger, for it
would make things impossible to heal if he let his anger
and disappointment do the talking. He kept reminding
himself that she was from a different time where people
behaved differently and he could not punish her for that,
no matter how he felt about it.

Yet, he could not help feeling angry at her, and at the

same time, he was disappointed with himself. He knew he was better off saying nothing. So, without a word, he turned and walked away.

Chapter 11

Life may change, but it may fly not;
Hope may vanish, but can die not;
Truth be veiled, but still it burneth;
Love repulsed,—but it returneth.

—*Hellas* (1821)
Percy Bysshe Shelley (1792–1822)
English poet

HIS FEELINGS WERE LIKE RAW EDGES, AND HIS HURT
was deep and painful. He knew it wasn't fair to keep
her here and he wished he could send her away, but he
cared too much for her to let her go. And it went against
his code of honor. He did not know why it bothered him
that she had known a man before him or that she loved
Mackinnon, but it did. In time, he would deal with it and
it would be a thing of the past, like a wound that heals,
but now it was new, raw, and festered.

He did not want to deal with it, and he knew her well
enough to know she would want to talk about it in that
calm, persistent, knowing manner of hers. But if they
talked about it with him feeling as he did inside now,
she would be repulsed and turn away. He needed time
to come to peace with what she revealed and not take it
out on her. So, he did the only thing left that he could

do. He began to avoid her. And that made him moody, which caused him to spend too much time in his study thinking and mulling things over with a dram o' *uisge beatha*, and then another and another.

Torn over the direction of things between them, he began to avoid dealing with other things as well, preferring instead to hunt with his cousins, and staying up late laughing and drinking in the great hall. Whenever Elisabeth or Ailis tried to talk to him, he threatened to have his knights haul them to their rooms and stand guard by the door.

Once Elisabeth cornered him and said, "Lord Kinloss! You listen to me. It is far better to talk about what bothers you than it is to keep it bottled up inside. Why are you behaving this way?"

He wanted to tell her, but he couldn't seem to bring himself to that point. He knew that because he tried it more than once and ended up drunk. Even now, watching her from where he stood kept him twisted in knots. She was so beautiful with her glorious hair gathered about her face like a dark thundercloud that he wanted to drag her into his arms and kiss the memory of Mackinnon away, but he warned her instead. "One more word and I will confine ye to yer room."

"So confine me, but you are not behaving like the Earl of Kinloss, the chief of your clan. I know you are angry and hurt, but this isn't the way to..."

"Silence!" He slammed his hand down on the desk and called for the two guards at the door. "Escort her to the hospital and tell her to use her abounding determination to change things there."

Ailis came to speak with him, but before she could

utter one word, he threatened her. "It would behoove ye to hie yersel' to the hospital as well. I want no lectures from ye."

She shook her head, her expression confused, and he hated himself for what he was doing, but he could not seem to stop. He began to sink deeper and deeper into the gloom that consumed him. He sent away those who criticized him or tried to change things, and that included most of the staff. And things slid downward after that.

And then, one afternoon, Ailis went to the hospital to find Elisabeth.

"I canna understand what is happening to my brother. I found him in the great hall with Duncan, and they were feeding crickets. The little black beasties were a-running all over the floor. Faith, I fear they will overtake the castle."

Elisabeth then shared with Ailis how concerned she was over the lack of attention to the castle. "He has sent much of the help away and those who are left try to avoid him. Things are looking dismal. The castle needs a good cleaning, but who will do it? It would take more than the two of us."

With no answers, they focused their energies on the hospital, where they spent the rest of the day trying to get their minds off what was happening inside the castle. Later that evening, when they returned, they avoided the great hall, as they had begun to do of late, and went straight to the kitchen to eat before going upstairs to disappear into their rooms. This became a pattern until one day Ailis came rushing into the hospital and asked Elisabeth to come quickly.

They both rushed back to the castle and into the great hall and came to a sudden stop. From what she could see, it seemed to Elisabeth that the beautiful great room had been turned into sort of a "Renaissance gymnasium" for sport—drinking, gaming, swordplay, and obviously on more than one occasion, shooting arrows into price-less wall tapestries, for arrows were hanging limply from several of them.

"Have they gone stark raving mad?" Elisabeth asked, turning toward Ailis.

"I fear that may be so. Have ye seen the peacock in the great hall?" Ailis asked.

"The peacock? No, you mean you've actually seen a live peacock in the great hall?"

"Aye, we've been invaded by one of the peacocks, and I fear the other eight we have may decide to join him."

A few days passed before Elisabeth met the ill-tempered peacock with an overly aggressive attitude. He was coming up the stairs as she started to go down. Unfortunately for the peacock, this was about the time that Elisabeth, not a timid, retiring creature to begin with, was primed and ready to take on the earl, his cronies, and his overly aggressive peacock all at the same time. The peacock walked on by in his unruffled elegance as Elisabeth slipped to one side and went to the kitchen to fetch a broom. She was worried that the peacock might encounter one of the children that resided here, and being very aggressive birds, they could do se-rious damage with their metatarsal spurs to an adult. She shuddered to think about one attacking a child.

So she carried the broom back to where she had seen the creature, and she engaged the peacock in a duel on the second floor. A battle ensued, with her swinging the broom at the irate peacock and him counterattacking and emitting a shrill, ear-splitting screech as she whacked him with the broom and chased him back down the stairs.

And she didn't stop there; rather she kept after him, ruffled plumage and all, until she drove him to the long gallery that led to the main entry. And then, to everyone's astonishment, for by that time a crowd had gathered, Elisabeth, who used to be quite a slugger for her high school softball team, hit a home run with the peacock through the castle door held open by Ailis and witnessed by Lord Kinloss, his cousins, and several of the Murray clansmen.

Broom still in hand, she turned around and asked, "Who wants to be next?"

It was the first act toward restoring peace in the castle.

"Weel, that was quite a hit ye delivered," one of the men named Ian said.

"Aye," Cailean agreed. "It was quite a feat for such a wee lassie. Mayhap it will become immortalized as the tale of 'Elisabeth and the Peacock,'" which was truly something, Cailean being very smart and studious and the quietest of the brothers.

"The best thing for that peacock would be to immortalize it with a wild rice stuffing," Elisabeth said, still feeling the effects of a rush of adrenaline. And then the castle erupted with such laughter that even her thoughts were drowned out.

Later that night, when she was lying in bed thinking about that arrogant peacock, she started laughing and wished she and Isobella were lying next to each other, as they used to do, so they could enjoy their reminiscing together. She sighed, about to fall into a pool of soggy melancholy, when suddenly she recalled Shelley's words regarding his visit to the home of Lord Byron in Italy: "I have just met, on the grand staircase, five peacocks, two guinea hens, and an Egyptian crane. I wonder who all these animals were before they were changed into these shapes."

That reminder made her worry a little about the other animals in residence at Aisling, being eight or ten deerhounds, five or six cats, an eagle, two red kites, and six falcons. Lord, what would they do if the entire menagerie was invited and decided to accept the invitation to take up residence inside the castle?

That was when she began to hope in earnest that the home run with the peacock would be the first step toward restoring the castle to its former normalcy, and over the next few days, there was so much talk regarding Elisabeth's episode with the peacock that she received smiles and a "thank you" from the help who were still in residence, the fortunate few who were not sent away by Lord Kinloss.

Ailis mentioned to Elisabeth that she had noticed a change in David, for he seemed in better spirits and even refused a glass of whisky with his cousins. He then told Ailis to enlist Elisabeth's help to "Bring back the fired help and get the castle back in shape."

"Catastrophe avoided," as Elisabeth said, and that night she slept for nine hours, straight through to the next morning.

Chapter 12

The month of May was come, when every lusty heart
beginneth to blossom, and to bring forth fruit;
for like as herbs and trees bring forth fruit and flourish
in May,
in likewise every lusty heart that is in any manner a lover,
springeth and flourisheth in lusty deeds.

—*Le Morte d'Arthur* (1470)
   Thomas Malory (?–1471?)
   English writer

ELISABETH WAS ON HER WAY TO THE KENNEL, FOR SHE had not been back since that fateful day when she told David about Ronan Mackinnon. She was thinking she was glad she told him, glad she got that out of the way, and glad also that things were back to normal. And she regretted the way things had gone between them. She understood now that he must care for her much more than she suspected, for it was not difficult to comprehend that his hurt over her rejection and the knowledge that her heart belonged to another had shocked him to the core and sent him spiraling into the depths of despondency.

She was happy things were back to normal around the castle and that they were progressing rapidly at the hospital as well. As for David, he seemed changed, although she did not see him as much as before, and to be honest, she did miss seeing him. There was something she sensed about him that intrigued and drew her to him, in spite of her not wanting to fall for him and have her heart get in the way of realizing the dream she had for the hospital, and that fact alone went a long way to ease the tumult she felt inside, which began to dwindle toward peaceful tranquility.

Still, she felt something strange, for it wasn't exactly desire, and it wasn't pity, but something more akin to a wrenching sadness, for there had been little joy or softness in his life and she wondered at the cause. What had he planned on doing before he inherited the title? Had he ever fancied himself in love? Was he as lonely inside as she thought him to be? Is that why he was hard on himself, which sometimes made him difficult to deal with?

And yet these very qualities made him a good leader and loved by his clansmen. She knew it wasn't fair for her to judge him by the standards of her time. She had learned much about the Highlanders and the hardships of their existence from Isobella during their conversations when the two of them were doing archaeological excavations in the cave on Mull. She also knew by heart the plight of Scotland's past: the strife and peril that walked beside them throughout time, the harsh climate of their land, the unforgiving hardness of the terrain, the angry battering of the sea, the penetrating gloom of mist, the loneliness of the barren mountaintops, and the sad memories of lives lost in battle on the moors and in deep glens. She knew of the centuries of harsh treatment at the shrewd hands of the English and the humiliation of being looked down upon by their

Lowlander countrymen. And yet, according to Ailis, he was loving, gentle, and kind to his sisters and grieved greatly over the loss of each of them, especially his twin, so recently taken.

She truly liked David and not just because he allowed her to open the hospital. In fact, she knew her feelings ran deeper than like, but she chose to keep that to herself. Mushy feelings always got in the way of things, and if it worked out between them, she knew her big-as-Texas heart was big enough to contain love for him and the hospital. Time would tell...

She did give some thought to the closed-in feelings she had around him, as if his protective feeling for the remnants of his family and his clan were held so tightly to his breast that there was no room for anyone to worm their way into that tight inner circle, for he was not one to open up and declare his feelings. Perhaps it was out of fear of being rejected and hurt, for he did not strike her as a cold or distant man, but more one who did not show his cards until after everyone else had laid theirs on the table. She could be wrong about all of this, of course, and perhaps he was simply the type who preferred a woman of aristocratic breeding—one who was as Celtic as the enchanted woods and fairy glens of the Black Isle. And he deserved such a woman.

Puppies! That's what she needed... a basket of warm, fragrant, wiggling little puppies who loved one and all, licked faces indiscriminately and, best of all, carried no baggage.

She opened the door to the kennel and stepped inside, then made her way to the stall where the pups were kept. She no more than reached there when she could feel his presence, which was absurd, she knew, but it followed her until she opened the stall door and stepped inside.

The deerhound stood and gave herself a shake, and then she poked her nose against Elisabeth's hand. Elisabeth dropped down to stroke the hound's head and spoke softly, "I think you are giving me sympathy, and for that I thank you. We women, no matter our species, must stick together, mustn't we?"

The hound nudged Elisabeth and gave her cheek a lick, and she heard a low, rumbling laugh. Her head jerked up and she saw why David rarely smiled. Women wouldn't be able to withstand the sight of it or the sound of his laugh, for it would draw them toward him as rats to the Pied Piper. And it was a breathtakingly beautiful smile that set fire to his eyes. No woman, and she meant *no* woman, no matter her age, could ever be impervious to it.

Something about that revelation disturbed her, and she rose to her feet feeling anything but immune to him. Strange, how the thought of some other woman going after him did not sit well with her. In fact she found it irked the hell out of her. Her heart pounded at the nearness of him and from the intensity of knowing his penetrating gaze was centered upon her. Her mouth was dry, and she was certain she could not speak. She made the mistake of looking at him and her heart seemed to stop, for she knew what he was thinking. He was too quiet, his gaze too intense, and he was standing way too close. She wondered if she was falling in love with him and had simply been too pigheaded to notice. Well, she could sure do worse...

She could see in his eyes that in spite of his

disappointment over learning about Ronan, he still held his affection for her. She was glad to know that final wedge of separation had not been driven between them. "It is good to hear you laugh," she said. "It's a beautiful sound. You should practice it more often."

A brief wave of melancholy seemed to settle over him before it moved on, but it was enough for her to see in his eyes that not all his wounds were healed, and she thought of the words of Homer, "And taste the melancholy joy of evils past: for he who much has suffer'd, much will know."

She was sorry he knew much about suffering, for she could see the residue of it lingering in the deep blue-violet of his eyes and it touched her, for he was such a strong and powerful man, and yet, he had a gentle side that was capable of being deeply wounded and she regretted the way in which she had been the cause of some of it, for one should never ease their own doubts and feelings by wounding others.

"I am glad to see you, for I have missed seeing you," and that was true, she realized, for she had missed the warm camaraderie that once existed between them.

"Have ye?" he said.

She wanted to smile at his Scots brevity. "Hmmm, I expected more than two words."

"Lower yer expectations." But, she did try to get it under control. "Yes," she said rather breathlessly. "I have tried, truthfully I have, and that is why the world seemed just a little more beautiful when I saw you just now. And then when I heard your voice, I knew that it was true."

"'Truthful words are not beautiful; beautiful words are not truthful.' Ye have studied Lao Tzu," he said.

"No, I have not, but I have studied Alfred Lord Tennyson, who said, 'Words, like nature, half reveal and half conceal the soul within.'"

"And ye are speaking from yer soul?"

"Yes, I suppose I am, for I regret that my words were not more carefully chosen so many times when I was harsh. My calling is to heal pain, not to cause it. Unfortunately, I am the outspoken twin who speaks before she thinks, often without taking the time to find the right words to soften the edge of my point. I did not mean to be cruel or to wound you."

She was tying his thoughts in knots. He was not prepared for this. His feelings for her were vast, silent, and deep like the waters of the North Sea, not shallow and bubbling over rocks like a narrow Highland burn. He feared what it could do to him, for how could he... how could anyone live with such intensity of passion as he felt for her? She was on his mind constantly. She plagued his sleep. He even felt guilty for offering her the abbey as a hospital, because he knew it was not for benevolent reasons, but because it was a way to keep her here.

All he thought about was making love to her, so much that even knowing of her love for Mackinnon did not matter as much as he thought it did at first. But, he was not sure of her or her feelings. Did she speak from the heart, or did she try to assuage his grief and relieve her own guilt? It did not matter if she was offering to make peace between them. They could never be friends, for his feelings for her were deep and far beyond that now. Yet, he did not want to risk his heart or reveal the tender shoots of his passion that lay coiled like a serpent in his chest, a master passion that devoured all others.

She toyed with some lace trim at the cuff of her sleeve. "My only thought was to be truthful, for I felt I owed you that much."

Silently, he studied her face for several moments before he said, "'Tis of no matter now, it is said and done."

"Yes, I suppose it is and I need to get back." She turned and walked away, and heard the snap of the kennel door and the tread of his footfalls coming behind her until he fell in step beside her. "It matters to me," she said. "And I want you to know I am sorry for the harshness of my words."

He took her elbow and she paused to turn toward him, her eyes questioning. He seemed taller than she remembered, and she was momentarily distracted by the white shirt he wore, loosely tied at the throat so that his smooth skin was visible. It was beyond rare to see him out of his mail or without a doublet. His dark hair was loose and damp, as if he had just come from a swim, and he seemed even blacker in the dimness of the kennel— something she blamed on the fact that everything about him seemed different and more intense than before. And she was certainly more aware of the manliness of him and the nearness. She was curious at the change in her feelings toward him. Had the rift between them given her the distance she needed to allow her true feelings to surface?

Not that she was falling in love with him, of course, but a nice, little romance wouldn't hurt things. She liked to be held, caressed, and comforted as much as any woman, and kissing rated very high in her book.

Having these feelings and knowing he could provide what she needed made her feel a part of Aisling, where before she was nothing but a stranger. If this were to be her home, she wanted to belong here. She realized she had been staring and felt a warm flush heating her face. She started to turn away, but his hand lashed out and caught her by the wrist. He yanked her against him, driving his hands into her hair as he turned her face toward his.

"Not this time," he said. "Ye willna get away this time." His mouth slanted across hers and kissed her deeply and thoroughly with such heat and passion that the kiss was hard, almost painful, to the point that it was exquisitely erotic and she felt all liquid inside. So much for her desire to run from him, and who was she kidding? She cared for him... more than she should and that made her cautious and wary. Yet, when she was with him like this, all of these things dissolved until there was nothing left but the wonderful way she felt when he touched her.

He must have sensed it, for he groaned and backed her against the kennel wall and pressed the long length of his body against hers, the hardness of him almost painful against her hip bone. Her arms came up and she stood on her toes and felt his hand cover her breast, and a shiver rippled across her, starting at her shoulders, and she felt the rapid escalation of her breathing. His hand tugged at her skirt, and a moment later, she felt his hand against her leg, then slipping around to grip her buttocks as he pressed himself against her. A thickness gathered in her throat, and she felt a flush of heat that seemed to extract all the energy she possessed. Weak now with yearning, she moaned and leaned limply against him.

His hand came around and tugged down her undergarment, and he found the place he sought and groaned, his fingers slipping inside, and she would have collapsed if he hadn't had a good grip on her. She was totally unprepared for the way she was overcome with an intense wildness to get closer to him, and even closer if that were possible. His lips kissed her neck, beneath her ear, then across her now bared shoulder, lightly nipping at her skin, before he found her mouth. She could feel the heat from him burning into her skin, searing with white-hot intensity. She decided he was a magician when it came to women for he could certainly bend one's will to his quite adroitly and… She forgot what she was thinking for he was kissing his way across her face, and she wanted him to curl his arms around her and hold her close and never stop.

He softly whispered the things he wanted to do to her, and her knees buckled and her mind was screaming, *Yes… yes, do it!*

"I want to feel you lying beside me with nothing on. I want to feel the satin of yer skin and to hear the way ye gasp when I come into ye. I have thought of naught since I first saw ye that day near the burn. I felt possessed by ye, by yer spirit and the woman ye are. Ye bind me and I am helpless to put ye from me."

Her knees buckled, and she was certain she would have fallen if he hadn't held her pressed against the wall of the kennel. His hand began to move faster, and she began to pant as she tilted her head back to rest against the wall, and it was only the weight of his body pressed against hers that kept her from falling. She began to press against the pressure of his hand, moving in rhythm with it, her breathing nothing more than short panting gasps, and she was afraid she was going to moan out loud from sheer agony of it. She felt cheated, for she wanted to feel his beautiful bare skin against hers, and then her body began to shudder and she knew she couldn't hold back. The moan came bubbling up and he captured it with his mouth, kissing her with almost brutal intensity as he drove her over the edge.

She was completely overwhelmed, both physically and mentally. All she could think about was him and how good it felt to be with him. He made her feel wanted and he had provided a home for her. What more could she ask for? Her arms slipped around his neck and she laid her head against his chest, listening to the wild beating of his heart and feeling too, the kiss he pressed upon the top of her head.

"My lass," he whispered against her hair, and her stomach knotted with the desire to feel him inside her. She had felt such wild, abandoned desire, and even now that she was sated, she yearned to be with him again, only in the cool, refreshing waters of the burn, with his beautiful, smooth skin slick and glistening as it had been that day when she first saw him as she was running from the MacLeans. She wanted to lie beside him in bed and to feel the luxurious weight of him upon her and the hardness of him as he came into her.

Suddenly, she felt his body harden, and he pulled back. "Someone comes."

She had not heard a sound, but she did not doubt the years of his knight's training. She pulled away and straightened her clothes and ran her hands through her hair. She was worried what she looked like and feared it would be obvious as to what the two of them were doing.

As if sensing that, he said, "I will deal with it. Give me a little time to speak wi' them, and then ye can leave without anyone being the wiser." He leaned forward and kissed her gently on the lips. "It is not easy to be wi' ye like this and stop. This is no' over, lass, and we will have our moment, doubt it not," he said, before he turned away.

She remained where she was, hearing voices but not able to decipher what they were saying. Once the voices died down, she slipped away and turned toward the abbey.

After she arrived at the hospital, she focused her thoughts. She thought it time to make another copy of the ledger, where the friars had set down the dosages and the recipes for mixing the medicines she would find useful, and put it in a safe place, for fires were not uncommon in this time period, according to Isobella.

As she worked, her mind kept drifting back to David, reliving each exquisite moment until she was ready to slap herself, since giving a mental slap to herself had not given her the desired effect. But, nothing seemed to help, for the scene with him seemed to play over and over in her head. She told herself she would keep her mind on preparing the hospital to heal the ill and the infirm, and not upon what it felt like when he touched her.

She thought of Ronan again and smiled, for she knew without a doubt that he was part of her past, and that was where she wanted him to be. She found herself praying that he was also moving on. He was a good man and she could only wish for him the best life had to offer and it was with complete honesty that she understood and accepted with all her heart that she truly wanted him to be happy, and that meant falling in love with his wife and allowing Elisabeth to fade into his past where she belonged.

At that moment, a strange thought crept into her mind. Was it possible? Did she lose Ronan because David was her true destiny? Or should she stop thinking about love and become more nunlike? Perhaps that would solve a lot of problems in her life, for her attempts at romance always ended up with her going full speed into a dead end.

She knew she could be reading things into this that were not there, for there was always the possibility that she wasn't destined to have either of them. And judging from the way her luck had been running of late, that seemed the most likely. However, it was also possible that she was a simpleton for trying to read anything more into it other than she and David were two normal people who desired each other and acted upon it, no strings attached. She frowned at that one. She wasn't a Puritan, but neither was she one to flip her skirts at the first sinuous coil of desire. She decided not to go there but rather to let it lie fallow and think about medicine, which, at the present, seemed a much safer way to go.

That was when the doctor in her kicked in and she chastised herself: Elisabeth, you are an idiot. What you experienced was the highest point of sexual excitement, an ordinary climax characterized by strong feelings of pleasure and consisting of intense muscle tightening around the genital area, experienced as a pleasurable wave of tingling sensations through parts of the body. You did not attain the euphoric transcendent state of overwhelming happiness and miraculous rapture.

Welcome back, Elisabeth R. Douglas, MD.

Chapter 13

When written in Chinese, the word "crisis" is composed of two characters. One represents danger and the other represents opportunity.

—Speech given April 12, 1959, in Indianapolis, Indiana
John F. Kennedy (1917–1963)

ELISABETH AND AILIS SPENT MOST OF THEIR TIME IN the abbey, but with just the two of them, progress was moving slowly. "Perhaps things will get better," Ailis said, "for Taran and Aleyn have been quizzing me of late. 'Twould seem their curiosity is soon to get the best o' them, and I would not be surprised to see them poking their heads aboot."

Elisabeth turned around with a pair of Viking forceps in her hand. "What kind of questions were they asking?"

"They were verra curious and asked me what we had discovered in the old abbey that kept us out here so much. I told them we had no' discovered anything, that we were only cleaning the place, but I didna think they believed me. I have a feeling they will come for a visit and poke their noses in here before long to see what we ha' found to hold our attention."

Elisabeth laughed. "Perhaps we should pretend to have found a treasure..." She paused and frowned.

"Well, maybe that isn't such a good idea after all, for they might want to dig up the abbey floor."

"They will be here before the week is over, I think."

Ailis was right. One by one the Murray cousins began to stop by, and Taran and Aleyn, the two youngest, were the first to pay them a visit. Whether out of boredom, curiosity, or a genuine desire to help, Elisabeth did not know, but she and Ailis were elated to see them and welcomed their help. "If you are so led to offer it," Elisabeth said.

Ailis and Elisabeth were leaning over a table with a drawing of the abbey. So far, they had sketched in the location for the kitchen, the infirmary hall, the laundry, the pharmacy, a storeroom, and a supply room in the tower, as well as places for seven beds along the length of each wall, with four rooms for patients who needed to be isolated.

"We are fortunate this was an abbey, for we already have so many of the rooms, like the kitchen, laundry, and storerooms. True, they all need a little work after being abandoned for so long, but that is so much easier than if it had simply been a chapel."

Elisabeth's and Ailis's excitement shot like a bolt of electricity into Taran and Aleyn, for they were immediately carried away by the momentum. They had heard Elisabeth and Ailis were going to make the abbey into a hospital, but they never expected that to happen. Only now, after seeing the progress and feeling the surge of excitement coming from Elisabeth and Ailis, they were curious as could be and so totally fascinated with the idea of a hospital that they were quick to volunteer.

Elisabeth and Ailis welcomed their help, and it was a blessing to have help with the heavier chores, which made progress move at a much faster pace. However, Cailean, who came once or twice to see how things progressed, did not show any interest in helping.

"He finds his books more important than being around yer hospital," Taran said. "Mayhap, Cailean will change his mind afore long."

"This isn't my hospital," Elisabeth said. "It is for all the Murrays and any others who need medical attention."

"Aye, I know that and so does Aleyn."

"Well, we shall get along without them," Ailis said.

Work on the hospital progressed well, but Elisabeth was concerned and voiced her concerns to Ailis. "We need to order supplies. I've finished the list and it is fairly long… plants for medicinal purposes, seeds to plant, herbs and exotic spices imported from other countries, opium from China. If I could go to Mull, I'm certain Alysandir Mackinnon would give me the money to purchase what we need."

Ailis shook her head. "I dinna think David will let ye go. Let me speak to him. If he willna let you go, then mayhap he will give us the money."

Ailis knew her brother well, for David had no qualms about it; in fact, he went to the abbey to speak with Elisabeth. "I understand you need to order supplies from Edinburgh," he said.

"Yes, we are close enough now that we should begin to stock the rest of the things we will need. I know this will be a great expense at first, but…"

"'Tis a guid cause and necessary to keep the clan healthy, and also to give succor to the poor." He began to walk around, as if he were inspecting their progress, so Ailis and Elisabeth joined him, explaining what each of the rooms was for and showing him the drawings they had done.

"I thought we would use this area," Elisabeth said, indicating the abbey courtyard, "for a garden to grow as many of the herbs as the weather here will allow."

"Ye have surprised me, Elisabeth, for I didna doubt ye could come up with such a workable plan, and yet ye have exceeded all my expectations."

"I could not have done it without Ailis," Elisabeth said, giving Ailis a smile. "And of course Taran and Aleyn are a wonderful addition for they are our strong arms."

"'Tis a fine hospital all of us will have here. I will send men to visit the abbeys and cathedrals to alert them that there will soon be a hospital at Aisling Castle. Duncan and Branan can make the journey to Edinburgh to acquire yer supplies as soon as they return from Mull."

As it turned out, they arrived from Mull the next afternoon, and shortly after their arrival, Elisabeth was summoned to David's study. When she entered the room, David leaned back in his chair. "Sit down," he said. "I suppose ye ken why I sent for ye."

"Yes, I heard that Duncan and Branan had returned."

"The Mackinnon vouched for ye and he sent this letter for ye from yer sister."

Elisabeth was so happy to have a word from Isobella that she forgot all about the fact that David would believe her story now. She reached for the letter and held it to her breast and closed her eyes, as if by doing so, she could absorb each precious word so that it became a part of her. "You cannot imagine what this means to me. I am so thankful you doubted my story, or I would never have had this. Thank you."

He leaned back a little further, quietly studying her. A shaft of sunlight coming through the mullioned window had fallen upon her, turning the skin exposed above the décolletage of her yellow gown to cream, dusted with gold. His gaze rested upon her throat, then dropped lower to the swell of her breasts. He saw her swallow, and he wondered if she knew he was thinking that he would like to put his lips there upon the warm, pale flesh.

He was feeling mellow after a dram of *uisge beatha*, and all he was thinking about was how much he wanted to remove every scrap of fabric covering her and to clear his desk with one swipe and lay her upon it. He imagined her thus, and her nearness, her desirability, and the fact that a part of him was responding to the present situation much faster than the rest of him did not help the situation. It also made him miss what she was saying.

She arose to her feet and said, "…So, I suppose I should be getting back to the hospital now."

He walked around the desk and stopped a few feet from her, debating whether he should see her on her way, or tear her clothes off and make love to her on the desk he had mentally cleared a few seconds before. For a moment, he felt as if time had frozen, for she looked at him with a questioning expression that remained in place, almost making him think she was waiting to see if he was going to make a move toward her or stand there like a simpleton.

He couldn't decide what he wanted to do, touch her or have her touch him, for both held a great deal of appeal at the moment. He felt as though he was treading on a thawing burn that was liable to give way beneath his feet at any moment. She was on his mind constantly, and he was consumed by the aching need to answer the question he had wondered about since that day she came upon him bathing in the burn and which was greatly intensified by her reaction to him in the kennel. Now the question looming was: What it would be like to make love to her, knowing she wanted him as much as he wanted her?

He saw her eyes widen, as if he had spoken aloud about all the things he had been thinking about, but he knew that was impossible. So, to break the line of his thinking, he said, "I will give Duncan and Branan a day to rest from their trip to Mull. They will leave day after tomorrow, and perhaps Cailean could accompany them."

A look of joy sprang across her face, that she gave a little yelp of pure elation, and the next thing he knew, she threw her arms around his neck and said, "Thank you, David… thank you… thank you…"

And then she completely surprised him when she came up on her toes, and placing her hands on each side of his face, she planted a kiss upon his mouth that had enough heat to fire up Vulcan's forge.

She must have realized at that point just what had happened, and she broke away from him and, backing up, she said, "I'm so sorry. I don't know what came over me."

"Elisabeth…"

"I just wanted to let you know how much it meant to me…"

"Elisabeth…"

"To have you say Duncan and Branan would go to Edinburgh, and…"

"Elisabeth…"

"For the life of me, I don't know what is going on with me. I've been acting quite strangely of late and saying and doing things I normally would never say or do. My life seems to be topsy-turvy and spinning like a top, and I'm trying to hang on, but it isn't looking so good. And worst of all, I think I'm starting to act like Izzy."

"Elisabeth…"

"I think I need to go now," she said, backing away.

Before she could turn away, David took over. He took her in his arms and held her close, while she babbled and got his shirt damp. He carried her to his big leather chair and sat down, cradling her close, until she sighed and twined her arms around his neck. He wasn't about to let her go to sleep now, and his hand began to tug at her skirts until he touched her leg, and he followed it upward until he heard her gasp.

She made a move to get up, but he held her fast. "Ye feel too good where ye are," he said, and he covered her mouth with a kiss when she opened it to respond.

"We can talk later," he said, and kissed her again… longer and deeper this time until she began to breathe rapidly and his hand began to move and he found the place he searched for.

"We can't… not here. Someone might come in."

"They wouldna dare."

She started to say something but he found a way to make her gasp instead. He gazed down at her enraptured face, and he felt an uncontrollable, irrational need to bend her to his will and make her respond, yet never giving her what she wanted, for he would bring her to the brink, then leave her wanting while he kissed her in every place he could reach, and then he would touch her again. And each time she responded much faster than the time before, until the last time, he barely touched her at all, and she was so mindless with wanting him that she cried out the moment his hand made contact, and she dug her fingernails into his back.

Breathless now, she dropped her head on his shoulder and bit his ear.

He drew back to look at her. "What was that for?"

"Torture," she said. "Pure, excruciating physical and mental torture."

"And here I thought you enjoyed it."

"I did," she said, kissing his neck. "So much I cannot wait until next time."

He drew his head back and stared down at her lovely face, more lovely now with the blush of pleasure upon it. Then, with a smile, his hand slipped beneath her skirts and slipped over her velvety skin until he found the place he sought.

"I didn't mean now," she whispered breathlessly.

He moved his hand against her. "Are ye sure?"

Later, she lay quiet and limp in his arms for some time, then stirred and started to get up, but he held her fast. "Not yet," he whispered against her hair. "Let me hold ye a little while longer."

"Why?" she asked, her fingers playing with the gold Murray crest ring on his finger.

"Because it may be a while before I have the chance to hold ye again. You seem to be spending more time in the abbey of late than ye do here."

She smiled and put her arms around his neck. "I did not realize you were in need of attention."

"Och! I am, but only from ye, lass. Ye ken I was beginning to wonder if ye would ever realize that."

She kissed his cheek. "Worry no longer," she said, nipping her way around his ear and neck.

"Come to bed with me," he said, hoarsely, and she burst out laughing.

Anger surged through him, for she had played him for the fool, leading him on and then coldly rejecting him. He opened his mouth to tell her what he thought of a woman like that, when he heard her whisper.

"It's not what you think, Lord Kinloss. Look..." She started laughing again.

"Wha..."

"The window," she whispered. "Look at the window."

He turned his head and saw the peacock sitting on the ledge, with his head bobbing right and left, up and down as he looked in the window. David was about to say something when he felt the tremors ripple over her body as she said, "A peeping peacock," just before she exploded with laughter.

He laughed with her, but in truth, he received more pleasure from listening to her. He kissed the top of her head and held her steadfastly, cherishing the moment and absorbing the beautiful sound of her laughter. He knew the moment had to end, but he was reluctant to let her go, for it was perfect... almost too perfect, and he feared this moment might never come again.

Two weeks later, Ailis and Elisabeth were in the hospital. It was midafternoon and they were in a celebratory mood, for Duncan and Branan had arrived with the supplies two days ago, and now everything had been unpacked and put away. For the past two hours, they had been arranging flowers and placing them throughout Aisling Hospital, for the abbot at Fortrose Cathedral was coming the next day to bless it.

Earlier, Duncan suggested they celebrate the coming occasion with a little whisky. Just the family members were present, for tomorrow, when the abbot arrived, the entire Murray clan and members of nearby clans would all be in attendance.

When they were all gathered there, David stood and gave a toast: "To Elisabeth Douglas, for her love and concern for her fellow man, for her desire to open this hospital, and for the persistence she possessed in persuading me that we needed a hospital. And to my sister, Ailis, who stood firm on the common ground of siding with another woman and prevented many an argument by convincing me I was being overly stubborn."

Elisabeth raised her glass and took one sip, then began to speak to everyone who came forth to congratulate her. And the biggest surprise was the big bear hug she received from Cailean, his green eyes alive with laughter when he admitted he had been terribly pigheaded about the hospital. "'Twould seem I have spent so much time in opposition to everything in the past, that I became quite fond o' the role. 'Tis a good feeling to be on the supportive side for a change," he said, and everyone laughed.

He looked as if he planned to say more, but at that moment, the door opened and several people burst into the room, following a man carrying a lad who looked to be about sixteen. A woman walked beside them, crying.

Elisabeth was shocked because she never dreamed she would have a patient so soon, and this one did look like he was in excruciating pain. She approached the man and woman. "Is this your son?"

"Aye, he isna well. 'Tis a fever and pain in the stomach."

"Has he been sick to his stomach or vomiting?"

"Aye, he did once, but no more."

Elisabeth put her hand on the boy's head. He was burning with fever. "We need to get him on a table so I can examine him," she said, but she knew he was in horrible pain, and with the fever and vomiting, she was thinking appendicitis. "How old is he?"

"Seventeen years," the woman said. "He is our oldest son."

The age was right, for appendicitis was most common among people ten to thirty years old, and it was the cause of more emergency abdominal surgeries than any other illness. She led them into one of the private rooms to shield everything from the growing number of people who were gathering. David and Ailis followed, along with their cousins. A short time later, David called Duncan aside and said something, and Duncan nodded and stood beside the door.

Ailis was looking rather lost, so Elisabeth began to tell her what was going on. "I think it is his appendix, but there are a couple of tests I can do that will confirm it. Do you know what an appendix is?"

"I know that in Latin the word means 'the part that hangs.'"

"That's very good, Ailis. A human appendix hangs at the end of the large intestine. It is located in the lower right portion of the abdomen. It has no known function. Removal of the appendix doesn't cause any harm to the body's function."

She looked at the lad, "What is your name?"

"Ian."

"Well, Ian, I am going to press on your... stomach." She almost said abdomen but decided to switch to stomach, which was a much older word. "I want you to tell me if you feel any pain." She tested for rebound tenderness first by placing her hand on his abdomen and pressing, then letting go.

The moment she released her hand, he writhed and said, "I dinna like ye to do that. It hurts."

"I'm going to do one more test." It was called Rovsing's sign. She put her hand on his abdomen again, this time on the lower left side of the abdomen. She pressed, then released, and he howled.

"Can you show me where it hurt?"

He pointed to the right side of his abdomen. She told Ailis, "You see I pressed on the left side of his abdomen, and when I released it, he felt pain, but when I asked where, he pointed to the right side. That is another indication of what is wrong with him."

She turned to David. "He has appendicitis. I'm certain of it."

When she saw the puzzled look on his face, she took him aside. "Appendicitis is an inflammation of the appendix. Once it occurs, there is no cure, so it is considered a medical emergency. If you get to it soon enough, the sick person recovers without a problem. However, if they do not have it taken care of quickly, the appendix can burst, causing infection and possibly death. It is quite common and anyone can get it, but it occurs most often between the ages of ten and thirty. His appendix has to come out. If it ruptures, it could kill him. I pray it has not ruptured already. Can you explain this to his parents?"

He nodded, and while David spoke with the parents, Elisabeth asked Ailis to go with her, and they moved quickly to the pharmacy where she gathered opium for pain and the instruments she would need to operate. These Ailis placed on a clean cloth on a small table next to the long table where the boy lay. She covered the instruments with another cloth.

"I am going to give you something for pain," Elisabeth said, "It will make you very sleepy and that is good. While you are asleep, I am going to make a small cut in the lower part of your stomach, about right here," she said, lightly touching the place. "I will remove your appendix, which is what causes you to feel so bad. I will keep giving you this sleeping medicine after it is over so you can sleep some more."

She brushed the hair back from his face and smiled at him. "You are a strong, young lad, Ian, and you are healthy. You will be much better when this is over. Are you afraid?"

He shook his head, and she smiled again and patted his hand. She turned to Ailis. "Hand me the opium and alcohol mixture," she said, as she picked up a spoon to feed him the amount she had calculated for his age, height, and weight.

Once he was asleep, she asked David if he would explain to Ian's parents that it was best to have the door closed to keep her from being distracted. "Tell them Ailis will come out from time to time to tell them how their son is doing. And tell them that Ian will not feel any pain."

Once he was asleep, Elisabeth used a clean cloth to wash a large area of Ian's stomach with soap and water, then dried it and cleaned it a second time with some of David's whisky. She used a sharp scalpel to cut an incision, pausing from time to time to let Ailis use the clean squares of cloth to blot away the blood. The appendix was a darkish red and highly inflamed, but thankfully, it had not ruptured. She removed it and closed the wound.

She cleaned the area, including the stitches, with alcohol, then lightly applied a mixture of mashed garlic to keep down infection. As she finished, she said to Ailis, "Stay with the lad while I go speak to his parents."

David and the parents were next to the door, and it looked as if there were even more people gathered than there were before. She smiled at the parents, then said to David, "It was his appendix and it was very close to rupturing. Thankfully, they brought him here just in time. He won't be able to go home for several days, as I will keep him here to make sure there are no signs of infection." David spoke to them and the woman started to cry. She took Elisabeth's hand and kissed it. Elisabeth smiled and said, "Come, would you like to see your son now?"

They followed her into the room and David stood back to make certain no one else came into the room, as

Elisabeth requested. He did not understand why that was necessary, but he did as she said.

"He will sleep for a while due to the medicine I gave him for pain. But as you can see, his color is good, and..." She put her hand on his forehead. "His fever is going down. Both are very good signs."

"I hope he can come home soon," the father asked.

"It all depends on how well he does, but he should only stay here for about three days so we can be certain he is free of infection. Then he can go home and return a week later for me to remove the stitches."

"He will be well then?" the father asked.

"He will be feeling much better, but full recovery usually takes four to six weeks. He is young and strong, and we have no complications, so it could be less."

When David returned with his cousins, Elisabeth had them take Ian to one of the beds in the ward so she could sleep on the bed next to it. After that was done, David left with the family, while Elisabeth and Ailis cleaned things up. As they worked, she noticed Ailis was on such a high, having taken part in her first surgical operation, and she had a million questions. But, eventually even Ailis began to run out of steam.

"I will be back in the morning and I'll have breakfast sent to ye," Ailis said. "Should I have anything sent for the lad?"

"No, that would not be wise. I will keep him on liquids for a day at least, just to observe how he does. You might see if the cook can make a clear broth for him from chicken or pheasant. And perhaps some milk."

Ailis nodded. "I will see ye in the morning."

Although tired, Elisabeth smiled and said, "Good

night, Ailis. I couldn't have done this without you," and she was rewarded by a beaming smile from Ailis.

Elisabeth checked on Ian again, and carried a ewer of water and a cup and placed it by the bed, in case Ian woke up during the night. He needed to drink a lot of liquids. She washed her face and hands and lay down, too tired to remove her shoes or pull the blanket over herself.

Sometime later, she was awakened by someone tugging at her shoe, and even in the dim light coming through the window, she saw it was David. "What are you doing here? You should be asleep like normal people."

"I wanted to be certain ye were getting some rest."

"As you can see, I was." She sat up and lit a candle, then stood to check on Ian. His brow was cool and his breathing steady. She pushed the long hair back from his face. "Poor lad, I know he was in so much pain. He will be sore for a while, but the pain will not return."

David came up behind her and wrapped her in his arms. "I wonder if he will ever know just how fortunate a lad he was. I am humbled by yer knowledge, the skill of yer hands, and the learning that took place betwixt yer time and mine."

"Oh, you have no idea," she said, turning toward him. "It would be a true wonderment to you, milord."

"I prefer David coming from yer sweet lips. 'Milord' sounds too formal."

"You're an earl! You are formal," she said, laughing.

He pulled her close and whispered, "Call me David. I love the way you say it."

"I've never known anyone with so many names." She started to say something more, but he was looking at her in a way that made her forget what it was.

"You are wonderment to me," he said, and turned her toward him. His kiss was tender and gentle, and the arms he wrapped around her strong and protective. When the kiss ended, she placed her head against his chest and her arms slipped around him. She had no idea what the future held for her or him, or even if she would remain here at Aisling, which made her think of her ghostly friend and confidant. Once again, Black Douglas was remaining in the background and making himself scarce, which usually meant there were rougher roads ahead. Because of this, she was gripped by uneasiness and a fear of the unknown, although she did not know exactly why.

She had no idea why her mind went off in that direction, other than she was tired and not riding herd on her thoughts. She closed her eyes and listened to the steady sound of David's heart beating and wondered how she would survive being separated from him, if it came to that. She didn't want to leave here. She didn't want to leave him. He was a good man. She had feelings for him, deep ones, but she wasn't certain if that was a deep and intense love that would last a lifetime, and sometimes she worried that this might be moving too fast, and David had yet to say anything more than that he simply desired her.

Still, the thought of being separate from him was like being bound and chained in a solitary room deep in the bowels of some dreadful dungeon. She knew that even then, he would be with her, as was the memory of Ronan, for memories, like history, could never be completely erased.

Chapter 14

Evil enters like a needle
and spreads like an oak tree.

—Ethiopian proverb

WORD OF THE HOSPITAL AT AISLING SPREAD FASTER AND further than anyone anticipated, and the only thing that saved it from being horribly overcrowded was its location, for the Black Isle was not as accessible as other shires due to its being surrounded by water on three sides: Cromarty Firth to the north, the Beauly Firth to the south, and the Moray Firth to the east, and on the fourth western side, its boundary was delineated by rivers.

Yet, in spite of the marvelous things going on with the hospital, Elisabeth could not shake the cloud of gloom and doom hanging over her head. She thought perhaps it was born of her feeling for David, for she did care for him more and more with each passing day, and he always seemed to be riding in the back of her mind. Usually, that thought was followed by the thought that she had also cared for Ronan, and look what happened to that.

Would David be taken as well?

Perhaps she was doomed… doomed to a life of unfulfilled and hopeless passion, or perhaps she was allowing her mind to wander off in a ridiculous direction when she should be enjoying each and every moment.

She gave herself a mental shake, for she had other things to think about. A new patient had just arrived by the name of Lord Leven, and he had a badly injured leg. Elisabeth had looked at it and told Ailis to ready things for surgery, for she feared the foot was in too bad a condition to save.

She began to gather the seeds for an herbal preparation she was about to make. She needed her wits about her, for what she was about to mix could be lethal if she made the slightest mistake, so the doctor in her took over.

Ailis came into the room. "I ha' everything set up for surgery."

Elisabeth turned her head and asked, "How is Lord Leven?"

"His wife is with him now, and it calms him, although I do feel sorry for her, puir woman. He isna a verra kind soul, ye ken. Still, it is a terrible thing to know ye are to lose yer leg at such a young age."

"Yes, it is horrible, but not as horrible as dying from it. If he had only come sooner, I could have saved it, but it's too late. The blood supply to the lower part of the leg and foot is damaged. My fear now is that it may not be possible for the tissues to heal even after I amputate. That is why I am not taking just the foot but part of the leg above it. He does have on his side the fact that he is young and healthy."

"Aye, he is young and so is Lady Leven, but I fear he will be difficult to deal with, for it willna be easy to accept the loss of even part of his leg."

"I agree," Elisabeth said, "but dying is a worse fate." She glanced back at the seeds awaiting her. "I will mix this now and we can administer it to Lord Leven. It will put him completely under... that is, he will be sound asleep."

Ailis stepped closer. "What is it that ye are preparing?"

"They are seeds from three poisonous herbs: black henbane, opium poppy, and hemlock."

"Hemlock! 'Tis what killed Socrates."

"Yes, it is what killed him, and by dying he made it famous," Elisabeth said.

"How did ye learn aboot it?"

"I learned about poisons in medical school, but I learned this recipe from the friars at Soutra Aisle. It is mixed by volume of three parts to one part to one part, respectively."

Ailis had that worried frown of concentration spread across her brow. "How do ye get it doon him?"

"That is why I had you fetch the draught of ale. We will mix the seeds in the ale and have him drink it, and he will fall into a deep sleep." She did not add that the friars had provided her with an ancient addendum, spoken in Middle English: *And thanne men may safly kerven him* (and then men may safely carve him).

Elisabeth picked up the mixture and followed Ailis out the door. She saw David standing a few feet away, with a pleading look in his eye. He had tried at length when they brought Lord Leven to the hospital to convince her to let Lord Leven be, for he was a hothead and rather arrogant. "Ye may save his life, but he willna thank ye fer it. 'Twould be best if ye let him be."

Well, she thought, it is too late to turn back now, so

she gave David a weak smile and said, "I took an oath to save lives. I cannot let him die knowing there was a chance I could save him."

"I hope ye dinna come to regret it, lass."

"So do I," she said. Then taking a deep breath, she stepped into the surgery room.

The mixture of herbs worked like a charm, and Lord Leven was completely out and wouldn't feel a thing. But, oh, he would upon awakening, so she would keep him on a less potent combination for the next few days to keep him quiet and resting as much as possible.

As far as the operation went, it was highly successful, and over the next few days, she was very relieved that there was no sign of infection, which did occur even in the twenty-first century. Due to the gradual reduction in pain medication, Lord Leven was awake most of the time, and as the medication continued to be reduced, his hostility and criticism escalated. Whenever his wife tried to smooth things over, he would turn on her until the poor woman sat silently at his side, her eyes downcast.

When it came time for him to leave, Elisabeth, Ailis, and David told him good-bye.

When he did not respond, his wife turned to him. "They have saved yer life. Can ye no thank them for it?"

His eyes were wild and his nostrils pinched as he turned on her, and for a moment Elisabeth thought he might strike the poor woman. "It is beyond me to comprehend why you think I should thank them for giving me a future as a cripple."

"I understand your hurt," Elisabeth said. "The loss of a limb is a terrible thing, but I had to remove it to save your life. If I had not, you would be dead now."

Lord Leven's nostrils flared, but he said nothing, before he turned and signaled for his entourage to follow. Moments later, they departed.

When the last of them was gone, Ailis said, "I have never met a more ungrateful person in my life." She looked at Elisabeth and said, "Dinna feel poorly about what he said. He is an ungrateful, hurtful man."

"I gave him his life back," Elisabeth said. "What he does with it is up to him, although I will say he does have a highly developed instinct for being unhappy."

It had been a long day, and as they walked back to the castle, they forgot about Lord Leven.

Later that evening, after the family had dined, David and Elisabeth played chess in David's study. It was a nice change for her and kept her mind off the unpleasantness with Lord Leven, which did visit her mind from time to time. However, before long, such thoughts took a backseat, for she was really into the game and focused upon it, especially when she began to make an interesting observation, for she had a sneaking suspicion that David was cheating.

"You let me win!" she said.

"Nae, lass, I didna. Ye beat me fairly and with no help from me."

She crossed her arms in front of herself and said, "David, I have *never* been a good chess player." Which was true.

"Ye never had a good teacher," he replied, laughter in his eyes.

"Oh," she said, laughing. "So you are heaping piles of praise upon yourself now? I had no idea you were so vain."

He had a mischievous gleam in his eye, as he said, "I take pride in my game, lass, but no' excessively so."

He laughed and offered her a goblet of red wine that had arrived by ship from France a few weeks ago, and they talked for a while. But before long, he put his glass down and held out his hand. Elisabeth tilted her head to one side and gave him a questioning look. "Come here," he said, softly. "I just want to hold ye and whisper in that pearly shell of an ear."

Shivers went over her whenever he waxed poetic like this. What followed was a rush of desire so strong that it left her hoping he would do more than ply her with words whispered in her ear. She smiled, stood, and placed her trembling hand in his, and he pulled her around the small game table and into his arms. She wished things could always be like this with him and that she would always be this happy. He kissed her soundly and long enough that she was ready to make love on the floor, if that was what he wanted, but he bit her earlobe gently and whispered, "Go to yer room and ready yersel' for bed, and I will join ye shortly."

Her heart pounded so loud that she feared he might hear it, for she knew he wasn't coming to her room for tea. *Am I ready for this? Oh yes, you are so ready...* That was true, and when she stood and walked out of the room with him, she kept repeating in her mind... *When he turns to go down the other hallway, do* not *take off running, and whatever you do, do not take the stairs two at a time. Remember what Alysandir's sister, Barbara, told you: A lady glides in a smooth, effortless manner, like a swan upon water...not clumsy as a puffin taking off or landing.*

She went to her room, thankful her customary bath

awaited her, and she undressed quickly and stepped into the warm water, wanting to bathe before it grew cold. Afterward, she dressed for bed, and when she climbed into it, she stretched and found a comfortable position, then sighed, for it had been a very, very long day, both physically and emotionally. That, coupled with the slow-spreading warmth of the wine, overpowered her and she fell sound asleep.

She did not awaken when he opened the door and came into the room, nor did she stir when he removed his clothes and slipped into bed beside her, but when she felt the weight of him on top of her, she stirred and said, "David..." And then she said groggily, still half asleep, "I think I'm too sleepy."

He chuckled. "Naught to worrit aboot, lass. I ha' a way to open those sleepy, green eyes and make yer soul sing," he said, and her eyes opened to see his face shadowy above hers. She smiled at him, aware that her heart was now pumping blood furiously to meet the demand that would soon be required of it. She put her arms around him and opened her mouth to say something, but he stopped whatever it was she was going to say with a kiss that made her forget all about talking.

She felt the press of his legs against hers, and she moved them to accommodate him, and he entered her swiftly, pressing himself against her until he could go no further. She felt the heat of each strong, sweeping movement, each rhythmic stroke that her body responded to, until she felt her body no longer belonged to her but completely to him, for she was powerless to stop as she lifted her hips, groaning at the exquisite feeling radiating through her.

Again and again he moved against her, and her body responded on its own, rising up to meet him, her legs encircling his and drawing him closer still. Something wild and wonderful was happening to her, and she felt as if she teetered on the edge of a deep precipice, and if she fell into it, she would never return.

She had never felt such an out-of-control response and she tried to pull away, but he held her fast. She wanted to tell him to stop, that she was going insane and couldn't handle it, but her breathing was running ahead of her thinking, gasping and panting, until her hands curled to grip the bedding beneath her. She wondered if anyone ever died from such exquisite sensation and need.

She felt the sweat-slickened body slide over hers, and her hands went around his back to caress the hardness of his firm buttocks, the skin so smooth, the muscles hard and unrelenting. And then the spasms came, rolling like storm-driven waves, riding high and crashing mightily against the shore, pounding and pounding repeatedly, until she cried out and felt the uncontrolled jerk of her body that seemed to separate itself from her and follow his lead.

"This is where ye belong," he said, taking her in his arms and rolling to his side, her head resting on his shoulder. He stroked her arm gently, as if he had to be touching her even now. "I find I am even jealous of the sun for looking down upon ye. Ye are in my thoughts constantly. I think aboot making love to ye when I should have my mind on what I am aboot. I am a prisoner of my own desire, and the thought of losing ye sets fire to my mind and stills my heart."

Her arms went around him and she wanted to tell him she loved him, but something held her back. Uneasiness settled over her and she wondered if Black Douglas was about and if he had bad news to deliver to her. She hugged David with all her might, and she fell asleep holding him tightly, as if by doing so, she could keep the magic of the moment and him in her life forever.

But when she awoke before daybreak the next morning, she saw that David was gone and the place where he had been was cold. She dressed and went to the hospital without breakfast. Since the hospital was once a chapel, there was a small altar room that had not been changed, for both she and Ailis felt it would not be right to do away with it, and besides, the sick and the infirm that entered the hospital would often desire the opportunity to attend to the spiritual side of their healing.

She paused just inside the door and lit a few candles. Although she was Presbyterian (which was not heard of yet) and not Catholic, she knew that to God, it would not matter. She knelt at the altar and prayed for guidance and answers to what troubled her soul, for she should be at her happiest moment after such a night of love-making, but something prevented her from feeling the uplifting joy that should follow it.

She prayed for strength and wisdom and guidance that she would make the right decisions, but she no more than said her amen when she had a clouded vision of a great black bird as it flew over the gentle terrain and sloping fields of the Black Isle before it disappeared into the mist that shrouded Mulbuie Ridge, and she knew it was a sign full of portent.

It was still early when she finished, so she blew out

the candles and went outside. The sun was rising in a glory of orange, red, and yellow, a dawn worthy of greeting the goddess Aurora. It had been a chill night, but the day would bring warmth, for already the first rays of sun breathed a white mist over the ancient tombstones where the Lords of Kinloss slept in silence below.

She turned once to glance back at the hospital, the gray granite fortress that echoed the voices of the past and the chants of friars. She walked past the gurgling mouths of grimacing gargoyles, and then she continued down a narrow trail through the foliaged tracery of towering trees to walk down a well-worn cart road before she turned onto a footpath, narrow and winding. The sky was clear and the sun casting its warmth in brilliant, rosy light that shimmered through the ragged edges of trees that looked sharp and black against the crisp blue of sky overhead. She heard the gurgling of Markie Burn before she saw it rattling down from the higher elevations, and she knew she was drawing near the beautiful little pool that was clear and fair as a fairy's haunt.

She sat on a rock and removed her sturdy shoes and wondered what her mother did with all her wonderful high heels left in her closet, especially the Jimmy Choos she found on sale at Nordstrom and never got to wear. She thought about all the clothes she had and her mementos like her cheerleader uniform and her diploma from medical school.

She needed to get her mind off such. Lord above! She didn't know what was happening to her. She wasn't the whiney, sniveling type, and had no reason to be so now when she had nice home, a wonderful hospital, and a strong, loving man whose sister was her best friend. *So what ails you, Elisabeth? Why can you not enjoy life's bounty that you have been given? Why do you fear the rap and knock of something evil trying to take it all away from you? You are stronger than that.*

Giving her head a good shake, she thought that maybe a good foot-dunking in the icy water of Markie Burn would shock some sense into her. She removed her shoes and knew the water would be cold, but the chill was actually comforting. She wondered if she was becoming a Scot in nature, for the cold did not bother her as much as it did when she first arrived. Suddenly, she felt another wave of homesickness and the niggling feeling that something was about to happen. She shouldn't be here. She did not belong. "You are not a Scot and you will never be a Scot," she said aloud. "You are a foreigner in a foreign land."

A whirlwind blew down from the mountain's brow and rattled through a stand of trees, sending a flutter of leaves floating down. "Och, so it is time fer a bit o' wallowing in self-pity, is it? I overestimated ye, lass, fer I thought ye to be made of a stronger constitution."

"Don't mess with me. I'm as cross as two sticks," she said.

"I was thinking cross as two crabs, but I will go with yer sticks if it suits ye." She turned her head and saw him, looking quite splendid and displaying a brilliant smile that made her want to shove him in the water. "So, which is it? Did you come here to gloat or gripe?"

Sir James smiled and walked over to a nearby rock and sat down, and her jaw dropped. "Why are you sitting down?"

He gave her a curious look and asked, "Why not? Ye are sitting doon."

"I'm not dead."

"Is sitting reserved only for the living?"

"Why would you need to sit? You're a ghost. Don't tell me your feet hurt?"

"Nae, they dinna… 'tis one of the benefits of ghosting, ye ken."

"So, why are you here? Just for a friendly chat? I will warn you that I'm not the friendly, chatty type, especially right now."

"Aye, I ha' been coming to the same conclusion over these past few days. What ails ye?"

"I don't know. Things are going very well for me, and I truly feel I have a home here. And David…"

His brows rose and she said, "Never mind about David. He is doing fine."

"Aye, I ken he is happy as a mudlark."

She gave him a serious stare, trying to decide if he had been present when she made love with David.

"Nae, I wasna," he said, "but I was aware o' it."

"Nothing escapes you, does it?"

"I wouldna be a good guardian if I didna keep up wi' ye."

"Well, see that you don't overdo it."

"So tell me what ails ye, in spite of everything being rosy wi' Kinloss?"

"It isn't anything that has happened. It's a feeling that I have, that something is *going to happen*."

"Have ye no heard that ye shouldna give the deil so much notice?"

"That's just it! I think he is giving me too much notice."

"'Sweet are the uses of adversity, which, like the toad, ugly and venomous, wears yet a precious jewel in his head.'"

She raised her brows at that one and said, "That sounds far too poetic for you."

He laughed. "Aye, flowery prose was never my calling. 'Tis Shakespeare, but I asked his permission to use it."

"*You what?* You asked Shakespeare? Truly?"

"Aye. 'Twould be plagiarism if I didna, would it not?"

She smiled. "I never thought of a ghost worrying about breaking the law." She sighed. "What was the rest of that quote? I remember memorizing it once, in junior high, I think."

"'And this our life, exempt from public haunt, finds tongues in trees, books in the running brooks, sermons in stones, and good in everything.'"

She sighed. "Sometimes I think I'm stuck in the toad ugly and venomous stage."

"'Twill not be much longer, lass, and yer trial by fire will be over. Just because the road darkens is no reason to turn back."

"What trial by fire?"

"Ye will ken when it arrives."

She raised her brows to hover over the direct stare. "And just how much longer will that be?"

"Weel, I canna say much aboot that, ye see. I can only encourage ye to stay the course when it does, and not let every little gale blow ye oot to sea."

She sighed and rested her chin in her hands and thought about their visit. "I'm glad you came. I needed to talk to someone."

"Aye, I *was* summoned to haste here forthwith."

"I worry about my future."

"Worry will change naught. Follow the path and dinna stray. It only lengthens yer journey when ye do."

"How will I know the path? Are you going to give me a hint?"

"Nay, ye should understand by now that ye will know it when the time comes, and if ye dinna, something will happen to get ye in the place ye were meant to be. Ye canna change yer destiny. Remember that. Change the things ye can change, and accept those which ye canna change. And keep a cheerful heart, no matter what."

Up went her brows. She did not like the sound of that. "What do you mean, *no matter what*?"

He stood and his image began to shimmer and sparkle, and then it faded like a million raindrops falling to the ground.

Things are often difficult before they are easy, lass...

His image was gone, so she leaned forward and started to pick up her shoes, then changed her mind. Instead, she removed her clothes and waded into the water. It was cold, but she would swim a bit and that would warm her.

She hadn't swum for very long when she felt something grab her leg and she screamed, just before she was pulled under and wrapped in David's arms. She shoved him away and broke the surface, gasping for air, her heart pounding faster than she thought possible. He surfaced and reached for her, and she splashed water in his face. "You frightened me to death! How did you know I was here?"

"A blind man crawling on all fours could follow yer trail, lass."

"Don't be clever. You aren't my favorite person of the day right now." She swam toward shallow water, but when she started to leave, his arm snaked around her waist and he pulled her against him.

"Yer slippery as a troot."

His hands were roaming everywhere. "I'm a little peeved at you, so don't try to be amorous."

"Peeved? Why?"

She pondered whether or not she should tell him what had been eating at her all day. But, she knew if she told him he would laugh and think she was being silly. "Besides, I'm freezing and I want to get out."

He put his arms around her and held her close, and soon his body began to warm her. Kissing her hair, he rested his chin on her head and said, "What bothers ye?"

"Why didn't you wake me before you left this morning?"

He pulled back and looked down at her upturned face. "Ye are upset because I didna wake ye? Did ye wish to get up early? Ye had somewhere to go?"

She wanted to hit him. Was he a blockhead? Without thinking, she blurted out, "No, I wanted... oh, never mind." She shoved at him and made a move to turn away, but he caught her and pulled her close, while he looked down at her. She swore to Zeus, if there had been the slightest hint of a smile on his face, she would have punched him then and there, but his expression was serious. Feeling ashamed, she lowered her head, preferring not to let him see her face, for fear he could read her thoughts.

He put his hand beneath her chin and tilted her face up, and for a moment he only searched it as if he would find answers written there. And then his look softened.

"Ah, lass… my lass… ye wanted me to make love to ye again."

It sounded so ridiculous and childish when he said it that she said, "We should go. Someone might see us."

"Shhhh… everything comes to those who wait."

She frowned, for that sounded very familiar.

He wrapped her in his arms. "Ye are a woman every man dreams of. How can I make ye understand that a lifetime of making love to ye twice a day would never be enough?" He wrapped her in his arms and pressed a kiss against the top of her head. "I canna promise to start each and every day off with lovemaking, lass, but I will promise to do my best."

She had a good comeback for that one, but David, smart man, took over and kissed her before she could speak. By the time the kiss ended, he was standing in chest-high water with Elisabeth's legs wrapped around him, and by that time, she forgot all about pushing him away.

His hands were cupping her backside and guiding their movement until she shuddered and buried her face against his neck. When she caught her breath, she bit him.

"*Owww!* Why did ye bite me?"

"Because I wanted the last word."

She decided there was no lovelier sound in the entire world than the sound of David Murray when he laughed.

Chapter 15

Do not be misled by the fact that you
are at liberty and relatively free;
that for the moment you are not under lock and key:
you have simply been granted a reprieve.

—"A Warsaw Diary" (1985)
Ryszard Kapuscinski (1932–2007)
Polish journalist

EVERYONE HAD LEFT THE HOSPITAL AND THE LAST
patient had gone home. It had been a long week.
Ailis and Elisabeth were both exhausted, but thankfully, toward the end of the day, things began to slow
down somewhat.

Elisabeth said good night to Ailis and began to blow
out the candles. She heard someone enter and turned
around. David stood there watching her. "I was beginning to think ye were going to stay the night."

She put her hands on her waist and kneaded her back.
"Not tonight. I am beyond tired of this place. It's been
a very long day. My back feels like an entire Roman
legion has used it for a footbridge."

"I know something that would be good for it," he
said, taking her in his arms and holding her close.

Her arms went around him, and she tilted her head

back and smiled. "I do wonder why we have a need for medicine at all, with the male of the species being quite capable of the sexual healing of everything from ingrown toenails to brain surgery. How are you at performing miracles?"

He took her in his arms. "Come here and let me show ye." His eyes were bright and teasing, and when he smiled, she was mesmerized by it. He was truly beautiful when he smiled, with his long, dark hair tied back, black lashes a woman would covet, and the barest suggestion of dimples that made her want to kiss him there.

"There are many who think yer work in the hospital is a miracle. Ye are a gifted healer, Elisabeth, but I canna say I am no' jealous of the time ye spend here, of the attention ye give to others, when I want all of yer attention all of the time."

"Now, that would prove to be rather boring for both of us."

"Never," he said and held her close, trying to lighten the heaviness he felt in his heart. Of late, Elisabeth seemed preoccupied, and he feared she was drifting away from him. His thoughts were interrupted by a vision of himself as a young boy, the day his favorite deerhound died. His mother wrapped him in her arms and said, "Dinna grieve so, David, for ye canna ever keep that which was never yours."

Had he been wrong about her, this beautiful gift of womanhood that had come into his life from another time and place? Had she never belonged to him because she was destined to belong to someone else? David knew she was loved by everyone at Aisling and considered a blessing from above, which she was. He was thinking about making love to her again tonight, as he watched her as she blew out the last candle and they left the abbey.

On the way back, she slipped her arm through his and leaned her head against his shoulder. She was suddenly overcome with the need to be close to him, for being with him gave her such peace, and she thanked God for putting this wonderful man in her life. She could not imagine what her life would be like without him.

An owl hooted and a breeze stirred the leathery leaves of the trees. The evening was cool, the castle dark, with only a few dim hints of light proving that any windows existed in the great fortress. When they stepped inside, all was quiet, with only the night guards and a torch bearer awake. David nodded at the torch bearer and they followed him wordlessly down the long gallery to the stairs. Once they reached the top, he opened the door and with a glance at the torch bearer said, "Light the candle by the bed."

A golden glow suffused the room with golden magnificence, for the light illuminated the gold and silver threads in the embroidered wall hangings. They stood silently waiting until the torch bearer left, then Elisabeth turned to say good night.

David kissed her, and she turned and went into the room and closed the door behind her. A short while later, she was in her gown and about to get into bed when the door opened. She heard the noise and turned quickly and, seeing David, released a ragged breath. "You scared me! Why did you come back?"

He crossed the room quickly and took her in his

arms. "I came back because I couldna leave ye." He took her in his arms and pulled her close. "Although I have thought aboot what I am going to say many times, I never seemed to find the right time to say it. I canna wait any longer, Elisabeth. Marry me and do me the great honor of becoming my wife."

She put her arms around him and held him tightly, as if by doing so she could keep him beside her forever, but her future, like theirs, was filled with uncertainty. "Oh, David, I love you, but I cannot marry you, at least not now," she said, whispering the words against the warm strength of his neck.

He pulled back and placed his forefinger beneath her chin and lifted her face toward his, while he searched her eyes, as if he could find the reason for her words there. "'Tis because of him, isn't it? Ye fancied yersel' over yer heartbreak at losing Mackinnon, only now ye realize ye willna ever stop loving him."

She shook her head, knowing this was painful for him, just as it was painful for her. She kissed the strong cords of his neck and tried to memorize the masculine fragrance of him. "No, you are wrong. I could never have made love with you if Ronan still claimed my heart. Of course he will always be a presence in my memory, for it is impossible to pretend he did not exist or that I did not love him, for I did and deeply. But it was never our fate to be together and I have left that heartache behind me. That does not mean it has been completely erased, any more than you can erase the memory of the family members you have lost."

"Then why say ye nay to my proposal?"

"I say it because I must. Not by choice but demanded

by the uncertainty of my fate. I don't know what the future holds for me."

"Whatever it is, we will deal wi' it together. I will always be by yer side, lass. I willna leave ye," he said, and swept her into his arms. He carried her to the bed and lowered her to stand beside it. The moon moved behind a cloud and the room grew darker.

"Take off yer clothes. I want to lie beside ye with naught between us."

She knew that was his way of saying he did not want to talk about it right now, and truthfully, neither did she, for she liked his idea ever so much better. "You first," she said, smiling.

If there was ever a time in history when men were modest, it wasn't in this century, for he stripped off his tunic and trews, and lay down to watch her.

Elisabeth blew out the candle, dropped her robe, and leaped into bed.

"St. Columba! I ha' never seen a woman who could snuff a candle and be in bed afore it got dark."

"Oh, David, you haven't seen anything yet."

"Truly?"

"Yes, truly," she said, and she proceeded to show him.

—⁓—

David awakened her the next morning with lovemaking, and she was as touched by his gentleness now as she had been by his passion the night before. She knew she was madly, hopelessly, crazily in love with him, and she enjoyed the moment, knowing he felt the same about her.

When she left the bed later, she decided to wear her dark green dress with the fabric that resembled

lightweight linen. It had large pockets, which she insisted upon for the hospital, and she wore it with only
one petticoat, which made moving around the hospital
much easier. Once she was there, she would put on
her apron.

She picked up the petticoat and stepped into it, and
then slipped on the dress. A few minutes later, she went
downstairs for breakfast, but before she could take her
first bite, Taran came rushing into the hall.

"Come quick!" he said. "They have brought a lass
burning wi' the fever. She doesna look like she will live
much longer."

Elisabeth rushed toward the hospital with Taran.
Once they arrived, he said, "I told the lassie's mother to
remove her clothes, leaving just her chemise."

"Excellent decision, Taran, for that is exactly what I
would have said. You are going to make a fine doctor
one day."

"Aye, if ye teach me," Taran said, as he held the oak
door open.

"Of course I shall teach you," Elisabeth said, rushing
through the door at a fast pace. "There is enough work
for a dozen doctors on the Black Isle," she said, hearing
the sound of Taran running to catch up with her.

Elisabeth washed her hands while she asked the
mother questions regarding her daughter. The girl's
name was Mary Morrison. She was sixteen and had been
sick for four or five days and running a fever. She had a
constant headache and complained of her neck hurting,
especially when she tried to turn it.

Meningitis… The dreaded word came immediately
to Elisabeth's mind, for the symptoms were aligning in

the right order... high temperature, the stiffness of her neck, the headache. True, the symptoms were all there, but to know for certain, she would need to run tests. Since that was not possible, her only other option was to make educated guesses on this one, because she had no access to the things she would need to draw spinal fluid or blood, or any way to test it even if she could.

There were two kinds of meningitis. The most common was viral and easier to treat. Unfortunately, she suspected the girl had the more dangerous type, bacterial meningitis, which could be life threatening without antibiotics, preferably given intravenously. However, there were no antibiotics and no IVs since they had yet to be discovered or developed. She would have to diagnose and treat this without any of the modern equipment she was trained with.

She paused, recalling one of her professors in a medical history course who wrote on the blackboard a quote from the ancient Greek physician Hippocrates: "Foolish the doctor who despises the knowledge acquired by the ancients."

Well, she wouldn't be foolish, for knowledge acquired by the ancients was all she had, at least when it came to medicines. Elisabeth turned away, drying her hands as she did, and approached the table where the girl lay, still as a corpse and very pale, her breathing quite shallow.

Elisabeth placed her hand on Mary's head. She was burning up, but without a thermometer, Elisabeth couldn't be sure how high her temperature was. If she were to hazard a guess, she would say around 104 or 105, and that was dangerously high. The major threat facing her now was hyperpyrexia, and that meant there would be permanent brain damage if the fever rose above 106. The fever had to come down immediately or the girl could go into convulsions, and they had no ice to pack around her burning body.

Elisabeth paused, thinking what the ancients might have done, and it hit her that there may be no ice available, but there was a burn not far away and the water, she knew from her swim, was very cold. She turned to Taran. "We have to get the fever down and quickly." She decided it would be best to give Mary the ancients' remedy for fever and decided to give her the maximum amount of willow bark now in order to get it into her system. She prayed that and the cold burn would work together to begin to bring down the fever. It was an ancient remedy that went back to the times of the ancient Greeks, for Hippocrates wrote of its medicinal properties. She glanced toward Taran. "Go to the apothecary and bring me the willow bark tablets we compounded."

Taran was back quickly, and Elisabeth mashed some of the tablets and mixed them with water. "Hold her head up. I need to spoon this into her mouth and pray she swallows it."

It wasn't easy, but when Elisabeth pushed the spoon of medicine toward the back of the girl's throat, her gag reflex caused her to swallow it.

When the mixture was all gone, Elisabeth turned around quickly and asked, "Can you carry her, Taran?"

"Aye, I am strong and she is a wee lass. Where are we taking her?"

"To the burn. We need to get her into the water."

"Faith! 'Tis no a guid time fer a bath, with the lass as

sick as she is. And the water is verra cold. 'Twill make her shiver."

"Right now, cold is what I want. We must hurry. Pick her up and come with me. Make haste, Taran. We haven't time to waste."

Elisabeth snagged a sheet and a couple of smaller cloths from the shelf as they walked out of the room. Several people followed, but she stopped long enough to say, "Her mother may accompany us. The rest of you will remain here."

When they reached the burn, Elisabeth handed the sheet to the mother. "You wait here and hold the blanket. We will get it wet and wrap her in it before we take her back to the hospital."

Elisabeth removed her shoes and waded out, then held out her arms and said to Taran, "Let me have her while you remove your boots."

Taran handed the girl to her and Elisabeth lowered herself until the water was up to her neck. Mary began to shiver. Elisabeth looked at the mother. "I know it is cold, but it will help lower Mary's fever and help to bring down her body temperature."

Taran joined her, and she handed the girl to him. "Try to lower her a little more to keep as much of the back of her head submerged as you can, while I bathe her face with a cloth." She dipped the cloth in the water and began to bathe the front and sides of the girl's neck, for it was good to concentrate on the areas where major veins and arteries were, and also where the carotid artery and jugular vein were near the surface.

"How long do we keep the lass here?"

"Until I see her fever has dropped," Elisabeth said,

deciding she would explain to him later that they had to bring the girl's heated body down to its core temperature, or she could convulse and suffer from deafness, brain damage or, in case of such a high fever, even death.

When Mary's fever had dropped sufficiently, they wrapped her in the wet blanket and carried her back to the hospital. Elisabeth decided to go with her gut feeling and treat the girl for bacterial meningitis. If instead she happened to have viral meningitis, the treatment for bacterial meningitis wouldn't hurt her. But, if she had bacterial meningitis and they treated her for the viral form, Mary could die before they had time to change directions and start the bacterial treatment.

Elisabeth was especially worried about the brain swelling, for meningitis attacked the brain and the spinal cord, and to bring it under control, she needed antibiotics. Ampicillin and penicillin G were effective against many of the bacteria strains, and in this time period they probably had fewer strains that had developed, so plain old penicillin would do wonders. Not that it would make any difference now, for penicillin wasn't going to be discovered until the twentieth century. And what a shame, for people in this time period would not have built up an immunity to penicillin like their descendants which meant it would be very effective. God, what she wouldn't give for a way to give Mary round-the-clock IVs, but she had no needles or tubes or bottles, and even if she had these things, she had no way to liquefy the penicillin so it could be given intravenously. The best she could do was to try and keep Mary hydrated by forcing water down her.

Elisabeth gave her another round of willow bark tablets, knowing she had done all she could do. She chose to spend the night at the hospital so she could make certain she kept giving her patient willow bark at the necessary intervals. That, at least, seemed to be helping to keep the fever down, along with the cold compresses she had been applying. But the fever was still too high, and Elisabeth was doing nothing to attack the bacteria that caused it. It was doubly frustrating to her, for she had the knowledge that medicines were possible, but she did not have the tools or the training and equipment to make her own.

By later that afternoon, the hospital had become a busy place, for all of the cousins, along with Ailis and David, had come to help with caring for the sick and carrying enough cold water from the burn to keep Mary's fever from rising any higher.

Once, Elisabeth left Taran to bathe Mary's face while she picked at the food David had delivered to her. When he came to see that she ate it down to the last morsel, she called him an ogre.

"Aye, and I may grow into a monster if ye dinna eat all o' it."

When she finished the last of it, he asked, "Canna ye come back to Aisling long enough to sleep a few hours?"

Although exhausted, Elisabeth shook her head and said adamantly, "No, her condition is too critical for me to even consider such. I cannot leave her."

David said he would remain with her, but Elisabeth insisted he return to Aisling. "There is nothing you can do here, and you need to get your sleep if you are going to keep things running smoothly. Besides, you would be a distraction for me. You can visit again tomorrow morning."

His arms went around her. "A distraction, am I?"

"Yes, and you well know it."

He massaged Elisabeth's neck and her head flopped against his chest, and it was heavenly to stay there even for a moment. When she pulled back, he kissed her. "Then I will have yer breakfast sent to ye here."

"I love you, David. I truly love you."

He crushed her against him. "I never thought to hear ye say that. I have loved ye for so long, and I feared ye wouldna ever be able to say those wirds to me."

She put her head against his chest, holding him to her for just a little longer, and she said, "I wish I could tell you that I love you a thousand times a day for the rest of my life, but…" He kissed her, stopping her words. A moment later, she broke the kiss and turned away to check on Mary.

Later, after she had given Mary another dose of willow bark tablets, Elisabeth sought a quiet place in the chapel area where she prayed for quite some time, seeking and beseeching for a miracle. "I know I cannot save her with my simple medicines. It is a horrible fate to be here with my training and knowledge and knowing what needs to be done, only to find my healing hindered for lack of medicines. If only I had the right antibiotic, Mary could recover within a week. I don't know what else to do. She is so young and I feel so helpless, for I fear she is dying."

She went back and told Taran to return to the castle and get some sleep. "There is nothing else we can do for her. It makes no sense for you to deprive yourself of sleep just to keep me company."

"I would rather stay here with ye. I can sleep on one of the empty beds so I'm here if ye have need of me."

"Alright, but only if you promise to go get some sleep now. I will wake you if I need you." She stopped by the bed where Mary's mother had been earlier in the day. She felt a twisting in her heart as she recalled the agony on the woman's face because she had to leave her child, but she had no choice, for she had to return home to care for her other children. Before she left, she begged Elisabeth to save her daughter.

Elisabeth sat beside Mary and continued to bathe her in cool water. She prayed. She cried. She got angry. She cried some more, then got up to mix another round of willow bark, knowing even as she did that it was pointless.

Only a miracle would save Mary now.

Sometime later, Mary's fever was approaching the critical zone again, and Elisabeth went to the apothecary. She was startled when she stepped inside, for sitting there on the table was a bottle of penicillin tablets, 500 mg.

For a moment, she was so stunned that she could only stand there as if frozen on the spot and stare at the all-too-familiar bottle.

"'Twould be better if ye gave it to the lass now. Ye can stare at it later."

Elisabeth whirled around and saw the twinkling blue eyes, and her own eyes began to blur, even though she wasn't the crying type. "If you weren't a vapor, I'd hug you."

"If the lass were not close to death, I might be tempted to arrange that."

"I don't know what to say."

"Weel, that is a first, but ye can fuss over me later. Go now. See to your lass."

She picked up the bottle and removed a pill, which she mashed and mixed with water. She turned and said, "Thank you," but no one was there.

She turned and hurried back with a smile in her heart. And somehow, she knew the Black Douglas saw it.

Elisabeth administered the first dose of penicillin and continued to give Mary five hundred milligrams every six hours.

When David returned the next morning, Elisabeth took him to the apothecary and showed him the bottle of penicillin.

He took the bottle and inspected it, then removed the lid, more intrigued by the plastic container than what was inside. When he finally looked at the pills, he looked at her with a curious expression upon his face. "This will kill the poison inside her?"

"We call it bacteria, but yes, it will kill it."

"Ye spoke to the Douglas last night?"

"Yes, I spoke with him, but not for long. By the time I finished mixing the first dose he was gone."

She rose up on her toes to kiss him and sent him back to work before she busied herself with the patients, for some were ready to be dismissed, and Ailis was talking to two families with sick children.

Throughout the day and that first night and all the next day, she administered the penicillin to Mary, and the next morning, when she returned to Mary's bedside, Elisabeth could see a hint of color on her face. She put her hand to Mary's forehead. It was much cooler. "Thank God, the fever is dropping."

David, who had been waiting on her, then ordered Elisabeth to go get some sleep. "I ken Taran can get that wee bit o' medicine doon the lassie's throat every six hours."

"He has already administered some of it to her, but I need to check on some of the other patients."

"You are going to bed," he said, and he picked her up and carried her from the hospital. She had fallen asleep by the time he reached the castle.

Six days after she came to the hospital at Aisling, Mary went home.

Chapter 16

When sorrows come,
they come not single spies,
but in battalions!

—*Hamlet*, Act IV, Scene 5 (1601)
    William Shakespeare (1564–1616)
    English poet and playwright

ELISABETH STRETCHED HER TIRED BACK AND LET OUT A long sigh. Perhaps she had been spending too much time in the hospital and needed some fresh air. She went in search of Taran and found him in the apothecary with his head bent over the notes and writings she brought with her from Soutra Aisle.

"It is heartwarming to see your interest in medicine, Taran. I was serious when I said you would make a fine doctor one day."

He grinned at her, pride glowing in his eyes. "I should like to go to the university to study medicine… perhaps Paris or Brussels."

She smiled. "I hope you will remain here for a while. I would miss your help and your dedication to your work here."

"I still have much to learn. Do ye ha' something ye wish me to do?"

"You can change the bandage on Cailean Matheson's leg. I am going to go for a walk down to Markey Burn, in case you need me."

"The fresh air will do ye good. Dinna worrit. I can take care of things here, unless we get another patient as sick as the last one."

She smiled at the excited expression on his face. "I hope that day never comes, just as I hope all our patients have such a happy ending as Mary. Send for me if you need me. Otherwise, I will stop by on my way back to see how things are going."

After she left and walked far enough that she could neither see, nor hear, the goings-on around Aisling, she felt some of the tenseness flow out of her. She reminded herself of the Biblical verse: "Physician, heal thyself," for she had put the healing of others ahead of caring for herself, ignoring the fact that she would be of no use to the infirm if she became ill herself. She felt like she could sleep for a week.

It did feel good to get some exercise and to be out of doors. She heard a sound of someone approaching, and when she turned, she saw it was Duff, one of the deerhounds. He came closer and pressed his wet nose against her hand. "So, you want to walk down to the burn with me, I gather. Well, come along then."

They continued on their way until Elisabeth could hear the sound of the rushing water, and then, quite suddenly, Duff stopped. She called him but he would not budge. She dropped down lower and gave him a pat, but still he did not move. "What's the matter, Duff? Change your mind about going with me?"

"He willna come while I am here," a familiar voice

said, and she stood and turned around to see the Black Douglas standing in all his shimmering radiance a few feet away.

She glanced back at Duff, who was lying down with his head resting on his paws, his eyebrows going up as he looked from her to Sir James and back again. "Yes, I suppose you are right. I heard the story about the dogs at Beloyn Castle and how they would not go near the painting of you."

His eyes were alive with mischief as if it was something he recalled with fondness, and then he said, "Aye, the story 'tis true. They wouldna come near the painting."

"Was that because they naturally sensed something, or because you put the fear of God into them so they would behave so?"

He laughed, and such a beautiful sound it was. "What do ye think?"

"I think you had a great deal to do with it. It was probably your way of getting our many-times-great-grandmother, Meleri Douglas, to become inquisitive about you. Am I right?"

He laughed. "Mayhap ye are."

She started to gloat a bit and say something like, "I knew it!"

But he quelled that idea when he said, "And mayhap ye are wrong."

"So, which is it?"

"Mayhap it is both."

She shook her head, as if by doing so, she could clear the bafflement from it. "How can it be both?"

"In ghosting, anything is possible... with a few exceptions, of course."

"Of course," she said, laughter dancing in her eyes. "And thank you for the penicillin, by the way. You have saved a life. I wish I could count on more, but I have a feeling that won't be the case."

"Aye, 'twas a one-time happening, for 'twould no' be wise to make a habit o' it."

"No, I don't suppose it would be wise. Because it would raise a lot of questions, and I might have a devil of a time explaining it, right?"

"Aye, evil gossip rides posthaste, while guid tends to dawdle."

"Why did you do it this time?"

"It is not the appointed hour fer ye to understand the way o' it."

"So will I eventually know, or are you just saying that to shut me up?"

"Weel, the latter has its merits, I canna deny that. Ye are cursed wi' the unwillingness to wait. *Wisely and slow; they stumble that run fast.*"

"Don't tell me you've read *Romeo and Juliet*."

"I ha' a lot o' free time."

She laughed. "Ahhh… the dreadful boredom of having nothing to do."

"'Tis good now and then to lie fallow for a while."

"Are you trying to frighten me, for you must know how I worry about the future."

"Nay, but ye canna fight that which is yer destiny any more than ye can read tea leaves before ye drink yer tea."

"Then answer me this, are you here now to warn me that something bad is going to happen to me?"

"Nae, lass, I ha' come merely to convince ye to stay

the course, to wait fer the silver lining when all seems
dark and gloomy."

"I like the silver lining part," she said, rather morosely. "It's poetic but difficult to get to the bank."

He laughed. "I have no doubt, lass, that ye will find a
way. Fear nae evil; ye are nae alone."

She had a clever comeback to that, but his image
began to fade and she knew from past experience that
he would not be summoned back.

Word of Mary's healing did indeed spread, and the hospital rarely had a vacant bed after that, for there was
an outbreak of measles and that meant many, many
children were brought there for her to treat. It was so
crowded that when one patient was sent home, there
were three waiting to take their place. Because she spent
so much time in the hospital, things were beginning to
grow more complicated between Elisabeth and David,
for he had grumbled more than once that he was sorry
they ever opened the hospital.

When he would come to visit her, he would complain that her supplies were stacked everywhere, and
there were so many people coming and going. "'Tis like
living in Edinburgh, and I grow quite weary o' tripping
over sick people."

"It is better than burying them," she replied.

Gradually things began to taper off and she knew the
measles outbreak was coming to an end, which pleased
David greatly. Late one afternoon, they were down to
only two or three patients, when Duncan Buchanan arrived with a twenty-five-year-old woman who turned out

to be his daughter, Maude. She had a terrible swelling on her throat. Elisabeth examined her. "Your daughter has a goiter, and it will continue to grow and should be removed. However, that will require surgery and I cannot operate without your permission."

"Aye, rid her of this evil thing."

Elisabeth felt a partial thyroidectomy would enable Maude's thyroid to function normally after surgery, and after carefully explaining the procedure, she operated. The surgery was a success and Maude was healing so well that three days later, Elisabeth informed her father that he could take her home.

It was almost dark when Elisabeth walked to the door of the hospital with them and stepped outside for some fresh air. She looked in the direction of Aisling Castle. Sheltered by a stand of Scots fir and pine, larch and shrubbery, the castle was not, at first, visible until one meandered down the lane and around a bend. Then suddenly it appeared: a venerable fortress of dark gray stone, cold and gloomy, with its thick stone mullions, strong battlements, arrow-slits, air holes, and machicolations, which represented the harsh realities of daily life. Yet it was also a startling combination of beauty and function, residence and fortification and comfort that exuded both warmth and luxury.

She heard a dog barking and looked off, just in time to see Duff come loping out of the trees. He greeted her by rearing up against her and almost knocking her down with his big paws. Overhead, she heard the caw of a crow and looked up to see it flapping away as a hawk approached. But the crow wasn't fast enough, and the hawk made fatal contact and flew away with it firm in its grasp. Man or beast... the motto was the same: hunt or be hunted.

She was about to return to the hospital when she heard horses approaching at a fast pace, and then several armor-clad soldiers rode by, their banner flapping as they rode toward Aisling. Since it did not concern her, for that sort of thing was a fairly normal occurrence, she returned to the hospital, tired and hungry. But so were Ailis and Cailean, so it made sense that the three of them could accomplish the important tasks and leave the cleaning to the two clansmen who would spend the night there.

She had not been there long when David sent word by Branan that her presence was needed. "That's all he said and nothing more?" she asked.

"Aye, that is all, but I did recognize the banner of the Earl of Bosworth."

Her heart sank at the sound of that name and she thought, Oh no! Please God, don't let my services be needed at Bosworth Castle. Her first thought was how David would react if she was summoned to the residence of Ronan Mackinnon. *But, what if it is Ronan who is ill? Well, why don't you go see why David wants you there, before you drive yourself crazy trying to wrestle invisible evils?*

It was dark when she returned to the castle and found Bosworth's men in the great hall, where they were finishing off a meal of roast lamb, which they washed down with goblets of ale. David was talking to them, his expression stiffly cordial but guarded, and that was not a good indicator of what was to come. Then she noticed a roll of parchment in his hand, and that disturbed her greatly.

Still clenching the document tightly, David said, "The Earl of Bosworth's daughter is gravely ill, and after hearing of your medical skill, he entreats ye to be his guest at Bosworth Castle so that ye might restore his daughter to good health. In case ye are wont to decline on the basis of his daughter's marriage to Ronan Mackinnon, he has supplied me with a request signed by the Duke of Albany, the King's regent, which is a more subtle way of issuing an order."

Her heart was beating so fast that she had trouble breathing, for she knew how painful this was for David to accept, but his hands were tied. "So, I am to go care for Bosworth's daughter by accepting his invitation as a guest, or I can be hauled there by force, is that it?"

"That would be my interpretation, yes," Lord Kinloss said.

"When must I leave?"

"They wanted to leave immediately, but I convinced them that after the day ye had and the lateness of the hour, ye would be in better condition to administer to Bosworth's daughter if ye were to leave at first light."

She turned to Taran, who was standing nearby and said, "Would you tell Cailean and Ailis that I need my saddle pouch of supplies, and to include one of the pouches of medicines that we have locked away?"

She glanced at David, who seemed to be engulfed in a cloud of melancholy, but she also saw that he tried to hide it, and she was saddened to think her going caused him angst. Was it because he did not trust her and thought she would rekindle an old flame? Or, would he always be this way any time she was asked to treat someone who lived further away? No matter which it was, she couldn't deal with that now. Her services were needed and she was commanded to go. There was no choice in the matter so she turned away, stopping long enough to tell the captain of Bosworth's men, "I will be ready to leave at dawn, and now I bid you good night."

She ordered a bath, thinking it might be the last one she would have time to enjoy for some time, and while she awaited its arrival, she packed a saddle pouch with her personal belongings, but not too many items, as if by doing so it would mean she would be there longer.

The bathing part was over quickly, but she lingered a while, her eyes closed as she replayed a mental tape of all that had been happening. She understood now why Sir James paid her that last visit, and she was thankful that he cautioned her that it would do no good to fight against her destiny. His last words to her were to stay the course and wait for a silver lining, even when all seemed dark and gloomy.

It seemed pretty gloomy to her now, but he had never been wrong in any of his warnings, and this was probably the first time that she was going to do her best to hold his word close to her heart. And speaking of her heart, it was nigh to cracking right now—a heart-wrenching grief for David, for she knew this must hurt, knowing she was going to reside for an undetermined time in the home of Ronan Mackinnon. Had it been reversed, she would have, more than likely, felt the same. So, how could she convince him that wherever he was would always be home to her? Her eyes blurred at the thought, for she realized that Aisling was home and that she had carved out a little slice of life for herself here. She hated the thought of leaving David, for his absence from her life would leave a terribly deep, dark emptiness within her.

She left the tub and slipped into her gown and thought of David, wishing she had a way to show him how very much she cared for him, some way to prove that it was he, and not Ronan, who resided in her heart.

And then she smiled...

———

David left the men drinking with his cousins and hoped they drank so much they would get a late start in the morning, and that would give her more time to sleep. He tried not to think in terms of Elisabeth being at Bosworth Castle with Mackinnon there, but of Elisabeth, the doctor, ministering to a sick woman.

It wasn't that he did not trust her. It was simply that no one had complete control over their heart. Love happened when people did not want it to happen, just as it did not happen when one wished it to. Love could not be controlled, nor could it be contained for long. It had a will of its own. It could make you happy, sad, or leave you wishing you were dead.

He just wished he had more time with her... time to open his heart to her... time to tell her all the things he should have told her before, but dawn was not many hours away. It would have to wait. As he approached his room, he kept thinking, love without trust is not love. Trust came at a great price, for it left one vulnerable. It was also a paradox, for one could not find true love without trust. By the time he reached his destination, he had decided that he loved her too much not to trust her. He wished he could tell her that now, but she would have a long ride ahead of her tomorrow and needed her sleep. It would have to wait until morning.

He entered his room and paused long enough to remove his clothes and lay them across the clothing chest. Guided only by instinct and a sliver of moon coming through the drapery, he felt his way along the side of the bed. He sat down and leaned forward, resting his head in his hands. He told himself the past belonged in the past, and Elisabeth was his future. She would return to him.

He lay back and brought his arm up so his forearm rested upon his eyes, for he hoped that would help keep them closed and usher in sleep, yet his mind wanted to rethink all the moments with her that he held sacred. God above, he would give anything to have just one more night. He knew sleep would not come to him this night, and he was about to get up when he felt the faint touch of something sliding along his arm...

"I love you, David. Only you and no other. I know you are the man meant for me and that is why things did not work before. It was the wrong man at the wrong time, and I know in my heart that you were always there waiting for me."

He felt that his heart had burst into a million little hearts that all pounded furiously within his chest. "My lass," he said, drawing her against him as he kissed the top of her head.

Emotion choked her throat when she spoke. "My heart aches at the thought of leaving you. I am so angry I wish I could tell Bosworth and Albany just what I think of them."

David rolled over and kissed her, his lips moving slowly across her face and throat. He nuzzled her ear and whispered love words, encouraging, coaxing, leading her to go on a wild journey of lovemaking with him, and she was so captivated and so in love with him at that very moment that she wondered where she would find the strength to ride away from him tomorrow.

"You are the man of my dreams, the man I was destined to love. It matters not that we were born centuries apart because of the wacky misalignment of some planet or a prank played by a playful muse. I have journeyed back through six centuries to set things right, for our lives were destined to be entwined. I could never leave you, David, for you are part of me. I love you... I love only you..."

Something happened to him, for it felt like a deep, underground river came gushing to the surface. It wasn't a gentle emotion, but a strong one that carried him along until he began to understand that this was real, and Elisabeth was real, and what they had together was all encompassing. It would endure.

"You were meant to be mine, and I knew it the moment I saw ye watching me by the burn that day, and that night in the cave... it was agonizing for me to keep my hands off ye. Leaving you at Soutra cut into my very soul, and the only thing I could do was to ride away from ye as quickly as I could, for I feared if I lingered, I would risk everything just to take ye wi' me and the world be damned." He did not speak the words. He breathed them as he brushed his lips against her throat. "I cannot imagine life withoot ye, and if ye didna return my love, I canna think what I would become."

She smiled, her hand stroking the strong arms that she so loved—arms that would slay dragons for her.

"And here I thought you could not wait to be rid of me and ride off."

"I will never be rid o' ye, for yer image is burned upon my heart."

She could feel the love he felt for her piercing her heart in a new way, for he was never a man to open his heart like this. She kissed him softly, her hands sliding over the hard musculature of his chest and lower, over the round firmness of his buttocks. He was so perfectly made in every way, and the best part was… he was all hers. He kissed her slowly and thoroughly, with such attention to detail, as if he could take the rest of his life doing it, and in a way, she wished he would.

His kiss was in her hair, moving across her brow and then covering her mouth, and he deepened the kiss as his hand came up to cover her breast, touching the sensitive points with his thumb and causing a tiny groan to escape her mouth. She moaned and moved beneath him, and she opened her mouth to speak words of love to him, but the words became a low moan when he deepened the kiss and moved his body above her, moving, pressing until she parted her legs.

The warmth of his breath washed over her, as if making room for the flurry of goose bumps that spread over her as his lips began to make lazy patterns across her skin. Each sensation traveled further and deeper than the previous one, and her breathing became more labored and shallow. She could see by the diffuse brightness in his eyes that he was reacting to her as much as she was to him, and the thought of it was as pleasing as it was powerful.

She closed her eyes, sensing the faint aroma of soap

on his skin before she was gently encircled in warm, comforting arms. The heat emanating from his body relaxed her, and she felt his gentle, caressing hands stroke her face and throat with inexhaustible patience, followed by a nuzzling kiss to the cheek.

It felt so perfect, so right that she knew she had been truly blessed. She had no thought of what was to come, only the thought that they were both naked, and with closed eyes she let her body lead the way. She opened herself to him, softly whimpered, and clung to him because she knew it could not last.

"I could spend all night just kissing you... everywhere. I want to make love to you and cannot maintain my sanity if I do not. I have thought of little else since the day you came into my life."

He kissed her breasts, first one and then the other, and she felt the softly breathed wetness that hardened them. The muscles in her stomach grew taut in response. He turned and shifted the angle of his body until he was lying full upon her and she knew the feel of the hard length of him, hot as a brand against her flesh. It felt so right to be with him like this, and yet, she did not want to dwell upon that.

David could feel the soft pliancy of her breasts pressing against the bare flesh of his chest with each breath she took. His hands wandered at will over the loveliness of her exquisite body and the response from her—a soft rapture that washed over him because of the magnificent throb of her intense passion. His mouth came to hers repeatedly before he dropped lower to kiss her breasts and take the hard points into his mouth. He wanted to touch her again and again until she was wild with wanting him, but at the same time he feared he was too raw with wanting her, too hungry for her, and too desperate because he feared this might well be for the last time. He knew then that he loved her, that he would give all that he owned to keep her here with him.

She had come into his life as strong as the wind blowing across the Highlands from Njord, the Norse god of wind, fanning the heated coals of his desire, and when her hand closed around him, he burst into flames, calling out her name. But before he could roll on top of her, she pushed him away and began kissing her way downward from his chest, and when she reached the place she sought and took him into her mouth, it splintered him into a million prisms of light and he reached for her and held her close.

"My lass, my only love," he said and he entered her. Flesh against flesh, warm and moist, fitting together in perfect union as if they had been missing, one from the other for all eternity, and now, after eons of searching, he had found that part of him that had been absent for so long. He ground his hips against hers and could hold back no longer. With a groan, he felt the surging release as his body tensed, and then he enjoyed the luxury of moving slow and relaxed inside her.

The sound of her passion went over him like a silent mist, a hypnotic harbinger of exquisite peace. There was nothing to match the joy of lying tangled in the long skeins of her silken hair, which seemed to wrap itself around him. They fell asleep for a time, trapped in that drowsy, sated feeling and the joy that comes with lying together after passion is spent. He thought this was the most perfect peace of all, and he wondered if he was dreaming and would soon awake to find she was already gone from him.

Later, when he opened his eyes, he breathed a sigh of relief, for he could feel the warm nearness of Elisabeth, and he stole a look at her, lying in a tangle of auburn hair. He kissed his way across the soft warmth of her neck and over the delicate wisps of hair curled behind her ear. Too strong… too overpowering… to the point that he was desperate to grasp, hold, and keep every possible memory he could make with her.

Hardened by desire, he felt as if he had drunk a magic potion, for already he wanted her, but before he could speak of it, she turned toward him and whispered, "Make love to me again," and her words curled seductively around him, as soothing as the warm waters of the Isle of Milos, flowing into the sea.

Later, when she lay nestled against him, her breathing even and steady, he held her close, afraid to let her go, as if she would remain beside him for as long as he could hold her to him. But soon Hypnos, the god of sleep, came upon them, and Elisabeth fell into a deep sleep where she was greeted by Morpheus, the god of dreams, who filled her mind with strange shapes and vivid colors that swirled around her, bright as a cluster of stars.

Elisabeth awoke early, while it was still dark, and she found comfort in the soft sound of David's breathing while she waited for dawn. She slipped out of bed, not wanting to awake him, and for a moment she stood beside the bed, gazing down upon him as if by doing so she could etch the memory of his beautiful, strong body and peacefully slumbering face into a part of her mind. And there it would remain, safely sequestered from anything she might face at Bosworth Castle.

She crept silently to the window and gazed out upon the mist that was beginning to fade in the thinness of early morning light, fragile and soft hued as gossamer. An uneasy breeze sent a dust devil spinning across the keep and sent a rush of wind through the castle parapets, then faded away to lonely silence.

Elisabeth fought against the loneliness she could feel rising in her throat, heralded by the steady pounding of her heart, for already she felt separated from David when she wanted so much to be with him. She put her hand to the wavy pane of glass, thinking how thin and fragile a barrier it was between the comfort of a familiar room and the cold unfriendliness of the unknown. A feeling of acute loneliness gripped her, and she faced the fright that tried to steal her composure and pushed it back to the dark confines of her mind. She would not crumble and play the weakling, for she was made of sterner stuff, she reminded herself. She was mindful of her ancestors who fled Scotland after the decimation of the Highlands following the Battle of Culloden Moor and the unknown they faced when sailing to a new home in America.

How odd it all seemed now and how distant, for she felt as though she had always been here and smiled at how very angry she had been at Sir James for inadvertently bringing her back with her sister. "I forgive you," she said and smiled, just before she frowned, for suddenly it occurred to her that it was beginning to seem that her coming back with Isobella had not been inadvertent after all.

I see Douglas's hand in all of this...

Confirmation came with a sudden whoosh of wind that swept down the chimney. It was reassuring to know that Sir James was never very far away, even if he did choose not to show himself.

Stay with me...

She turned away from the window and saw that David was awake and watching her. "Come back to bed. I want to hold you for a little while longer." She slipped into bed beside him and laid her head on his shoulder, and they talked quietly until the castle came awake and they knew their time together had come to an end.

Chapter 17

I had else been perfect,
Whole as the marble, founded as the rock,
As broad and general as the casing air,
But now I am cabin'd, cribb'd, confin'd, bound in
To saucy doubts and fears.

—*Macbeth*, Act III, Scene 4 (1606)
  William Shakespeare (1564–1616)
  English poet and playwright

ELISABETH PULLED HER HANDS FROM HER POCKETS, lifted her skirts to accept a boost into the saddle, and settled her cloak about her so that it covered her properly. Already she could feel the coolness of a breeze upon her hands and she wished she had thought to bring her gloves, for there was still an early morning chill in the air. She glanced at David and smiled brilliantly, wanting to assure him that she was at peace and already looking forward to the day she returned home to Aisling.

Then she pulled the reins to guide her horse around to fall in with the armored escort in front and behind her, as they rode slowly across the keep and under the portcullis gate and toward the abbey. As they passed, she nodded at Taran. He was standing in front of the hospital with all of his brothers and the clansmen who volunteered to help him. And then she saw dear, sweet Ailis standing on the stones that bordered the walk, and she recalled her vow to keep the hospital running, if it took the entire castle to do it.

They were soon past the hospital and on a narrow trail. She had been told they were riding to the western part of the Highlands, which she knew fairly well, although she had never been to Bosworth Castle. She did remember the beauty of the wild granite peaks, the wide span of moors, the glens and gurgling burns, and the poor Highlanders in small villages who gathered along the wayside to stare at the sight of newcomers. She could almost read the curious stares as if they were asking themselves, "What did the lass do to find hersel' riding wi' the armed soldiers of the Earl of Bosworth?"

As a reminder of what she left behind, she would forever keep locked in her heart the expression on David's face as they left, for it bespoke the control it took to keep himself from calling his men to arms to bring her back, and Boswell be damned. Reality began to set in when she turned around to look back and saw that the turrets of Aisling Castle were now out of sight, swallowed by the dense foliage of trees. None of the men riding with her spoke more than necessary, and while they were mannerly and hospitable, they were not prone to talk, so she entertained herself by taking note of the fact that there was beauty even in the rough terrain they traversed. She did steal a glimpse a time or two at the man riding beside her, who nodded his head and remained silent.

Soon, she saw no more red sandstone priories or flat, rolling countryside and thick woodlands, for the terrain became rougher and more inhospitable, as if doing its part to prepare her for the journey that lay ahead. They pushed on through landscape of such stark grandeur that it made her feel small and insignificant. The sun seemed less inclined to appear here, and when it did, it was more intense.

And Scotland would not be Scotland without rain, which seemed to come down harder and harsher than it did on the Black Isle. She wondered if that was only because everything about the land was hard and harsh. But the wind whistling down from the high corries reminded her of the Atlantic storms that would come out of nowhere to sweep over Màrrach Castle. That ushered in thoughts of Isobella, and she wondered how big her son was by now.

Occasionally they passed a monastery or abbey, and one in particular was exceptionally beautiful and small, but rather like a dollhouse made of roughly hewn stone, and a time or two, they passed a small village huddled below the protective brow of a gloomy castle. Then the terrain began to be more sparsely populated and gaunt, where swiftly flowing burns seemed to thunder down the steep slopes, only to slow to a calm trickle in the bare hills huddled around a lonely loch or a cluster of twisted pines or a desolate moor.

And it looked like it might rain, for the sky began to darken and thunder rumbled in the distance. She pulled the hood of her cloak over her head just before the skies threw open the doors to heaven, and the rain came swiftly down, cold and in pounding sheets that seemed in no hurry to let up. With the arrival of the inclement weather, her spirits began to slip, and she had to force herself to think of wonderful memories from her past so that she would not despair or feel abandoned and forgotten.

They splashed across a burn and up a steep, slippery side, and she was grateful to her sure-footed hobbler, for he did not slide as did some of the heavier horses. Only once, when they made a steep descent, did the gelding lose his footing and slide, but he recovered quickly and Elisabeth made it a point not to look down to see just how far she could have fallen.

By the time the rain let up, the sun was starting to drop in the sky and the air was moist and warmer. One of the men rode up beside her and handed her an oatcake, which she accepted with a smile and a pleasant, "Thank you for your kindness, sir."

"Ye are welcome, mistress," he said, before he turned his horse to take up his place behind her.

They hadn't ridden much further when they came to another steep descent, and about halfway down, in a small clearing, a snake slithered from behind a rock and one of the horses reared, throwing the rider against a sharp boulder that pierced his armor and left his arm bleeding. By the time she reached him, blood was dripping from his hand.

"'Tis naught," the man said.

"It will not be naught for long," she said, "if you don't let me see how bad it is. You are losing too much blood. You could bleed to death before we reach our destination." She turned to one of the other men. "In the pouch behind my saddle there is a small bundle, rolled up and secured with a cord. Bring it to me," she said, in the authoritative manner of the physician that she was.

An expression of indecision settled upon his face, and

he looked at the wounded man, who nodded and said, "Fetch it!"

The soldier went to her horse and returned a few minutes later with her medical supplies. "Can you remove his breastplate so I can see his entire arm?" she asked, and the man did as she asked.

There was a nasty gash from his elbow that ran half the distance to his shoulder and was bleeding profusely. "This wound must be closed. I can suture it, with your permission, of course. If you refuse, you will, without a doubt, bleed to death before we reach Bosworth Castle."

He nodded and extended his arm, which she steadied on a smooth section of a large, jagged boulder. She ripped away part of her underskirt and told one of the men to wet it. When he returned, she wiped away the blood on his arm, careful not to get too close to the damaged skin.

She then poured a bit of powder from a small vial over the wound and offered an explanation as to what it was: "This was given to me by the friars at Soutra Aisle. It will help to keep down infection." She then took a needle and threaded it and began to suture the wound. When she finished, she bound it with another part of her underskirt and used the ribbon from her chemise to hold it in place. "That will have to do until we reach Bosworth Castle."

"I thank ye fer yer kindness, mistress," the soldier said. Then he mounted and with a nod in her direction, he rode off. Soon, she was back on her horse and they continued on their way as if nothing had happened, riding until after darkness settled around them, and she wondered if they would ride all night. The thought

no more than formed when she noticed a glimmer of
lights through the trees and found herself hoping it was
Bosworth Castle, for a chance to lie down somewhere
would be heavenly, and she was so very, very tired, for
already she had dozed off and might have fallen from
her horse if one of the men had not pushed her back,
which awakened her.

It had been a very long day, but she was happy to
arrive, even after dark, rather than stopping to make
camp. Some of the exhaustion began to leave her, or
perhaps it was just overridden by pleasure of knowing
their journey was about to end, for the horses began their
descent into an open area. Soon they were on a trail that
led to the castle, which she hoped would be their final
destination, for she had no way of knowing if this was
indeed Bosworth Castle or simply a stopping-off place,
but as long as she was able to dismount for the night,
she did not care.

A short while later, they arrived at a massive castle
that would rival any she had seen. She inquired, "So,
this is Bosworth…?"

The man whose arm she sutured and saved from
bleeding to death replied, "Aye, 'tis Bosworth, mistress."

"Can you tell me where we are… what part of
Scotland this is?"

"Ye are on the western coast o' Scotland, mistress,
near Loch Carron, not so verra far from the Isle of
Skye," he said, with a nod, which she interpreted as a
"thank you" for saving him from bleeding to death.

She started to dismount, but before she could, he
helped her from the saddle, which was a good thing,
for her legs were a bit rubbery. When her feet touched

the ground, she had to hold his arm and wait a moment before trying her legs. In the meantime, she stood there, looking at the imposing structure towering around them. In the predawn light it seemed to be frowning down upon her, not that she cared, for she wasn't planning on making her home there. She had her own home and a castle much lovelier than this one, and it came with a resident Prince Charming, and the thought warmed her.

One of the soldiers came to escort her. But the man whose life she saved put a detaining hand on the arm of the soldier and said, "I will take the lass inside."

The soldier nodded and turned away, and the wounded soldier guided her into the castle. Upon entering, she was met by a well-dressed man, whom she assumed was the steward, and when she glanced at her escort, he nodded respectfully and turned away.

"If ye will come wi' me, mistress, I will show ye to the room we ha' prepared fer ye."

It was a lovely corner room, well furnished, with a warming fire, and the most blessed thing of all was a tub that was being filled with warm water. She turned to watch two men carry in her baggage, and a maid went quickly to where it was placed and began to unpack Elisabeth's few belongings. She was about to inquire about her medical bag, but a servant walked in with it.

Elisabeth eyed the tub and wished everyone would stop hovering and leave so she could relax before the water cooled, but that might have to wait, for another servant entered with a large tray of food, which was placed on a nearby table. That was followed by another servant who carried a decanter of wine and a silver goblet. So far, so good, she thought.

The woman who saw to her baggage said, "The earl wishes ye a good night's sleep and plans to meet wi' ye on the morrow. Will there be anything else ye might be needing, mistress?"

Elisabeth smiled and said, "No, you have gone far beyond my expectations. Please convey my gratitude to the earl."

Everything passed quickly after that, for after her bath, she ate a most welcome meal accompanied by wine, which made her terribly sleepy, and the bed was delightfully soft, and then she was out like the proverbial light, and the first part of her journey had come to an end.

The next morning, Elisabeth opened her eyes to the sound of a woman bringing her breakfast, followed by another woman who carried in clothes for her. After she ate, her hair was dressed and she put on one of several new dresses that were delivered to her as a gift of gratitude, and she was thankful she brought both of her aprons. She thought the dresses far too nice for her doctor routine, but she did not want to offend the earl by wearing one of her working dresses, so she chose a gown that was actually quite lovely, of green silk trimmed with cream lace.

She no more than finished dressing when she was escorted to meet the Earl of Bosworth, a squat, awkward figure of a man with a face as ugly as a plowed field, but his eyes were not the gentle kind, for they seemed to regard her with suspicion, which she supposed was normal, considering who his son-in-law was. She couldn't help wondering if he felt the least bit guilty.

"I welcome ye to Bosworth Castle, Mistress Douglas,

and I thank ye for coming on such short notice. My daughter, Judith, is gravely ill and we ha' no idea what it is that ails her. I am beholden to ye for gracing us wi' yer company and pleased that ye were able to come so quickly."

"I pray that I will be able to help your daughter, your lordship. And now, I suppose I should see to Judith so I might give you a swift diagnosis as to what ails her."

Bosworth nodded, and then said, "I have asked her husband, Ronan, to come and escort you to Judith's room. He is looking forward to seeing ye again."

"It will be a pleasure to see him again as well, since we are related by marriage and both claim our proper places as aunt and uncle of the child born to Isobella and Alysandir."

"Aye, I understand that ye were there for the birthing of the laddie."

She smiled. "That I was, and I have never felt so blessed as when he tried out his new set of lungs."

Bosworth chuckled and then looked toward the door and nodded for the guard to open it, and Ronan stepped into the room.

Elisabeth's heart skipped a beat and time spun backward. Two years had done little to change him, although he did look older and the bloom of youth was no longer upon his cheek. The memory of their love, the agony of being separated, the suffering of thwarted desire. It all came rushing back—only this time were nothing more than memories. She had loved him once and deeply, and he loved her, but they weren't the same people they were back then.

Ronan… once so dear to her. She did not wish him to suffer. She ached at the sadness in his eyes, and she knew he still loved her. She looked down for a moment to gain her composure, as if she could break the chain of memories that connected them. She thought of the days after he was gone, of the wrenching pain and how horribly she had suffered over his absence, the feeling that her life was over.

And then, along came David…

David… a weight was lifted and she knew she had made the right choice. Ronan was her past, but it was David who was her future. David, solid as a granite crag, enduring, steadfast, and unyielding in the face of hardship, and he loved her with all the ageless strength and endurance of the Scottish hills. She mustered her courage, for Ronan would know the moment she spoke that she no longer felt the same. She looked at him and said truthfully, "Ronan, how good it is to see you again. I am so sorry to hear about Judith's illness. Please know that I will do everything possible to have her well again."

A lapse of silence caused her heart to pound, and just when she thought he could find no words to say, he spoke. "'Tis good to see ye again as well, Elisabeth, and I ken ye willna fail to do everything possible to save Judith, fer I remember so many times when I was privileged to see the results of yer skill as a doctor."

But, this wasn't the Ronan she remembered and she knew their marriage had not been blessed with love, and that pained her, for he deserved so much more. Then he added, "I can think of no better hands in which to place the care of Judith than yours."

Chapter 18

So, so, break off this last lamenting kiss,
Which sucks two souls, and vapours both away,
Turn, thou ghost, that way, and let me turn this,
And let ourselves benight our happiest day.

—"The Expiration," *Songs and Sonnets* (1635)
  John Donne (1572–1631)
  English metaphysical poet and divine

ELISABETH WAS ACCOMPANIED TO THE ROOM OF JUDITH
Mackinnon by a woman known only as Bairbre, who
served as a healer and midwife to the castle. Bairbre
was a woman of solid stature with an ample bosom and
a wealth of graying hair, neatly done up. She had obviously been a handsome woman at one time, with her
haughty nose and thick brows that arched over her dark,
watchful eyes.

As they walked toward Judith's room, Elisabeth
took advantage of the time to ask Bairbre about
Judith's condition.

"She ha' been complainin' aboot her back hurting fer a fortnight. She hasna had much appetite and
feels poorly."

That wasn't much to go on, so Elisabeth asked a few
more questions and learned Judith had been throwing

up, but that seemed to have stopped a few weeks ago. "Any fever?"

"Mayhap a wee bit o' fever and one morning there was a wee bit o' bluid on her gown."

Blood... Hmmm... now we are getting somewhere. "Did Judith ever mention that she might be with child?"

Bairbre seemed surprised at that question, for her lustrous dark eyes grew wide. "Nay, mistress, she didna mention anything aboot that, and I dinna think she would have kept something like that a secret from me or her dear husband."

Elisabeth was about to ask another question, when Bairbre said, "This be her room," and she opened the door and stepped inside. "I ha' brought the physician to see ye and she will ha' ye feelin' better in no time," she said.

Elisabeth approached the bed. Judith was smaller than she anticipated, and she appeared to be quite slender, with light brown hair that was spread like a cloud about her head. She had a pretty face and lovely hands, and she seemed to be rather shy, but Elisabeth knew that could be simply the fact that she had been the reason Elisabeth's hopes of marrying Ronan were dashed, when he was snatched away and forced to marry her. Elisabeth hoped not, for she had not expected that she would like Judith, but she found nothing about her that she considered negative, for Judith seemed gentle, shy, rather sweetly natured, and sick.

"Hello Judith, I'm Elisabeth Douglas and I hope to help you get well. Bairbre said your back has been hurting you for some time. Is it still bothering you?"

"Aye, it hurts all the time and I canna find a way to make it stop. Nothing I take to ease the pain helps."

Elisabeth stopped at a basin and picked up a ewer of water and poured some in the basin, then carefully scrubbed her hands with a bar of soap. She turned to Bairbre and asked for a clean cloth to dry her hands. She turned back to Judith, drying her hands as she asked, "Is there any chance you could be with child, Judith?"

Judith glanced at Bairbre and then back at Elisabeth. "I thought mayhap I was at one time, but then I decided I wasna."

Elisabeth asked several more questions about her general health, pregnancy symptoms and the bleeding, and the amount of time that had lapsed during all of this. At last, she said, "I would like to give you an examination so I can discover why you are feeling so poorly. May I?"

Judith nodded and Elisabeth proceeded with the examination, wishing she had the proper medical instruments, tests, and medications. However, she would have to make do with the supplies she brought from the hospital at Aisling.

Good luck was on her side, and the supplies she had proved to be enough, for Judith was indeed pregnant, or at least she had been. Unfortunately, Elisabeth had to be the one to inform her that the baby had been dead for some time—about two months was Elisabeth's best calculation. The worst of it was that Judith was now bleeding more heavily, which weakened her, and she was terribly uncomfortable due to the severe cramping.

The first thing Elisabeth had to do was to tell her the baby had died and that the fetus was the cause of her pain and bleeding. "Sometimes, a woman will never know and the fetus is simply absorbed by the mother's body. Unfortunately in your case, you have an advancing infection, so the fetus must be removed before you will be able to regain your health. To do nothing would be fatal."

The procedure would normally be followed with a D & C, but Elisabeth did not have the tools to perform a true D & C, so she would come as close to it as she could. Even in the twenty-first century, there were women who chose not to have the D & C to clear the uterine lining after a miscarriage or missed abortion, where the baby died but a miscarriage did not spontaneously occur. By having a D & C, which scraped the wall of the uterus, there was also the fear of weakening the uterine wall or doing some damage, such as a perforation with the sharp tools used.

Elisabeth pushed Judith's hair back and patted her perspiring face with a cloth. "I am going to give you something to ease the pain in your back. Do you understand what I explained about the things I will have to do to make you well and healthy again?"

Judith nodded and said weakly, "Aye, I understand and I thank ye fer yer kindness."

Elisabeth could see she was hurting, so she administered the opium to kill the pain and help her sleep. Like the seventeenth-century physician Fabricius, she considered the use of hooked instruments for extracting a fetus to be dangerous, so she had a pair of forceps, made while at Aisling, that were spoon-shaped. Not as good as those in the twenty-first century, but the best available to her in this time period.

While she waited for the opium to take effect, she held Judith's hand until she began to grow groggy, and then Elisabeth moved to the window to look out on the grounds of Bosworth Castle. It did not occur to her to think about Judith in any other way than as a patient, for she did not dwell upon the fact that she was the woman who had stolen the man Elisabeth loved, and she was glad for that... Now, when she and David paid a visit to Màrrach, she would never worry about how it would be when they ran into Judith and Ronan.

She was a woman and a doctor, and she knew the highlights of today were tomorrow's shadows and that everything was in a constant motion of change; therefore nothing was constant in life except change. As the proverb said, *Life is a bridge. Cross over it, but build no house upon it*.

She turned away from the window. Judith still was getting close to being completely under but not there yet, so Elisabeth's thoughts returned to David. She wondered what he was doing at this very moment and had the warming thought that he was thinking of her. Giving herself a mental shake, Elisabeth set aside the thoughts of her private life to once again assume the role of the healer and to answer the call of the physician that still ran strong within her.

It was a source of joy in her life, this being used for a purpose. Therein lay her greatest satisfaction, for in stretching herself beyond ordinary limits and using her knowledge and abilities, she had found a way to know that she had accomplished something. Healing... it was her center, her orientation, her proof that love and life were the most precious gifts of all.

A gust of wind whooshed down the chimney, carrying the faintest scent of flowers. She relaxed, knowing

Black Douglas was there, lurking in the background and watching over her like a protective guardian, which, in a way, he was. She checked Judith again and saw she was sleeping soundly. Elisabeth paused long enough to say a prayer for the dead child and the parents, before she devoted herself to the task of extracting the tiny baby that was never destined to be part of their world.

She held it in her hands, an infant so small, and one never destined for the breathing world. Nor was it given the chance to form a smile or grasp a finger or even to be given the privilege of struggling to be born. Created in a loveless union of dutiful passion, it led not a charmed life but slipped silently into the world, unknown and unwelcome, never taking a breath or releasing a cry, fated to be untimely extracted from the mother's womb, naked, alone, and dead.

For a moment, Elisabeth held the wee baby boy in her hands, holding it as one would a squalling newborn, and whispering a prayer and then an apology for the breath never taken. Tears gathered and she was suddenly overwhelmed with wretchedness and the unfairness of life and death, knowing the hopes, dreams, and wishes we are all born to enjoy would never become hopes, dreams, and wishes for this tiny scrap of humanity that never fully formed.

Short swallow-flights of song that dip their wings in tears, and skim away…

How appropriate were Tennyson's words for the shortness of life. A tear slid from her face and fell upon the baby, and she prayed it would wash away the pain so Ronan and Judith could move on and put the past behind them. Her wish for them no more than settled in her mind when she felt the lifting of a great weight that held her pinned to the past, as if it had suddenly become a boulder that rolled away, taking with it all the sorrow and wretchedness that lay in the past. With a sigh, she placed the baby in a tiny basket and covered it, then checked on Judith, who still slept soundly.

As if on command, the gloom of clouds that had hovered over the castle throughout the day seemed to clear, and a brilliant shaft of sunlight pierced the room to land precisely upon the place on her breast where her heart resided. And she knew the warmth of it had penetrated her heart as well, for she had never known such peace.

And suddenly he was there, Sir James Douglas, his form so pale and translucent it could have been a vapor, and she realized it probably was, it was soon apparent he was visible only to her, for the nursemaid stood quietly by, noticing nothing.

Thank you, her heart whispered, for she saw it as a very significant and portentous sign regarding the future... her future.

His smile was brilliant and filled her with warmth, and then his image began to sparkle like a million sunlit dewdrops that rose from a spangled sea, and it hovered like a rainbow for only a moment, and then, like rain, it fell back into the sea. She turned and handed the small basket to the midwife, then turned her attention to Judith.

Ronan had informed the midwife that he would be waiting with a priest in the adjoining room, and to bring the babe there. Elisabeth stayed with Judith until she was awake enough to be told that everything was over, and then she explained the recovery period and how long she should wait before resuming sex or trying to get pregnant again. She could see the expression on Judith's face was a mixture of shame and regret.

Elisabeth pushed the damp hair back from Judith's face and said, "We have all made mistakes in our lives, and we all have regrets we would like to expunge from our memory. Don't let the past dictate your future. I have forgiven you. That should be enough to set your heart free. If it is not, then you must forgive yourself. Ronan was part of my past, a man I loved deeply, but sometimes things happen that go beyond our control and we can either accept them and move on, or wallow in them and destroy our lives and the lives of those around us. I know in my heart that he was never meant for me, and what happened was a way of turning me toward the man I was destined to love for all time."

"I feel so guilty for I robbed ye of yer husband on yer wedding day, and I canna believe that ye could ever forgive me."

"And yet, I have managed to do just that." Elisabeth smiled and said, "It did not happen right away, mind you, for I had to take a journey and discover who I was and why I was here. So, I left Màrrach Castle, and I took my grieving heart on a journey to find a way that I could practice medicine. I ended my journey at Aisling Castle, where I have opened a hospital, and I know in my heart that is where I was supposed to be. My life is there now, with my work and the man I love, for it was Lord David Murray, the Earl of Kinloss, who loved me enough to give me my dream, and I now run a hospital that was once an abbey. He is the one I have trusted with my heart.

"You should feel neither shame nor remorse, and if

you must do penance, I can only ask you to do it by being a good and faithful wife to your husband and a loving, devoted mother to your children. Do not ruin your chance of happiness over guilt, for I can truthfully say, had I married Ronan, I would have never fulfilled my destiny."

Tears rolled down Judith's face, and she took Elisabeth's hand and kissed it. "Bless ye," she said.

"You already have," Elisabeth said, and turned away. After pausing a moment, she turned back and said, "I will send Ronan in to see you now, so dry your eyes and let him comfort you, and in doing so, you will know your loss was not in vain, for I truly believe that wee babe will bring the two of you together."

Elisabeth left the room and went across the hall where Ronan waited, having been joined by the Earl of Bosworth. Elisabeth walked through the opened door and paused. "I bring you good news. Judith is awake and feeling much better. She is completely out of danger, and the best part is, she will be able to bear more children. She will need a few days of rest. After that, she will be able to resume her normal life."

She paused, then looked at Ronan and said, "You can go to your wife now. She grieves over the loss of the baby, and only you can ease her pain."

Ronan nodded and she saw the grateful expression on his face. She smiled and started to leave the room, for she was still feeling the effects of her journey and the long day she had. She turned to the earl and said, "I would like to leave for Aisling Castle in a few days, for I am most anxious to see Lord Kinloss and return to my work at the hospital."

The earl nodded and said, "I owe ye a great debt, Elisabeth Douglas, and I shall find a way to repay ye."

She smiled. "There is no need. Saving Judith's life and knowing she will bless you with many grandchildren is payment enough. And now, I will take my leave and return to my room for a much needed nap."

"I will have yer escort ready to leave once ye decide when that will be. And now, I shall go visit my daughter."

———

The first blush of morning had barely settled itself over the turrets of Bosworth Castle when Elisabeth gasped and sat up straight in her bed. She gazed around the room and felt disappointment to see she was still at Bosworth Castle, when she was hoping she would find herself in her room at Aisling and that David would soon be paying her a visit. She was consumed with a longing to see him and to feel the strength of his arms around her and to know that her long, unbelievable journey would end there... in David's arms, and there she would remain, for she could not imagine being separated from him ever again.

She felt such a powerful, overwhelming need to be with him: a heartfelt desire to have him near her, not just for the present, but for all time. She wanted to see his face and learn once again the texture of his skin when she touched it, the feel of his lips upon hers and his words of desire whispered against her skin. She felt a tight coiling in her stomach and knew the knot of desire so strongly that when she closed her eyes, she could feel the touch of his hand upon her and the passion his touch could evoke. *David...*

There was so much she wanted to tell him, and she was so very happy that her departure for Aisling would begin shortly. With that thought to inspire her, she threw the bed coverings back and sprang from the bed, tangling her leg in the sheeting, and went sprawling.

She eyed the red spot on her knee and rubbing it, thought, well, the day is off to a good start. She then imagined what a sight she must be, her hair mussed, arms akimbo, legs sprawled, gown riding up to her thighs and…

Oh my God! There he was… in all his shimmering glory, a very young version of the Black Douglas in full armor and looking ready for battle, and she prayed it wasn't against her.

She tugged at her twisted gown and tried to sit up, but the expression on Douglas's face was fair to glowing with amusement, and the hilarity of it sent her into peals of laughter once again. Finally, when she gathered enough breath to speak, she said, "You always seem to catch me at the best possible moment."

A look of amusement settled upon his face and his eyes sparkled with blue fire. "'Twould be beneficial if ye would tell me if ye wish to be on yer feet, or do ye prefer to spend the morning in yer present sprawl?"

"Truthfully, I do feel the need to get up, but I don't seem to be going about it in the right way, and now that you are here, well…" The words were no more than uttered when she felt herself literally rising off the floor, and with a tilt forward, her feet planted themselves firmly on the stone floor beneath her.

"Ahhh," she said with a relieved sigh, "that is ever so much better. I don't suppose you would show me how to

do that, would you?" She looked down, making certain
her gown was in place.

"Dinna worrit, all yer particulars are covered, if that
is what ye are concerned aboot."

"Oh, I'm not. After all, you are a ghost and far removed from earthly yearnings."

His dark brows rose like two carets over his questioning eyes. "'Twould seem ye think a ghost has no
recollection of that which lies deep in the heart's core."

She frowned and crossed her arms over her chest.
Something fishy was going on here, for she had never
seen him looking so young and it had been a while since
he had worn the Douglas armor. "Okay, out with it. Are
you all frisky with youth and dressed to the nines in your
best suit of polished armor so you can soften the blow of
some bad news you have to give me?"

"What makes ye think I ha' bad news to impart?"

"Well, it does seem to draw you out of hiding from
time to time. While I'm waiting, tell me about my sister.
How does she fare?"

"The lass blossoms. Motherhood agrees with her."

"And why the younger version of yourself, which I
like, by the way?"

"'Tis one o' the privileges o' ghosting to appear
whenever, wherever, and in whatever form, dress, or
age ye fancy."

"You make ghosting sound like something one
should aim for."

"Nae, lass, ye canna neither aim nor ask."

"Then how did you come to be one?"

"Weel, I dinna ken aboot that," he said. "All I remember is one moment I was lying on the battlefield

on the moors o' Spain, mortally wounded, and the next thing I felt no pain and I saw two of my friends leaning over me whilst the others were battling on, but no one seemed to notice me when I walked amongst them and disappeared, leaving my puir lifeless body to be cared for by the others."

"So, where did you go? How did you learn about the ghosting rules and such? I would think it would be put into your head, rather than by attending some sort of ghosting school."

His smile was brilliant, "'Tis sorry I am, lass, but ghosting has its rules, as ye ken, and I canna tell ye all the secrets o' it."

She shrugged. "I know we've had a nice little chat, but I'm not sure what I learned from it."

"Weel, that makes two o' us."

And then he vanished.

Chapter 19

No cord nor cable can so forcibly draw,
or hold so fast,
as love can do with a twined thread.

—*The Anatomy of Melancholy* (1621)
   Robert Burton (1577–1640)
   English poet, essayist, and playwright

IT WAS EARLY IN THE MORNING, TWO DAYS LATER, when they prepared to leave, just as the dawn was inching across the dark fringe of trees, motionless in the distance. The air was still and as silent as the departing night. Now the gray morning inched slowly forward, cautiously creeping down the flanks of crags, cloaked in a thick misty fog spilling downward toward the firth.

Elisabeth stood on the steps, pressing her cold hands against the warmth of her body beneath her woolen cloak, reminding herself that she had faced the unknown before and survived. A feeling of loneliness swept over her, for she seemed to always be on the move without a place to truly call home, but that was all about to change, for soon she would see David again, and feeling the strength of his arms around her would make everything she had been through fade into the past where it belonged.

After watching the preparations for a while, she was surprised to see that this was a much smaller escort than the group that brought her here, for there were only four men. She smiled to herself, wondering if they had thought they needed more men since she had basically been ordered to come here and they thought she might be difficult to deal with.

She watched the grooms hustling to and fro with blankets and saddles as they prepared the horses, while an occasional clank of a bridle cut through the early morning silence. She heard the ring of spurs as someone approached, and before she could turn to see who it was, someone touched her elbow and said, "Mistress, we are ready to leave now. Allow me to help ye into the saddle."

She'd had her first horse (and it wasn't a pony) when she was four, but who was she to help usher out chivalry by telling him she could mount by herself as easily as he could? She never thought she would feel this way, but she loved being treated like a lady, so she said, "I would greatly appreciate your assistance. Thank you."

He nodded and took her by the elbow and escorted her down the steps to where her horse awaited her.

Most of the men were already mounted by the time she was helped into the saddle, and they seemed as eager as her to begin their journey. So she gathered the reins and held them loosely in her hand while she waited for the signal to ride, which she assumed would come once the last of Bosworth's men were mounted.

Almost immediately, those to the front were off at a lope, which was a relaxed, smooth gait, due to the horses' long strides, and quite easy to maintain for long distances. Her horse seemed to know when it was time to go without her urging. They fell into rhythm with the other horses, and their journey began. She found herself riding beside a soldier she thought of as weather-beaten, for he was an older man with leathery skin and he had that easy way of seeming to become one entity with his horse, which reminded her of the weather-beaten cowboys back in Texas. She smiled as she wondered what he would do if she offered him a chew of tobacco. Not that she ever chewed any, of course, but it was a nice thought and mindful of the home and culture she left behind.

After a while, when the monotony of it began to settle in, she tried to focus on David and her reunion with him at Aisling. She truly thought of it as home now, and already she thought of the people there as family, for they had endeared themselves to her with ease. She anticipated seeing them all and basking in the warm, hospitable welcome that she knew awaited her there, not to mention the sheer joy of knowing she had her head on straight when it came to David and she hoped that he would never again feel that Ronan was a threat to the love she bore him. She had much to be thankful for, including the fact that the sidesaddle had yet to be invented so she was allowed the privilege of riding astride, which is what she was accustomed to, having been brought up on a ranch in the hill country near Austin.

Austin... how odd and far removed that sounded to her now, for she rarely thought of her life in the twenty-first century, and she wondered how she would feel if she suddenly found herself back in Texas.

Would you want to go back?

A shiver crossed over her, for it was a question she had for some time avoided for she truly dreaded answering it. There was a time, of course, when she wanted nothing more than to find herself back home, but that all seemed part of her past now, and not her future. She thought of the people she could help with her knowledge of medicine and knew there was no longer a reason for her to wonder, if the question was put to her, would she choose to go or stay. She thought of her wonderful, strong knight and could not imagine being separated from him. David was her life now, and her future. She could not leave him any more than she could leave Isobella, for how could she separate herself from her twin?

They rode into a clearing and she could hear the gurgle of a burn tumbling over rocks nearby. She was thinking this would be a good place to find some privacy, but she hated to ask them to stop just for that however, she could not go on indefinitely without stopping, so she opened her mouth to speak, just as she heard the leader say, "We will stop here to rest the horses and to have something to eat."

"Something" being the usual: an oatcake, a strip of dried beef, and water, and then they would mount up and be off again. She followed their lead to a place of jutting boulders that she thought was perfect, for it would give her more privacy than a stand of trees. Once they stopped, she dismounted and said, "I need a moment of privacy."

The leader nodded and said, "'Twas what I had in mind when we stopped here. The other side o' that boulder should afford ye all the privacy ye need."

On the other side of the boulder, the waters of the burn poured over a small cliff into a pool below. She spotted a tangled screen of rather prickly looking bush and thought it the perfect place.

She wasn't there long and knew the men were probably still seeing to their horses, so she walked a ways to get a closer look at the little waterfall. What happened next passed with such rapidity that it was no more than a blur. One moment she was walking, and the next thing she knew, an arm lashed out to encircle her like a band of steel, while a hand clamped over her mouth. "Scream and I will cut yer throat, lassie. Do ye ken?"

She nodded, thinking the sound of a scream wouldn't have reached Bosworth's men on the other side of the huge bolder, not with the noise coming from the burn tumbling into the pool. Besides, she wouldn't risk her life needlessly, so silent she would be. She felt herself being thrown across a saddle. Her abductor mounted behind her, and spurred his horse forward and into the trees. After a while, they came to more open terrain and he stopped and allowed her to sit in front of him, which was tremendously more comfortable than having her ribs crushed riding the other way.

They crossed the open glen toward another stand of trees, which they entered. "I don't suppose you will tell me where you are taking me."

"Ye will find oot soon enough."

He was right, for before too long, they stopped at an old, deserted hunting cabin where she thought they would at least rest before moving on. Instead, they dismounted and he secured his horse before he led her toward the cabin. She was terrified he was going to rape her there, and she was trying to decide what chance she had of outrunning him when the door of the cabin opened. God help her, but she was actually happy to realize she had once again been captured by the MacLeans, for there stood old Angus MacLean himself, looking rather pleased to see her.

"Welcome to my temporary abode," he said. "I hope yer ride here was a pleasant one."

"No, it was not. I was terrified he was going to do all manner of horrible things to me before he killed me. How dare you put me through something like this! If you were going to take me prisoner again, why didn't you do it the way you've done before? At least, accustomed as I am to your previous kidnappings, I would have recognized you and not been so terrified. And, how, in God's name, did you know where I was?"

"'Tis sorry I am, lass, but it was time for a change of tactics, fer a repeat o' the past would make it obvious to the Mackinnon that I was behind it. I ha' taken great care to arrange things so that Kinloss and the Mackinnon do not suspect ole Angus MacLean had anything to do wi' it. And to answer yer question, I heard that ye were summoned to Bosworth Castle, so we kept our eye on ye, and when ye were well away from there, I had Lachlan follow ye until he found a suitable place where he could seize ye and bring ye here."

"Why didn't you do it yourself?"

Angus stroked his chin as if in thought. "Ah, lassie, 'tis a disappointment ye are, fer I figured ye for a smarter lass than that. If I captured ye, Bosworth's men would ha' recognized me, and the earl's men would have reported it to Bosworth, who would have told Lord Kinloss, who would have notified Alysandir Mackinnon, and… weel, ye can see what a passel o' trouble all of that would ha' been. This way, I can take ye back to Duart, and no one will know I ha' ye, and I willna have to worrit aboot Mackinnon or Kinloss coming to yer rescue until I have ye all married to Fergus and then it will be too late."

"You aren't still stuck on me marrying Fergus, are you? No priest would dare force a marriage on a woman who refused to say anything resembling a marriage vow, and on top of that, I refuse to say one word that would unite me with him. As soon as I return to Aisling Castle, I will marry the Earl of Kinloss."

"Ah, lassie, ye disappoint me again, fer I already have a priest that will stoop that low."

"I would think a forced marriage would be grounds for divorce," she said, thinking it wouldn't be too many years in the future when Henry VIII had his marriage to Catherine of Aragon declared null and void so he could marry Anne Boleyn. Of course, she wasn't exactly the Queen of England, either. She sighed and decided to let the matter settle in her mind before she stepped into the arena of distress. For now, she would make the most of it; she knew the best way to deal with Angus was to charm him, so charm him she would.

After all, she had been their prisoner before and Fergus had wanted to marry her then, and she managed to be rescued by Alysandir before the wedding could take place. And if nothing else, she still had Sir James hovering out there somewhere.

They readied themselves to begin their trek to the Isle of Mull, and she had no idea how long that would take, for she wasn't certain exactly where they were. She only knew they had taken a different route on the way back than they had taken on the trip to Bosworth Castle, due to flooded rivers that would be too dangerous to cross.

Before mounting again and riding for what seemed an eternity, she noticed that the sun began to drop lower, leaving the crags in deep shadow. She managed to learn the name of one of them by asking Angus, who replied in a hospitable fashion.

"'Tis Creag an Duilisg, that begins at Loch Achaidh na h-Inich," he said, "and it gives me pleasure to see ye taking an interest in yer surroundings."

She remained quiet, for she did enjoy seeing new parts of Scotland whenever she traveled. Even as a child, she had always been one to notice her surroundings. This seemed odd to her parents, for they thought it would have been Isobella who took such an interest in her surroundings, due to her becoming an archaeologist. But, it always held a special allure for Elisabeth, for even now, in spite of her being a prisoner of MacLean, she was absorbed with the surrounding terrain and how it gradually changed as one went along, in such a slow manner that one hardly noticed it.

She did recall Isobella saying that the landscape and place names of these Northwestern Highlands seemed intimately connected to their Celtic heritage. As they passed by the island-scattered bay of a loch, she was in awe of the sweeping vistas of both sea and snow-covered mountains, framed by forested hillsides that melted into crags that seemed to reach down to the deep, dark waters of the Atlantic. Being able to see the sea, even from so far away, meant they were getting closer, but they were still quite a distance from the Isle of Mull and the Western Highlands.

"Where are we exactly and what loch is that?"

He looked in the direction she was pointing and said, "That would be Loch Carron."

She knew Loch Carron was a sea loch on the west coast of Ross and Cromarty, where the River Carron entered the North Atlantic. She also knew they would have to stop somewhere for the night, for it was too great a distance to ride before nightfall.

They rode through a sodden wooded area, thick with foliage and deep, dark shadows, which did little to help with the lifting of her spirits. It began to rain again, hard and pelting, which stung her face and her hands, holding the dripping reins. Her fingers were red from the cold and she would give anything to stop and take her gloves out of her pouch, but she knew it would only take up precious time. All in all, she was more than ready to get wherever it was that she was going, for she was beginning to feel like a lost gypsy.

Without thinking, she reached up to touch the coin around her neck, as she often did without thinking. Only this time it was different, for when she reached for the coin, it was not there. "Oh my God! I've lost my necklace!"

Angus turned his head toward her, seemingly in no hurry to ask, "Where do ye think ye lost it?"

"I don't know," she said, feeling so upset over losing one of the few things she had that came with her from America. "It was irreplaceable."

Angus turned toward her. "Weel, dinna surrender to

grieving over yer loss just yet. Mayhap we will find it and all yer worry will be fer naught. When did ye see it last?"

"This morning, when I put it on just before we left. I was half asleep, and I must not have tied it tight enough. I don't suppose we could backtrack and look for it."

"Nay, lass, ye ha' covered too much terrain for anyone to search for something so small. We shall get ye another necklace to take its place."

"No, you could never take its place," she said, remembering the day it was given it to her. "And I do have another necklace… a lovely diamond cross given to me by one of the friars at Soutra. I wear it frequently, but this necklace was given to me a long time ago."

Her thoughts returned to the present when they splashed across a meandering burn and the trail narrowed considerably on the other side. Thankfully, this was where Angus declared they would stop and made camp. The rain had halted and what was left of the sun cast long, eerie shadows through the surrounding trees. But she was thankful to be on solid ground again and to have something to eat. Dinner was a roasted rabbit, which she found palatable, but it did not stretch very far and she found herself hungrier after eating the tiny morsel than she was beforehand.

Wordlessly, she bedded down in the place indicated, which was blessedly near the fire. She stared at the fire and recalled the day David had rescued her from the MacLeans and they spent the night in the cave. Much as she was doing now, she had lain with her arm curled beneath her head and watched the fire burn, while inside, she yearned for David to come and lie beside her.

And later, when he did just that, she wanted him to kiss her, and he did so. She closed her eyes and thought how desperately she wanted David to find her and prayed that he would do so. And then she fell asleep, not in the arms of David as she had done that night, but surrounded by Angus and his men who guarded her.

They started at first light the next morning, and when the sun was high in the sky, they came to the point where they left their horses so they could go by boat to Mull. She was reminded of the Highlanders' saying, "*Guid gear comes in sma' bouk*," which meant the same as "good things come in small packages," and before long, she thought she had never felt anything as good as putting her foot on Mull soil.

They obtained the horses the MacLeans kept on the other side. Once again, she mounted her horse and they continued their ride until she began to recognize familiar terrain and knew that Caisteal Màrrach was not much more than a day's ride away. It was comforting to know it was that close. That was a good feeling, for it did give her peace of mind to think that she was at least on the same island as her twin.

———

When they discovered Elisabeth was missing, Bosworth's men followed the trail of her abductor as far as an old hunting lodge. From there, they followed the trail of three horses to the point where they entered the burn, but before they could track them further, it began to rain, so they turned back and rode home to Bosworth Castle, where they informed Lord Bosworth that Elisabeth had been abducted.

"God's eyeballs! How could she be taken right from under your noses?" He did not wait for an answer, and after hastily writing two letters, he dispatched riders to deliver one to Alysandir Mackinnon on the Isle of Mull and the other to Lord Kinloss on the Black Isle. And then he told his son-in-law, Ronan Mackinnon.

"Where were your men when she was taken?" Ronan asked.

"They followed her abductor's trail to an old, abandoned hunting lodge. It seems there were two people waiting at the lodge, for they followed the trail of three horses away from there, then lost the trail where it entered the burn."

"Where was the hunting lodge?"

"Aboot a day's ride from Creag an Duilisg, where Loch Achaidh na h-Inich begins."

"Hmmm..." Ronan said, thinking to himself, and then he asked, "I hope it was the trail of her abductor they followed, for I would think many a traveler would make good use of an abandoned hunting lodge, which is probably why they chose such a rendezvous."

"Aye, 'twas a guid choice they made. So I ken there is no way o' knowing fer certain just who took her and where they took her. Mayhap Kinloss or Alysandir will receive a ransom note in the near future."

Ronan's first guess was that the MacLean had something to do with it, since he had a habit of taking Elisabeth whenever he could, but it was a bit far-fetched, for how would he know where she was? Ronan also knew that Angus MacLean always loved putting on a show, surrounded by his men, for what was the glory in an abduction if one did not receive credit for it? And that made him think that perhaps it wasn't MacLean, unless MacLean planned for him to think that.

A week passed and no ransom note had arrived, but on the eighth day, Lord Kinloss did arrive with several of his men. He met with Bosworth and Ronan, and Ronan was surprised to find that he liked Kinloss, and he was relieved to know Kinloss did not seem to hold a grudge against him for having once loved Elisabeth or for his wife being the cause of Elisabeth being at Bosworth Castle. It was obvious to Ronan that Kinloss was deeply in love with Elisabeth and determined to find where she had been taken.

Later that evening, after Bosworth had retired, Ronan and David sat in the great hall after the evening meal was served. They were drinking wine and discussing Elisabeth's capture and the possibilities of how it was carried out and by whom. That was when Kinloss told Ronan about the time the MacLeans had captured Elisabeth when she was on her way to Soutra Aisle, and how she had slipped away and he had rescued her and delivered her to the hospital there. "Do ye think he has kept an eye on her since then?"

Ronan nodded. "I wouldna put it past him. He has been determined to force a marriage between her and his son, Fergus, but I think the old fool uses that for an excuse because he enjoys having her around. It has become like a game with him, and he probably has his spies aboot who report her whereabouts. I am sure, if he has her, that he is gloating aboot it right now."

Kinloss replied, "He can gloat all he wants, as long as the bastard doesn't force her to marry Fergus. I can promise you that if he has her, I will take her back."

"How will ye go aboot it?"

"I plan to ride to Mull and speak with yer brother, Alysandir."

"I will go with ye," Ronan said, then added, "I would give anything if we had even a wee bit of proof what direction the bastards took after they captured her. It could have been anyone—a puir Highlander looking to make money from her capture… possibly from prior knowledge. And we both know that MacLean has taken her more than once in the past and could easily do so again. And there are always brigands about who would recognize her as a woman of quality and hope to profit from it, although they should have contacted us by now."

Kinloss nodded, then added, "And there is always the possibility that we would not want to consider: she was taken because she is a beautiful and desirable woman of good breeding—the kind he would never have, and so he abducted her and took her to the hunting lodge for one purpose only."

Both of them knew but chose not to mention what could have happened to her had it been the latter.

The two of them continued talking, taking time to consider even the wildest of ideas in order to satisfy themselves that they had left nothing out. After a while, the kitchen help began to clean away the dishes. As one of the women passed by carrying an armload of tankards that reached all the way to her chin, Ronan held up his goblet and said, "Bring us another ewer of wine."

"I will fetch it right away, sir," she said and she hurried off.

She was back in a few minutes, minus the tankards

and carrying the ewer of wine, which she placed on the table. She had no more than released the tankard and started to turn away when Kinloss's hand lashed out and grabbed her by the wrist. He jerked her toward him and asked, "Where did you get that necklace? And by God, dinna ye lie to me!"

She looked terrified and glanced from Kinloss to Ronan, as if she thought he might help her, but all Ronan said was, "God have mercy! It's Elisabeth's coin!"

"Aye," Kinloss said, not taking his hard stare from the girl's face. "I am going to ask you one last time where ye got it, and ye better tell me the truth."

"M-my friend gave it to me, your Lordship. I swear he did."

"*When* did he give it to you?" Ronan asked.

She looked from one to the other, and then said, "Aboot a week ago… maybe more."

"And where did he get it?" Kinloss asked.

"He said he found it, your Lordship. Honest he did."

Ronan immediately said, "Who is your friend? Tell me his name?"

"Dugal MacAlpin is his name, sir."

"Where does he live?" Ronan asked.

She looked a bit confused when she responded, "Why he lives here, sir. He is one of His Lordship's soldiers."

"Do you know where he found it?"

"Aye, he said he found it in a hunting lodge."

"It belongs to Elisabeth Douglas, the doctor who was here to help my wife. I'm sure Dugal told ye Elisabeth was captured."

"Aye, sir, he did tell me that. He said they followed the tracks to a hunting lodge and that was where he found the necklace." She reached up and untied the necklace and offered it to Ronan, who pointed to Kinloss.

"Give it to His Lordship," he said. "He was waiting on Elisabeth's return to the Black Isle, where they are to be married. So ye can understand why he would want the necklace back."

"Aye, sir, I do understand, and 'tis sorry I am aboot my having it on and causing ye grief."

Kinloss gave her a smile that relaxed the lass, and then he said, "To the contrary, it is a good thing ye wore it, fer it may help us to find out where she has been taken."

They sent for Dugal MacAlpin who verified that he did find the necklace. "I didna think aboot it belonging to the doctor. I just put it in my pocket because aboot that time, someone shouted that they found the tracks of their horses, so we left quickly so we could follow them, for it looked like it would rain soon."

They offered him a glass of wine and found Dugal to be a congenial sort who gave them a detailed account of their journey from the time they left Bosworth Castle until they tracked horses of Elisabeth and her captor to the burn, and they abandoned the search. "We searched both sides o' the burn for some distance, looking fer the tracks of their three horses, trying to find where they came oot o' the water, but it began to rain and since that would erase any visible tracks, it made no sense to keep searching."

They thanked Dugal and sent him on his way with a tankard of ale.

"So what now?" Ronan asked.

Kinloss did not have to think about that, for he quickly replied, "I want to take the same route the soldiers took with Elisabeth. I'd like to see the hunting lodge to look for any traces of her having been there… other than the necklace."

Ronan nodded, and then asked, "Do ye think she left it a-purpose?"

David did not have to think upon that, for he remembered quite well the day Elisabeth showed him the necklace, recalling also how few things she possessed from her former life and time. To her it was priceless. "Nay, I think it meant too much to her to risk losing, but we won't know for certain until we find her."

Ronan relaxed and his expression softened, as if there was little doubt that the phrasing Kinloss chose when he said, "*We won't know*," included him. "Considering the fact that the hunting lodge is not all that far from Creag an Duilisg, where Loch Achaidh na h-Inich begins, and that it is on the way to Mull, I think a trip to Mull would be beneficial. And another thing, it is a common occurrence to board horses on both sides o' the Sound, so they probably would have left their horses and taken a boat across the Sound, and picked up their horses they had left on the other side. If that be the way o' it, then it wouldna be difficult to find the place where the horses were picked up and who it was that took them. I will go wi' ye and if we find oot it was Angus MacLean, then we can go to Màrrach and put together a plan with the help of Alysandir."

Kinloss nodded. "'Tis a good plan," he said, "and the most logical. Let us plan to leave at first light."

—⁓—

The original part of the hunting lodge was constructed of wattle and daub, which meant the wooden frames filled with clay did not age well and had fallen into neglect, but a more recent addition of stone was not as dilapidated as they had expected, but it had obviously been abandoned some time ago.

Kinloss stirred the ashes in the fireplace. "I don't think they stayed here very long. These predate the time that Elisabeth was here. The weather is growing colder, and a fire would have indicated they stayed here long enough to go to the trouble to gather wood and build a fire."

"Aye," Ronan said, "'Twould seem this was a temporary stop."

"There isna evidence, other than Elisabeth's necklace, that anyone has been here for quite some time," Kinloss said, "fer cobwebs abound and the wind has swept doon the chimney and scattered ashes aboot, yet there were no footprints. 'Tis a puzzlement. If ye ha' just taken a captive, ye wouldna travel this far and stop at a hunting lodge when ye needed to put as much time as ye could between ye and those who would come searching."

Still thinking, he added, "Unless this was a prearranged place to meet, where Elisabeth would either be handed over to the person who hired him, or to meet up with his cohorts or clansmen, which means we still dinna ken if we are looking for one man or several. Mayhap we missed an important clue, for remember Dugal MacAlpin told us Bosworth's soldiers said they followed the *tracks* at the hunting lodge, so that might indicate more than one horse."

"Hout! You are right! And later, he mentioned three horses, and it didna stick out at the time, but three horses would mean they met someone else at the lodge."

"Curse the deil!" Kinloss said. "For that would mean we are looking for only one other person, which doesn't necessarily indicate the MacLean's involvement. 'Tis rare indeed for MacLean to venture forth withoot his men clustered aboot him."

"It doesna disprove it either," Ronan said. "Angus is a sly old fox. He could have met them at the cabin, or he could have sent one of his men to meet them."

Kinloss nodded in agreement. "Either way, we canna say for certain that the MacLean was involved, or how many men he had with him."

"Aye, we can only speculate at this point, but once we reach Mull, if the MacLean is involved, someone, somewhere should have seen them."

Suddenly, Ronan had an idea. "The best place to find oot is at the place where they would have crossed the Sound of Mull, for ye canna ride across the Sound. They would either have someone take them and their horses across, or leave those horses and cross by boat, then pick up the horses they previously left on the other side."

"Well then, I see no reason to linger here any longer. Let us be away from this place," Kinloss said.

Chapter 20

Stone walls do not a prison make,
Nor iron bars a cage;
Minds innocent and quiet take
That for an hermitage;
If I have freedom in my love,
And in my soul am free,
Angels alone that soar above
Enjoy such liberty.

—"To Althea, from Prison" (1642)
  Richard Lovelace (1618–1657)
  English Cavalier poet

AFTER RIDING ALL DAY, ELISABETH WAS HAPPY TO SEE the orange face of the sun slowly making its descent behind the trees that topped the hills in the distance. She felt a twinge of loneliness, for their zigzag tops reminded her of the rickrack trim on her mother's green Christmas apron.

A ruffle of wind stirred in the trees, their lofty branches a dark silhouette against a darkening sky, and she wondered if it was truly the wind or Sir James passing by, just to let her know she wasn't alone. She decided to go with the latter, for it did take the burden of loneliness away.

She was anxious to reach Duart. At least she would be off the horse and would have a nice room with a clean bed, which was much better than riding to the monotonous clip-clop of hooves and the murmur of occasional conversation among Angus and his men.

It was almost daybreak when they arrived at Duart Castle. Elisabeth was relieved to see it standing atop a crag, just as it always had, with a proud and defiant frown like a sentinel guarding the Sound of Mull. She was happy to finally see the castle gates and to listen to the grinding sound as they opened, granting them entry. As they rode past the gatehouse, Angus nodded to the guards, who greeted him with a friendly "Welcome home!" to their chief.

Sudden awareness came rushing upon her, for everything seemed the same as she had seen it the day she left. Everything was familiar to her, even the sound of horseshoes ringing against the cobblestones and the occasional echo of a metal bit clanging as an anxious horse tossed his head.

Not all the castle was asleep, however, for the heavy doors were opened to them as they approached, and upon entering, she paused long enough to greet the steward and hand him her cloak. The interior light from torches was scant and as smoky and dim as she remembered, and all was eerily quiet to one as accustomed to the sounds of the night as she had become.

She was surprised to feel a rush of emotion as the cold, clammy hand of loneliness reached out to touch her, and David never seemed so far away. She wondered if he knew she had been captured, or if he would suspect that it was the MacLean, for although Angus did not tell her the reason for his waiting for her at the hunting lodge, she had a suspicion it had something to do with throwing David off track, for she knew his first thought would be to go to Màrrach to confer with Alysandir about her disappearance.

"Welcome home. I see yer trip bore just the fruit ye were looking for," the steward said.

"Aye," Angus said. "All in all, it was well worth the journey." Angus then gave him instructions to make ready Elisabeth's room that had been designated for her before he left.

"I will see to it right away."

Around her, she could hear the sounds of the castle coming to life, for a door slammed somewhere distantly and the tread of feet hurrying down the stairs could be heard. She smiled to herself, remembering Isobella telling her about her first visit here and how terrified she was of Angus MacLean, he was the stuff of myth and nightmare, and Isobella had imagined him as a pirate, his beard full of lit cannon fuses, the ends of his pigtails smoking, pistols jammed in his bandoliers, and a bloody sword in his hand.

Elisabeth remembered there was a time when she thought of him as someone who stepped from the pages of myths and fairy tales herself, for he did seem the quintessential monster, to be honest, there was a time when she was also terrified of him, for he certainly looked the part, with a face expressionless enough to have been carved from granite. And beneath his thick, dark brows were eyes as black as a moonless night. He seemed to have stepped out of a nightmare and was sure to frighten children, but his bark truly was worse than his bite, and in spite of all the hell he put her through, she rather liked him… this tall, dark, and swarthy man with shaggy black hair and heavy-lidded, piercing black eyes that missed nothing.

The MacLean turned to her once the steward was gone, and with eyes that did seem to twinkle, he said, "I trust ye remember the way to yer room. Ye will find everything there, just as ye left it."

"Yes, I think I can find my way there, and I will be glad to sit down on something besides a hard saddle." She turned away and hurried up the stairs, then turned down the dimly lit hallway, going to the very end where her corner room was. The door was open, and the candles and fire were lit. A tray on a nearby table held an assortment of breakfast items, from scones to tatties, smoked salmon, and porridge, and she was reminded of the saying, "*S mairg a ni tarcuis air biadh*," which meant, "He who has contempt for food is a fool."

She was hungry enough to eat a live caterpillar, so she ate enough to satisfy her hunger and drank the milk, foregoing the wine, which had a tendency to keep her awake. A lovely blue linen gown lay on the bed, and she knew the trunk would contain some of her old clothes and some new. But, right now she was interested only in the gown and some sleep.

—⁓—

Fergus MacLean heard that Elisabeth Douglas was back in residence and he knew his father would soon be pushing him to pay her court, or to at least try to be friends with her, for as Angus said, "Friendship oft leads to love." And if there was anything Fergus knew, it was that he would soon be out of favor with his father for his refusal to officially court Elisabeth Douglas.

To be honest, Fergus dreaded even seeing her, for she always looked at him like he was a leper or worse, and she went to great length to avoid him. Oh, he knew the stories his father filled her head with, of how "Fergus is in love wi' ye," which made Fergus mount up and go hunting, for he preferred to be away from Duart, especially when she was in residence. He was at home in the out-of-doors, fishing, hunting, or settling disputes among clansmen. Away from the castle he was in complete control. He could relax around a shy Heilan' coo and dodge leaping bucks, and he enjoyed talking with the clansmen who were always grateful for the game he provided them.

The times when he was around her, he was quiet and listened to his father ramble on about his fancy plans for him and Elisabeth. Many times he overheard his father telling her how much "Fergus loves ye," and he avoided her even more. It was pleasant while she was gone, but now that she was back, there was a problem, for he was a well-trained knight now and capable of making his own decisions. He was not going to let his father force him to marry Elisabeth Douglas, in spite of his vow to honor his father.

He knew Angus would have something planned today that would put him in the path of Elisabeth, so he left Duart before dawn to go hunting. It was late when he returned, and having missed the hour to dine in the great hall, he was about to go to the kitchen to find something to eat when he passed the great hall and saw everyone seated, as if they were waiting. He hoped to God they were not waiting on him.

"Fergus, we ha' been waiting to dine wi' ye, so come in and sit doon next to Elisabeth. I ken ye ha' much to say to her now that she is back."

Fergus was still in his mail, but he did remove his hauberk and stopped long enough to wash his hands before making his way to the table, with the eyes of everyone in the room upon him. When he reached his place, he glanced at Elisabeth and said, "Good eventide to ye, Mistress Douglas. I trust ye had a pleasant journey that wasna overly tiring."

Elisabeth sat back in her chair and studied him for a long moment before she replied, "Good evening to you as well, Fergus. It is nice to see you again. I understand you were out hunting today. Did you have good fortune?"

"Aye, I did."

She tried not to smile, for he may have changed physically, but he was still a man of few words, at least around her, which she attributed to his being in love with her.

Elisabeth watched him break apart his bread and dip a piece of it into the bowl of soup. He had changed so much. Gone was the tall, slender young man, who seemed too quiet and retiring to ask a woman to dance, let alone to marry, which seemed reason enough for his father to do his talking for him, including how he wore his heart on his sleeve, first for Barbara and then for her.

She couldn't get over the fact that the slender frame had filled out quite majestically, for there were muscles where they should be and a knight's sinewy strength everywhere else. He was taller than she remembered, and while he was still reserved and quiet, there was a sense that he was as manly and strong as any knight, including those who were loud and boisterous.

He had his father's dark coloring, but his eyes must have come from his mother, for they were a strange color that was almost a combination of aqua and green. Strange that she had never noticed that before, but then she always did tend to ignore him, or give an uninterested glance or a bored look, whenever she saw him. All in all, she was truly astounded that he had changed so much in a couple of years.

She gave her attention to her meal and was hoping someone would be the first to leave so she could follow shortly, for she did not want Angus to feel the effects of too much wine and to start on his wishes for a marriage between her and Fergus. As it turned out, it was Fergus who was the first to leave, quietly slipping away when his father was well into a story with someone at the end of the table.

Elisabeth found her chance to leave after a couple of others had departed, for she did not want Angus to make some comment that she was slipping away to meet Fergus, as he had said once.

Chapter 21

From the desert I come to thee on a stallion shod with fire,
And the winds are left behind in the speed of my desire.
Under thy window I stand, and the midnight hears my cry:
I love thee, I love but thee, with a love that shall not die
Till the sun grows cold, and the stars are old,
And the leaves of the judgment Book unfold.

—"Bedouin Song" (1872)
   Bayard Taylor (1825–1878)

DAVID AND RONAN CROSSED THE SOUND OF MULL, AND a coin to a youth gave them the answer to their question, for the MacLeans had come to Oban by boat and mounted their horses and left for Duart Castle, with a beautiful woman "wi' long, reddish brown hair, and she was complainin' a lot."

David smiled, for if she was complaining, she was in no danger. They arranged for horses for themselves and set out for Màrrach Castle, which was less than a day away if they rode hard and made few stops along the way. Ronan would guide them; he would enjoy seeing his family, and they would have the opportunity to meet with Alysandir and the rest of his brothers so they could put together a plan to take Elisabeth from Angus MacLean for the second and, hopefully, the last time.

Darkness descended upon them before they reached
Màrrach, but they were blessed with a full moon and a
clear, calm night with ample moonlight to guide their
way. David caught the scent of saltwater and knew they
were getting close, for Màrrach Castle overlooked the
Atlantic. Before long, he caught a glimpse of the silhouette of the castle rising out of the base of a summit
of rock, whose base lay beneath the cold depths of the
Atlantic, according to Ronan.

David knew the history of Màrrach for it was a castle
with a long past, more than worthy of respect due to its
age and the secrets contained within its dark, gray granite walls. It was the ancestral home of the Mackinnons,
who were descendants of Celtic tribal chiefs who came
from Ireland during a time of feudal greatness. He
knew also that in Gaelic, the name Màrrach meant an
enchanted castle that keeps one spellbound, usually with
a labyrinthine maze of passages.

Like Duart Castle, Màrrach Castle had never been
penetrated, not even when the Vikings swept down from
the North to raid the sparse population of the island.
This was because it was a large, fortified structure built
on the quadrilateral plan, with curtain walls about eight
feet thick and thirty feet high. Tonight, the corbelled
battlements and square turrets seemed etched in black
against a lighter night sky.

They stopped at the portcullis gate, while Ronan
called out his name as he rode up to the gate so the
guards could see his face in the light of their torches.

"'Tis Ronan Mackinnon," one of them called out.
"Open the gate!"

Soon, they walked into the penetralia and the

innermost part of the castle and followed the torch-lit hallway toward the great hall, for they could tell by the happy chatter that the residents had gathered for the evening meal. A moment after the two of them entered the room, lit by an ample number of tallow candles glowing from sconces that lined the walls, there was a shout: "May God be praised! 'Tis Ronan!"

Almost immediately he was surrounded by his family, which was much larger in number than David's. As he grinned at the smothering reception Ronan was receiving, David took a few steps back to keep from being crushed himself. Luckily, the welcome died away and Alysandir greeted David like a member of the family, which he hoped to God he would soon be when he had Elisabeth back in his arms, and there he would keep her.

A beautiful, copper-haired woman hurried toward him and gave him a warm greeting, then a hug, as she said, "Lord Kinloss, it is an answer to prayer to finally meet you, but I do not see my sister."

So this is Elisabeth's twin... so like her, and yet so different, but he liked her warm and friendly manner and he could tell that she thought favorably of him.

"But, where is Elisabeth?" she asked.

"That is what we have come here to tell ye," Ronan replied. "Angus MacLean captured her as she traveled from Bosworth Castle to return to Aisling."

"Let us go to my study where we can meet to discuss where we go from here," the Mackinnon said, and Alysandir turned and led the way, talking to Kinloss as they went, with Ronan and his brothers in tow.

After all had been served a round of wine, Alysandir asked David and Ronan to fill in the details about why

Elisabeth went to Bosworth Castle and how she ended
up in the hands of Angus MacLean, if that was indeed
the person who abducted her. Once he understood all
that had happened, he explained to David the situation at
Duart and why it was considered impenetrable.

They discussed several possible scenarios but found
flaws in each of them, so they decided it was best to
get a good night of sleep and give time for the news of
Elisabeth's capture to settle in their minds.

"We will meet again on the morrow after we break
fast," Alysandir said.

Elisabeth's interest in Fergus continued to grow, not in
a romantic way, for no one could take David's place in
her heart. It was simply that she was terribly curious
over the change in him, so she began to make subtle
inquiries, or to listen whenever she heard someone mention his name. Before long, she was stunned to think that
she had terribly misjudged him by allowing his father's
boasting and determination to see them wed, to sway
her opinion, without making any effort to simply ask
Fergus why he was so determined to marry her. There
was no doubt in her mind now, that Fergus had *never*
been in love with her and that made her wonder if he
had actually been pining over Barbara Mackinnon as
she was told the first time she was captured. Truth was,
based upon the opinions and stories of others around
Duart Castle, that Fergus MacLean was an honorable
man, a faithful knight and respectful to his father, in
spite of the terrible burden Angus placed upon him, first
by fabrications concerning Fergus and his overfocused

devotion to Barbara, and later by Angus's desire to see him marry Elisabeth.

Elisabeth felt terribly guilty for her part in this, especially for not recognizing that Fergus had never acted like a man desperately in love with her. But, there was still the fact that Barbara had fancied herself in love with him at one time, and apparently Fergus felt the same about her. So, Elisabeth made inquiry to one of her maids.

"Oh, my dear child," Alice said. "That was years ago, when they were no longer children but not yet adults. It was never a true romance, although they both thought themselves in love. Time cured them both, but I think Barbara's head was filled with his father's stories to the point that she believed that Fergus would never get over loving her. Puir lad, no wonder he has always been a wee bit reserved and shy around women. He was probably terrified of ever falling in love with anyone after that."

"He does not have someone he fancies?"

Alice made a face that spoke volumes. "Lord above! I ha' never heard o' him showing interest in anyone. He is the first to take the lead in battle. He is the biggest provider of game for the castle and for those less fortunate, and he is legendary for his generosity and kindness toward them."

After Alice left, Elisabeth decided to pay a visit to the garden, for it was a favorite of hers and of Isobella's when she spent some time here. She glanced out the window and the garden looked so inviting, for the fountain was gurgling and what looked to be the same peacock was still strutting, but the kittens she remembered were gone. No matter, she would go park herself on the bench and enjoy the sunshine and an opportunity to make vitamin D.

She entered the garden from the far end and walked through the vegetable garden, which was starting to look like winter was on its way. She rounded the corner and jerked to a stop, for her favorite bench was taken by no other than Fergus, who seemed to be deep in thought. She turned to leave quietly, and then she stopped. If she ever wanted answers to her questions, this was the time, for Angus had ridden away from the castle at dawn and Fergus was in the garden, sitting just a few feet away. So, she turned in his direction, and when she stepped onto the graveled pathway, his head jerked up.

When he saw her, he stood and she knew he was going to leave. "Fergus, please don't go. I would like to talk to you, for I am ashamed that I did not try to do so when I was here before."

A look of indecision passed over his face, and for a moment she thought he would leave, but in the end, because of his knightly honor and being duty-bound to deal kindly with women, he remained where he was. When she reached the bench, she sat down and said, "Please, sit down beside me, for I have something I would like to say to you."

She saw the muscle working in his jaw, for he was obviously still trapped at a moment of indecision, before he finally sat down, careful to seat himself at the farthest point away from her that he could without toppling off the bench altogether.

When he was seated, she said, "First, I would like to start off with saying that I am terribly ashamed to admit that I owe you an apology and have owed it to you since I was first brought here. I misjudged you terribly and I hope you can forgive me for it."

"'Tis naught to forgive, for I remember no ill treatment or slightings from ye," he said. "So, fret not aboot it."

"Oh, but I do. I allowed myself to form an opinion of you based upon the opinions and the comments of others. I have only recently come to learn that being in love with Barbara and her being in love with you was something that occurred many years ago, at an age when we fall in and out of love with each beautiful or handsome face we see."

He lifted his head and tilted his head back, to stare upward as if he was recalling that time of tender feelings. "'Twas a long time ago and I no longer think upon it."

She had gone this far and she might as well finish, so she ignored his comment and went on. "When I was here before, I rarely saw you and only had polite conversation with you on rare occasions. I misinterpreted your reserve, thinking you were so in love with me that you were overwhelmed and unable to declare your feelings. I see now that I was so overawed with my own charm that made you love me that I never took time to know the real you.

"When I returned this time, I was stunned at the change in you, for you are a man of great physical prowess, a knight of the first order, an expert marksman and hunter of game, kind and benevolent toward your clansmen and the less fortunate. I regret I did not take the time to become friends with you before, and I hope that by extending the hand of friendship toward you now, we can let go of the past and become friends. I am going to marry the Earl of Kinloss, who is probably searching for me right now. It is my hope that once we have been reunited, you would be present at our wedding."

"I thank ye fer yer kindly spoken wirds, and in my heart, there is naught to forgive, but if it eases yer heart to hear it spoken, then I do forgive ye for any misconceived slight ye feel ye did. It grieves me that my father keeps ye here, for it goes against all I believe in and hold dear. I take an oath before ye now, that I will help ye leave Duart, but I must think upon it. Mayhap, it would be wise for us to meet here from time to time so my father will think a miracle has occurred and the two o' us have opened our hearts, one to the other."

"Why do you think your father has created this ongoing situation concerning you and your feelings toward certain women? Surely, that serves no purpose. What does he hope to gain from it?"

"He was raised on the stories of family feuds, and there have been many in the past between the MacLeans and the Mackinnons."

"But why perpetuate a feud that should have died out a long time ago? And why do it at your expense?"

"He grows old... I think he misses the way things were, so he turned his thoughts toward seeing me married, believing it would fill the loneliness he feels for the past that dwells inside. He created his own feud, hoping the real thing would someday come along. As for using me as justification, it may have been the best reason he could think of."

"You were a saint to endure it for so long."

"He is my father. It is my duty to honor him."

She closed her eyes, recalling the many times Izzy

would tell her of the days of yore and the code of honor knights lived by. It wasn't the first time she had heard such, of course... she had seen her share of knight movies like *Robin Hood, Braveheart, Excalibur, King Arthur, Henry V*, and *Camelot*. But it was the first time she saw the knights' code in real time, and she felt so terrible knowing how much Fergus must have suffered from the ridicule.

Choked by emotion, she said, "You are a man of tremendous honesty, with integrity in your beliefs and actions. It is one thing to accept responsibility for your own actions, but it is heroic to accept it for the actions of others." She stood and gave him a kiss on the cheek. "My heart is gladdened over having the privilege to speak with you, and I thank you for your generous spirit and the ease with which you forgive. It is a marvelous attribute. I am happy to meet here anytime to build upon our friendship, and I cannot thank you enough for your being you."

Neither of them noticed Angus watching them from the parapet wall, so they could not see the slow smile that spread across his face.

Chapter 22

Look from thy window and see my passion and my pain;
I lie on the sands below, and I faint in thy disdain,
Let the night winds touch thy brow with the heat of my
  burning sigh
And melt thee to hear the vow of a love that shall not die
Till the sun grows cold, and the stars grow old,
And the leaves of the judgment Book unfold.

—"Bedouin Song" (1872)
  Bayard Taylor (1825–1878)

THREE DAYS LATER, THE SISTER OF ANGUS MACLEAN
arrived late in the afternoon. She was the same sister
who was married to David's uncle, although she preferred life in a convent over marriage, and had come to
Duart Castle to visit. Elisabeth was surprised to see she
wore a pale blue habit, very much like the one Elisabeth
had worn at St. Leonard's.

The castle help was bustling about, for Angus was
in high spirits over the blossoming romance between
Elisabeth and Fergus, and now his dear sister was here,
so he ordered the preparation for a grand celebration and
splendid meal to be served in the great hall.

In her room, Elisabeth was trying to decide what
dress to wear, for her heart was not in it and she did not

feel like faking a romance with Fergus any more than Fergus did, but as she told him, one has to do what one has to do.

She was about to remove her clothing when someone knocked at her door. She was astounded when she opened it and Fergus was there. He slipped into the room before she could ask him what he wanted.

He handed her a pouch. "Put this on, and be verra sure you put the cloak on."

She was stunned and had no idea why he was asking her to put something on with a cloak, but before she could ask, he answered the question for her.

"As ye ken, my aunt is here, so I took the liberty of borrowing one of her habits and I took her cloak. Tonight is the perfect time for us to leave, while all the festivities are beginning and everyone will be in the great hall. If they miss us, at first they will think we ha' slipped off to be alone. I pray that we can put enough distance between us by the time they discover we are gone."

"But they will know your aunt wouldn't leave so soon after her arrival and on the night of a big feast for her."

"I will tell the guards that ye wish to visit the graves of my MacLean ancestors, so that ye might pray for their souls before tonight's feast."

She gave him a hug and said, "Fergus MacLean, besides being a knight beyond compare, you are a genius!"

Mel Gibson couldn't have produced a better script for a castle escape, if he had the original cast of *Braveheart* and *Robin Hood* put together, for everything went off without a hitch. They chose to leave just before the banquet began, when all the help was in the great hall and

the guests were dressing for the evening. Elisabeth was
to bring his aunt's hooded, convent cloak in the pouch
and wear her own cloak to cover the blue habit, in case
she met anyone while leaving her room. They would
then meet in the outer bailey, behind the stable, where he
would be waiting with the horses. There, she would remove her own cloak and put on his aunt's, and he would
escort her through the castle gate.

It was perfectly scripted and acted, and even the castle guards at the gate did their part, and the two of them
were through the gates and on their way before the first
guest arrived in the great hall. Once they were well away
from the castle and out of sight of anyone who might
be on the parapet walls, they broke into a steady lope,
which the horses could maintain for a longer distance
than they could if at a full run.

She had to hand it to Fergus, for he had it planned
well. Cunning knight as he was, he did not take the
customary trails one would use to go to Màrrach Castle
but a different route that was longer, but not one Angus
would expect them to take, since speed would be of the
essence. They rode all night and the next day, stopping
at intervals to rest the horses and exchange mounts, for
Fergus in his mail was much heavier than Elisabeth, so
his horse would be tired before hers. He was pleased
to know she had been raised around horses and was an
accomplished rider, for riding a trained war horse was
not something most women would tackle.

They arrived at Màrrach after midnight, and when
they entered the castle, the steward informed them
that Lord Kinloss and Ronan Mackinnon were both at
Màrrach. Never had she been gifted with better news.

Just knowing David was here lifted a tremendous burden from her.

She arranged for a bath to be delivered to her room and made one request. "Please give the best of care to my dear friend, Fergus MacLean, for I would not be here if it were not for him."

"I can assure ye that it will be done, Mistress Douglas."

She turned then and gave Fergus a hug and said she would find a way to repay his kindness toward her.

"Mayhap, I will hold ye to yer wird, mistress," he said with a warm but tired smile.

They parted and Elisabeth hurried to her room, and was surprised to see Sir James sitting on the end of the bed when she opened the door. "It is amazing to me," she said, closing the door, "how you always seem to be about when things are going well and painfully scarce when they are not. Are you here after the battle is over to shoot the wounded? I have been in a terrible situation, in case you haven't noticed."

"Aye, I noticed, but ye handled everything well enough on yer own, did ye not?"

"Yes, but it could have been a bit easier."

"Or worse…"

"Okay, then why are you here after the ordeal is over?"

He stood and his image, while not in solid form, was beautifully bright so that he almost looked human, but she noticed an odd look in his eyes. Her brows narrowed. "Don't tell me you have come to say good-bye."

He smiled, his eyes lighting up as he said, "The worst is behind ye, and ye do ha' in yer room a man waiting who is more than capable o' helping ye now."

She felt a heavy weight inside and her chest felt

constricted, as if her heart was suddenly twice its size and had no room to beat. She had always given him a piece of her mind and did her fair share of complaining, and yet, he was always there, even if she could not see him. "It isn't easy to accept the fact that I will not see you again. I don't suppose you could pay me a short visit now and then... even if it's just a whirlwind or two?"

His countenance brightened. "I might find a need to admonish ye wi' a ruffled leaf now and then."

She laughed. "I shall miss your wonderful sense of humor. I would have enjoyed having you for a friend in real life."

"Friendship knows no bounds. Not even the grave can end it. Now, give me a simile and bid me adieu, so ye can ready yersel' to pay a visit to yer laddie, who grieves sorely over losing ye."

"I will, but first I must claim my hug, for you hugged Isobella."

"'Tis a blessed thing that the two o' ye were no' quintuplets," he said, his form changing before her eyes. She went to him and he opened his arms and she felt a surge of warmth pass through her, and all the weariness from her travels vanished. "I cannot ever thank you enough."

"Aye, ye can. Ye can name yer first son after me. I was thinking mayhap the name Douglas Alysandir Murray has a nice sound to it."

She leaned back. "My firstborn will be a son?"

"Everything is possible," and his form began to fade, but before it disappeared, he reached up to the top of his tunic and removed one of the blue stars and offered it to her. "'Tis a wedding gift fer ye to remember that the two o' ye are stronger together than apart."

She opened her hand, and he placed it there, but what she saw was not the star, but a chain with a star sapphire set in gold.

She looked up to thank him, but all she saw was a blue, swirling vapor as it floated through the window and vanished.

She looked down at the necklace and turned it over. On the back it said *Ne Oublie*...

She smiled. The Graham motto: *Ne Oublie*... Never forget.

As if she ever could.

Chapter 23

My steps are nightly driven by the fever in my breast
To hear from thy lattice breathed the word that shall give
  me rest.
Open the door of thy heart and open thy chamber door,
And my kisses shall teach thy lips the love that shall fade
  no more
Till the sun grows cold, and the stars are old,
And the leaves of the judgment Book unfold.

—"Bedouin Song" (1872)
  Bayard Taylor (1825–1878)

LORD KINLOSS LAY ACROSS THE BED BUT HE COULD NOT sleep. When Isobella gave him a choice, he thought sleeping in Elisabeth's bed was a good idea, but then he decided there would be too many memories of her there, and he wouldn't be able to sleep. So he chose the other so he could fall asleep quickly without tortuous thoughts.

It didn't work… Thoughts of her surrounded him, and even the bed seemed to carry the scent of her. Try as he might, he could not sleep for imaginings of her lying beside him in this bed, wearing a lovely sleeping gown that he would slowly remove. Her memory accompanied him wherever he went, and his emptiness over losing her was deeper and more painful than any wounds inflicted in battle.

The thought of her becoming the bride of Fergus MacLean drove him mad. He prayed he would find her before that could happen, for he knew if he did not, he would never get over the loss. Over and over, the images of moments with her played in his mind and he could not sleep for her memory would grant him no peace.

He put his arm over his eyes and thought of her, and he could smell the sweet fragrance of her hair, the smooth warmth of her leg lying close to his. On it went, memory after memory, until the images in his mind began to grow faint and the pounding of his heart eased. And as always, his last thoughts were of her.

Elisabeth... always Elisabeth...

He closed his eyes and she was there, coming toward him through a purple haze of heather, her long hair whipping in the wind, her skirts swirling about her. He moaned and slid his arm to the other side of the bed, as if by virtue of desiring it, she would be there. God, he wanted her to the point of desperation, and he longed to touch her. But the bed was empty and any thought of sleep this night vanished.

He left the bed and poured himself a glass of wine and moved to the desk, but instead of sitting down, he leaned against it, his back to the door, for it afforded him a magnificent view through the window he opened earlier. The air here was fairly cold, but the moisture from the Atlantic tempered it, and the coolness seemed to clear his head. He finished the first glass of wine and poured another, and wondered how many times had Elisabeth seen this same view from her room, and did she feel as humbled by the vastness of the night sky as he.

This was the picture that greeted her when Elisabeth opened the door quietly and slipped inside. She was thankful for the rumble of thunder that greeted her, for she had not wanted to wake him.

She gently closed the door behind her and almost gasped when she saw him sitting on the corner of the desk. He stared out the open window, while the wick of candle burned low on the desk, as if it danced upon the whisper of a breeze entering the room. He was clad only in his trews, and she was mesmerized by the play of muscle when he lifted the goblet he held in his hand.

The thunder was closer now, and the smell of rain was in the air as she tiptoed up behind him, glad she was barefoot. She had almost reached the desk, when he leaned his head back and released a deep sigh, as if he was relieved of a burden.

"I had given up hope of finding ye in time," he said. "I feared ye were married by now and forever lost to me."

She stared at the back of his beloved head, the hard muscles of his back, and his beautiful long hair. "Did you doubt that we were meant to be together—that I came back in time to find you?" Her voice was not quite as steady as she wanted it to be, and she did not want to break down and cry. But she had been through so very much these past weeks and the fear of losing him forever had taken its toll. How could it not when she feared all she would have left was the memory of having loved him?

"Aye, the thought entered my mind. Ye must admit we ha' had a damnable time o' it," he said, and reaching around, he took her arm and led her around to stand in front of him. For some time, he simply looked her over, studying her as if trying to decide if she was real and not the teasing of a dream. He pulled the cord on her cape and pushed it from her shoulders.

"Ye are even more beautiful than I remembered, in spite of yer image being a constant presence that invaded my thoughts. It was torment to be apart from ye and not knowing."

"I suffered the same torment, for it was being apart from you, and since I've been told Ronan is here, I hope that means you no longer believe he has my heart or that you consider him a threat."

"Aye, he is an honorable man."

"I am sorry for everything that has happened... for what you have been through."

"'Tis naught compared to the pain o' losing ye. When I received word that ye had been captured..." He leaned his head back and she saw the muscles working in his jaw, and she knew his anguish. "I couldna bear the thought of never seeing ye again."

She lifted her chin to look at him, so he would see the truth in her eyes. "It was the same for me," she said, "for I died inside, a little more each day I was away from you."

There was an element of sadness about him, one that seemed to cling to him like a low-lying cloud hugs land. He held her face cupped between his hands, his gaze traveling over her face as if he was committing each feature to memory. "I never knew love could be so all encompassing, so overwhelming, or that the absence of it could destroy a man so easily."

"I am sorry it all happened and I know it was worse for you because you were left in the dark about everything. At least I knew what was happening to me, although it was not easy. I knew you would come to search for me, but I was frightened you might find me too late. I wish I could undo what has been done, but I cannot. I can only promise to love you, and keep on loving you more each day than I did the day before. I want nothing as much as I want to spend each day of my life with you, to never be separate again."

His arms went around her and he drew her close, his words fanning her hair, his breath warm upon her neck. "When you rode out of my life that day, it was the most difficult thing I've ever done, to walk away from ye, knowing I might never see ye again. The only glimmer of hope I had to hold on to was remembering your assurance that there was naught between ye and Mackinnon, but I also knew that seeing him again might have changed things fer ye."

"Well, at least the news that I was back in the hands of Angus MacLean satisfied that fear."

"Nay, lass, fer I had a new worry. The moment I saw Ronan was no longer a threat, I then had to worry that Fergus MacLean would be married to ye before I reached Mull."

Her eyes met his and when they did, the pain she saw there seemed to fade away, replaced by a warm, teasing look. "Faith! I ha' never know a lass so mired in marriage proposals. For a while I thought I might ha' to take up my sword and fight off yer suitors if I was to win yer hand."

"You have always had my hand, my heart, and

everything else." She smiled and put her arms around his neck, drawing him close so she could place a kiss upon his lips, and then she whispered teasingly, "And I pray to God that nothing else will come between us before we can return home and put an end to all of this by finally getting married."

"Dinna worrit aboot that," he said. "I solemnly vow that naught will come between us from this moment forward. I willna risk losing ye, nor will I pass through the gates o' Màrrach Castle again... until ye are my wife. If I ha' learned anything, it is the enduring power of procrastination."

Her heart pounded with joy. "You mean to have a wedding here at Màrrach?"

"Aye, I do. I shall speak wi' Alysandir aboot having the wedding here and will request it be performed by his uncle Lachlan."

She threw her arms around his neck and gave him another kiss, then frowned, as if there was a problem with that idea. "But, what about Ailis? We cannot marry without her present, and your cousins, too."

He kissed her back, and his words whispered against her mouth, "We will have Ailis here, and my cousins, too, but we will need to see if some o' yer friar friends can run the hospital in their absence."

"That would be wonderful to have everyone here. I'm sure Alysandir would send some of his brothers to invite them."

"Fergus might also enjoy a visit to Aisling and a tour o' yer hospital."

She gasped. *Fergus... Ailis...* Her eyes lit up and her lips curved into a smile.

He chuckled and whispered, "Oh, no, I ken what ye are thinking…"

"Well, of course you do, and I'm not surprised, you know. You always seem to know me better than I know myself, as I recall, which can be terribly troublesome at times, for it does away with the prospect of surprise. And another thing, I would like…"

"Shhhh…"

"But this is concerning Ailis, and you know how much I…"

"Elisabeth…"

"Well, don't you think it would be a wonderful idea if…"

"We will discuss all of that after."

She was about to ask him after what, when he took her by the hand. He led her toward the bed and silenced her with a kiss as he slipped the gown from her shoulders and it fell to the floor. Elisabeth did not say anything more, for David found something she liked more than talking.

The Road Not Taken

Two roads diverged in a yellow wood,
And sorry I could not travel both
And be one traveler, long I stood
And looked down one as far as I could
To where it bent in the undergrowth.
Then took the other, as just as fair,
And having perhaps the better claim,
Because it was grassy and wanted wear;
Though as for that the passing there
Had worn them really about the same.
And both that morning equally lay
In leaves no step had trodden black.
Oh, I kept the first for another day!
Yet knowing how way leads on to way,
I doubted if I should ever come back.
I shall be telling this with a sigh
Somewhere ages and ages hence:
Two roads diverged in a wood, and I—
I took the one less traveled by,
And that has made all the difference.

—Robert Frost (1874–1963)
  U.S. poet

Epilogue

Freskin Castle
Moray, Scotland, 1535

"*CUIMHNICHIBH AIR NA DAOINE BHO'N D'THAINIG SIBH.*"
Remember the people from whom you have come...

Over the years, many things haunted Elisabeth, but one of the most haunting was the memory of this phrase in Gaelic that her father taught her. This set her to thinking about a legacy they could leave behind, and she decided on a portrait of the Murrays and the Mackinnons that her parents might one day see.

And today she would see the realization of it. After two weeks of rain, everyone in Freskin Castle had awakened to greet a gloriously sunny day. Lady Elisabeth Murray, Countess of Kinloss, was thinking it was about time. The end of the rain meant Robert Davidson could finish painting the family portrait, and they could all return home to Aisling Castle.

It had been over a year ago when Elisabeth first spoke to Isobella about the idea of each of them having a family portrait painted, with their names listed on the back, along with the last verse from Robert Frost's poem, "The Road Not Taken." The portraits were to remain in their respective castles, for one day, six hundred years in the future, they were certain their parents would travel to Scotland to find out what happened to their twin daughters who simply vanished. It was the sisters' greatest hope that their parents would discover the portraits hanging in the ancient castles of the Mackinnons and the Murrays, and they would know what truly happened to the twin daughters the day they disappeared.

They knew their mother would recognize Frost's poem, for it was one of her favorites, and she would know the Elisabeth and Isobella in the paintings were her daughters, for no one in sixteenth-century Scotland could possibly recite a verse of Robert Frost poetry written in the twenty-first century.

The day finally arrived when the rain was gone, and now the Murrays were all gathered outside the walls of Freskin Castle, in Moray, Scotland, just across the firth from the Black Isle. They all loved to spend time at Freskin because it had been in the Murray family for centuries and was actually older than Aisling. But Freskin would never be held with the same fondness they held for their beloved home, Aisling Castle, and the hospital there.

Once the six children were in their places, the hard part began, for they had to remain perfectly still, or as reasonably close to it as possible, which was difficult with three boys and three girls, ranging in age from their eighteen-year-old son down to the youngest son, age eight. But, miracles do occur, and the last of the children were miraculously where they should be and Robert Davidson picked up his palette and began to paint. These final strokes would complete the painting that would tell the tale of Elisabeth Douglas, who left Texas in the twenty-first century and found her husband in sixteenth-century Scotland.

Fortunately, the weather lasted until the portrait was finished at last, and all the children seemed to vanish. Elisabeth watched them race toward the castle and shook her head. "I forgot to remind the girls that they were supposed to act like ladies in those dresses."

"I believe the correct phrase is, '*A lady glides in a smooth, effortless manner, like a swan upon water…not a clumsy puffin taking off or landing.*'"

She laughed and the Lord of Kinloss put his arm around her shoulders, as the two of them watched their children disappear into the castle keep. "I dinna ken why ye expect them to exercise restraint, when their mother is bound by the motto: Exuberance in all things is best."

She thought about that for a moment, for exuberance took one many places. It was the gift of joie de vivre, the delight of being alive, and its gift was the pleasure of adventure, enjoyment its reward. She cocked her head to one side and studied his face. "I don't seem to remember that motto. Did you just make it up?"

He laughed and turned her to face him. "What do ye think?"

"I think you made it up."

He smiled and said, "Aye, I did, but it fit the occasion."

"Perhaps it is good to be that way, for if Isobella and I weren't so exuberant, we wouldn't have come back in time, and you would have never known I existed."

He wrapped her in his arms and pulled her close so he could look into her eyes. "My love, if you did not exist, all the fame, fortune, and possessions in the world would have no meaning."

Chapter 1

I can call spirits from the vasty deep.
Why, so can I, or so can any man;
But will they come when you do call for them?

—*Henry IV, Part 1*: Act III, Scene 1
  William Shakespeare (1564–1616)
  English poet and playwright

St. Bride's Church
Douglas, Lanarkshire, Scotland
In the year 1515

THE LANARKSHIRE HILLS OF SCOTLAND LACK THE SHARP AND ridgy majesty of the rugged Highland mountains, for they resemble rounded loaves of bread fresh from the oven, all huddled together. The lonely hills are somehow irresistibly attractive, with their pasture-covered slopes and fairylike meadows, where clear streams murmur through rolling undulations of thick woodlands, and the wood mouse and roe deer reside. Here, the sterner features of the north give way to a grace of forest and tenderness of landscape, where the gentle Douglas Water flows.

Alysandir Mackinnon thought it a good day as he rode across the rolling hills, accompanied by the rhythmic clang of his sword tapping against his spur, while

larks, hidden among the leathery leaves of trees, broke
into song as he passed beneath the heavy branches.
A glance skyward told him the sun had passed its zenith,
as it dipped behind a cloud to begin its slow descent into
afternoon. Just ahead, spangles on the river danced and
sparkled their way downstream.

Alysandir pushed back his mail coif. Sunlight brought
out the rich darkness of his black hair and the vivid blue
of his eyes. He turned toward his brother Drust. "We
will follow the river until we find a place to ford."

Drust followed Alysandir's lead and pushed back his
own coif, the shiny links of mail almost matching his sil-
very, blue-grey eyes. He wiped the sweat from his face
and gave a silent nod. They continued and drew rein at a
point where the terrain sloped gently downward toward
the river, before it narrowed to make a meandering turn.

"This looks like as good a place as we have seen,"
Alysandir said, and he spurred his mount forward and
plunged into the water. His horse staggered with the
first splash and the water washed over his hocks, but
Gallagher was a hobbler, a sturdy Highland pony known
for its stamina and ability to cover great distances over
boggy and hilly land at high speed. Alysandir only had
to spur the horse lightly as he urged him slowly forward
until Gallagher gained his footing as the water rose over
the stirrups.

When they reached a point where the water became
deeper than they expected, Alysandir was about to
turn back, but Gallagher leaped ahead with a mighty
splash, and they began the climb upward toward the
opposite bank.

Wet and dripping, they rode into town and attracted a

great many curious stares from villagers who gawked as if they rode into town to slay a dragon or two. Although a small town, Douglas was large enough to have a two-story tavern with a stable out back and streets that were fairly busy at this time of day. They rode between uneven rows of buildings stacked on each side of curving streets that had been laid out more than three hundred years before.

They passed a steep cobbled path that ran through an archway to a small, walled garden next to a house in ruins, and as they threaded their way among carts, wagons, barking dogs, clucking chickens, and the occasional darting child, they observed the slow progress of a lone rider coming toward them. He was leading a prisoner riding a hobbler, the unfortunate wretch bruised and blindfolded, with his hands bound behind his back. Alysandir wondered what the Highlander's crime had been—probably no more than trying to eke out a living in a harsh and unforgiving land.

Just ahead, near the center of town, stood St. Bride's Kirk, where mail-clad heroes of yesteryear lay entombed within, most of them with the surname Douglas. But Alysandir's fiery thoughts centered not upon the long-dead knights but upon his own desire to be away from the Lowlands, Douglas, and Lanarkshire, and back in the Highlands and his home on the Isle of Mull.

Drust, meanwhile, was giving his attention to a young lassie with copper-colored hair who was standing in the kirkyard and holding a bonnet full of eggs. Alysandir caught a glimpse of her standing beneath the graceful branches of an old tree and felt a strange yearning tug at him, but he hardened his heart and dismissed her. Aye, she was a beauty and his body stirred at the sight of her, but he still wasn't interested. The sound of Drust's voice cut into his thoughts.

"That lassie with the russet ringlets is a beauty, and she has taken a fancy to ye, Alysandir, for already she has wrapped ye in her tender gaze."

"I am leery of any lass standing under a wych elm," Alysandir replied.

"I know ye have no desire ever to have a woman in yer life again, but just suppose ye did find yerself in a position where ye were forced to take another wife. What virtues would ye seek?"

"Ye ken I have no desire to marry again. Not ever."

"So make up a list just to keep me happy. We've naught else to do right now."

Alysandir did not know why his brother insisted on having high discourse with him. Of late, Drust had been making too many inquiries as to Alysandir's unmarried state. "Ye are becoming a great deal of trouble, Drust. Next time, I will let Ronan or Colin ride with me."

"Fair enough," Drust replied as a wide smile settled across his face. "I will start the list. Loyalty would be one, am I right?"

Loyalty. The word evoked pain. "Aye."

"Ye canna stop there," Drust said with a teasing tone. "Give me the rest."

"I will give ye the virtues that any man should want in a woman, but only if ye promise to keep quiet the rest of our journey."

"Aye, I agree. Now, give me the virtues."

"Chastity, loyalty, honesty, wisdom, strength, courage, honor, intelligence, confidence, and a strong mind.

A woman who knows when to yield as readily as she knows when to take a stand. A woman equal to the man in question, not in might but in nature, virtue, and soul. She would possess a true and steadfast love for him, and in return, she would have his undying love, respect, and honor."

"What aboot silence and obedience?"

"If a man had a woman's love in the truest sense of the word—which I have yet to see any proof of—then he would have all the others for they are but parts that make up the whole."

"I hand it to ye, brother. I didna think ye could give me one virtue, yet ye named many. Surely ye miss having such a woman."

Alysandir pinned him with a cold stare. "I never had such a woman, so how could I miss her?"

"Ye changed once. Perhaps ye can change again."

"Changed? In what way?"

"I remember when ye would as soon tryst in the kirkyard as in a hayloft. How is it that knowing what ye or any man would want in a woman, ye refuse to find her?"

"'Tis easy enough to answer, for such a woman does not exist."

The words were barely uttered when the faintest echo of a man's laughter reached their ears. The sound of it seemed to break into a thousand pieces and fall like tinkling glass. Alysandir and Drust exchanged glances as the laughter faded and a slight wind stirred the heavy branches of the old wych elm.

As they rode on past St. Bride's Kirk, a tossing and rustling of the leaves sent a chill wafting down upon them. Across the way, a startled flock of sheep bolted, running across the meadow and up the hill to the pasture on the other side. The hair on Alysandir's neck stood, and his scalp felt as if it were shrinking. "Did ye hear the laughter?"

"Aye, I heard it and felt the cold wind that blew through the trees. Unless my senses deceive me, there is an oddity aboot."

"What oddity is that?" Alysandir asked.

"We are riding by the crypts of the ancients. Perhaps they wish us to pass by quickly and not linger."

Alysandir laughed. "Perhaps ye are letting yer imagination take the lead. The Mackinnons never had a quarrel with any Douglas, living or dead."

"What aboot the laughter? Ye heard it as well as me," said Drust.

Alysandir's face looked drawn as he replied, "Mayhap it was the bleating of a winded sheep."

"Aye, and mayhap it was not." Drust gazed at the river.

Alysandir knew his brother was thinking about the Douglas Water that flowed through the village of Douglas, past the ruins of Douglas Castle. The name Douglas Water came from the Gaelic *dubh-glas*, which meant black water. The Norman Douglases took their surname from the river in the twelfth century. Superstitious Drust was probably searching for some connection between the laughter they heard and the Douglases. Let Drust think what he would, especially if that would keep him quiet for a while.

The brothers rode on in silence, taking no notice of a dark shadow that came out of nowhere to pass overhead, mysterious and foreboding as the cry of a raven as it darkened the sky. Thunder rumbled in the distance, yet there was no scent of rain in the air. Engrossed as they were with their own thoughts, they did not turn back for one last look at St. Bride's Kirk. If they had, they would have seen a pale mist, of a greenish tint, that bubbled up from beneath the old kirk door.

True Highland Spirit

by Amanda Forester

—— ❧ ——

Seduction is a powerful weapon...

Morrigan McNab is a Highland lady, robbed of her birthright and with no choice but to fight alongside her brothers to protect their impoverished clan. When she encounters Sir Jacques Dragonet, she discovers her fiercest opponent...

Sir Jacques Dragonet is a Noble Knight of the Hospitaller Order, willing to give his life to defend Scotland from the English. He can't stop himself from admiring the beautiful Highland lass who wields her weapons as well as he can and endangers his heart even more than his life...

Now they're racing each other to find a priceless relic. No matter who wins this heated rivalry, both will lose unless they can find a way to share the spoils.

—— ❧ ——

"A masterful storyteller, Amanda Forester brings new excitement to Scottish medieval romance!"—Gerri Russell, award-winning author of *To Tempt a Knight*

For more Amanda Forester books, visit:

www.sourcebooks.com

The Highlander's Prize

by Mary Wine

Clarrisa of York has never needed a miracle more. Sent to Scotland's king to be his mistress, her deliverance arrives in the form of being kidnapped by a brusque Highland laird who's a bit too rough to be considered divine intervention. Except his rugged handsomeness and undeniable magnetism surely are magnificent...

Laird Broen MacNichols has accepted the challenge of capturing Clarrisa to make sure the king doesn't get the heir he needs in order to hold on to the throne. Broen knows more about royalty than he ever cared to, but Clarrisa, beautiful and intelligent, turns out to be much more of a challenge than he bargained for...

With rival lairds determined to steal her from him and royal henchmen searching for Clarrisa all over the Highlands, Broen is going to have to prove to this independent-minded lady that a Highlander always claims his prize...

"[The characters] fight just as passionately as they love while intrigue abounds and readers turn the pages faster and faster!" — *RT Book Reviews*, 4 stars

For more Mary Wine books, visit:

www.sourcebooks.com

The Highlander's Heart

by Amanda Forester

───────── ❧ ─────────

She's nobody's prisoner

Lady Isabelle Tynsdale's flight over the Scottish border would have been the perfect escape, if only she hadn't run straight into the arms of a gorgeous Highland laird. Whether his plan is ransom or seduction, her only hope is to outwit him, or she'll lose herself entirely...

And he's nobody's fool

Laird David Campbell thought Lady Isabelle was going to be easy to handle and profitable too. He never imagined he'd have such a hard time keeping one enticing English countess out of trouble. And out of his heart...

───────── ❧ ─────────

"An engrossing, enthralling, and totally riveting read. Outstanding!" —Jackie Ivie, national bestselling author of *A Knight and White Satin*

For more Amanda Forester books, visit:

www.sourcebooks.com

Sins of the Highlander

by Connie Mason with Mia Marlowe

❧

ABDUCTION

Never had Elspeth Stewart imagined her wedding would
be interrupted by a dark-haired stranger charging in on
a black stallion, scooping her into his arms, and carrying
her off across the wild Scottish highlands. Pressed against
his hard chest and nestled between his strong thighs, she
ought to have feared for her life. But her captor silenced all
protests with a soul-searing kiss, giving Elspeth a glimpse
of the pain behind his passion—a pain only she could ease.

OBSESSION

"Mad Rob" MacLaren thought stealing his rival's bride-
to-be was the perfect revenge. But Rob never reckoned
that this beautiful, innocent lass would awaken the part of
him he thought dead and buried with his wife. Against all
reason, he longed to introduce the luscious Elspeth to the
pleasures of the flesh, to make her his, and only his, forever.

❧

*"Ms. Mason always provides a hot
romance."—RT Book Reviews*

www.sourcebooks.com

About the Author

Since her first publication in 1988, *New York Times* bestselling author Elaine Coffman's books have been on the *New York Times, USA Today* Top 50, and Ingram's Romance bestseller lists and won nominations for Best Historical Romance of the Year, the Reviewer's Choice Award, Best Western Historical, and the Maggie. She lives in Austin, Texas.